"I can't get you

"I know what you're

"I doubt that." Hayes looping around the he gently drew her to him. "Because if you could see what I was up to, then you'd know I was about to kiss you."

He brushed his lips over hers, then pulled back to gaze into her eyes. "Sorry, I couldn't resist."

"You don't have to treat me as if I'm made out of glass and might break," she said. "I'm a lot stronger than I look."

"Is that right?" He looped an arm around her waist and pulled her to him right there in the street between their vehicles. Her full lips parted in surprise. Her sweet, warm breath comingled with his own. She let out a soft moan as he tasted her. Drawing her even closer, he deepened the kiss, demanding more.

8

RESCUE AT CARDWELL RANCH

BY
BJ DANIELS

Published in Great Britain 2014
by Mills & Boon, an imprint of Harlequin (UK) Limited,
Eton House, 18-24 Paradise Road, Richmond, Surrey, TW9 1SR

© 2014 Barbara Heinlein

ISBN: 978-0-263-91360-6

46-0614

Printed and bound in Spain
by Blackprint CPI, Barcelona

New York Times bestselling author **BJ Daniels** wrote her first book after a career as an award-winning newspaper journalist and author of thirty-seven published short stories. That first book, *Odd Man Out,* received a four-and-a-half-star review from *RT Book Reviews* and went on to be nominated for Best Intrigue that year. Since then, she has won numerous awards, including a career achievement award for romantic suspense and many nominations and awards for best book.

Daniels lives in Montana with her husband, Parker, and two springer spaniels, Spot and Jem. When she isn't writing, she snowboards, camps, boats and plays tennis. Daniels is a member of Mystery Writers of America, Sisters in Crime, International Thriller Writers, Kiss of Death and Romance Writers of America.

To contact her, write to BJ Daniels, PO Box 1173, Malta, MT 59538, USA, or e-mail her at bjdaniels@mtintouch. net. Check out her website, www.bjdaniels.com.

This one is for David Rummel,
who makes me laugh with his stories and his wonderful
joy for life. You definitely make our lives more fun.

Chapter One

From the darkness, he heard the sound of high heels tapping quickly along the pavement, heading in his direction, and smiled. This could be the one.

If not, he would have to give it up for the night, something he couldn't bear doing. For days his need had been growing. He'd come here tonight because he couldn't put it off any longer—no matter how dangerous it was to hunt this close to home.

Since it had gotten dark, he'd been looking. He hated to think of the women he'd let get away, women in their tight skirts and low-cut blouses, women who'd just been asking for it.

But waiting for the right woman, he'd learned, was the smart thing to do. It took patience. Tonight, though, he found himself running short of it. He'd picked his favorite spot, the favorite spot of men like himself: a grocery-store parking lot at night. Once he'd parked next to her car—he knew it was a woman's car because she'd left her sunglasses on the dash and there was one of those cute air fresheners hanging from the mirror— he'd broken the bright light she'd parked under.

Now the area was cast in dark shadow—just the way he loved it. He doubted she would notice the lack of light—or him with his head down, pretending to be packing his groceries into the trunk of his large, expensive vehicle. Women were less afraid of a man who appeared to have money, he'd discovered.

At the sound of her approaching footfalls, he found it hard not to sneak a peek at her. *Patience.* This would be the one, he told himself. He already felt as if he knew her and could easily guess her story. She would have worked late, which was why she was still dressed as she had been this morning, in high heels. She wasn't pushing a cart so she wasn't shopping for her large family.

Instead, he guessed she was single and lived alone, probably in a nice condo since she drove a newer, pricier car—the kind independent, successful single women drove. By the sound of her footfalls, she carried only one small bag of groceries. He could already imagine his hands around her throat.

The footfalls grew closer.

He'd learned a long time ago not to act on impulse. Snatch the first one he saw and bad things happened. He had a scar to prove it. That run-in had almost cost him dearly. Not that she'd gotten away. He'd made sure of that. But she'd wounded him in more ways than one. It was why he'd come up with a set of rigorous guidelines he now followed to the letter. It was the reason, he told himself, that he'd never been caught.

He closed his eyes for a moment, imagining the look in her eyes when she realized she was about to die.

This woman *had* to be the right one because his need had grown to the point of urgency. He went over his guidelines, the memory of his only mistake still haunting him.

He wouldn't let himself be swayed by an alluring whiff of perfume. Nor would he risk a woman carrying anything that could be used as a weapon at a distance like an umbrella.

Then there was her hair and attire. It would surprise most women to know that what made her his target was her hairstyle. There was a reason women with short hair were not common prey of men like him. Give him a woman with a ponytail—a recent trend that filled him with joy—or a braid or even a bun—anything he could bury his fingers in and hold on for dear life.

Clothing was equally as important. She had to be wearing an outfit that would come off easily and quickly because he often didn't have a lot of time. Of course, he always carried a pair of sharp scissors, but a woman in a blouse and a skirt made his life so much easier, even with a blade handy.

Now as the sound of the high heels grew closer, he readied himself with growing anticipation. He was betting this one was wearing a nice short skirt and a button-up blouse. Tonight, he could even handle a matching jacket with the skirt. No blue jeans, though. They were such a pain to get off.

Her cell phone rang. She stopped walking. He groaned since if she'd been just a little closer, she would have already been in his trunk, her mouth duct taped as well as her wrists and ankles.

He cursed her cell phone even though it often made things easier for him. Women who were distracted—either digging in their purses for their keys or talking on their cell phones or unloading their groceries—were oblivious to the fact that he was already breathing down their necks.

He silently urged her phone call to end. Just a few more steps and he would grab her by the hair, overpower her and have her in the trunk of his car before she even knew what was happening. Once he got her to the place he had picked out down by the river...well, that was when the real fun would begin.

His next victim was still on the phone. She sounded upset, so upset that she'd stopped walking to take the call. She would be thinking about the call—not him right next to her car.

The call ended. She began to walk again, right toward him. He doubted she'd even noticed him bent over his car trunk, pretending to be taking care of his groceries.

He heard her vehicle beep as she unlocked it. Any moment she would walk within a few feet of him on his right. He would have only an instant to make his decision. An instant to see what she had in her hands, what she was wearing, how long her hair was. Even with his meticulous planning, there was always the chance that this could be the one woman who would surprise him. The one who would fight back. The one who would get away and ruin his perfect record.

His heart began to pound with excitement. He loved this part. None had ever gotten away—even the one who'd scarred him. He was too smart for them. They were like sheep coming down a chute to slaughter, he thought, as he looked up and saw her start past him.

Chapter Two

McKenzie Sheldon came out of the grocery store thinking about work. Not work, exactly, but one of the men at her office.

She was going to have to do something about Gus Thompson. The warnings she'd given him had fallen on deaf ears. The man had reached the point where he was daring her to fire him.

Shifting the single bag of groceries to her other arm, she began to dig for her keys when her cell phone rang. She stopped and pulled out her phone, saw it was her receptionist and said, "What's up, Cynthia?"

"You told me to call you if I was having any more problems."

McKenzie let out an angry breath. "Let me guess. *Gus.* What has he done now?" she asked with a disgusted sigh.

"I'm sorry, Ms. Sheldon, but he won't leave me alone. If I work late, *he* works late. He always insists on walking me to my car. I've told him that I'm not interested, but it seems to make him even more determined. I make excuses to avoid him, but—"

"I know. Trust me. It isn't anything you're doing."

"He scares me," she said, her voice breaking. "Tonight I looked out and he was waiting by my car. I'm afraid to try to go home."

She started to tell Cynthia that she didn't think Gus was dangerous, but what did she know? "Is he still out there?"

"I don't know." Her receptionist sounded close to tears.

"Call the police. Or if you want to wait, I can swing by—"

"I don't want you to have to do that. I'll call the police. I wanted to talk to you first. I didn't want to make any trouble."

"Don't worry about that. Gus is the one making the trouble. I promise you I'll take care of this tomorrow." She heard her receptionist make a scared sound. "Don't worry. I won't mention your name." She thought of the night she'd looked out her window at her condo. Gus had been sitting in his car across the street. He'd seen her and sped off, but she'd wondered how many other nights he'd been out there watching her house. "I should have fired him a long time ago."

"But he's your best salesman."

McKenzie let out a humorless laugh. "Hard to believe, isn't it?"

"Still, I wouldn't want to be blamed for him losing his job."

"You won't. Trust me. I have my own issues with him." She snapped the phone shut, angry with herself for letting things go on this long.

She had talked to Gus after that incident outside her house. He'd shrugged it off, made an excuse and she hadn't seen him again near her place. But that didn't mean he hadn't been more careful the next time. There was just no reining Gus in, she thought as she found her keys and started toward her car.

She wasn't looking forward to tomorrow. Gus wouldn't take being fired well. There would be a scene. She really hated scenes. But this was her responsibility as the owner of the agency. Maybe she should call him tonight and hire security until she could get Gus Thompson's desk cleaned out and the locks changed on the doors at the agency.

With a sigh, she hit the door lock on her key fob. The door on her SUV beeped. Out of the corner of her eye, she barely noticed the man parked next to her, loading his groceries. His back to her, he bent over the bags of groceries he'd put in his trunk as she walked past him.

She was thinking about Gus Thompson when the man grabbed her ponytail and jerked her off her feet. Shocked, she didn't make a sound. She didn't even drop her groceries as his arm clamped around her throat. Her only thought was: *this isn't happening.*

HAYES CARDWELL FELT his stomach growl as he walked down the grocery-store aisle. The place was empty at this hour of the night with just one clerk at the front, who'd barely noticed him when he walked in. The grocery was out of the way and it was late enough that most people had done their shopping, cooking and eating by now.

His plane had been delayed in Denver, putting him down in the Gallatin Valley much later than he'd hoped—and without any food for hours. He still had the drive to Big Sky tonight, one he wasn't looking forward to since he didn't know the highway.

Being from Texas, he wasn't used to mountains—let alone mountain roads. He was debating calling his brother Tag and telling him he would just get a motel tonight down here in the valley and drive up tomorrow in the daylight.

He snagged a bottle of wine to take to his cousin Dana Savage tomorrow and debated what he could grab to eat. The thought of going to a restaurant at this hour—and eating alone—had no appeal.

In the back of the store, he found a deli with premade items, picked himself up a sandwich and headed for the checkout. His Western boot soles echoed through the empty store. He couldn't imagine a grocery being this empty any hour of the day where he lived in Houston.

The checker was an elderly woman who looked as tired as he felt. He gave her a smile and two twenties. Her return smile was weak as she handed him his change.

"Have a nice night," she said in a monotone.

"Is there a motel close around here?"

She pointed down the highway to the south. "There's several." She named off some familiar chains.

He smiled, thanked her and started for the door.

MCKENZIE HAD TAKEN a self-defense class years ago. Living in Montana, she'd thought she would never need the training. A friend had talked her into it. The highlight of the course was that they'd always gone out afterward for hot-fudge sundaes.

That's all she remembered in the split second the man grabbed her.

He tightened his viselike grip on her, lifting her off her feet as he dragged her backward toward the trunk of his car. The man had one hand buried in her hair, his arm clamped around her throat. He was so much taller, she dangled like a rag doll from the hold he had on her. She felt one shoe drop to the pavement as she tried to make sense of what was happening.

Her mind seemed to have gone numb with her thoughts ricocheting back and forth from sheer panic to disbelief. Everything was happening too fast. She opened her mouth and tried to scream, but little sound came out with his arm pressed against her throat. Who would hear, anyway? There was *no* one.

Realization hit her like a lightning bolt. The parking lot was empty with only one other car at the opposite end of the lot. With such an empty lot, the man who'd grabbed her had parked right next to her. Also the light she'd parked under was now out. Why hadn't she noticed? Because she'd been thinking about Gus Thompson.

She saw out of the corner of her eye that the man had moved his few bags of groceries to one side of the trunk, making room for her. The realization that he'd been planning this sent a rush of adrenaline through her.

If there was one thing she remembered from the

defense class it was: *never let anyone take you to a second location.*

McKenzie drove an elbow into the man's side. She heard the air rush out of him. He bent forward, letting her feet touch the ground. She teetered on her one high heel for a moment then dropped to her bare foot to kick back and drive her shoe heel into his instep.

He let out a curse and, his hand still buried in her long hair, slammed her head into the side of his car. The blow nearly knocked her out. Tiny lights danced before her eyes. If she'd had any doubt before, she now knew that she was fighting for her life.

She swung the bag of groceries, glad she'd decided to cook from scratch rather than buy something quick. Sweet-and-sour chicken, her favorite from her mother's recipe, called for a large can of pineapple. It struck him in the side of the head. She heard the impact and the man's cry of pain and surprise. His arm around her neck loosened just enough that she could turn partway around.

McKenzie swung again, but this time, he let go of her hair long enough to block the blow with his arm. She went for his fingers, blindly grabbing two and bending them back as hard as she could.

The man let out a howl behind her, both of them stumbling forward. As she fell against the side of his car, she tried to turn and go for his groin. She still hadn't seen his face. Maybe if she saw his face, he would take off. Or would he feel he had to kill her?

But as she turned all she saw was the top of his baseball cap before he punched her. His fist connected with her temple. She felt herself sway then the grocery-store parking lot was coming up fast. She heard the twenty-ounce pineapple can hit and roll an instant before she joined it on the pavement.

From the moment he'd grabbed her, it had all happened in only a matter of seconds.

HAYES STEPPED OUT into the cool night air and took a deep breath of Montana. The night was dark and yet he could still see the outline of the mountains that surrounded the valley.

Maybe he would drive on up the canyon tonight, after all, he thought. It was such a beautiful June night and he didn't feel as tired as he had earlier. He'd eat the sandwich on his way and—

As he started toward his rented SUV parked by itself in the large lot, he saw a man toss what looked like a bright-colored shoe into his trunk before struggling to pick up a woman from the pavement between a large, dark car and a lighter-colored SUV. Both were parked some distance away from his vehicle in an unlit part of the lot.

Had the woman fallen? Was she hurt?

As the man lifted the woman, Hayes realized that the man was about to put her into the *trunk* of the car.

What the hell?

"Hey!" he yelled.

The man turned in surprise. Hayes only got a fleeting impression of the man since he was wearing a baseball cap pulled low and his face was in shadow in the dark part of the lot.

"Hey!" Hayes yelled again as he dropped his groceries. The wine hit the pavement and exploded, but Hayes paid no attention as he raced toward the man.

The man seemed to panic, stumbling over a bag of groceries on the ground under him. He fell to one knee and dropped the woman again to the pavement. Struggling to his feet, he left the woman where she was and rushed around to the driver's side of the car.

As Hayes sprinted toward the injured woman, the man leaped behind the wheel, started the car and sped off.

Hayes tried to get a license plate but it was too dark. He rushed to the woman on the ground. She hadn't moved. As he dropped to his knees next to her, the car roared out of the grocery parking lot and disappeared down the highway. He'd only gotten an impression of the make of the vehicle and even less of a description of the man.

As dark as it was, though, he could see that the woman was bleeding from a cut on the side of her face. He felt for a pulse, then dug out his cell phone and called for the police and an ambulance.

Waiting for 911 to answer, he noticed that the woman was missing one of her bright red high-heeled shoes. The operator answered and he quickly gave her the information. As he disconnected he looked down to see that the woman's eyes had opened. A sea of blue-green peered up at him. He felt a small chill ripple through him before he found his voice. "You're going to be all right. You're safe now."

The eyes blinked then closed.

Chapter Three

McKenzie's head ached. She gingerly touched the bandage and closed her eyes. "I'm sorry I can't provide you with a description of the man. I never saw his face." She'd tried to remember, but everything felt fuzzy and out of focus. She'd never felt so shaken or so unsure.

"Is the light bothering you?" the policewoman asked.

She opened her eyes as the woman rose to adjust the blinds on the hospital-room window. The room darkened, but it did nothing to alleviate the pain in her head. "It all happened so fast." Her voice broke as she remembered the gaping open trunk and the man's arm at her throat as she was lifted off her feet.

"You said the man was big."

She nodded, remembering how her feet had dangled above the ground. She was five feet six so he must have been over six feet. "He was…strong, too, muscular." She shuddered at the memory.

"You said he was wearing a baseball cap. Do you remember what might have been printed on it?"

"It was too dark." She saw again in her memory the pitch-black parking lot. "He must have broken the light because I would have remembered parking in such a dark part of the lot."

"Did he say anything?"

McKenzie shook her head.

"What about cologne?"

"I didn't smell anything." Except her own terror.

"The car, you said it was large and dark. Have you remembered anything else about it?"

"No." She hadn't been paying any attention to the car or the man and now wondered how she could have been so foolish.

The policewoman studied her for a moment. "We received a call last night from your receptionist about a man named Gus Thompson."

McKenzie felt her heart begin to pound. "Gus works for me. You aren't suggesting—"

"Is it possible the man who grabbed you was Gus Thompson?"

McKenzie couldn't speak for a moment. Gus was big. He also had to know, after numerous warnings, that she was ready to fire him. Or at least, he should have known. Could it have been him? Was it possible he hated her enough to want to hurt her? "I don't know."

"We found a car registered to him, a large, dark-colored Cadillac. Did you know he had this car?"

"No. But his mother recently died. I think he mentioned she'd left him a car."

"He never drove it to work?"

"No, not that I know of." Again, she hadn't been paying attention. She knew little about Gus Thompson because she'd chosen not to know any more than she had to. "I saw him parked outside my house one night. I spoke to him about it and I never saw him again, but I can't be sure he didn't follow me sometimes." She thought of one instance when she'd noticed him driving a few cars behind her. But Bozeman was small enough that it hadn't seemed all that odd at the time.

The policewoman raised a brow. "You never reported this?"

McKenzie tried to explain it to herself and failed. "I guess I thought he was annoying but harmless."

"Did you ever date him?"

"Good heavens, no."

"But Gus Thompson probably knows your habits, where you go after work, where you shop?"

She nodded numbly. Gus could have followed her many times and she wouldn't even have noticed. She'd been so caught up in making her business a success....

The policewoman closed her notebook. "We'll have a chat with Mr. Thompson and see where he was last night at the time of your attack."

"He wasn't at the office last night when you sent a patrolman over there?" she asked.

The policewoman shook her head. "He'd already left. Your receptionist was unsure when."

McKenzie felt a shiver, her mind racing. Could it have been Gus who'd attacked her? She swallowed, her throat raw and bruised from last night. Gus was big and strong and she knew he resented her. To think she'd almost reassured Cynthia that Gus wasn't dangerous. He could be more dangerous than she would have imagined.

"I used to work with his mother when she owned the agency," she said. "I inherited Gus. He is my best salesman, but I know he felt his mother should have left him the business and not sold it to me."

The policewoman nodded. "This could have been building for some time. We'll see what he has to say."

She had a thought. "I hit the man last night several times, but I'm not sure I did enough damage that it would even show." She described the ways she'd hit him.

"Don't worry. We'll check it out. In the meantime, you'll be safe here."

As the policewoman started to leave the room, McKenzie said, "The man who saved me last night..." She had a sudden flash. *You're safe now.* She blinked. "I'd like to get his name so I can thank him."

"He asked that his name be kept out of it."

She blinked. "Why?"

"There actually are people who don't want the notoriety. I can contact him if you like and see if he might have changed his mind. What I can tell you is that he just happened to fly in last night and stop at that grocery store on his way to see family. Fortunately for you."

"Yes. Fortunate." She had another flash of memory. Warm brown eyes filled with concern. *You're safe now.*

"The doctor said they're releasing you this afternoon. We're going to be talking to Mr. Thompson as soon as we can find him. Maybe going to the office isn't the best idea."

"I *have* to go into work. I was planning to fire Gus Thompson today. Even if he wasn't the man in the parking lot last night, I can't have him working for me any longer."

"Why don't you let us handle Mr. Thompson. We have your cell phone number. I'll call you when he and his personal items are out of your business. In the meantime, I would suggest getting new locks for your office and a restraining order for both yourself and your business."

She must have looked worried because the officer added, "You might want to stay with friends or relatives for a while."

"I have a client I need to see tomorrow south of here. I could go down there tonight and stay in a motel."

"I think that is a good idea," the policewoman said.

"Look what the cat dragged in," Tag Cardwell said as Hayes walked into the kitchen on the Cardwell Ranch. "We were getting ready to send the hounds out to track you down."

"Hey, cuz," Dana said as she got up from the table to give him a hug and offer him coffee. It was his first time meeting his cousin. She was pretty and dark like the rest of the Cardwells. As Tag had predicted, he liked her immediately. "We thought you'd be in last night."

"Ran into a little trouble," Hayes said and gladly took the large mug of coffee Dana handed him.

"That's Texas-speak for he met a woman," his brother joked.

Hayes told them what had happened and how it was after daylight before he left the police station. He didn't mention the strange feeling he'd had when the woman had opened her eyes.

"Is she all right?" Dana asked, clearly shocked.

For months, Tag had been talking up Montana and its low crime rate among all of its other amazing wonders.

"She regained consciousness in the ambulance. Last I heard she was going to be fine—at least physically. I'm not sure what a close call like that does to a person."

"Have the police found the man?" Dana asked, and hugged herself as if feeling a chill. Hayes thought about what his cousin had been through. She had personal experience with a psychopath who wanted to harm her.

"Unfortunately, the police don't have any leads. I wasn't able to get a license plate or even the model or make of the car the man was driving." He felt exhausted and stifled a yawn. He'd been going on nothing but adrenaline and caffeine since last night. "Hopefully, the woman will be able to give the cops a description so they can get the bastard."

"You look exhausted," Dana said. "I'll make you breakfast, then Tag will show you to your cabin. You two don't have anything planned until late afternoon, right?"

"Right," Tag said. "I'm taking my brother to see the restaurant space I found."

"Then get some rest, Hayes. We're having a steak fry tonight. Our fathers have said they are going to try to make it."

"That sounds great." He wasn't sure he was up to seeing his father. Harlan Cardwell had only been a passing figure in his life. Tag, who was the oldest, remembered him more than the other four of them. Harlan had come to Texas a few times, but his visits had been quick. Being the second to the youngest, Hayes didn't even remember his uncle Angus.

Hayes felt emotionally spent, sickened by what he'd witnessed last night and worried about the woman. He kept seeing her staring up at him with those eyes. He mentally shook himself as Dana put a plate of silver-dollar-sized pancakes with chokecherry syrup in front of him, along with a side of venison sausage and two sunny-side-up eggs.

He ate as if he hadn't eaten in days. As it was, he'd never gotten around to eating that sandwich he'd purchased at the grocery store last night. After he'd been plied with even more of Dana's amazing buttermilk pancakes, his brother walked him out to his rental SUV.

"So how are the wedding plans coming along?" he asked Tag as they got his gear and walked up a path behind the barn into the pines to his cabin.

He'd flown in a month early to talk his brother out of opening a Texas Boys Barbecue joint at Big Sky. The five brothers had started their first restaurant in a small old house in Houston. The business had grown by leaps and bounds and was now a multimillion-dollar corporation.

All five of them had agreed that they would keep the restaurants in Texas. But in December, Tag had come to Montana to spend Christmas with their father and had fallen in love with both Montana and Lily McCabe. Nothing like a woman and a little wilderness to mess with the best-laid plans.

It was now up to Hayes, as a spokesman for the other three brothers, to put Tag's feet firmly back on the ground and nip this problem in the bud.

"It's going to be an old-fashioned Western wedding," Tag was saying, his voice filled with excitement. "I can't wait for you to meet Lily. She's like no woman I have ever known."

Hayes didn't doubt it. He'd never seen his brother so happy. All of the brothers had the Cardwell dark good looks. Add to that their success, and women were often throwing themselves at one of them or another. Except for Jackson, none of them had found a woman they wanted to date more than a few times. They'd all become gun-shy after Jackson had bitten the bullet and gotten married—and quickly divorced after he found out his wife wanted nothing to do with their newborn son.

Hayes couldn't wait to meet this Lily McCabe to find out what kind of spell she'd cast over his brother—and possibly try to break it before the wedding.

GUS THOMPSON HAD never been so angry. The bitch had called the cops on him. He glanced toward the empty receptionist's desk at the front of the real-estate office. It didn't surprise him that Cynthia hadn't come in today. Stupid woman. Did she really think he would blame *her?*

No, he knew Cynthia didn't do *anything* without checking with her boss.

So where the hell *was* McKenzie Sheldon? No matter what was going on, she was usually at work before him every morning. *She must have had a rough night,* he thought with a smirk.

Where was everyone else? he wondered as he checked his watch. Had they heard about the police coming by his house last night?

When the front door opened, he turned in his office chair, the smirk still on his face since he'd been expecting McKenzie. He felt it fall away as he saw the cops. Hadn't it been enough that an officer had shown up at his door last night, questioning him about stalking the receptionist at the office? Now what?

"Mr. Thompson?" the policewoman asked. Her name tag read P. Donovan.

"Yes?" he asked, getting to his feet. He saw them look around the empty office.

"Are you here alone?"

"Everyone seems to be running late this morning," he said, and wondered why that was. Because they'd all been given a heads-up? Gus noticed the way both cops were looking at him, scrutinizing him as if he had horns growing out of his head.

"We'd like to ask you a few questions," the woman cop said. "Ms. Sheldon has asked us to first see that you remove your belongings from the premises."

"What?" he demanded. "The bitch is *firing* me? Has she lost her mind?"

P. Donovan's eyes went hard and cold at the word *bitch.* The word had just slipped out. He'd known McKenzie had it in for him, but he'd never dreamed she'd fire him.

"I'm her biggest-earning salesman," he said as if

there had been a mistake made and he hadn't made it. Neither responded. Instead, he saw the male cop looking around. "What?"

"Are there some boxes in the office you can put your belongings into?" the cop asked.

Hadn't either of them been listening? "She can't do this." Gus heard the hopelessness in his voice. He hated nothing worse than the feeling that came with it. He wanted to break something. Tear the place up. Then find McKenzie Sheldon and punch her in the face.

The male cop had gone into a storage room. He came back with two boxes. "Please take only those items belonging to you personally. We'll watch so we can tell Ms. Sheldon."

Gus gritted his teeth. McKenzie didn't even have the guts to face him. Well, this wasn't the last she'd see of him. He'd catch her in a dark alley. He started to shovel the top of the desk off into one of the boxes, but the male cop stopped him. T. Bradley, the name tag read.

"Leave any inventory you've been working on."

He grabbed up his coffee mug and threw it into the box. The couple of tablespoons of coffee left in the cup made a dark stain across the bottom. The same way McKenzie's blood was going to stain the spot where they met up again, he told himself.

His personal belongings barely filled one box. That realization made him sad and even angrier. This business should have been his. When he was a boy, he used to sleep on the floor of the main office when his mother had to work late. This place had been more like home than home during those years when she'd been growing the business.

"Is that everything?" P. Donovan asked.

He didn't bother to answer as T. Bradley asked for his key to the building.

"Ms. Sheldon has taken out a restraining order against you," the cop said. "Are you familiar with the way they work?"

He looked at the cop. "Seriously? Do I look like someone who is familiar with restraining orders?"

"You are required to stay away from Ms. Sheldon and this building. If you harass her—"

"I get it," he snapped, and handed over his key. As he started toward the door, T. Bradley blocked his way.

"We're going to need you to come down to the police station with us to answer a few more questions."

"About what?" The receptionist, bloody hell. "Look, I haven't done anything that any red-blooded American male doesn't do. I like women." He realized they were staring at him. "Come on. She liked it or she wouldn't have led me on."

"Whom are you referring to?" P. Donovan asked.

He frowned. "Cynthia. The receptionist. She was threatening to call the cops last night, but I didn't really think she'd do it. Why would you ask me that? Who else called the cops on me?"

"Didn't she ask you to leave her alone?" the woman cop asked.

He shrugged. "I thought she was just playing hard to get."

"What about Ms. Sheldon? Did you also think she was just playing hard to get?" T. Bradley asked.

Gus closed his eyes and sighed. So she'd told them about that time she'd caught him in her neighborhood. "There's no law against sitting in your car on a public street. I didn't even realize she lived in the area. I was looking at the house down the block, okay?" Not even he could make the lie sound convincing.

"Let's go," P. Donovan said and led him out of the building as if he were a criminal. In the small parking lot, he saw his colleagues waiting in their vehicles for the police to take him away.

He wanted to kill McKenzie.

"Please open the trunk of your car, Mr. Thompson," T. Bradley said as Gus started to put the box in the backseat.

"Why?" he demanded.

"Just please open it," P. Donovan said.

He thought they probably needed a warrant or something, but he didn't feel like making things any worse. He cursed under his breath as he moved to the back of the vehicle and, using his key, opened the trunk. It was empty, so he put the box in it. "Satisfied?"

It wasn't until T. Bradley rode with him to the police station and they had him inside in an interrogation room that they demanded to know where he'd been last night after he'd left the office.

"We know you didn't go straight home," P. Donovan said. "Where did you go?"

So much for being Mr. Nice Guy. Through gritted teeth, Gus said, "I want to speak with my attorney. *Now.*"

Chapter Four

He'd failed.

Failed.

The word knocked around in his mind, hammering at him until he could barely think.

You got too cocky last night, you and your perfect record.

It wasn't his fault. It was the woman's. The fool woman's and that cowboy with the Southern accent who'd rescued her.

That rationale didn't make him feel any better. He'd had one woman who'd fought back before, he thought, tracing a finger across the scar on his neck. But he hadn't let her get away and she'd definitely paid for what she'd done to him.

The possibility of not only failure, but getting caught was what made it so exciting. He loved the rush. But he also loved outsmarting everyone and getting away with it. Last night should have gone off without a hitch. The woman was the perfect choice. He'd done everything right. If he hadn't had to knock her out… Even so, a few more seconds and he would have had her in the trunk. Then it was a short drive to the isolated spot he'd found by the river.

His blood throbbed, running hot through his veins, at the thought of what he would have done to her before he dumped her body in the Gallatin River. He had to kill them for his own protection. If he were ever a suspect, there couldn't be any eyewitnesses.

Except last night he'd left behind *two* eyewitnesses— the woman and the cowboy. Had either of them gotten a good look at him or his vehicle? He didn't know.

A costly mistake. He mentally beat himself for not waiting until he could leave town before grabbing another one. The northwest was like a huge marketplace, every small town had perfect spots for the abduction and the dumping of the bodies. Small-town sheriff's offices were short on manpower. Women weren't careful because people felt safe in small towns.

Also, he had the perfect job. He traveled, putting a lot of miles on the road every year with different vehicles at his disposal. He saw a lot of towns, learned their secrets at the cafés and bars, felt almost at home in the places where he'd taken women.

But last night, after a few weeks unable to travel, he'd been restless. The ache in him had reached a pitch. His need had been too strong. He'd never taken a woman in his hometown. One wouldn't hurt, he'd thought. No, he hadn't been thinking at all. He'd taken a terrible chance and look what had happened.

He gingerly touched the side of his head where she'd hit him with whatever canned good had been in her grocery bag. Fortunately, other than being painful, the bruise didn't show through his thick hair. His shin was only slightly skinned from where she'd nailed him with her high heel and his fingers ached. No real visible signs of what she'd done to him. Not that he didn't feel it all and hate her for hurting him.

It could have been so much worse. He tried to console himself with that, but it wasn't working. The woman had made a fool out of him. It didn't make any difference that he shouldn't have gone for so long since the last one. But it had begun to wear on him. Otherwise, he would never have taken one this close to home. He would never have taken the chance.

The television flickered. He glanced up as the news came on. This was why he couldn't let them live, he thought, as he watched the story about a botched abduction at the small, out-of-the-way grocery store the night before. He waited for the newsman to mention the woman's name and put her on camera to tell of her heroic rescue by the cowboy. He wanted to see the fear in her eyes—but more than anything, he needed her *name*.

The news station didn't put her on air. Nor did they give her name or the cowboy's who'd rescued her.

Furious, he tried several other stations. He'd gotten a good look at her last night after he'd punched her and had her on the ground.

But he foolishly hadn't bothered to take down her car license number or grab her purse. He hadn't cared who the woman was. She'd been nobody to him. But now he was desperate to know everything about her. All the others, he'd learned about them after their bodies were found. It had never mattered who they were.

They'd already served their purpose. Now it was inconceivable that he didn't know the name of the only woman who'd ever gotten away.

Without her name, he wouldn't be able to find her and finish what he'd started.

STANDING IN THE hospital room half-dressed, McKenzie tried to still her trembling fingers. The morning sun was blinding. Her head still ached, but she'd kept that from the doctor. After the police had left, he'd made her spend the night in the hospital for observation. Today, though, she had to get back to work. It was the only thing that could keep her mind off what had happened. Worse, what could have happened if someone hadn't stopped the man.

"Let me," her sister said and stepped to her to button the blouse.

She stood still, letting her big sister dress her—just as she had as a child. "Thank you. I wouldn't have called but I needed a change of clothing before I could leave the hospital."

Shawna shook her head. She was the oldest of nine and had practically raised them all since her mother had been deathly ill with each pregnancy, especially with her last baby—McKenzie.

"Mac, I would expect you to call because I'm your *sister* and, after what you've been through, you need your family."

She didn't like needing anyone, especially her big sister. "I didn't want to be any trouble."

Her sister laughed. "You have always been like this."

She straightened McKenzie's collar. "You've never wanted to be any trouble. So independent. And stubborn. There. You look fine."

She didn't feel fine. From an early age, just as her sister had said, she had been fiercely independent, determined to a fault, wanting to do everything herself and driven to succeed at whatever she did. She was still that way. Nothing had changed—and yet, after last night, everything felt as if it had.

It was as if the earth was no longer solid under her feet. She felt off-balance, unsure—worse, afraid.

"Are you sure you're ready to leave the hospital?" Shawna asked, studying her.

"The doctor says my head will hurt for a while, but that I should be fine. I need to get to the office and reassure everyone. I had to fire one of my employees today." She swallowed, her sore throat again reminding her of the man's arm around her neck. Had it been Gus Thompson? The thought made her blood run cold. "I'm sure everyone is upset."

"You can't worry about them right now. You need to think about yourself. Just go home and rest. I can stop by your office—"

"No, this is something I need to do myself." She saw her sister's disappointment. Shawna lived to serve. "But thank you so much for bringing me a change of clothes."

"What do you want me to do with the clothes you were wearing?" she asked, picking up the bag. Her pretty new suit was blood-splattered from the now bandaged head wound. So was the blouse she'd been wearing.

"Throw them away. I don't want them."

She felt her older sister's gaze on her. "There doesn't seem to be anything wrong with the suit or the blouse. Once I get them clean... It seems a shame—"

"Then drop them off at Goodwill."

Her sister nodded. "Are the police giving you protection?"

"They really can't do that. Anyway, there's no need. If it was someone I know, then they don't believe he'll try anything again with them involved. And if it was random...then the man could be miles from here by now."

Shawna didn't look any more convinced than McKenzie felt. "I guess they know best."

"I'm going to stay in Big Sky tonight. I have a client I need to see up there this afternoon so I'll spend the night and come back tomorrow."

"Do you want me to go home with you to your condo and wait while you pack?"

She thought of her empty condo. "No. That's not necessary." But even as she said it, she was already dreading facing it alone. "I know you need to get back to your job." She stepped to her sister and hugged her. Shawna had never married. But she kept busy with three jobs as if needing to fill every hour of her day doing for others.

"You've done enough," McKenzie said. Her big sister had always been there for her from as far back as she could remember. It made her feel guilty because she felt her sister had been robbed of her childhood. Shawna had been too busy raising their mother's babies.

"If you need anything..."

"I know." Sometimes she felt as if Shawna had made

a life in Montana so she could watch over her. All the other siblings had left, stretching far and wide around the world. Only she and Shawna had stayed in the Gallatin Valley after their parents had passed.

But her big sister couldn't always protect her. Before last night, McKenzie would have said she could protect herself. Last night had proved how wrong she was about that.

GUS THOMPSON WOULD never forget the humiliation he'd been put through at the police department. "Don't you know who I am?" he'd finally demanded.

They had looked at him blankly.

"My photo is all over town on real-estate signs. I am number one in this valley. I sell more property than any of the hundreds of agents out there. I'm *somebody* and I don't have to put up with this ridiculous questioning."

"You still haven't told us where you were last night." The woman cop was starting to really tick him off.

He looked to his attorney, who leaned toward him and whispered that he should just tell them since it would be better than their finding out later. "I went for a drive. I do that sometimes to relax."

"Did you happen to drive by the River Street Market?"

"I don't remember. I was just driving."

"We searched your car… Actually, the car that is still registered to your mother, and we found a gas receipt." The woman cop again. "You were within a quarter mile of the grocery last night only forty-two minutes before the incident involving Ms. Sheldon."

"So what?" he snapped. "Aren't you required to tell me what I'm being accused of? Someone steal McKenzie's groceries?"

"Someone attacked and attempted to abduct Ms. Sheldon."

"Trust me. The guy would have brought her back quick enough." Neither cop smiled, let alone laughed. He raked a hand through his hair. "Why would I try something like that in a grocery-store parking lot when I could have abducted McKenzie Sheldon any night right at the office?"

His attorney groaned and the two cops exchanged a look.

"Come on," Gus said. "I didn't do anything to her. I swear." But he sure wanted to *now*. Wasn't it enough that she'd fired him? Apparently not. She wanted to *destroy* him. Something like this could hang over his head for years—unless they caught the guy who really attacked her. What was the chance of that happening? Next to none when they weren't even out looking for him.

He pointed this out to the cops. "Get out there and find this guy. It's the only way I can prove to you that I'm innocent."

They both looked at him as if they suspected he was far from innocent. But they finally let him go.

Once outside the police station, Gus realized he didn't know what he was going to do now. Of course, another Realtor would hire him. The top salesman in Gallatin Valley? Who wouldn't?

Unless word got around about Sheldon's attack—

and his firing. Everyone would think it was because he was the one who'd attacked McKenzie. How long would it take before everyone knew? He groaned. Gossip moved faster than an underpriced house, especially among Realtors.

McKenzie Sheldon better hope she hadn't just destroyed his reputation—*and* his career.

"I'M ANXIOUS FOR you to see the building I found for the very first Big Sky Texas Boys Barbecue," Tag said later that afternoon. "The Realtor is going to meet us there in a few minutes."

Hayes had taken a long nap after the breakfast Dana had made for him. He'd awakened to the dinner bell. Dana was one heck of a cook. Lunch included chicken-fried elk steaks, hash browns, carrots from the garden and biscuits with sausage gravy.

"This is the woman who should be opening a restaurant," Hayes said to his cousin.

"Thanks, but no, thanks," Dana said. "I have plenty to do with four small children." As if summoning them, the four came racing into the kitchen along with their father, Hud, the local marshal. The kids climbed all over their father as Dana got him a plate. It amazed him how much noise kids seven to two could make.

Tag's fiancée, Lily McCabe, came in looking as if she was already family. She declined lunch, saying she'd already eaten, but she pulled up a chair. Introductions were made and five minutes later, Hayes could see why his brother had fallen in love with the beautiful and smart brunette.

"We'd better get going," Tag said, checking his watch. He gave Lily a kiss then rumpled each child's hair as he headed for the door. Hayes followed, even though there was no purpose in seeing this building his brother had found for the restaurant.

They weren't opening a barbecue place in Big Sky. He wasn't sure how he was going to break it to his brother, though.

The road from the ranch crossed a bridge over the Gallatin River. This morning it ran crystal clear, colorful rocks gleaming invitingly from the bottom. Hayes watched the river sweep past, the banks dotted with pines and cottonwoods, and wished they were going fishing, instead.

At Highway 191, Tag turned toward Big Sky and Hayes got his first good look at Lone Mountain. The spectacular peak glistened in the sun. A patch of snow was still visible toward the top where it hadn't yet melted. This morning, when he'd driven to the ranch, the top of the peak had been shrouded in clouds.

"Isn't it beautiful?" Tag said.

"It is." All of the Montana he'd seen so far was beautiful. He could understand why his brother had fallen in love with the place. And with Lily McCabe.

"Lily was nervous about meeting you earlier," Tag said now, as if reading his mind. He turned toward Lone Mountain and what made up the incorporated town of Big Sky.

Hayes could see buildings scattered across a large meadow, broken only by pines and a golf course. "Why would she be nervous?"

"She was afraid my brothers wouldn't like her."

"What is the chance of that?" Hayes said. He had to admit that Lily hadn't been what he'd expected. She was clearly smart, confident and nice. He hadn't found any fault with her. In fact, it was blatantly clear why Tag was head over heels in love with the woman.

But Lily had reason to be nervous. She was backing Tag on the restaurant idea. A math professor at Montana State University in Bozeman, she didn't want to move to Texas with her future husband. A lot was riding on what Tag's brothers decided. Their not wanting a Montana barbecue place had nothing to do with liking or disliking Lily.

"Is she going to meet us at the restaurant building site?" Hayes asked, wondering how involved the bride-to-be was planning to be in the barbecue business. After the fiasco with Jackson's wife, the brothers had decided no wives would ever own interest in the corporation. They couldn't chance another ugly divorce that could destroy Texas Boys Barbecue. Or a *marriage* that would threaten the business, for that matter.

"No, she's doing wedding planning stuff," Tag said. "Who knew all the things that are involved in getting married?"

"Yes, who knew," Hayes agreed as his brother turned into a small, narrow complex. He saw the For Sale sign on a cute Western building stuck back in some pine trees and knew it must be the one his brother had picked out.

"Good, McKenzie is already here," Tag said just an instant before Hayes saw her.

He stared in shock at the woman he'd seen the night before. Only last night McKenzie had been lying at his feet outside a grocery store as her would-be abductor sped away.

Chapter Five

"Hayes, meet McKenzie Sheldon, Realtor extraordinaire," Tag said. "McKenzie, this is my brother Hayes."

McKenzie smiled, but she wasn't sure how convincing it was. Her sister had tried to talk her into moving this meeting to another day. Maybe she should have listened. She hadn't felt like herself all day.

While she'd tried to put what had happened last night out of her mind, she kept reliving it. Now she felt jumpy and realized it had been a mistake to take the attitude "business as usual" today.

But she couldn't bear the thought of hanging out at the condo all day when she knew nothing could take her mind off last night in that case. Her first stop had been the office where she'd assured everyone that Gus Thompson would no longer be a problem. While she was there, the locksmith came and changed all the locks, which seemed to reassure some and make others at the office even more nervous since Gus hadn't gotten along with any of his coworkers.

Then she'd gone to her condo, packed quickly for overnight and driven to Big Sky to meet her client.

She'd worn a plain suit with a scarf to cover the bruises on her neck, but the gash on her temple where the man had slugged her still required a bandage if she hoped to hide the stitches.

As she caught her reflection in the empty building window, she saw with a start that she looked worse than she'd thought. How else could she explain Hayes Cardwell's reaction to her? His eyes had widened in alarm as he put out his hand.

He looked like a man who'd just seen a ghost. He'd *recognized* her. How was that possible when he'd only flown in yesterday?

"Pleased to meet you, Ms. Sheldon."

Tag had told her that his brothers shared more than a love of barbecue. The resemblance was amazing. Like Tag, Hayes Cardwell had the dark hair and eyes, had the wonderful Southern accent and was handsome as sin.

She thought of Ted Bundy as she took Hayes Cardwell's large hand, hers disappearing inside it, and saw his dark gaze go to the bandage on her head. "I had a little accident last night."

"You're all right, though?" He still held her hand. She could feel herself trembling and feared he could, too.

She put on her best smile. "Fine." Then she finally met his gaze.

His eyes were a deep brown and so familiar that it sent a shudder through her. Even though she'd told her sister that there was nothing to worry about, she was well aware that the man who'd attacked her last night could be closer than she thought.

HE'D STAYED HOME from work saying he didn't feel well, even though he knew that might look suspicious if he was ever a suspect. But he was too anxious and upset over last night to go to work today.

There'd been nothing of use in the morning paper, only a short few paragraphs.

Police say a man tried to abduct a 28-year-old woman about 10:35 p.m. last night in the River Street Market parking lot.

The man attacked the woman as she came out of the market and attempted to put her into the trunk of his vehicle. He is described as over six feet with a muscular build. He was wearing a dark-colored baseball cap and driving a newer-model large car, also dark in color.

If anyone has information, they should contact the local police department.

He knew he should be glad that the information was just as useless to the police. She hadn't gotten a good look at him, which was great unless they had some reason to withhold that information. That aside, nothing in the news was helping him find the woman.

Too restless to stay in the house, he decided to go for a walk in his northside neighborhood to clear his head. The houses were smaller on this side of town, many of them having been remodeled when the boom in housing came through years before.

House prices had dropped with the mortgage fiasco, but so many people wanted to live in his valley that prices had never reached the lows they had elsewhere. He was glad he hadn't been tricked into selling his house for top dollar. He could have found himself in a house he couldn't afford. Instead, his small, comfortable home was paid for since he lived conservatively.

Everything about his lifestyle looked normal on paper. He'd attended Montana State University right there in Bozeman. He'd bought a house after he graduated with a degree in marketing and had gone to work for a local company. He was an exemplary employee, a good neighbor, a man who flew under the radar. If caught, everyone who knew him would be shocked and say they never would have suspected him of all people.

As he walked around his neighborhood, he saw that more houses were for sale. It made him upset to think that his older neighbors were dying off because more college students would be moving in. Constant temptation, he thought with a groan.

He promised himself the next time he took a woman it would be in another town. Even better, another state. He couldn't take the chance so close to home ever again. If there *was* another time. Last night's botched abduction had left him shaken. She'd jinxed things for him. If he didn't find the woman and fix this—

At a corner he hadn't walked past in some time, he saw that another house had gone on the market. But that wasn't what made him stumble to a stop next to the strip of freshly mown lawn.

There she was! He could never forget that face and now there she was. Right there on the real-estate sign in the yard, smiling up at him as if daring him to come after her.

McKenzie Sheldon of M.K. Sheldon Realty.

"ARE YOU ALL RIGHT?"

McKenzie nodded, even though she was far from all right. Did she really think she recognized this man? She hadn't seen the face of the man who'd tried to abduct her so she couldn't have seen his eyes. This man's eyes were…familiar and yet she'd never met him before, had she? Would she look at every man she met and think he was the one who'd attacked her?

Hayes Cardwell was staring at her with concern and something else in his expression. Compassion?

It was the very last thing she needed right now. Tears welled in her eyes. She felt lightheaded and groped for the wall behind her for support.

"If you'd prefer to do this some other time," Hayes said.

She shook her head. "No, I'm fine. It must have been something I ate." In truth, she hadn't eaten anything since the day before. No wonder she felt lightheaded. But she'd toughened it out through worse, she told herself, remembering when she'd taken on the agency.

Tag Cardwell hadn't seemed to notice her no doubt odd behavior. He was busy looking in the windows of the building, anxious to get inside and show his brother the space.

"I think you're going to like this location for your restaurant," she said, turning away from Hayes Cardwell's dark, intent gaze and what she saw there. "Let me show you. It's perfect for what you have in mind."

Her fingers shook so hard, she didn't think she was going to be able to put the key in the lock. A large, sun-tanned hand reached around her and gently took the keys from her.

"Let me do that," Hayes said. His voice was soft, his Southern accent comforting and almost familiar.

She was going mad. She could smell his male scent along with the soap he'd used to shower that morning. He was a big man—like the man last night who'd attacked her. She touched her bruised throat and closed her eyes against the terrifying memory.

He opened the door and she stumbled in and away from him. Her cell phone rang and she was startled to see that it was the police department.

"I need to take this. Please have a look around." She scooted past Hayes and back outside, leaving the two men alone inside what had been a restaurant only months ago. Her phone rang again. She sucked in a deep breath of the June mountain air and, letting it out, took the call. As she did, she prayed the man had been caught. She couldn't keep living like this.

"Ms. Sheldon?" the policewoman asked.

"Yes?"

"I spoke to the man who intervened last night during your attack. He still would prefer to remain anonymous."

"You're sure he wasn't involved?"

"Involved? No. The clerk at the store was a witness. He was leaving the store when he saw the abductor try-him out. It appalled him that she thought she could just fire him and he'd go away. Well, she was dead wrong about that.

Unfortunately, the forty-mile drive had taken longer than he'd expected. Summer traffic. He'd forgotten about the damned tourists so he hadn't been able to beat McKenzie to the restaurant—which had been his intent.

Fifty minutes later, he'd parked next to a small grocery in a space where he had a good view of the restaurant with the M.K. Realty sign out front. He'd arrived in time to see two men pull up in an SUV only moments after McKenzie.

He'd been forced to wait, telling himself it might work out better. He would grab her after her showing. He could get a lay of the land before he did anything stupid. More stupid, he thought, thinking of Cynthia, the receptionist. She wasn't even that cute.

While he had no patience for waiting, he was surprised when the showing only took a matter of minutes. He had to laugh. Boy, had that not gone well. And now McKenzie had just lost her best salesman. She would definitely regret firing him, probably already did.

He saw his chance when the two men McKenzie had shown the property to got into their SUV and drove away. The restaurant location was somewhat secluded, separated from the other businesses by pine trees.

Once he got her alone, she'd be forced to listen to what he had to say.

As he started his vehicle, planning to park behind her car so she couldn't get away, he saw her looking around. Was she worried he might show up? Or was she looking for the man who'd attacked her last night? Her gaze skimmed over him in his vehicle where he still sat, motor running. He looked away, glad he'd driven his silver SUV that looked like everyone else's around here.

When he'd dared take a peek again, she was headed for her car. He couldn't let her just drive away. His best chance of talking to her was here rather than back in Bozeman.

Gus shifted the SUV into gear. He told himself all he wanted to do was tell her what he thought of her firing him, of accusing him of attacking her, of treating him like an employee rather than appreciating what he did for M.K. Realty.

He just needed to have his say. He wasn't stupid enough to touch her. Or threaten her. He had the right to have the last word. She couldn't just get rid of him in such a humiliating way and think he was going to let it pass.

But as he'd started to drive up the road to the empty restaurant, another vehicle pulled in and parked next to her car. Annoyed, he saw that he would have to wait again. He hadn't come all this way to give up. He killed his engine with a curse. If he couldn't get to her now, then soon. She would hear him out, one way or another.

MCKENZIE HATED THE scared feeling she had as she hurried to her car. Her gaze took in the activity lower on the hillside. She told herself she'd just imagined someone watching her. Down the road, there were families in vans with laughing and screaming children, older people trying to park in front of one of the small businesses that dotted the meadow, a young couple heading into the grocery store.

Everywhere she looked there were people busy with their own lives. It was June in Montana, a time when in Big Sky, it seemed everyone was on vacation. No one had any reason to be watching her.

Still, she gripped her keys in her fist until her hand ached as she neared her car. She wanted to run but she was afraid that like a mad dog, the person watching her would give chase. She couldn't see anyone watching her and yet the hair rose on the back of her neck. The afternoon sun had sunk behind Lone Mountain. Shadows moved on the restless breeze through the pines next to the building.

Fear was making her paranoid, but she couldn't shake off the feeling that the man from last night hadn't left town. Nor had he forgotten about her.

She reached the car, opened the door and climbed in, fumbling in a panic to get the door locked. The moment she did, she realized she hadn't looked in the backseat. Her gaze shot to the rearview mirror. She swiveled around. The backseat was empty.

Hot tears burned down her cheeks. She began to shake uncontrollably.

At the sound of a vehicle approaching, she brushed at her tears and tried to pull herself together. She was trying to put the key into the ignition, when the tap on her side window made her jump.

Her head swung around and she found herself looking up at Hayes Cardwell. She cursed herself. He would see that she'd been crying. She felt a wave of embarrassment and anger at herself.

"Are you all right?" Hayes mouthed.

She lowered the window a few inches. "I—"

"I know. That's why I came back. There's something I need to tell you."

"If it's about the restaurant space—"

"The police called me and asked me again if I would mind if they told you that I was the man who found you last night at the grocery store."

She felt her eyes widen in alarm. "You—" The brown eyes. A flicker of memory. *You're safe now.*

"I can't imagine what you're going through, that's all I wanted to say. I was worried about you. But I didn't want you thinking…"

She nodded, unable to speak around the lump in her throat. He'd seen her reaction to him. It was the reason he'd decided to tell her. He didn't want her thinking he was the one who'd hurt her. Her eyes burned again with tears.

"Call the police. I understand why you would suspect me. I'll be over here when you finish if you want to talk or anything." He stepped away from her car.

She put the window up and dug out her phone. When the patrolwoman came on the line she asked, "The man who saved me last night? Was his name Hayes Cardwell?"

"So he *did* contact you."

"It's true?"

"Yes. He and his brothers own a chain of—"

"Barbecue restaurants in Texas."

"That's right. He also works as a private investigator in Houston. Like I said, we checked him out thoroughly. Plus, we have an eyewitness who saw him rescue you."

"Thank you." She disconnected and, pulling herself together, climbed out of the car.

Hayes was standing at the edge of the building, looking toward the Gallatin River. In the afternoon sun, the surface of the water shimmered like gold. The scent of pine wafted through the June air. There was nothing like Montana in the summer.

"I'm so sorry I suspected you." He'd never know how much. "The police told me that I owe my life to you. Thank you."

He turned to look at her, kindness in his dark eyes. "No, please, don't feel bad. I didn't tell you so you could—"

"Thank you?"

He shrugged, looking shy. "I just happened to be in the grocery store."

"I didn't mean to make you uncomfortable."

"I'm afraid I'm the one who made you uncomfortable. I apologize for staring earlier. I was just so surprised to see you again."

She nodded and touched her bruised neck, remembering the man's arm around her throat and fighting for breath.

"Are you sure you should be working this soon after what you've been through?" he asked.

"I needed to keep my mind off…everything."

"Is it working?"

She gave him a weary smile. "No," she said and

looked away. "I've felt jumpy all day and I haven't been able to shake the feeling that someone is…watching me." She glanced around again, the feeling still strong. She shivered, even though the afternoon was warm.

What if the man from last night wasn't through with her? Wasn't that what had been in the back of her mind all day?

HAYES LOOKED PAST her. He saw people coming and going at a nearby small business complex. No one seemed to be looking in this direction, though.

"You say you feel as if someone's watching you?"

She nodded. "I know I'm just being paranoid—"

"Your best defense is your instincts. Don't discount them."

She stared at him and tried to swallow the lump in her throat. "You think he'll come after me again?"

"I don't know. Is there any way he knows who you are?"

"I… The police think it might be a man I worked with. I fired him today. I have a restraining order—"

Hayes scoffed at that. "Restraining orders can't protect you from a predator. Where are you staying?"

"I checked into a motel up here for the night—"

He shook his head. "My cousin Dana owns a ranch not far from here. She recently built several guest cabins. I'd feel better if you'd consider staying there—at least until the police have a chance to catch this man." Hayes knew from experience that there was little chance they would catch him—unless he did turn out to be this man she'd fired.

"I couldn't impose."

"You wouldn't be imposing, trust me. My cousin Dana loves a full house and you would be doing me a favor."

She cocked a brow. "How's that?"

"I wouldn't have to worry about you the whole time I'm in town."

McKenzie smiled. It was a nice smile, a real one, and he was suddenly aware of how attractive she was. She had long hair the color of caramel. Most of it was pulled up with a clip at the nape of her neck, but a few strands had escaped, framing a face that was all girl-next-door—from the sprinkling of freckles that dusted her cheeks and nose to the wide-set tropical-blue eyes. But it was her mouth that kept drawing his attention. It was full, her lips a pale pink. Right now she worried at her lower lip with her teeth.

She had the kind of mouth a man fantasized about kissing.

He roped in his thoughts, telling himself not to make a big deal out of this coincidence. But he couldn't shake the memory of the first time he'd looked into her eyes. And now here she was, Tag's real-estate agent. As a private detective, he'd never bought into coincidences. This was definitely one that had him thrown off-balance.

"You'll like my family and you'll be safe." After that, he didn't want to think about it. Maybe the police would get lucky and catch the man.

"Are you sure about this? I know you didn't want to be involved…"

"I *am* involved," he said and smiled. Maybe more

involved than he should be, he thought. "Do you need to stop by your motel to cancel your reservation?"

"I hadn't checked in yet. I can call."

"Why don't you follow me to the ranch, then, and meet the Cardwells. Trust me. You're going to love them and feel at home there."

"WHAT?" TAG SAID as they stood in the ranch house living room later. "McKenzie is the woman you saved?"

Hayes nodded.

"Talk about a small world. So you decided to bring her back to the ranch?"

"Look, I know you're upset with me about the restaurant—"

"I'm just trying to understand what you're thinking. Since you're only going to be here a couple of days, how do you intend to keep this woman safe?"

"I don't know what I was thinking, okay? She was scared. When I went back and found her, she was losing it, all right? She thought someone was watching her."

Tag looked skeptical.

"I think she was probably imagining it, but she's terrified this predator will come for her again. Who wouldn't be?"

"You did the right thing," Dana said from the doorway. "I'm glad you brought her here. It isn't like we don't have plenty of room. I put her in the cabin next to yours, Hayes. She can stay as long as she wants."

"With the wedding coming up July Fourth—"

Dana cut Tag off. "Your brothers can always bunk together if they haven't caught the man who attacked her by the time Jackson, Austin and Laramie arrive. I told her she is welcome to stay as long as she wants to and that is that."

Tag didn't look happy about it. "It makes it pretty awkward since, from what I can gather, we aren't going to buy the restaurant space."

Dana looked to Hayes. "Is that what you and your brothers have decided?"

"We're still discussing it." That wasn't quite true but he really didn't want to get into this right now. If he couldn't talk his brother out of this, then he'd contact the rest of the guys and let them deal with it. His job had been to come up here and check out the situation and if at all possible, put an end to it.

"Why don't you take McKenzie for a horseback ride?" Dana suggested to Hayes. "It's beautiful up in the mountains behind the ranch and it will take both of your minds off your problems."

He was glad for anything that let him escape more discussion about the restaurant, so he jumped at it. "Good idea."

He found McKenzie standing outside on the wide Western porch, leaning on the porch railing and looking toward the mountains beyond. At his approach, she turned to smile at him.

"Thank you," she said, turning to him. She'd changed out of the suit she'd been wearing earlier into jeans and blouse. "This place is beautiful. I feel…safe here and I adore your cousin Dana."

"Everyone does. I thought you'd like it here. That

was the plan. Dana suggested a horseback ride up into the mountains. What do you say?"

"Really? I'd love to." She sounded so excited he couldn't help but smile. He was reminded again of that moment last night when he'd looked into her eyes and felt…something.

"Great. Dana said she has two gentle horses that should be perfect for us greenhorns."

"Speak for yourself," McKenzie said. "I grew up riding and I suspect you did, too," she said, eyeing him. "Or is that Stetson and those boots just for show?"

He laughed. "I've ridden a few horses in my day."

Dana came out of the house then with a pair of boots she thought would fit McKenzie. They all visited as she led them up to the corral and got them saddled up for their ride.

Hayes noticed that McKenzie's step was lighter. He felt uncomfortable playing hero protector, but he preferred that to worrying about her. He'd learned as a private investigator to follow his own instincts. If she felt she was being watched, he knew there was the chance she probably was.

Chapter Six

He couldn't believe his good luck at finding McKenzie Sheldon's face on that real-estate sign. He took this as an omen that things were going to work out, after all.

Whistling all the way back to his house, he planned his new strategy. From the description the newspaper had run of the attacker, he felt assured that McKenzie hadn't gotten a good look at him. Which meant she wouldn't know him if she saw him again. But he had to be sure before he moved forward.

He checked the real-estate listings and found an open house she was hosting on Sunday, day after tomorrow. But to his delight, he saw that she was going to be the featured speaker at a real-estate conference being held at the university right here in town tomorrow.

He imagined that she was scared after last night. He just hoped she didn't cancel her speech or her open house or have someone else host it. Given the fight she'd put up last night, he had a feeling she wouldn't. He liked that about her and couldn't wait to see her again.

Excited now and much relieved, he felt better than he

had since his failure the night before. But he wouldn't be satisfied until he fixed this.

From as far back as he could remember, he couldn't bear failing. He supposed that was his parents' fault. They'd expected so much of him—too much. He would have given anything to make them happy, and he'd certainly tried for years. But he'd only disappointed them time and time again.

The thought left a bitter taste in his mouth.

His parents weren't the only ones. He'd also disappointed his girlfriends. The thought of them made his stomach roil. He'd never known what they wanted from him. It was this secret that women kept among themselves. They would get that self-satisfied smirk on their faces, mocking you for failing.

"I should have expected as much from you," his high school girlfriend used to say. And when he begged her to just tell him what she wanted, she would add, "If you don't know, then there is really nothing more I can say."

The bitches had played their games with him throughout high school and then college. He'd tried to understand them. Even with his longest relationship after college, four years, he'd continued to disappoint. Nothing was ever good enough. And the nagging…

That was really when things had started to change. After his breakup following four years of torture, he'd picked up a woman at the bar and taken her for a ride out into the country. All he'd wanted was sex and a little peace and quiet. But it had proven too much to ask. She'd started going off on him, about how she should have known at the bar that he was a loser. He'd told her to get out of his car.

"Out here? No, you take me back to the bar where I left my car right now," she'd said.

He remembered looking at her. How ugly women were when they scowled like that. "Get out of my car right now or I am going to kill you."

She'd started to argue, but something in his expression had stopped her. She got out and began to cry, yelling obscenities as he backed up to leave. "I'm going to tell on you! Everyone is going to know about you!"

He'd hit the brakes, then threw the car into first gear and hit the gas as she began to run. That had shut her up. He'd chased her down the road until she'd had the sense to run into the trees. He'd been so calm as he'd turned off the car and gone into the trees after her.

She'd been easy to catch.

That was when he'd officially quit trying to please other people. Now he only worried about making himself happy. And what would make him happy was finding McKenzie Sheldon and finishing what he'd started.

McKenzie shifted in her saddle as she stared across rows of mountaintops to the sunset. The waning sun had left streaks of pink, orange and gold that fanned up into Montana's big sky.

"It's breathtaking." She turned to look at Hayes. "Thank you for bringing me up here. You were right, your family is so inviting, especially Dana. This was so kind of her."

"She is one in a million, no doubt about that."

"You all seem so close. My family is spread out all over the place. I only have one sister here in town and I don't see her much. My fault. I work all the time." She let out a sigh.

"I never met the Cardwell side of my family until this trip," Hayes said. "My mother left my father when us boys were very young and took us to Texas to live. We only saw our father on occasion, so this is my first time in Montana—and meeting my cousin Dana."

McKenzie couldn't help being surprised. "You seem so at home here."

He chuckled at that. "Montana does that to a person. Look at my brother. He intends to stay, restaurant or no restaurant."

"You're opposed to opening a Texas Boys Barbecue here?"

"It's complicated."

"I'm sorry, I shouldn't have asked." She looked toward the sunset and breathed in the sweet scent of the tall pines around her.

"No, it's fine. It's just that we started small, in an old house in Houston, and the business just…mushroomed. My brother Laramie has a head for that end of it and runs the corporation so the rest of us can pursue other careers."

"I understand you're a private investigator in Houston?"

He nodded. "Maybe it's just me, but our little barbecue joint has grown into something I never wanted it to be. Adding another one in Montana… Well, it was never in the plans. We swore we would at least keep them all in Texas."

She said nothing, hating that she had a dog in the fight. This was something the brothers would have to sort out among themselves. Meanwhile, she feared Tag would lose the restaurant space and clearly he had his heart set on his own business in Big Sky.

"It makes it all the more difficult because there are five of us," Hayes said. "Do you come from a large family?"

She laughed. "Nine children."

His eyes widened in surprise. "Imagine all of them having to agree on something."

"Impossible."

Hayes nodded, but he looked upset by the situation. "Your brother is still going to marry the woman he loves and stay in Montana no matter what happens with the restaurant, right?"

"Seems so. I just hate to disappoint him, but it isn't as if he needs a job."

"Some people just enjoy working," she said, realizing how true that was. She couldn't imagine retiring, say, ten years from now even though she probably could. What would she do all day if she did?

"I suppose we should head back," Hayes said as the sky around them began to darken. The breeze stirred the thick pine boughs and McKenzie felt a chill, even though the day was still warm. "Sorry to dump my problems on you."

"Yes, I have more than enough of my own," she

joked. "Seriously, it was nice to think about someone else's for a while."

"I'm glad you're staying here on the ranch. Dana has invited us for a cookout tonight. You'll get to meet the rest of the family."

"I don't know how I will ever be able to repay her," McKenzie said.

"Just being here makes her happy since I think she gets starved for female companionship with all these Cardwell men around."

As they rode back toward the ranch, she couldn't help but notice the pines shimmering in the waning light. In the distance, she could see Lone Mountain, now a deep purple.

She couldn't remember a time she'd enjoyed a man's company the way she did Hayes Cardwell's. He wasn't hard to look at, either, she thought with a hidden smile, surprising herself. No man had turned her head in a very long time. And he really had taken her mind off last night.

But as they rode into the darkening ranch yard, she felt another shiver and tried to shake off that feeling of being watching again.

HAYES NOTICED HOW quiet McKenzie was at supper. Fortunately, his father and uncle hadn't been able to make it to the ranch so she'd only had to meet a few of the family members. He could tell she was exhausted. The ride, though, had put some color back into her cheeks.

After dinner, the two of them headed for their respective cabins on the mountainside behind the house and he asked, "Would it be possible for you to take a few days off? I'm anxious to have a look around the area and thought you might want to come along."

He could see that she saw through his ruse right away.

She smiled politely, though, and said, "I am speaking at a real-estate convention tomorrow at the university before several hundred people."

That had been his fear. "You can't get someone else to do it for you?"

"Are you kidding?" She laughed. "This has been planned for months."

He nodded. "So it's been widely publicized."

She frowned. "You can't think that the man who attacked me would come to something like this, hoping to harm me."

He wasn't sure what to think. "I don't like it because it will be hard to protect you in a crowd like that."

"Hayes—"

"If you're going to tell me that you don't want my protection, save your breath. I'm going with you."

"You'll be bored to tears."

"I hope so. I'm sure your speech will knock 'em dead, but with any luck, it will be uneventful."

"This conference is important. It's about growth in Montana, especially in this Big Sky area," she said as they neared her cabin.

Moonlight filled the canyon, casting long shadows from the pines. A breeze stirred the boughs, sending the sweet scent of pine into the night air. Overhead stars glittered above the canyon walls.

McKenzie met his gaze and smiled. "Good for *both* of our businesses, actually. There's a lot of money that has moved into Montana. A Texas barbecue restaurant at Big Sky wouldn't have made it maybe even five years ago. Now, though?" She raised an eyebrow.

"I know you aren't just saying that to sell the building we looked at."

"That building would already be sold if your brother hadn't put down money on it," she said.

Hayes's brow shot up. "Tag put money down on it?"

She realized she'd let the cat out of the bag. "I'm sorry, I got the impression it was his own money and merely to hold it until you could all see it."

"I knew he had his heart set on this, but…" He shook his head as they reached her cabin.

A small lantern-shaped light cast a golden glow from the porch over them and the wooden lattice swing that moved restlessly in the light breeze. Dana and Hud had the half-dozen guest cabins built to look as if they'd been there for a hundred years. They were rustic on the outside but had all the conveniences of home inside.

"I hope you and you brothers can work this out," McKenzie said.

"Me, too."

"Thank you again for everything," she said as she looked past him toward the old two-story ranch house below. "I've loved getting to know some of your family and the horseback ride… Well, I can't tell you how much I needed it, needed all of this."

"You know, Dana said you are welcome to stay as long as you want."

She smiled at that. "That is very sweet of her, but with Tag's wedding just weeks away… No, I need to get back to work."

"I understand. What time is this conference tomorrow?"

McKenzie told him and reluctantly agreed to his following her to her condo and then to the university.

"I hope you didn't think I was trying to strong-arm you into the restaurant site," she said.

He shook his head. "I didn't. McKenzie, I was thinking we should have dinner some night before I return to Texas."

"I would enjoy that."

He waited for her to enter the cabin and turn on a light before he started through the pines to his own cabin. As he walked, he pulled out his cell phone and called his brother Laramie. It was such a beautiful June night and he wasn't tired at all. If anything, he didn't want the night to end. He couldn't remember being this…

For a moment, he didn't recognize the emotion. Happy. He laughed to himself. He felt…happy.

"Tag has his heart set on opening a restaurant here," he said without preamble when his brother Laramie answered.

"We already knew that. What did you think about the location he picked?"

"What is the point of discussing that if we don't want to open one in Montana?" he demanded. "Wait a minute. He called you, didn't he?"

Laramie sighed. "He wanted to make sure I was flying in for the wedding in a few weeks so I could see the site and we could talk. You didn't tell him what we decided, I take it? Is this just a case of you not wanting to play the bad guy?"

"No, I'm actually reconsidering." Hayes told himself it had nothing to do with McKenzie Sheldon and much more to do with Montana. He was falling for the state. He wouldn't be here long enough to fall for the woman, which was another reason not to stay too long. Fate might have thrown them together, but then again, he didn't believe in fate, did he? "Tag made some good points."

"So would the location work?"

"The location is fine. Actually better than fine. And maybe Big Sky is ready for Texas barbecue, but is this really something we want to do? What's next, Wyoming? Minnesota?"

"Tag said that people from all over the world visit Big Sky and a lot of the homeowners have sophisticated tastes."

Hayes laughed. "You aren't really implying that our barbecue requires a sophisticated taste."

"Maybe not, but our beans definitely do."

They both laughed.

"So tell me about his fiancée," Laramie said.

"She's pretty, supersmart, has a great job and owns her own home here in Big Sky. And she's definitely wild about our brother."

"Sounds like our Tag hit a home run."

Hayes sighed. "She's nice, too. I liked her."

"I heard you found a woman up there, as well."

"*Found* being the operative word." Hayes told his brother what had happened.

"Crazy. I thought there wasn't any crime up there."

"Low crime. Not *no* crime." He'd reached his cabin. As he climbed up the steps and sat down on the porch swing, he said, "I'm thinking I might stick around for a while." It surprised him that he'd voiced what had been in the back of his mind.

"So it's like that," Laramie said.

"It's...complicated."

"Be careful, Hayes," his brother warned. "You know what Jackson went through with his marriage."

He did. His wife had left him right after their son was born, only to come back three years later and try to take Ford away from Jackson. "Could you fly up now instead of before the wedding?"

"Not going to happen. Let's remember that I'm the brother who keeps Texas Boys Barbecue Corporation going."

"We never forget that," Hayes said. Laramie was the business major, the brother who'd gladly taken the reins when the business had begun to take off. True, it had grown more than any of them had anticipated since then, but Laramie was still the best brother to be in charge. And there was that added benefit that none of them forgot. Laramie allowed the rest of them to do whatever they wanted, never having to worry about money.

"You know how thankful we all are that you took it on," he said, not that Laramie needed reassurance. His brother loved what he did and continued to make the corporation more than profitable.

"What about Austin?" Hayes had to ask.

Silence, then Laramie said in a worried tone, "He's on a case down by the border. I haven't been able to reach him for several weeks now."

Hayes let out a curse. When Austin got on a case, it was all-consuming. They often went for weeks, even months, with no word from him. He only seemed to take on the most dangerous cases. They'd almost lost him more than once.

"I thought he was working fewer hours for the sheriff's department."

"You know him better than that," Laramie said. "I'm sure he will do everything possible to make the wedding, though."

Hayes sure hoped so, but of the five of them, Austin was the loner of the family and possibly the most stubborn. "When are Jackson and Ford flying in?" He knew Jackson and his five-year-old son wouldn't miss the wedding, even though weddings were the last thing Jackson was interested in attending after his marriage had gone so awry.

"A few days before the wedding. Ford is excited about riding horses at the ranch. Apparently, cousin Dana promised him his own horse while he's up there."

"So what do you want me to do about Tag and the restaurant site?" Hayes asked.

"If you've already weakened, I'd say it was a done deal."

As Hayes disconnected, he thought about walking

back to McKenzie's cabin and telling her to get the paperwork for the restaurant site ready. It was pretty much a done deal if Laramie was getting behind it.

But he stayed on his cabin porch. He could tell her tomorrow or maybe even the next day. It would give him an excuse to see her again. Not that he needed one. What was that old Chinese proverb? *He who saves a life is responsible for it.*

The woman brought out his protective instincts. He knew it was because she was so strong, so determined, so capable of taking care of herself under normal circumstances. But the man who'd attacked her had shaken her world and left her afraid and vulnerable.

Hayes told himself that whoever had tried to abduct her in the grocery-store parking lot was probably long gone.

But what if he wasn't? What if it was this man she'd fired?

He swore softly under his breath. It seemed that tomorrow he was going to a huge real-estate conference where a predator could be anyone in the crowd. And to think he'd actually considered leaving his gun in Texas, asking himself, *what were the chances he would need it in Montana?*

Chapter Seven

The moment they reached what McKenzie called the "field house," a huge, circular, dome-shaped building on the Montana State University campus, Hayes saw the parking lot and knew this was going to be a security nightmare.

As they entered the building, they were surrounded by people, many of them coming up to McKenzie. There were pats on the back, handshakes, people brushing her arm in welcome as she made her way down to the exhibits.

"Are you all right?" McKenzie asked when they finally got to M.K. Realty's booth.

"It's not me I'm worried about."

"You've been scowling since we got here," she said. "Haven't you ever heard of safety in numbers?"

She seemed to be at ease, as if she'd forgotten the attack, but Hayes wasn't fooled. He could see past the bravado. She was putting on a show, determined that her attacker wasn't going to change anything about her life.

But he already had. She either was pretending otherwise or the reality of it hadn't hit home yet.

"Sorry," he said. "I'll try to lighten up. Or at least look as if I have."

She gave him a grateful smile and squeezed his arm. "I really do appreciate that you're here."

Let's see if you do when this day is over, he thought, wondering how he was going to keep her safe in a place this packed with people.

As she had a word with her employees at their booth, he watched the crowd. He had some idea of who he was looking for. A large man, over six feet, strongly built.

He'd had a few cases involving these types of men. While he knew the general type, there were always exceptions. He wasn't going to make the mistake of trying to pigeonhole this one.

The place was filled with men, most of them alone. Any one of these men could be here to hurt McKenzie. The thought rattled him so much that he didn't hear her saying his name. When she touched his arm, he jumped.

She gave him a pleading look. She was trying so hard to hold it together. She didn't need him wigging out on her.

"He could be miles from here," she whispered as she stepped close. He felt her breath on his ear and shivered inwardly. Just the light scent of her perfume had his pulse thrumming.

Today she'd worn a business suit with a white blouse under the jacket that accentuated her olive skin and the thin silver necklace around her neck. At the end of the chain, a small diamond rested between the swell of her breasts. She'd put makeup on the bruises at her neck, hiding them enough that no one would notice. Diamond studs glittered on each of her earlobes with her hair pulled up off her long, slim neck.

She'd chosen a shade of lipstick that called attention to her full mouth. No way could this woman possibly blend into this crowd.

"Are you listening to me?" she asked.

He nodded, although his thoughts had been on the way the suit skirt hugged her shapely behind, dropping below her knees to her long legs and the matching high heels on her feet. McKenzie was the whole package. Any man in his right mind would want this woman.

As it was, somewhere in this building could be a man completely out of his mind who, if he got the chance, would hurt her and bury her in a shallow grave somewhere.

"Why don't you stay here? You'll be able to see me from here." She pointed to a raised area where she would be giving her speech.

Before he could object, she took off through the crowd. He went after her, fighting his way through the throng of people. He caught a glimpse of her head as she neared the platform and knew he wouldn't be able to catch up to her before she was on stage.

McKenzie couldn't help being irritated with Hayes. She needed his strength right now. Seeing the worry in his eyes only made her more aware of what had happened to her two nights ago.

But she'd put it behind her, convinced the man had been traveling through town and was now miles from here.

She cut through the crowd, not stopping even to say

hello to people she knew. She was in the people business. It really did matter who you knew when you sold real estate, she was thinking as she neared the side of the raised platform and the podium and microphone waiting for her.

Rows of chairs had been placed in front and were already full. She'd been honored when asked to speak. Some of the older Realtors resented her because she'd climbed so fast.

She thought of Gus Thompson's mother. She'd been McKenzie's mentor and had taught her the ropes.

"Of course they don't like it," she'd said once when McKenzie had mentioned that some of the Realtors had given her the cold shoulder. "Just keep your chin up and don't lose sight of where it is you want to go."

It had been good advice. She hadn't made enemies along the way and was glad of that. Instead, she'd kept her nose to the grindstone, working hard and now knew she had the respect of her peers. Several of the older Realtors gave her a nod as she passed.

She made her way to the stairs at the back of the platform near the wall and had started up the stairs when her hair was grabbed from behind. Her head jerked back. She heard the sound of something sharp cutting through her hair an instant before the pressure on it was released.

Fighting to keep from falling back down the couple of stairs she'd climbed, she swung around, thinking she must have caught her hair on something.

There were people everywhere but none were paying

any attention to her. Nor could she see anything that might have caught in her hair.

Her hand went to her long, blond mane. In the middle of the back of her head she felt a place where a huge chunk of her hair had been chopped off only inches from her scalp.

She looked down to see a few long strands on the stairs along with the clip she'd used to put her hair up this morning.

Her body began to shake. Someone had grabbed her from behind and chopped off a huge chunk of her hair? It was inconceivable. But then so was what had happened to her the night in the grocery-store parking lot.

On the stage, one of the Realtors was checking the microphone as she got ready to announce the guest speaker.

McKenzie looked again at the people milling past. No one seemed to pay her any mind. No one had a hank of her hair in his hand. But she knew it could have been any one of them.

She quickly stepped back down the stairs to retrieve her clip. Her fingers trembled as she pulled her hair up as best she could and anchored it with the clip.

She could do this. She would do this. She wouldn't be scared off. She wouldn't let whoever had done this win.

SOMETHING WAS WRONG. Hayes watched McKenzie walk onto the stage smiling. But he knew her smile and that wasn't it.

His heart began to pound. He shouldn't have let her out of his sight. The darn woman. She was so stubborn, so sure she could handle this on her own. She hadn't been out of his sight for more than a few moments—not until she'd gone behind the raised platform.

Whatever had happened must have occurred there. But with so many people around...

He watched her walk up to the microphone. He could see her trying to pull herself together. She looked down at her notes. Even from a distance he thought he saw her hands trembling.

She laid her notes down on the podium and leaned toward the microphone. Her voice was clear and true as she looked up at the crowd gathered to hear her speak.

Hayes had admired her, but right now he was in awe of her courage and fortitude. He could practically see the determination in her shoulders, in her voice, in those amazing eyes of hers. She stood there and gave her speech with probably more spirit than she would have if something hadn't happened before she'd stepped up to that microphone.

She was beautiful, a woman to be reckoned with, and Hayes knew he wasn't the only man in the audience who thought so.

When she finished, she was met with applause and even a standing ovation.

She beamed, raising her chin into the air, her eyes bright. The look on her face filling him with fear.

If the man who'd attacked her was somewhere in that crowd watching her, McKenzie was letting him know she wasn't scared of him and that she was far from defeated.

It was the kind of challenge that would only antagonize her attacker—and get her killed.

HAYES WAS WAITING for her as she descended the stairs behind the platform. She saw his expression and had to look away to keep from breaking down. He knew. How, she had no idea.

He took her arm without a word and led her toward the closest exit. She kept a smile on her face, nodding to people she knew. Hayes didn't slow down until he had her out the door and almost to his rental car.

"What happened?" he asked the moment he had her safely in the passenger seat with him behind the wheel.

She reached up and unclipped her hair. It fell past her shoulders except for the part that had been whacked off. She put down the car's visor mirror and got her first look at the damage that had been done.

Hayes let out a curse.

The savagery of the act more than the loss of the hair brought tears to her eyes. "It will grow back. It's just hair."

He let out another oath. "He's telling you that he's not done with you. He's telling you—"

"I know what he's telling me," she snapped as she turned to face him. "It's just hair. He won't get that close to me again."

Hayes pulled off his Stetson and raked a hand through his own hair as if he was too angry to speak.

"You can't give him another chance at you," he said after a moment. "Today? It was too dangerous. You need to cancel your appointments until the police find this guy."

"What I need is a haircut."

His expression softened as he met her gaze. He must have seen how close she was to tears and how badly she was fighting not to cry. "Where do you want me to take you?"

"A friend of mine owns a salon. I'm sure under the circumstances she will be able to squeeze me in."

"After that, we need to talk," he said as he started the car and pulled out of the lot, wondering if her attacker was watching them drive away.

HE PUT THE fistful of McKenzie Sheldon's hair to his nose and smelled the sweet scent. She'd probably shampooed it this morning in the shower. He let himself imagine her standing under the warm spray for a moment. He would never see her like that, arms raised as she gently worked the shampoo into her long, blond hair.

Rubbing the hair between his fingers, he studied it in the light of the men's room. It was hard to know the exact color. Pale summer sun, he thought. Too bad he couldn't show the hair to someone who would know what to call it.

He would keep the hair. Maybe he would tie a ribbon around it. Not even an hour ago, it had been growing on her head. That thought stirred the need within. He ached with it and wasn't sure how much longer he could go without fulfilling it.

Someone came into the men's room. He put the hair

into the pocket of his jacket, careful not to let any of it escape. He'd lost some of the strands on the stairs as it was. He didn't want to lose any more.

The idea of cutting her hair hadn't even crossed his mind until he'd grabbed hold of it as she'd started up those stairs. He'd wanted her to stumble. Maybe even fall. He had needed to know if she would recognize him when she saw him. The idea of her falling into his arms was just too mouthwatering to pass up.

He'd told himself that just touching her again would be enough. But then she'd gone behind that platform out of sight of the cowboy she'd come with, the same one, he suspected, who'd saved her at the grocery-store parking lot.

Seeing his chance, he'd grabbed her hair, felt its silky smoothness… He always had his scissors with him, sharpened to a lethal edge. When he'd grabbed her hair, felt it in the fingers of his right hand, his left had gone for the scissors.

At that moment, he'd wanted a piece of her—since that was all he was going to get until he could catch her alone.

Now, feeling better than he had since the night he'd failed, he left the bathroom one hand deep in the pocket of his jacket where he kept the scissors, the other gently caressing her hair. It was enough for today, he thought, anxious to get out of the building so he could be alone.

Soon, McKenzie Sheldon. Very soon and it will be more than your hair that I have my hands on.

"ARE YOU SURE you don't want me to take your open

house today?" Jennifer Robinson asked when McKenzie called the office.

"No, I can handle it, but thanks, Jennifer." She wasn't looking forward to the open house. Someone had tried to scare her yesterday.

Now she looked at her short curly hair in the mirror. Hayes had complimented her hairdo when she'd come out of the salon. "It looks good on you."

She'd always hated her natural curly hair, brushing it straight every morning after her shower. It felt odd, the loss of weight she'd become used to. She raked her hand through the curls and told herself she liked it better short—a lie, one she told herself every time she remembered the sudden feel of her head being pulled back, then the sound of something sharp cutting through her long hair before her head snapped forward again.

It had happened so fast.

And could again, Hayes had reminded her. She knew he was angry with her for taking off yesterday without him with her—and for not hiding out. He didn't want her hosting this open house today. He didn't understand. She couldn't hide. She refused to let this man take away everything she'd worked so hard for.

"At least come back to the ranch tonight," Hayes had pleaded yesterday after the conference. "I can keep you safe there."

She'd been scared and shaken enough that she'd agreed to go back up the canyon to Cardwell Ranch rather than return to her condo. Her evening had been so relaxing and enjoyable she'd never wanted to leave. Dana's husband, Marshal Hud Savage, had cooked steaks outside on the grill and they'd all eaten on the wide porch to enjoy the beautiful night.

She'd been completely captivated by the Cardwells, especially Hayes. He had an easygoing way about him that appealed to her. It amazed her that she'd thought there was anything threatening about him. It was his eyes. She'd remembered them from the night of the attack. They had been comforting. Just like his words. *You're safe now.*

Only she wasn't.

She reminded herself of that as she drove from Big Sky into Bozeman, determined to get on with her life.

"At least let me take you to your open house," he'd argued.

"You can't be with me 24/7 and I refuse to hide under a rock. He's trying to scare me."

"Until he tries to abduct you again and kill you. McKenzie, he knows who you are."

His last words had sent an icy chill through her. *He knows who you are.*

But she didn't know who he was. He could have been anyone in that crowd yesterday.

Angry with herself for letting her thoughts take that turn, she told herself she would put the attack behind her. Big words, she thought as she drove up in front of her condo and just sat there, engine running, surprised how hard it was to face going inside. She knew it was crazy. The attack hadn't even happened here. And yet she had the crazy fear that he would be inside, waiting for her....

Getting out of her SUV, she gripped her keys as she made her way to the front door. She noticed her neighbor had already gone to work. A quiet had settled over the four units. She'd picked this condo because of all the pine trees and the creek that meandered past it.

Now, though, the thick pines made her nervous and the babbling stream quickly put her nerves on edge. She got the key into the lock and pushed open the door.

She wasn't sure what she'd expected to find. Maybe the place ransacked. Everything looked exactly as she'd left it. She stepped in. An eerie silence settled around her. She'd always loved coming home. The condo had been decorated simply with light colors that made the rooms feel welcoming. She'd always felt at peace here.

Now, however, she opened her shoulder bag and took out the pepper spray she'd bought yesterday. Holding it, she moved quickly through the two-story condo, checking closets and bathrooms and even under beds until she was sure she was alone.

She was trembling more from fear than from the effort of searching the spacious condo. The fear made her angry with herself. She couldn't keep living like this.

When her cell phone rang, she jumped. Stilling her heart, she took the call. It was her sister.

"How are you doing?" Shawna asked.

"Fine." The lie seemed to catch in her throat. "Not as well as I'd hoped."

"If you need company—"

"No, I'm keeping busy. I have an open house today."

"Work as usual, huh? That's my little sis. Well, if you need anything, you know to call."

"I will. Thank you."

As she hung up, she saw that Gus Thompson had left a message. She braced herself and played it.

"We need to talk. Call me."

Just the sound of his voice made her stomach ache. What did he think they needed to talk about? And why was he so insistent? She still couldn't believe he was the man who'd attacked her, but maybe she just didn't want to. She'd worked with him for years. Surely she would have known he was dangerous, wouldn't she?

McKenzie quickly showered and changed for her open house, determined not to let Gus or anyone else keep her from her work. She had a business to run. She had to go over everything she needed, afraid that as distracted as she was, she would forget something important. The open house needed to go off just right. This was a major sale for a contractor she liked working with, so she hoped to get an offer before the day was out.

Hurrying so she could get to the house early, she exited her front door and was just pulling the door closed after her when the man stepped out of the shadows.

HAYES SWUNG BY the restaurant site before heading to McKenzie's open house. He wanted to see the traffic flow in the area and take another look around. The other day, he'd been distracted and determined they weren't buying the space. But after talking to his brother Laramie, he'd tried to reach Austin. He'd been told that Austin was on a case and couldn't be reached. He couldn't help worrying about him.

He felt at loose ends. His attempt to talk McKenzie out of hosting the open house today had fallen on deaf ears. Did she really think that by pretending none of this was happening it would stop this bastard? All she had to do was look in the mirror to see just how close the man had gotten to her—again.

He'd been shocked last night after dinner when she'd told him about the open house, but he'd tried not to argue with her. He'd seen the way she could dig her heels in. Look at what had happened yesterday. Maybe his concern *had* put her in more danger. He was determined not to let that happen again.

"Can't someone else host it?" he'd suggested.

"I could get someone else to do it, but…I can't." She'd shrugged as if it was hard to explain.

"I get it," he'd said. "You're like my brother Laramie. We've offered to help with the load, but…"

"He has it handled."

"Yep, and he does a fine job of it. I noticed that you own your realty company." She was young to have accomplished so much so quickly. He wondered if she'd had help and decided not. It was that tenacity about her that intrigued him. But also frustrated him because her determination not to let her attacker interfere with her life put her in danger.

"It was a lot of hard work, but when you want something badly enough…" Her voice had dropped off and he'd realized she was thinking about the man she'd fought off repeatedly the night of her attack. Neither would have given up. If Hayes hadn't come out of the store when he had…

"What kind of open house is it?" he'd asked to derail her thoughts—and his own.

"A brand-new, state-of-the-art, spacious, three-thousand-square-foot executive home overlooking Bozeman with beautiful views of the Spanish Peaks."

He'd laughed and she'd joined him. He was glad she could laugh at herself.

"I did sound like a Realtor, didn't I?" She sighed. "Bad habit."

"Let me guess. All restaurant-quality appliances and granite countertops in the massive kitchen. I had the flu recently and found myself watching some of those home shows on television. Talk about over the top."

She'd nodded in agreement. "You do see a lot of… extravagance in some of the homes in this area, too. Gold faucets, heated driveways, dual master suites."

"You love what you do," he'd said as if he'd just seen it.

She'd smiled, tears in her eyes. "That's why I can't let him stop me."

"Or me stop you," he'd said, and she'd nodded before she'd leaned over and gently placed a kiss on his cheek.

Their eyes met and locked and for one breath-stealing moment he'd almost taken her in his arms, even though he knew he wanted a lot more than a kiss. Fortunately, or unfortunately, they'd been interrupted by the kids running in to say good-night as they headed to bed.

The moment had been lost, filling him with regret and relief at the same time. His life was in Houston. He reminded himself of that now.

Determined to get at least the barbecue joint settled, he called Jackson. Ford answered the phone. The five-year-old sounded so grown-up. Hayes tried to remember the last time he'd seen his nephew. It had been too long, that was for sure.

"Hey, kid," he said. "What have you been up to?"

Ford was a chatterbox on the phone. Hayes listened to stories about sports, the trouble his nephew had gotten into and how they would be flying to Montana for his uncle Tag's wedding to some girl before Ford launched into an excited story about the horse Dana had picked out for him to ride once he got to Montana.

Finally, Hayes had to ask if he could speak to the boy's father.

Jackson came on the line.

"How much of that can I believe?" Hayes joked.

His brother laughed. "Ford's into Texas tall tales I'm afraid, just like his uncles. What's this I hear about Laramie supporting the Montana restaurant?"

"I talked to him last night. Tag's convinced him. I have to admit, I've weakened, as well."

"What about this future bride?"

Hayes could hear the concern in Jackson's voice. He'd gotten burned badly. He didn't want to see his brother Tag go through a divorce.

"She's nice. I liked her. She's got plenty of her own money, a good job, a nice house up on the mountain behind Big Sky. Clearly, they are crazy about each other."

Jackson snorted. He knew crazy.

"I'm standing in front of the restaurant space right now. I think we should move ahead with this."

Jackson sounded surprised. "What changed your mind?"

"I actually think it's a good business decision. Also, I guess I want to do this for Tag."

"Is everyone else in agreement?"

"Can't reach Austin. Nothing new there." But he figured Austin would go along with whatever was decided. He had little interest in the business, too involved in being a sheriff's deputy and saving the world.

"As long as Tag's new wife isn't involved in the business in any way, I'm good with it," Jackson said. "I still have time to meet her and see what I think before he can get the place open."

No one was more cynical than Jackson.

"I think this is the right thing to do," Hayes said, checking his watch. "I'll tell the Realtor when I see her."

GUS WAS GLAD he'd scared her. He took enjoyment in McKenzie's shock and fear. How did she think he felt being interrogated by the police and suddenly out of a job?

"Gus." She said his name on a frightened breath, her hand going to her chest as she stumbled back against her closed condo door.

He'd seen her lock it so he knew she wasn't going to be able to get back inside away from him until he had his say. He closed the distance, forcing her up against the door, towering over her. She'd cut her hair. It surprised him. He'd always thought she liked it long. He wondered what had precipitated this? Out with the old, in with the new? Had she already replaced him at the agency?

"What do you want?" Her voice actually squeaked. Where was that ball-breaking woman he'd worked for the past six years?

"What do I *want?*" he repeated. "I want to know why you're ruining my life."

Some of her steel returned to her voice. "This isn't the place to talk about this."

He laughed. "Where would that place be, McKenzie? You've taken out a restraining order against me so I can't go near the office or you."

Some of the color came back into her face. "It should be obvious why I had to do that."

"Because you think I'm some kind of psycho? Do you really think I attacked you in a grocery parking lot?"

"I don't know. Were you at the conference yesterday?"

"Why? Were you attacked again?" He smirked. "Do you really think I can show my face at a real-estate conference right now?"

He could tell she didn't believe him. "I thought I saw you there."

"Well, you were wrong. The same way you were wrong to fire me."

"I'm sure I wasn't the first person you've stalked. You've been harassing my receptionist. I told you that if I had to warn you again…"

He looked at her in disbelief. "Maybe I was *interested* in you, did you ever consider that? I came by your house that day to ask you out, but about the time I finally got up my nerve, you saw me. Your expression… Well, let's just say I knew my answer."

The woman he'd known was back. Anger flared in her eyes. She moved away from the door, forcing him to take a step back. "It's too bad you didn't take no from Cynthia."

He felt off-balance, something she'd made him feel way too many times. "I don't expect you to believe this, but she led me on. She liked me flirting with her."

"Up to a point, I'm sure that was true."

"And yet you fired *me*."

"It was a combination of things, Gus, not just a couple of incidents and you know it. You've always resented working for me."

He nodded, finally seeing it. His own anger boiled to the surface. "You were just waiting for my mother to die so you could get rid of me. As long as she was alive, you wouldn't dare."

"That isn't true." McKenzie looked at her watch, dismissing him. The old McKenzie Sheldon, businesswoman, had come back. "You're going to make me late for an open house and there really is no point to this discussion. I'm not changing my mind. If you promise to leave me alone in the future, I will write you a recommendation, not that you need one. You're a great salesman. Just stop trying to sell yourself to women who aren't in the market."

"That's it?"

"You brought this on yourself, Gus." She slipped past him.

He had no choice but to let her go. As he watched her drive away, he felt as if she'd punched him in the gut. He knew the best thing he could do was leave her alone, take the recommendation and start looking for another job.

But this still felt unfinished to him.

HE STOOD OUTSIDE the open house for a moment, wondering who could afford such a home—and what the commission would net McKenzie Sheldon. Probably more money than he made in months. He would never admit that that alone made him want to hurt this woman. The woman was obviously very successful. It would seem small of him to want to destroy her simply out of jealousy.

But a part of him had to admit, he liked to target successful women. He liked bringing them down. He smiled to himself, thinking how many of them he had made beg for their lives. They weren't so arrogant and sure of themselves then.

People were coming in and out of the open house. Beautiful June days probably brought more people out than stormy, wintery ones, he thought. He waited and fell behind a group of five. Being a salesman at heart himself, he quickly sized them up. The elderly married couple looked serious about home buying. The two women behind them were just gawkers. The lone man who'd led the way looked like another Realtor.

Once inside, he cut away from the others. The elderly couple made a beeline for McKenzie and the flyer she was handing out. He only got a glimpse of her. The last thing he wanted to do was get caught staring at her.

His plan had worked beautifully. He would wait until there were a lot of other people going through the house so he blended in. But at some point, he would have to get close enough to McKenzie Sheldon so he could look into her eyes and find out whether or not she recognized him.

Even a hint of recognition and he would get out of there. The best plan was to park a few blocks away and walk. Not that he expected her to chase him out to his car. Or even scream.

The house was no surprise. Every room was large and over the top with expensive features and furnishings. He wandered around, saw the older couple inspecting the fixtures and heard the two women oohing and ahhing over the kitchen.

As spacious as the house was, he felt claustrophobic and knew he couldn't take much more of this. He was working up his nerve to return to the main entrance and get one of the brochures from Ms. Sheldon, when he came around a corner and almost collided with her.

She pretended the encounter hadn't startled her, but he'd seen the terror flash in her eyes. Nice eyes, more green than blue today. Those eyes widened and for just a moment, he feared she'd recognized him. She was blocking the hallway and his way out. A fissure of panic raced along his nerve endings. Perspiration dampened his shirt and hairline.

He told himself that if she opened her mouth, he'd hit her. There wasn't anyone else around. He'd punch her hard enough to knock her out and then he'd push her into one of the bedrooms and leave quickly. He balled up one fist and took a breath.

But she didn't scream. The flash of terror had only lasted an instant then she'd looked relieved and relaxed a little.

"Sorry," she said. "You startled me."

Not as much as I did a few nights ago. He looked

right into those aquamarine waters. Not even a hint of recognition. He almost laughed since just an instant before he'd been planning to knock her senseless and make his escape.

"I'm sorry," he said. "We both must have been distracted."

"How do you like the house?" she asked, covering her initial reaction to him.

"It's beautiful." *Just like you.* She blew him away. She was much more striking than her photo on the real-estate signs. There was a sweetness about her. Strength? Oh, he knew her strength and her determination only too well. Sweet, strong and successful—his perfect woman.

"You might want one of these." She held out a flyer.

"Yes," he said and smiled. "Thank you. Oh, and do you have a business card?"

She brightened. "Of course. I usually have one stapled to the flyers. I forgot this morning. I have one in my purse if you'd like to follow me." She headed back toward the entrance. He followed her, admiring the part of her body he had some history with.

From under an entertainment counter, she pulled out her purse, removed a business card and handed it to him. The card was thick, nicely embossed. He rubbed it gently between his fingers. A business card told a lot about a person.

He carefully put it into his shirt pocket and folded the flyer she'd given him.

"Is there anything else I can help you with?" she asked.

"No, I think I have everything." He smiled. "But you'll be hearing from me."

McKENZIE WAS JUST about to ask the man for his name when the front door opened and her attention was drawn away as she saw Hayes Cardwell come through the door.

A mixture of pleasure and relief filled her at the sight of the big cowboy. He wore jeans, a Western shirt and a gray Stetson over his longish dark hair. Unlike yesterday, he looked more relaxed.

Almost instinctively, she started to move toward him, but remembered the man who'd shown an interest in the house. She turned her attention back to him. "I look forward to hearing from you if you have any questions about the house or would like to see any others."

"Next time, I'd like to bring my wife along. I'll give you a call," the man said, glancing at Hayes before he quickly moved off.

McKenzie turned to Hayes. She always felt she had to be "on" at open houses. Even though she loved her job, sometimes it wasn't just her high-heeled shoes that made her hurt. Her face often ached from smiling so much.

"Decided you wanted a kitchen with all stainless-steel appliances and granite countertops?"

"Can't imagine living without them."

She chuckled at that. "You're saying you don't have them at your house in Houston?"

"I live in an unremodeled house in the older part of Houston."

She cocked an eyebrow at that.

"I have…humble tastes."

"Nothing wrong with that," she said. "Excuse me a moment." McKenzie saw a few more people she needed to talk to before they left. The elderly couple sounded interested. She gave them her business card. As she started to go look for Hayes, she saw the man she'd spoken to earlier before Hayes had come in.

The man was walking away when he suddenly stopped and turned to look back at her as if he'd known she'd be there framed in the front window, watching him. He gave a slow, vague kind of smile. She quickly stepped back out of sight, even though she feared he'd seen her. His smile had almost been mocking, as if he'd put one over on her.

She'd dealt with enough people at open houses that she had a pretty good sense of who was genuinely in the market for a house and who wasn't. The man had seemed interested and yet he hadn't asked any questions about the house—unlike the elderly couple. Maybe he *had* just been putting her on.

McKenzie went to find Hayes, annoyed with the man and herself. He might have fooled her once, but she would be watching for him at her next open house.

HAYES LOOKED AROUND the large residence, killing time until the open house was over. Several men came through. Any one of them could have been McKenzie's attacker.

At four o'clock, he found McKenzie finishing up with a couple and waited as she packed up to leave.

"Dinner. You name the restaurant," he said.

"I really should—"

"Work?" He saw her hesitate. "I figured since we both need to eat…"

She brushed a lock of hair back from her face. She'd dressed up for the open house, taking extra pains with her appearance. Probably to give herself more confidence. But under the surface, he would see that she was still running scared.

"Hayes, I appreciate what you're trying to do…."

"*Eat?* I like to do it three times a day, if possible."

"You know what I mean." She sighed. "You can't protect me forever, especially since you will be leaving soon."

He nodded. "So that must mean I'm just hungry, don't you think?"

She laughed. "Are you always so determined?"

"Always." He led the way out of the house and waited while she locked up. "By the way, how long do we have on that restaurant space at Big Sky?"

"Changed your mind?" she asked as they walked toward their vehicles.

"Tag isn't changing *his* mind." They'd reached his rented SUV. "Why don't you leave your car," he suggested. "I'll be happy to bring you back after dinner."

"Okay. Just let me put my things away."

He watched her put the flyers in the passenger seat and helped her place the Open House signs in the trunk. But as they finished, he noticed her look past him and frown. He turned but didn't see anything out of the ordinary.

"Is everything all right?" he asked.

"Hmm," she said distractedly. "Just someone I saw earlier at the open house. He must live in the neighborhood. It's nothing."

They ate a nice dinner, talked about everything but her attacker. Not that it kept the man from being present. Hayes doubted the attack was ever far from either of their minds.

He'd hoped McKenzie would be staying in the cabin at Cardwell Ranch, but she couldn't hide out, given her career. Not that a woman like her would let herself hide out forever, anyway, and the man might never be caught. Still, he didn't like the idea of McKenzie staying in her condo alone.

He'd told his brother he was staying until the wedding. It was only a few weeks away and if they were going ahead with the restaurant, he could help out. At least that was his excuse. In truth, he couldn't leave McKenzie. Not yet, even though she was right. He couldn't stay forever. Maybe it was best for her to start adjusting to living with never knowing when the man might reappear in her life.

"Dinner was wonderful," she said as they left the restaurant. "And a great idea."

"Thanks. I'm just full of great ideas," he said with a chuckle. "Like this one. I wish you would come back up to the ranch tonight."

She shook her head as he pulled up behind her car where they'd left it earlier for the open house. With the houses so far apart, the neighborhood was dark in the huge spaces between streetlamps. No lights burned in the house she'd shown earlier. With the houses bordered by tall, dense trees or high hedges, there were lots of places for a man to hide, he thought.

How many houses just like this did she show alone? He hated to think. In other places, he'd heard that real-estate agents now worked in twos to be safer. But this was Montana. People felt safe here.

"Thank you for the offer," she said. "I appreciate it, but I have a lot to do tomorrow."

He nodded, not surprised.

She opened her car door. "Have your brother give me a call about the restaurant space."

So that was how it was going to be? Business as usual? The woman was stubborn as a mule. She refused to take some time off, leave the state or at least town for a while. There was no way he could keep her safe and he couldn't just walk away.

He got out and caught up to her, catching her hand to turn her toward him. "I have a favor." She raised a brow. "I need a date for the wedding."

"Your brother's wedding?"

"Yes."

She shook her head. "I'm not your responsibility. I told you, you can't keep me safe."

"It's more complicated than that," he said as he touched her cheek. "From the moment I first looked in your eyes…" His words died off. She was staring at him. He shook his head. "Maybe I can't get you out of my mind—"

"I know what you're up to."

"I doubt that," he said, and leaned toward her, his hand looping around the back of her neck as he gently drew her to him. "Because if you could see what I was up to, then you'd know I was about to kiss you."

He brushed his lips over hers, then pulled back to gaze into her eyes. He'd been captivated by those eyes two nights ago. That hadn't changed. "Sorry, I couldn't resist."

"You don't have to treat me as if I'm made out of glass and might break," she said. "I'm a little battered right now, but I'm resilient and strong, a lot stronger than I look."

"Is that right?" He looped an arm around her waist and pulled her to him right there in the street between their vehicles. He kissed her like he meant it this time. Her full lips parted in surprise. Her sweet, warm breath comingled with his own. She let out a soft moan as he tasted her. Drawing her even closer, he deepened the kiss, demanding more.

McKenzie came to him, fitting into his arms as she answered his kiss with passion. He felt desire race in a hot streak through his veins. He didn't want to ever stop kissing her.

But when she pulled back, he let out a shaky breath. "Wow," he said and laughed.

She sounded just as breathless. She met his gaze in the moonlight. "Hayes, what is this?"

"*This?* This is crazy. Worst possible timing ever."

McKenzie nodded agreement.

"And yet, from the first moment I looked into your eyes..."

She shook her head. "I...I really can't.... Hayes, I'm

not sure of anything right now and quite frankly, I'm suspicious of your motives."

"My motives for kissing you? It was just a kiss, right?"

She studied him openly in the dim light.

"Quite the kiss, though, wouldn't you say?" he asked, grinning.

She smiled at that. "Quite the kiss."

"Glad you agree. I'm still going to follow you home and make sure you're all right."

She looked as if she wanted to put up a fight, but no longer had the energy to. "Thank you," she said as she turned and started for her car. He watched her. She seemed a little wobbly on her high heels, strange for a woman who lived in them. He hoped the kiss had smacked her silly the way it had him. He'd kissed his share of women, but none had lit a fire in him the way McKenzie's kiss had.

As she reached the car, she hesitated. He saw her glance back at him, then reach for something on her windshield. His pulse leaped. Something was wrong. He was running toward her as she took what looked like a folded sheet of paper from under the wiper blade.

Chapter Eight

McKenzie had been shaken even before she found the note. The kiss had her whirling. It had been a while since a man had kissed her. She couldn't recall anyone who'd made her surrender so completely to a kiss before, though. She'd felt...*wanton,* and that wasn't a word she would have used about herself. She'd also felt out of control and that scared her.

Hayes had her blood running hot. He'd sparked something in her that made her ache for more. That alone was enough to turn her already crazy world upside down. She'd been content with her career, with her life, with an occasional date. Hayes had changed all that in just one kiss. Now she wanted...Hayes Cardwell. Bad timing or not.

But she questioned whether he was interested in her as a woman. Or if he was just hardwired to protect the woman whose life he'd saved because he was a Texas cowboy and a gentleman.

When she'd found the note under her windshield wiper, at first she'd thought it was an advertisement.

Instead, scrawled words had been written on the sheet of paper.

I'm watching you.
This time you won't get away.
I am going to miss your long hair.

The paper began to shake in her fingers. She had *felt* him watching her. It hadn't been her imagination. He was out there and he wasn't through with her.

She read the words again, all easily visible in the diffused light from the closest streetlamp. All her bravado fell away. The man wasn't giving up. He was out there. Maybe even watching her right now, wanting to see her fall apart.

McKenzie slumped against her car as she looked out into the darkness, unable to pretend any longer that she wasn't terrified. She'd thought she could go on as if nothing had happened. As if nothing kept happening.

Suddenly, Hayes was at her side, his arms coming around her. "What is it?" His gaze took in the sheet of paper trembling in her fingers. Using his sleeve, he took it from her. "Get in my car. I'll call the police."

She nodded and started for his rental SUV. Earlier, she'd told him how strong and resilient she was. She didn't feel either right now. She wanted to lose herself in his strong arms. For so long she'd made her way alone, determined not to lean on anyone, not to need anyone. Right now, she needed Hayes—and more than just to protect her.

Behind her, she heard him on the phone. Her gaze

swept through the dark neighborhood. A breeze stirred the tree boughs, throwing shadows everywhere. Was he out there watching her? Enjoying tormenting her?

McKenzie quickened her step, grabbed the passenger-side door handle and flung it open. She practically threw herself into the car, slamming the door behind her. Heart pounding, she tried to catch her breath. Anger mixed with fear, a deadly combination that had her wiping furiously at her tears.

She'd never felt helpless before. It was a horrible feeling, one she couldn't bear. Somehow, she had to make it end, and falling into bed with Hayes wasn't the answer as much as she would have liked to.

As Hayes finished his call and climbed into the SUV behind the wheel, she turned to him. "I have to find this man."

"I've called the police. They're on their way. They'll see if they can get a print off—"

"He won't have left fingerprints on the note he left for me. He's too smart for that." She shook her head. "Nor do I believe the police will find him. That's why I have to."

Hayes stared across the seat at her. "What are you saying?"

"I need to set a trap for him."

He held up a hand. "Hold on."

"No, I can't let him continue to torment me. I have to find him and put an end to this, one way or another."

HAYES DIDN'T KNOW how to tell her, but decided honesty might be the best approach. "I would imagine he will find you before you find him." He saw her reaction to his words. "He's fooling with you because you made a fool of him the other night. He has only one option. He needs to right this. Which means there's a really good chance that he isn't some psycho passing through town who just happened to see you the other night. He's a hometown psycho who isn't finished with you."

Her lower lip quivered for a moment before she bit down on it. "You sound as if you've dealt with this kind of…person before."

He nodded. "I've crossed paths with several. They're calculating, cunning and unpredictable—and extremely dangerous."

She leaned toward him and he was reminded of their kiss. He could smell her clean scent and remembered the feel of her in his arms. "Help me set a trap for him. I don't want to wait until it's on his terms."

"It's not that easy—"

McKenzie drew back. "I'm sorry. I shouldn't have asked. You have your brother's wedding and you're leaving town—"

"Do you really think I can leave you now?" He thought of that strange feeling the moment he'd looked into her eyes three nights ago—not to mention the kiss just moments before. He took her hands in his, reveling at the touch of her skin against his. This woman made him feel things he'd never felt before, never dreamed he would ever feel.

"I can't let you go after this man alone. I'm staying until I know you're safe." He wasn't sure he could leave even then and that scared him more than he wanted to admit.

He thought of his brother Tag coming to Montana for Christmas and falling for Lily. Now Tag was getting married and talking about settling in Big Sky. Hayes had thought his brother was nuts to leave behind everything like that.

Hayes felt as if his head were spinning. All he knew for sure was that he had to protect this woman—whatever it took. He couldn't think beyond that, didn't dare.

"I won't be safe as long as he's out there. You said so yourself. I don't see that I have a choice."

A car turned onto the street. The headlights washed over them. Hayes glanced in his rearview mirror as the cop car pulled up behind them.

Hayes didn't have a choice, either. He leaned over and kissed her quickly before climbing out with the note that had been left on her windshield. Like her, he doubted there would be fingerprints on it. Just as he doubted the police would be able to find this man, given how little they had to go on.

The only thing Hayes didn't doubt was that the psycho would be coming for McKenzie.

THE POLICE OFFICER bagged the note her attacker had left and promised to let her know if they found any prints. McKenzie could see that Hayes wasn't holding out any more hope than she was.

The cop walked around the neighborhood, shone his flashlight into the bushes and trees, but to no one's surprise, found nothing.

"He's right," Hayes said after the officer left and he walked her back to her car. "The best thing you can do right now would be to take a long vacation somewhere far away from here."

They stood under Montana's big sky. Millions of stars glittered over their heads and a cool, white moon now buoyed along among them. The June night had turned crisp and cool. This far north even summer nights could chill you. Especially if there was a killer on the loose.

"Do you really think the man would forget about me?" She didn't give him a chance to answer because they both knew that answer. "I can't run away. I would always be looking over my shoulder. No, I have to end this here and soon."

Hayes groaned. "How did I know you were going to say that?"

She shrugged and met his gaze, losing herself in his dark eyes. It would have been easy to get on a plane with him and go to Texas and pretend none of this had happened.

But it *had* happened. Not to mention, she had a business here, people who were counting on her. She wasn't going anywhere—not that Hayes had given her the Texas option to begin with.

She felt strangely calmer as she leaned against the side of her car and looked at the Texas cowboy standing by her. Once she'd settled down enough so she could actually think clearly, she'd made the decision quickly—just as she'd done with her business.

She couldn't wait around for this horrible man to try

to abduct her again and do nothing. If Hayes wouldn't help her, then she would figure out something on her own. She'd been on her own and done all right. She wasn't going to let one crazy psycho change that.

"I have another open house tomorrow." She held up her hand before Hayes could argue. "As you said, he knows who I am. He also knows where I am going to be. For all I know he was one of the people who came through the house earlier. I could have talked to him." She shuddered at the thought and hugged herself.

"I wouldn't be at all surprised that he was one of the men who came through today," Hayes said. "Seeing you feeds whatever it is that drives him. He likes seeing you scared. He'll play with you until he's ready to make his move, until an opportunity presents itself."

She was no fool. She was still scared, but knowing that the man wanted her scared made her determined not to let her fear hold her back. "So you're saying it could be a while before he makes his move?"

"Possibly. Unless you give him the opportunity he needs—like at an open house. You do realize this is speculation based on what I know about men like this. As I said earlier, they're unpredictable. I could be completely off base. There is no way to know what he will do next."

She nodded, considering this. "He feels safe because I didn't see his face the night he attacked me. If you're right about what drives him, he won't be able to stay away."

Hayes took off his Stetson and raked a hand through his thick, dark hair. She recalled the feel of those fingers when he'd taken the nape of her neck in his hand during their kiss.

"If you're determined to do this, then I'm staying down here in the valley tonight. I'm also going to the open house tomorrow," Hayes said.

She shook her head. "He won't make his move as long as you're around."

He stuffed his hat back down on his head and stepped to her to take her shoulders in his hands. "He's just waiting for the chance to get you alone again. He will make that happen with or without me around because he knows I can't watch you all the time. I'll be there tomorrow, like it or not."

McKenzie knew she didn't have the strength to tackle this tonight. "All right," she agreed. She had mixed feelings about having Hayes around. On one hand she would definitely feel safer, but he was a distraction she couldn't afford right now. She had to think clearly.

"He'll come to the open house tomorrow."

Hayes nodded in agreement. "That would be my guess. He's trying to build up his confidence. Being around you and you not knowing how close he is…well, that will make him feel more in control."

"Is there any way to get photos of everyone who comes through the open house?"

"Consider it done. I'll also talk to the police about running the license plates of those who show up."

She smiled at him. "I do appreciate what you're trying to do to keep me safe." She sobered as she looked into his handsome face. "I don't like involving you in this. If this man is as dangerous as we both suspect—"

"Don't worry about me. I'll follow you to your condo. But first let me check your car."

McKenzie watched him look under and around her car before popping the hood and checking the engine. "You can't think he'd put a bomb under my hood."

"Not really. But I do think he might disable your car so it stalls on the way to your condo and while you're trying to figure out what is wrong…"

She got the idea. Distraction. That's how she'd fallen into the man's snare the first time. A memory of the dark night at the grocery-store parking lot flashed before her. She'd been fiddling with her keys, her mind on the phone call and Gus. Gus, she thought with a silent curse. Maybe she should have called the police after she found him on her doorstep at the condo. Was this note merely him trying to scare her? Or was it from the man who'd tried to abduct her?

As she looked out into the darkness, McKenzie wasn't sure who would be caught in the trap she hoped to set for her would-be abductor. Whoever he was, she didn't feel him out there watching her. But he had been there. A psycho who, for whatever reason, had set his sights on her.

AT HER CONDO, McKenzie unlocked the door while Hayes surveyed the neighborhood. He hated that there were too many places for a man to hide. Also, because Bozeman was so small, he had to assume that the man knew where she lived.

He had McKenzie remain by the door until he could check to make sure they were alone in the condo. The place was neat and clean and sparsely furnished. He got the feeling that she didn't spend much time here other than to sleep.

The lower floor consisted of a kitchen, dining room, living room and half bath. Upstairs he found a full bath and two bedrooms. Just the right size for a single woman who worked all the time.

"Can you tell if anyone has been here?" he asked her when he returned to where he'd left her downstairs just inside the door.

She glanced around, clearly startled by the question. "I don't think so. How would he have gotten in?"

"I didn't see any forced entry, but if the man is someone you know and has access to your keys…"

"You mean like an old boyfriend?" She shook her head. "No one has a key to my condo. Nor can I recall anyone having access to my keys."

"Good." He met her gaze. "Do you own a weapon?"

She swallowed and looked uncomfortable. "I have pepper spray, Hayes." His name seemed to come of its own volition. She appeared surprised as if she, too, had just realized that she'd never said it before. "I also have a spare bedroom, if you want to…" She looked away.

"Thanks," he said without hesitation. He was planning to stay, whether she liked it or not.

"The spare bedroom—"

"I know where it is," he said.

She nodded. "I can't take being afraid all the time."

"We'll find him." Even as he said it, Hayes hoped he wasn't promising something he couldn't deliver. He *would* find him, but before the man got to McKenzie? That was what worried him.

She glanced at her watch. "Would you like a drink? I could use one." She headed for the kitchen.

He followed. As she pulled out a bottle of wine from the refrigerator, he said, "I'm going to need to know about everyone who came through the open house today—at least all of them you can remember. Do you have something I can write on?"

She poured them each a glass of wine before removing a notebook and pen from the small desk in the corner of the kitchen. They sat down in the living room on furniture that felt and smelled new. He doubted she had many—if any—guests over, including men. No time to date, he suspected.

That also explained why the man who had attacked her had chosen her. A businesswoman with a lot on her mind. She was a classic case of the perfect female victim. Had the man been following her? Or had he picked her at random? Hayes wished he knew. It would help find the bastard.

"Okay, from when the first person came in after you got to the open house…"

She nodded, took a sip of her wine and began to go through them. He quickly weeded out the women and most of the couples.

"There was that one man near the end…" She stared thoughtfully into space for a moment. "You might have seen him. I was talking to him when you arrived."

Hayes recalled a tall man with a head of thick, brown hair and light-colored eyes. He looked like a former football player. In fact, Hayes recalled wondering if the man had played for the Bobcats while attending Montana State University. He'd been wearing a Bobcat jacket.

"Early forties, big, not bad-looking?"

She nodded. "He seemed interested in the house—until I saw him later when he was leaving."

Hayes frowned. "What changed your mind?"

"You're going to think I'm silly, but he hadn't driven to the open house. I realized he must live in the neighborhood."

"He could have parked some distance away."

She nodded. "I suppose, but as I was watching him walk away, he seemed to sense me watching him and turned. It was his expression… This is where you're going to think I'm nuts, but he turned to look back, right at me as if he knew I would be there watching him, and the look on his face…" She took a drink of her wine. "It was as if he'd put something over on me."

Hayes felt a fissure of unease move through him. "You think it could have been the man who attacked you?"

"He was big enough." She shook her head. "I don't know. He mentioned that he had a wife."

"Probably to put you at ease."

"Maybe. It's just that he seemed…nice, gentle even, almost shy."

"Ted Bundy seemed the same way to *his* victims." McKenzie finished her wine and poured them both another glass. "Why would he take a chance like that, not just coming to the open house, but actually talking to me?"

"Maybe he wanted to see if you recognized him."

She cupped the wineglass in her hand as she felt a shudder move through her. "Is it possible I was that close to him again and I didn't know it?" That alone terrified her. Could she really not sense the danger?

"It's why the cops take video of people at crime scenes and funerals. Criminals like to return to the scene of the crime. In your case, be close to one of their victims."

"He is safe—until he tries to abduct me again." She shivered. "If he doesn't try again, he'll have gotten away with it." She felt her eyes suddenly widened in alarm. "There have been others, haven't there?"

"More than likely. But that can help. If we find out who this man is, maybe we can place him wherever those other abductions took place."

"You think he *killed* them."

Hayes didn't answer. He didn't have to. "I'm sure the police are looking into other abductions or missing persons around the area.... I'll check with them tomorrow. Tell me about tomorrow's open house."

"It's out in the country. It's fairly...isolated."

"Then I'm definitely going to be there. Don't worry, I'll be discreet. You won't even know I'm around. I'll want to go out earlier than you. Will you be going to your office in the morning even though it's a Sunday?"

"Yes. My job isn't eight to five. Nor five days a week."

"Neither is mine, so I get it," he said, and finished

his wine. His gaze met hers and she felt that bubble of excitement rise inside her, along with a longing that she knew only this man could fill. She wanted him, but not like this. Maybe once this was over...

As if sensing her thoughts, he said, "It's late. We should get some rest." He got to his feet.

"The bed is made up in the spare room. There are towels in the bathroom cabinet...."

"Thank you. I'm sure I have everything I need."

Wasn't that what the man at the open house had said?

Hayes met her gaze. "I'll be right down the hall if you need me."

She nodded. She *did* need him. It was that need that kept her silent as she watched him head upstairs. She heard him go into the bathroom and turn on the shower. She could hear water running and closed her eyes at the thought of Hayes naked in her shower. The Texas cowboy had done something no other man had. He'd reminded her she was a woman, a woman with needs other than her career.

McKenzie poured herself another glass of wine, finishing off the bottle. Normally, she had only one glass before bedtime. Tonight, she didn't mind indulging. Better to indulge in wine than in what she would have liked to indulge in. Her life was complicated enough without getting any more involved with Hayes Cardwell than she already was.

The wine made her feel lightheaded. Or was that her fantasies? Upstairs, Hayes came out of the bathroom. She heard him walk down the hall to the spare bedroom. She waited for him to close the door, but he didn't.

Shutting her eyes, she tried not to think about him lying in bed just down the hall from her own bedroom. A wild yearning raced through her as out of control as a wildfire. Her need quickly became a burning desire as it mixed with the wine already coursing through her veins.

McKenzie had always prided herself on thinking logically. She assessed every situation, looked at it from every angle then made a decision based on the facts— not emotion.

With Hayes, she knew she wasn't thinking rationally. She wanted him, needed him, like no man she'd ever met.

But she wouldn't act on it. Couldn't. At least until the crazy after her was caught. Even then, she wasn't sure she could let herself go. She'd been so wrapped up in her business that she hadn't given much thought to men. Now she couldn't stop thinking about Hayes Cardwell, but she would force herself to. She needed her wits about her and if she gave in to whatever this was between them... The thought made her ache.

She wouldn't let herself go there.

Feeling on moral high ground, she took the empty bottle and the glasses into the kitchen. She tossed the bottle in the trash and hand-washed the glasses, dried them and put them away before she went up to bed. Alone.

HAYES WOKE TO the sound of a phone ringing. He'd had a devil of a time getting to sleep, knowing McKenzie was just down the hall—and that there was a psychopath out there after her. If the man who'd come to the open house was her attacker, then he was definitely brazen. He was practically daring them to catch him.

The phone rang again. He heard McKenzie fumbling to answer it.

"Hello?"

Silence.

"Hello, who is this?"

Hayes was out of bed and down the hall to her room in a matter of a few strides. He reached for the phone. She handed it to him, those amazing eyes of hers wide and terrified. All the color had drained from her face and the hand that relinquished the phone had trembled.

He could hear heavy breathing as he put the phone to his ear. The man on the other end of the line chuckled softly. To his surprise, McKenzie jumped out of bed and ran to the window.

"Who is this?" Hayes demanded.

The chuckle died off. He could almost hear the anger in the breathing just before the call was disconnected. He checked caller ID. Blocked.

"It was him," McKenzie said, turning from the window. She wore a short cotton nightgown that left little to the imagination—not that Hayes's imagination needed any help.

He'd always thought of himself as a strong man. But right now he felt helpless against emotions that threatened to overpower him when he looked at this woman. "McKenzie." He said her name as if that alone could put distance between them and keep him from taking her in his arms.

She turned to him, her voice breaking as she said, "I heard something else besides his breathing." Her gaze locked with his. "I heard my neighbor's wind chimes. He called from those pines below my bedroom window."

Chapter Nine

Gus Thompson was lost. He'd driven around town tonight feeling as if his life were over. The last place he'd wanted to go was home to an empty house. He still couldn't believe everything had changed in an instant.

He was thirty-eight years old. Not even in his prime. He would get another job. At least that's what he told himself. And yet just the thought of approaching other Realtors had turned his knees to jelly. He'd never had to actually ask for a job before. His mother had seen that he had jobs from the time he was sixteen. Nepotism wasn't something he'd ever thought about—until now.

If his mother were alive, she would have put in a call, got him on somewhere and he'd just show up for work. She'd had those kinds of connections. Even better, his mother would have made McKenzie pay. Her wrath would have rained down like a firestorm on M.K. Realty. She might even have put dear McKenzie out of business just for spite.

But his mother was gone and he was jobless and lost. And all because of McKenzie Sheldon.

He hadn't known where he was driving until he

found himself in her neighborhood. Parking down the block, he'd cut the engine, having no idea what he was going to do when she returned. Their "talk" earlier had left him cold. He needed more from her than a luke-warm recommendation. He was a great salesman, but if there were even a whiff of gossip that he was diffi-cult to work with or that he hit on women in the office, it would kill the deal.

McKenzie had to hire him back. It was the only way.

As that thought settled over him, he'd seen her come up the street and pull into her drive. He'd started to get out, afraid how far he would have to go to get her to agree to rehire him, when an SUV had pulled up in her drive next to her vehicle.

Gus had ducked back into his car as he watched the Texas cowboy get out. McKenzie and the man headed for her front door. "What the—" They'd disappeared inside. A few minutes later, the cowboy had come back out and driven his vehicle into her garage.

It was the same cowboy he'd seen her with at Big Sky. The same man he'd followed to the Cardwell Ranch only to have neither appear again even after Gus had waited an hour.

Determined to wait this time, though, he settled in. The cowboy would leave before daylight, he told him-self. He must have fallen asleep because something awakened him. He sat up to find it was the middle of the night. All the lights were off inside the condo—just like the other condos on the block.

Angry and frustrated and feeling even worse, he was about to leave when he noticed something odd. A man had been sitting in an old panel van up the street. Gus watched him get out and head into the trees next to McKenzie's condo. A few moments later, Gus saw a light flash in the trees. Not like a flashlight. More like a small screen, making Gus suspect the man was making a call on his cell phone next to her condo.

How many men did McKenzie have on the string? he wondered. Definitely the cowboy.

So who was the man in the trees? His heart began to pound as he realized it could be the same guy who'd attacked her.

Before he could react, the man came out of the trees, walking fast. He jumped into the van. Gus hurriedly started his car, a plan crystallizing as he drove. If this guy was McKenzie's attacker and he could catch him, she would have to give him back his job.

HAYES, DRESSED ONLY in jeans, ran back to his room and grabbed his gun after the call and what McKenzie had heard on the other end of the line. He raced down the stairs and out the front door. If she was right, the man had been right outside her condo in the dense trees.

But as he reached the trees, he heard tires squeal and looked out on the street as a large car sped past. This time, though, the car passed under a streetlamp and he was able to get the license plate number.

Back in the condo, he found McKenzie wrapped in a fluffy white robe and matching slippers. She stood hugging herself at the front window.

"Did you…" Her words died off as she saw his expression. "He got away."

"I got his license plate number as he was speeding off." Hayes was already dialing the police. He asked for the same officer who they'd talked to earlier and told him about the phone call and the car.

"Give me a minute," the cop said as he ran the plate. "The car belongs to Ruth Thompson. Wait a minute. It's the same car Gus Thompson admitted to driving the night Ms. Sheldon was attacked."

"She has a restraining order on him."

"I see that. I'll make sure he gets picked up."

"Thank you." Hayes hung up and turned to look at McKenzie. "Did you actually see him in the trees?"

She shook her head. "He was just a shape. Large."

"The car that I saw racing away was Gus Thompson's mother's." She groaned. "Is it possible he also made the phone call?"

She seemed to think for a moment. "The man didn't say anything, he just…breathed." She closed her eyes and sighed. "It would be like Gus to try to torment me. He's furious that I fired him. So you think it wasn't the man who attacked me?"

"Not unless that man was Gus Thompson."

"WHAT THE DEVIL?" He looked in his rearview mirror, surprised that the car he'd seen earlier was still following him. He knew it couldn't be either McKenzie Sheldon or the cowboy he'd seen her with before. So who was it?

Not the police or they would have already pulled him over.

He had spotted the tail right away, but hadn't thought

anything of it. He had too much on his mind to care. What was the cowboy doing at her house? He could only imagine. He gritted his teeth, remembering the male voice on the phone. The Texas accent had been a dead giveaway. It had to be the same cowboy, the one who'd rescued her at the grocery-store parking lot. The same one he'd seen her with before. And now the man was in her condo with her? Close enough he'd gotten on her *phone?*

A wave of disgust and fury washed over him like acid on his skin. He'd never taken women out of any kind of anger. If anything, it was about control. So this scalding fury made him feel impotent. He had to do something about this situation and soon.

But how could he get control again—and quickly? If he acted out in anger, he would be more likely to make a mistake, one that could cost him dearly. No, he had to rein in his emotions. He couldn't let this woman and her hero cowboy get to him.

But even as he'd thought it, he felt his blood boiling. How dare the two of them! It was as if they were laughing behind his back. Mocking him. Now the cowboy had something that belonged to him. The woman was *his,* not some stupid bystander's who'd come to her rescue.

He had to think, plan. The woman had known he was outside her window. How? He remembered the way she'd stood at the window at the open house, watching him leave. He'd sensed her watching him. Had she also sensed how close he was to her tonight?

Or had it been something else? That's when he

remembered the wind chimes. He'd noticed them when he'd been waiting in the trees. They had been tinkling lightly so he hadn't paid much attention. But right when she'd answered the phone, a gust had caught them... *She'd heard the wind chimes.* The woman was more astute than any of the others, a worthier prey. It should have filled him with pride since she was now his.

The only thing spoiling it was the cowboy.

He thought of how he'd planned it, borrowing the old van he sometimes used at work, waiting until she'd be asleep before he'd called. He'd wanted to wake her, to catch her off guard. He hadn't known she wouldn't be alone.

A curse on his lips, he glanced again in his rearview mirror. The car was still with him! The driver had been staying back, but clearly following him. It was one reason he hadn't gone home. Instead, he'd been driving around, trying to clear his head and ditch the tail. But the fool was still with him.

It couldn't be the cowboy, could it? No. Then who? He reached under the seat for the tire iron he kept there, and was about to throw on his brakes and see just who was following him when he caught the flash of cop lights behind them.

Fear turned his blood to slush—until he realized that the cop wasn't after him, but whoever had been following him. He kept driving up another block before he turned and circled back. He had to know who'd seen him at the condo. Who was stupid enough to put himself in jeopardy?

Fortunately, as he drove by, neither the cop nor the

man bent over his car's hood being handcuffed paid any attention to him.

The man being arrested wasn't the Texas cowboy, but he did look familiar.

AFTER HAYES LEFT the condo this morning, McKenzie locked the door behind him as he'd ordered. She was still upset that the man who'd called last night had been right outside her condo. *He knew where she lived!*

But if the man was Gus… She still couldn't believe that even though the police had called to tell her that the car Hayes had seen speeding away belonged to Gus Thompson and that Gus had been arrested, but was expected to be out on bail soon.

"I really don't like you doing this open house," Hayes had said this morning before he left. "This nutcase is going to strike when you least expect it."

"Then I will have to be on guard all the time."

Once ready for the open house, she called to remind him that she had to stop at her office.

"I'll meet you there," he said.

"That really isn't necessary."

"I'll be the judge of that."

Only Cynthia and another real-estate saleswoman were in the office this morning. The others either had open houses or had taken the day off. She'd always felt a sense of euphoria when she walked into her office. She'd worked hard for this agency and felt a sense of pride that she'd done it alone through hard work.

But today she felt edgy. She couldn't forget for a moment that she was being hunted like an animal. It set her nerves on end and made her start whenever the phone rang.

McKenzie knew she had to pull it together. Last night she'd been angry, filled with a determination to track down this bastard and stop him. But in the light of day, she was too aware of how ill-prepared she was. She'd gotten lucky the other night and had been able to fight the man off—at least long enough that Hayes had seen what was going on and had saved her.

She couldn't count on his saving her again. That's what he was trying to tell her earlier at the condo.

And yet when she saw him drive up, she'd never been so happy to see anyone. "I told you I was driving myself," she said, glancing at the clock. The open house wouldn't start for several hours.

"There's somewhere we need to go." He sounded mysterious, but she followed him out to his SUV and climbed in. He drove out into the country, down a narrow dirt road until they were back into the foothills away from town.

When he stopped, she glanced around. "What are we doing?"

"You really think you're ready for this?" he asked as he pulled out a gun.

She felt her eyes widen in alarm. He held the gun out to her. "You ever fired one before? I didn't think so. You think you can kill someone?"

"Is this really necessary? I have pepper spray that I carry—"

"Pepper spray isn't going to stop this guy. I've seen the way you grip your keys when you get out of the car.

If he gets close enough to grab you, your keys aren't going to stop him, either. You're going to have to kill him or he is going to kill you."

She stared at the gun for a moment. Then she swallowed the lump in her throat as she reached for it. Her hand trembled. She stilled it as she got a good grip on the pistol.

"Will you show me how to fire it?"

He'd raised a brow. "You really think you can do this?"

"I don't think I have a choice, do you?"

He took the gun from her. "Come on, then." Climbing out he led the way to a gully where he set up a half-dozen rusted beer cans on rocks. "Familiarize yourself with the gun. Here is how you load it. Here is how you fire it."

Turning toward the cans, he showed her how to hold the gun and take aim. She did as he had done, looked down the barrel and pulled the trigger. The gun kicked in her hand, the shot going wild.

"Don't close your eyes when you pull the trigger," he said.

She tried again, holding the gun tighter. The next shot was closer. The third one pinged into a can, knocking it to the ground. She felt a surge of satisfaction, missed the next shot, but centered the cans on the next two.

Feeling cocky, she turned to look at him. "Well?"

"You killed a few old beer cans. You will have only a split second to make the decision whether to pull the trigger or not—and that's if you can pull the gun fast enough when the man surprises you," Hayes said. "He'll be counting on those few seconds when you hesitate."

"WHERE ARE YOU?" Tag asked, not long before noon. "I checked your cabin. It hasn't been slept in."

Hayes was driving north, leaving Bozeman and traveling out into the country past wheat fields broken by subdivisions. "I stayed at McKenzie's last night. Quit smirking. Nothing happened—at least not what you're thinking."

"Oh?"

He found the road he needed and turned down it. The sun had cleared the mountains to the east this morning and now splashed the valley in gold. "This guy who attacked her is still after her. She's determined to find him before he finds her. I'm helping her."

"Did you read something on a fortune cookie that says if you save someone's life, you're responsible for it?"

"I can't just leave her," Hayes said as he saw the house come into view.

"Really? That's all it is, just you needing to play hero?"

"I can't get into this right now. I'll call you as soon as I know something definite, but I might be staying until your wedding. Also, I told McKenzie we will take the restaurant building at Big Sky. I haven't talked to Austin but—"

"Was this McKenzie Sheldon's doing? Never mind. Whatever the reason you've changed your mind, I'm glad. You won't be sorry."

"I hope not."

"Now try not to get yourself killed before my wedding."

As Tag hung up, Hayes sped up the SUV, driving past the house and up the road for a half mile before he turned around and headed back, going slower this time.

The ranch-style house was huge, sprawled across twenty acres with a guesthouse, barn and stables behind it, along with an assortment of outbuildings. All kinds of places for a person to hide. He noticed there was also a dirt road that went up into the Bridger Mountains behind the house.

As he drove on by the house a second time, he called McKenzie. "Get someone to do the open house for you. It's too dangerous."

Gus had been arrested last night for violating the restraining order. But McKenzie had received a call earlier, warning her that he was already out on bail.

What had Hayes upset was what else the policewoman had told her. "He swears he saw a man beside your condo last night using a cell phone. He says he was chasing the man when he was arrested."

"Did he get a good look at the man?" McKenzie had asked.

"He says he didn't."

The policewoman hadn't believed Gus about any of it.

Hayes didn't know what to believe. Gus could be behind both the note on McKenzie's car and the call last night. Gus was angry, according to the police, which gave him reason to want to torment his former boss, even if he wasn't the man who'd attacked her.

"It wasn't Gus," she'd again said this morning on the drive back from shooting the gun.

"But Gus would know about the convention speech and the open house," Hayes had argued. "And he was definitely at your condo last night."

"You said he sped away. You didn't see another car?"

He hadn't been looking for another car once he'd seen Gus speeding away.

"I went by Gus Thompson's house," he said now. "He's not there. This open house is in the paper with your name on it, right?"

"It's not Gus."

"Okay, then if true, I would say you have two angry men after you now. Which is yet another reason you shouldn't do the open house."

"The police are going to have a car in the area of the open house."

"The area is too large and there are too many places a man could be hiding."

"*You'll* be there."

Her words hit him at heart level. "Why do you think I'm so worried?"

"I trust you."

Her first mistake. He opened his mouth to speak, but shook his head, instead. A part of him was touched by her words. Another part was afraid he would fail her.

"Hayes?"

"I'm still here."

"I know. I'm grateful."

He sighed. "Let me know when you leave the office for the open house. Keep your phone on. I won't stop worrying until I know you made the drive safely. Then, once you get here, I can really start worrying."

"So you agree with me that he'll show?"

"He'll be here. He couldn't possibly pass up such a perfect location with all these places to hide. The question is where."

GUS WAS NO longer angry at McKenzie. He was *furious.* She hadn't really had him *arrested?* Not when he was following the man who he assumed had attacked her.

When he'd first gotten released from jail he'd thought about just letting the crazy bastard get her. She deserved it, right?

After a while, though, he'd tamped down his fury, focusing instead on the look he'd see on her face when he caught her stalker. When he *saved* her.

He dug the handgun from the drawer beside his bed. He'd bought the pistol at a gun show years ago. The gun was loaded, but he grabbed another box of ammunition.

As he walked through the kitchen, he grabbed a sharp knife. He put the knife in the top of his boot. Today he'd worn jeans, hiking boots, a long-sleeved shirt. He had some dirty business to get done today.

In the garage, he walked past his mother's car to his SUV. He felt like a commando going into battle. The man after McKenzie had been at her condo last night. That had been a gutsy move. So Gus figured, given where the open house was being held, that the man would show. All Gus had to do was get there early for a place to hide out and wait. It would be like shooting fish in a bucket—barrel, whatever.

He'd checked out the house and grounds when the ranchette had first come on the market, so he knew where to park the SUV so it wouldn't be noticed. There was literally a forest that backed up to the property. He knew the perfect spot where he would be able to see anyone coming.

McKenzie grew more anxious as she neared the ranchette. She remembered what Hayes had said last night. But her car seemed to be running fine. However, she was relieved when she reached the turnoff to the house.

She didn't see Hayes anywhere around, but then again, she didn't expect to. He was here, though, she assured herself. The property was twenty acres, just as Hayes had said. While she'd seen the place before, she found herself looking at it from a totally different perspective than she had the first time.

Now she saw all the places a man could hide and wait for that moment when she was alone. And she would be alone some of the time because the asking price of this place was high enough that she didn't expect a lot of viewers.

Fear rippled over her, dimpling her skin and giving her a chill as she got out at the turnoff to put up the Open House sign. She couldn't help looking over her shoulder, hurrying to get the sign up and back into her vehicle as quickly as possible.

She was shaking by the time she climbed behind the wheel again. Did she really think she could do this? To catch this man she would eventually have to come face-to-face with him. He had to be caught in action. Her heart began to pound at the memory of his arm around her throat, the way he'd picked her up off her feet—

Turning down the road, she heard another vehicle. An SUV turned down the long drive behind her. She glanced at the car's clock. Her first viewer was early. As she pulled in, she saw that the car had slowed as if to study the place at a distance. Hurrying, she climbed out, taking everything with her as she moved toward the empty house. Her heart hammered in her chest as she opened the door and felt a blast of stale, cold air hit her.

She had to calm down. Taking a few breaths, she reminded herself how far she'd come. She hadn't gotten her success by being a wimp. She straightened her back as she put down the flyers and turned to watch the SUV cruise slowly up the road toward her. The sun glinted off the windshield so she couldn't see the driver.

This could be him.

Or he could already be in the house waiting for me.

Chapter Ten

Last night had been a close call. Some fool had chased him. Fortunately, the police had pulled the man over. He'd gotten a good look at the man's familiar face but it wasn't until he got home that he placed him. He'd seen Gus Thompson's face enough times when he'd been perusing the real-estate ads looking for McKenzie Sheldon's smiling face.

Just the thought of her made him feel better. But he couldn't ignore the fact that the man had given him chase last night. Did McKenzie now have *two* men protecting her? That made his stomach roil. It was bad enough that the cowboy kept getting in his way. Now this other fool?

To settle himself down, he thought about the open house and Ms. Sheldon. He would see her again today. Unfortunately, just seeing her wasn't helping much anymore. He needed more. He smiled in memory of the terror he'd seen on McKenzie Sheldon's face last night when she'd found the note and what he'd heard in her voice when he'd called and woken her up.

But even that wasn't enough. He had to get his hands on her.

True, she had needed a reminder that he was still here, that he was still coming for her. It had been a dangerous thing to do, calling attention to himself that way. But he relished in the fear, both his own and, of course, hers.

He'd been curious to see, after the note and the phone call, whether or not she would go ahead with the open house today. The listing was out in the country, miles from town and enough acreage and buildings that not even her cowboy or Gus Thompson, real-estate salesman extraordinaire, could keep her safe.

She'd proven to be a worthy opponent. But today would tell if the woman was equal to the challenge.

He'd already decided that he had to show up at the open house. She might be suspicious of him after yesterday since he'd been one of only a handful of men who'd come alone to the open house.

Today he would assure her she had nothing to fear from him.

After all, the one thing he could do well was *act* normal. He'd spent his life fooling people—even those closest to him. He knew exactly how he would play it and couldn't wait.

HAYES FELT HIS stomach tighten as viewers began to arrive. When he'd spoken to the police earlier, they'd agreed to run the plates of those attending the open house. They'd asked the sheriff's department to send a car out to the area, as well.

Given the price of this so-called ranchette, he'd thought that number would be low. He'd been surprised by the turnout.

Most were just curious, he was betting. But some actually appeared to be interested, walking much of the grounds, looking in the many structures. He'd heard that expensive houses in the area had continued to sell, even during the recession. It was easy to understand why people fell in love with Bozeman's charm, along with the beautiful valley, the nearby mountains and inexhaustible outdoor entertainment.

He took down each license plate number and snapped a photo of the people attending. He had a half dozen written down when the man drove up. He recognized the man right away as the one he'd seen talking to McKenzie the day before at the open house. Was this her attacker? He was dressed in jeans, boots and a Western shirt and had a cocky way about him.

As the man climbed out of his SUV, he glanced around as if taking in the place for the first time, then he headed for the front door.

McKenzie HAD BEEN talking to a middle-aged couple and turned to find the man directly behind her.

"I'm sorry. I didn't mean to startle you." He held out his hand. "Bob Garwood."

McKenzie battled back her initial surprise and took his hand. It was cool to the touch, the handshake firm. She even found her voice. "It's nice to meet you, Mr. Garwood."

"Please, call me Bob." He let go of her hand and

glanced around the living area. "I like this much better than yesterday's listing. How many acres?"

"Twenty. Most of it is now leased for hay."

He nodded. "That's great." His gaze came back to hers. "Mind if I take one of those?"

She handed him a sales flyer. Her hand was hardly shaking.

"Sheldon, right? McKenzie Sheldon. I almost called you last night. You gave me your card with your cell phone number, remember?"

She nodded numbly. If this was the man who'd attacked her, then he *had* called her last night. In fact, he'd been outside her condo. Her heart began to pound harder.

He smiled. "This might seem a little forward, but I wanted to ask you to dinner sometime."

"I don't date clients."

His smile broadened as he pulled out his card and handed it to her. "Good thing I'm not a client yet."

With that he walked away, his gaze going from the sales flyer in his hand to the house as if he seriously was looking for something to buy. She glanced down at the card. Robert Garwood. Apparently, he sold high-tech workout equipment for gyms.

"Are you all right?"

She jumped before she recognized the voice and turned to find Hayes behind her. "How long have you been here?"

"Long enough to hear him ask you for a date."

She let out a nervous laugh. "Maybe that's all he was doing, just hitting on me."

"Maybe. I'll run his name. Bob Garwood, right?"

She nodded as a few more cars pulled up out front. Two women climbed out of one vehicle, a couple out of another and one man, alone.

"You remember him from yesterday's open house?" Hayes asked.

The men's faces were all starting to blend together. "I think so."

"I'll be close by if you need me," he whispered and left.

McKenzie braced herself as the man who'd just arrived looked at the house, then started up the walk. She recognized him as being one from yesterday's open house. As she took a closer look at the couple, she realized the husband also looked familiar.

"Holler if you need me," Hayes said and left out the back way.

McKenzie jumped as the front door opened. She plastered a smile on her face as the group entered. The lone man took a flyer, gave her a nod and moved off through the house behind the two women. The husband she recognized from the day before came up to her.

"You're a busy woman," he said. "Didn't I see you yesterday at an open house in town?"

She nodded, wondering if he really didn't remember. He was large and there was something about his light blue eyes that made her feel naked. He was the one who'd acted as if he was pulling something on her yesterday.

His gaze locked with hers and she felt a shiver move

through her. She tried to repress it as she handed him a sales flyer.

He nodded, his gaze still on her as if he was trying to place her.

McKenzie tried to pull herself together. She'd been so determined last night, so sure she wanted to trap the man. But being this close to a possible suspect…

He was still looking at her.

"Jason?"

"Sorry," he said, turning to the woman with him. "I was just lost in thought for a minute there." He let out a self-deprecating laugh. "I'm Jason Mathews. This is my wife, Emily."

She shook the wife's hand, then Jason Mathews's. He had a firm handshake and held her hand a little too long, making her even more nervous.

"I was surprised when Jason suggested we buy something larger," Emily said. She was a small woman with dark hair and eyes. Her handshake had been limp and cold. As she spoke, she kept looking at her husband. "We own a house in town that's paid for, but I would love a place in the country. This might be too much for us, though. I hate to even ask what it costs."

Jason Mathews smiled at his wife. "Well, let's have a look. You might be surprised what we can afford." He gave McKenzie a conspiratorial wink and handed her his card before leading his wife toward the kitchen.

McKenzie tried to catch her breath as she glanced down at the card in her hand. Jason Mathews. Under his name was: Antiquities Appraiser and his business number.

She groaned inwardly as she realized how foolish she had been. The man apparently really was interested in buying a house. With a sigh, she turned to welcome more people into the house.

But every man who came in alone to see the ranchette made her wonder if he was the one she had to fear.

THERE WERE TOO many people here. He finally found himself alone next to one of the outbuildings and took a breath. He couldn't believe how smooth he'd been when he'd seen McKenzie Sheldon again. It had taken some of the sting out of failing. He couldn't wait to get her alone.

Talking to McKenzie Sheldon had his blood running hot, though. He felt his need growing, worse this time because of his failure. Just the thought of his hands on her bare skin— The things he would make her do. The things he would do to her.

A flash of light caught his attention. He stepped back into the shade of the building and cupped his hands to look up the hillside toward the forest. There was someone up there in the barn loft. The flash must have been binoculars. A cop? Or that damned cowboy?

He'd known the cowboy would be here protecting McKenzie. It irritated him, but would give him such satisfaction when he stole the woman from the cowboy right in front of his eyes. He smiled just thinking about it.

In the shadow of the building, he waited and watched, hoping for a glimpse of whoever was hiding up in the barn loft. Finally, his patience paid off. He caught a glimpse of a face and swore.

It was that man who'd followed him last night from McKenzie's condo, the same man he'd witnessed getting arrested. Obviously, Gus Thompson had gotten out of jail.

He didn't need to speculate on who the man was looking for. Stupid fool.

A hot well of need rushed through his blood. The women he took fulfilled a variety of his needs on several levels. At first, killing them had been just a precaution, but over time he'd begun to enjoy that part, as well.

If he couldn't have McKenzie just yet, well, maybe he could satisfy at least one of his yearnings.

GUS CAUGHT MOVEMENT out of the corner of his eye. He had found the perfect spot in the barn loft. Through a small window, he had been able to watch the property as well as the comings and goings at the house. He'd picked the barn because he'd known that few people would come all the way up the hillside to the big barn, let alone climb up to the hayloft.

A few had made the hike but only given the barn a cursory look. The stables were much more interesting, and even some of the outbuildings. But since the place was immaculate, all the buildings painted white with dark green trim, it was easy to see that everything was well maintained.

He could sell this place in a heartbeat, he thought with aching regret. What did McKenzie know about selling this property? It should have been his listing.

He was thinking that when he saw movement off to his right in the pine trees. Gus turned, fear making his movement jerky. He'd forgotten why he was here for a moment and that kind of distraction was just when the man who had attacked McKenzie would take advantage.

But to his surprise, there was no one in the pines next to the barn. The breeze stirred the branches, casting shadows over the dry needles on the ground.

He reminded himself that he couldn't get caught here by anyone or he would be going back to jail.

He might have convinced himself that he'd imagined the movement if he hadn't heard a sound below him. As his heart began to pound, he pulled the pistol he'd brought and moved cautiously toward the hole in the floor where the ladder came up.

He'd lied to the cops about the man he'd seen at McKenzie's condo. Even though it had been dark and the man had been dressed in a hooded black sweatshirt, he'd gotten a pretty decent look at him in the streetlamp. Once he saw him again, he'd know him.

He heard nothing below him. He thought about going down the ladder when he realized there was another way up into the loft—a second ladder on the other side of the large stack of hay.

Gun ready, he cautiously moved in that direction. The smell of the hay and dust filled his nostrils. As the floor beneath his feet creaked, he couldn't hold back the sneeze. He stopped and listened again. No sound other than the breeze in the pines nearby.

There was no one. He felt both relieved and disappointed. His only hope of getting his job back was saving McKenzie, he thought as he heard a slight rustle in the stack of hay next to him.

HAYES MENTALLY KICKED himself as he walked the perimeter of the property one last time. The open house had ended almost an hour ago but there were some visitors who were just now leaving. He'd texted McKenzie just moments ago. She'd texted back that she was fine. He tried to relax since the stragglers were either couples or several groups of women. No lone male. At least not one who he'd seen.

Earlier he'd found tracks coming from the road behind the house. But with the property bordering the forest, there were too many places to hide for him to search for a vehicle. He couldn't be sure that the tracks weren't from the owner or one of the people viewing the house and property.

He'd also found a place where someone had stood for a while on a rise with a view of the house. The boot tracks were men-sized, but they could belong to anyone. He felt as if he were looking for a needle in a haystack. He couldn't even be sure the man who'd attacked McKenzie was even here.

Since arming her with the gun, he'd had his misgivings. The gun had been more about making him feel better than any real protection for her. Now he hoped he hadn't made things worse and she shot some innocent fool who surprised her.

But he couldn't watch her all the time. Was it wrong to want her to have a fighting chance? Whether or not the gun would give her that…well, he couldn't say. It would all depend on when her attacker decided to strike again.

He was about to head for the house when something

caught his eye. For a moment, he almost ignored it. He was anxious to get to McKenzie. The last of the viewers were leaving. That would mean she was alone.

Staring up at the barn, he saw what had drawn his attention. The barn had four small octagonal windows across one side on the loft level. He saw now that there was something in one of the barn windows that hadn't been there earlier.

Hayes glanced down the hillside toward the house, torn. Whatever was in the barn window probably was nothing. He needed to get to McKenzie. And yet... He quickly texted her.

Everyone gone?

Yes.

He could almost feel the relief in that one word.

Lock all the doors and wait for me.

Pocketing his phone, he walked quickly up the hillside toward the barn.

Earlier it had been hot, but now with the waning sun, the air felt cool. He could smell the pines, hear the breeze rustling the boughs. As he neared the barn, he slowed. A prickling at his neck made him pull his weapon before he stepped into the cool, hollow darkness.

The inside of the barn was empty. He glanced overhead to the loft, then at the ladder. There was fresh manure on several of the steps. Someone had been up there, someone who'd come in through the corral where the horses were kept.

At the foot of the ladder, he saw that there was another way up into the loft—a second set of stairs, these much easier to climb. Moving to them, he began to climb, the only sound inside the cavernous barn the pounding of his heart.

Hayes slowed near the top, weapon ready. The moment he peered over the top, he saw the man sprawled on the loft floor, the strewn hay around him discolored with the man's blood.

As he eased up through the opening to the loft floor, he saw that the man's throat had been sliced from ear to ear. From the color of the blood straining the hay, he hadn't been dead long.

Hayes hurriedly surveyed the area, then careful not to contaminate the scene, checked the man's wallet and identification.

Gus Thompson, the man McKenzie had fired.

Chapter Eleven

As Hayes came through the door, McKenzie turned, clearly startled. Hayes saw her hand go to the gun in her bag, but stop short when she recognized him. Relief washed over her features as she dropped the bag and stepped into his arms.

"You're shaking," he said as he hugged her to him.

"The deputies wouldn't tell me anything, just to stay in the house. I saw the ambulance. I was so afraid it was you. What happened?"

"It's Gus Thompson. I found him in the barn on the property."

"Gus?"

"He's dead. He was…murdered."

McKenzie shook her head in obvious disbelief as she stepped out of his embrace. *"Murdered?"*

"The sheriff's department is investigating. That's all I can tell you."

She looked as stunned as he'd been when he'd ID'd the dead man. "What was Gus…?"

"Your guess is as good as mine."

"If he was the one who attacked me..." Her voice trailed off. "He wasn't."

"It doesn't appear so, but he definitely seemed to be stalking you. It could be he crossed paths with your attacker."

"So my attacker was here! He was someone who came through the house."

"Maybe. As I told you, with a property this size, he may have sneaked onto the place without anyone seeing him."

"Except Gus." She shivered. "I can't believe he's dead."

"I'm sure the deputies will want to question you about who came through the open house."

"But I don't know *anything*. A half-dozen men came through alone, but that isn't unusual."

"What about that man who asked you out? Bob Garwood."

She shook her head. "He's not the first man who came to an open house hoping to get a date with the Realtor. There were other men who could have been the one who attacked me." She described several of the men who'd come through. "There was one, Jason Mathews. He gave me a funny feeling, but he came through with his wife, Emily, so...."

"I'll check him out along with the others but there is a good chance the man who killed Gus didn't come into the house."

"You took down all the license plate numbers?"

"I did. I've turned them over to the sheriff's department." He hated to get her hopes up. If he was right about this man, the killer had gone years learning how to not get caught. He was good at this and he knew it. "We might get lucky, though."

McKENZIE HAD STOPPED trembling, but she was still shocked and shaken. After she'd talked to the deputies, Hayes had followed her back to her condo. She'd worked so hard, determined to be successful and independent. She hadn't wanted to need anyone. Now her carefully built world was coming apart at the seams, and it scared her more than she wanted to admit how dependent she'd become on Hayes Cardwell.

She had to get control of her life again. That meant she needed answers—even those she knew she didn't want to hear. "You said you were going to do some research to see if other women… There have been others, haven't there?"

"Maybe you should sit down," he suggested as they moved into the living room.

She shook her head, crossing her arms over her chest as if she could hold back the fear that filled her. "Just tell me."

"More than two dozen have disappeared over the last ten years. The more recent ones match your profile."

"*My* profile?"

"Successful, single businesswomen who work late, shop late, have a lot on their plates."

She tried to swallow the lump in her throat. "I'm his type, that's what you're saying. Did any of them…?"

"None got away. I believe you might be the first."

"Then they are all…"

"Still missing."

She tried not to imagine the other women. "In other words, they're probably dead." She waited, seeing that he knew more than he was telling her.

"Several have turned up in shallow graves. They all went missing mostly out West. I suspect this man travels with his job. Since you have been the only one who he attempted to abduct in this area, I think there is a good chance that he lives here." At her frown, he added, "Predators don't normally hunt in their backyards. Too dangerous."

"But he *did*."

Hayes nodded. "With what I know about his type, he probably can go for a length of time and then something just snaps or builds to the point where he can't help himself."

"So I just happened to be in the wrong place at the wrong time."

"Probably."

"But now he knows who I am and if I'm the only one that ever got away…"

"That's why you can't stay here."

She shook her head. "How long do you think I can hide from him, Hayes? I have a business to run. I need to work."

He shook his head. "I don't have all the answers."

"I know." She looked into his kind, handsome face. He hadn't asked for any of this. All she wanted to do was bury her face in his strong chest. In his arms, she felt safe. But Hayes wouldn't always be there to hold her and protect her. It was one reason she had to know everything she could about the man after her.

"You talked to the police about Gus?" She saw the answer on his face. "Tell me."

"The coroner said Gus was hit with a piece of pipe. The blow wasn't enough to kill him, but probably knocked him down, at least stunned him long enough for the killer to…" Hayes met her gaze. "Are you sure you want to hear this?"

"I got the man killed."

"That's not true and you know it. You had a restraining order against him. If Gus had stayed away, he would still be alive today."

She stepped to the window, her back to him, her mind reeling. "What was Gus doing in that barn?"

"The police think he was spying on you. They found binoculars near the window and a bag with candy bars. It was the bag I saw in the window fluttering in the breeze that made me go up to the barn. He had hooked it on a nail next to him. When the breeze came up…"

She turned to look at him. "Why would he spy on me?"

"You said he wanted to talk to you. Maybe he thought he could get you alone and convince you to give him back his job." Hayes shook his head. "Who knows."

"The police think his killer was the man who tried to abduct me, don't they?" She didn't wait for him to confirm it. "Gus swore to the police that he followed him last night after the man called me from down in the pines by the wind chimes. If he was telling the truth, maybe he wasn't there spying on me but looking for the man. But why would Gus do something like that?"

"Maybe he wanted to play hero and it got him killed."

"If he was looking for my attacker, that means he could recognize him. *Gus lied to the police.*" That shouldn't have surprised her. It would be just like Gus. Tears filled her eyes. "This is all because I fired him."

Hayes stepped to her and took her in his arms. She didn't fight it. She rested her cheek against his chest, soaking in his warmth, hoping to chase away the chill that had settled in her, even for a little while.

"McKenzie, none of this is your fault. Gus made some very poor decisions. That's what got him killed."

"Playing hero, isn't that what you called it?" she asked as she pulled back to look into his dark eyes. "So anyone who tries to protect me—"

"Don't," he said, as if seeing where she was headed with this.

She shook her head and stepped away from him. "He'll come after you next. I can't let that happen."

"I'm not Gus. He wasn't trained for this. I am."

"I want you to go back to Texas."

"AIN'T HAPPENIN'," HAYES said. "I'm staying right here and there is nothing you can do to drive me away, so don't even try."

She looked up at him, her eyes brimming with tears. "I couldn't bear it if anything happened to you because of me."

He reached her in two long strides and took her shoulders in his hands. "Nothing is going to happen to me. Or to you. We are going to catch this guy." He could see that she didn't believe that. He wondered if he did himself.

"I thought if we set a trap for him… I thought today…" Tears spilled down her cheeks. She had a swipe at them. "It was a stupid idea and look what happened because of me."

He could see her fighting to be strong. He'd never met a more courageous woman. "It wasn't stupid. He was there, just as you'd thought he would be. Unfortunately, Gus was, too. Listen, I have a plan. It's dangerous—"

She laughed, but there was no humor in it. "More dangerous than waiting around for him to attack me again after what he did today?"

"If I am right about this man, he's had some experience at this. He'll *expect* a trap. He knows the police and now sheriff's department are involved. I'm sure he knows I'm involved, as well."

"What are you saying? That he'll lie low for a while?"

He nodded. He didn't want to tell her that killing Gus would have relieved some of the killer's…tension. The man would be satisfied for a while. "But whatever drives him will eventually reach the point where—"

"He'll try to grab some other woman!"

"No. He can't move on until he's finished with you."

"You don't know that."

"Not positively, but based on what I know about these types of predators…" He held her gaze. "But understand. The longer he goes, the more dangerous he will be."

"Then you need to go back to Texas. Like you said, he knows you're involved. If he killed Gus because he thought he was in the way…"

"Who knows what happened with Gus. The truth is, I believe you're the only one who will be able to satisfy his need."

McKenzie swallowed. "This plan you have…"

"Right now, you're too accessible. He can fill some of his need too easily by simply seeing you and seeing that you're afraid or cutting off part of your hair as a souvenir. You need to hide out for a while. The longer we let him dangle, the more his confidence will decline. He won't know where you've gone. Then when you surface again…he'll make mistakes."

She felt her eyes fill with tears. "At least that's what you're hoping for."

He nodded, not telling her what else he was hoping for.

"So I hide out until…until what?"

"Until he can't take it any longer." Hayes pulled her into his arms and stroked her back. He was hoping that he would find the bastard before that happened. "You have to trust me." He drew back to look into her eyes. "Do you trust me, McKenzie?"

She nodded.

"Then the two of us are going to Cardwell Ranch."

HE LICKED AT a spot of blood on his wrist that he'd missed and smiled. When he closed his eyes he could feel the warm flow of blood running over his fingers. But the best part was the look in Gus Thompson's eyes when the man realized he was going to die—and with his own knife.

The fool had gone for a knife in his boot after his gun had been taken away from him. It had been too easy to cut his throat. True, killing him had been a risky thing to do, especially killing him in the barn loft. But the dried hay would make it hard for forensics to find anything. Not to mention all the people who had tromped through that place.

He was reasonably sure he'd pulled it off without a hitch. He'd wiped off most of the blood on his hand in the hay, having cut the man's throat from behind him. Then he had slipped out of the barn to wash his hands in the hose on the back side of the barn.

He'd been careful not to leave any footprints next to the faucet. The police would suspect that he had to clean up. The creek would probably be their first choice, the hose behind the barn too obvious.

Either way, he'd managed to clean himself up and leisurely walk back to the house without causing anyone to take note of him.

All in all, it had been an amazing day. He felt better about everything. Now all he had to do was finish McKenzie Sheldon and life would be back to normal. Well, as normal as his life could be, under the circumstances.

But he was in no hurry. Killing Gus Thompson had filled his growing need. Now he could just relax and watch McKenzie sweat. With her former salesman's death, she would be terrified. He chuckled. And her cowboy would realize he was no match for him.

Soon he would call and ask to see a house. He knew exactly which one he would want to see. When he'd gotten home from the open house, he'd searched the paper and internet for a listing in the area that would work to his advantage.

As he picked up her card and ran his fingers over the dark engraving, he had no doubt that Ms. McKenzie Sheldon would accommodate him in every way possible.

Chapter Twelve

Dana met them at the ranch house door. "I am so glad you decided to come back."

McKenzie couldn't help being touched by the warm welcome, but she still had misgivings about being here. It must have showed in her face because Dana hugged her and said, "I have something I want to show you in the kitchen," leaving the men in the living room. Because it was late, the children were already in bed. The large, two-story ranch house was quieter than McKenzie had ever heard it.

"I know that you didn't want to come here," Dana said, the moment the kitchen door closed behind them.

"Only because there is a killer after me. I couldn't bear it if I brought my troubles here and put your family in danger."

"We've had our share of trouble at this ranch, believe me, and I'm sure we will again," Dana said. "For me this place has always been a sanctuary. If it can be for others…" She smiled and took McKenzie's hands in her own. "Then I'm glad. My mother loved this ranch, fought for it. It's that Old West spirit that lives here in this canyon. Hayes did right bringing you back here."

McKenzie wasn't as sure of that. But she had to admit, she felt safer here and more at home than she did even in her condo as the two of them joined the men.

"We're going down to the Corral tonight," Dana said as if the idea had just come to her. "You dance, don't you, McKenzie?"

She started to shake her head.

"Not to worry," Hayes said. "I'll teach you Texas two-step."

"It's Saturday night in the canyon," Tag said. "You really do not want to miss this. Isn't that right, Lily?" His fiancée laughed and agreed.

McKenzie couldn't help but get caught up in their excitement. "Saturday night in the canyon. How can I say no?"

Hayes smiled at her. "It's going to be fun, I promise."

She didn't doubt it. The Cardwells were a family that had fun; she could see that. She found herself smiling as they all piled into a couple of rigs and drove up the canyon to the Corral Bar.

"I forgot to mention that my father and uncle are playing in the band," Dana said as they got out.

McKenzie could hear the music, old-time country, as they pushed through the door. The place was packed, but Hayes pulled her out onto a small space on the dance floor, anyway.

The song was slow, a mournful love song. He took her in his arms, drawing her close. She'd danced some in her younger days, mostly with her sisters, though.

Hayes was easy to follow and she found herself relaxing in his arms and moving with the music.

"You're a fast learner," he whispered next to her ear, making her smile.

They danced the next couple of songs, the beat picking up.

"Are you having fun?" Hayes asked.

She was. She laughed and nodded as he spun her, catching her by the waist to draw her back to him. She loved being in his arms and it wasn't just because she felt safe there. She was falling for Hayes Cardwell.

"Here, you need this after that last dance," Tag said, handing each of them a beer as they came off the dance floor. "Some nice moves out there, little brother." He winked at Hayes. "Who knew he could dance?"

"He is a man of many talents," McKenzie agreed as she tried to catch her breath. Just being around Hayes made her heart beat faster and her pulse sing. When he looked at her like he was doing now… "He just taught me the Texas swing."

"Come to Texas and I'll teach you all kinds of things," Hayes said, meeting her gaze and holding it.

She laughed that off but she could tell he was serious. Texas? She didn't think so. She hadn't spent years working her tail off to get her business where it was to pack up and move.

And yet when she looked into his dark eyes, she was tempted. She told herself it had only been an off-handed remark. They hardly knew each other. A woman would be crazy to pack up and move clear across country because of a man, wouldn't she?

HAYES COULD HAVE bitten his tongue. He'd seen his brother's surprised expression. He'd been joking. Or at least he thought he had when he'd started to suggest it. But by the time the words were out of his mouth...

He shook his head and took a long drink of his beer. From the moment he'd looked into McKenzie Sheldon's eyes he'd been spellbound. He couldn't explain it but the woman had cast a spell on him.

The band took a break and Dana and McKenzie headed off to the ladies' room together. He decided it was as good as any time to go over to say hello to his father and uncle.

"I heard you were in the canyon," his father said, giving him a slap on the back. Harlan Cardwell was still strong and handsome for a man in his sixties.

Tag had bonded with their father on his visit to Montana last Christmas. Hayes only had vague memories of occasional visits from his father while growing up.

"Good to see you," he said, then shook his uncle Angus's hand. The two had been playing in a band together, Tag had told him, since they were in high school.

"I've gotten to know Dad better," Tag had said when their father's name had come up. "He's a loner, kind of like Austin. He and his brother are close, but Uncle Angus doesn't even see his own daughter Dana that much."

"So you're saying our uncle is just as lousy a father as our own?" he'd asked Tag. "That's reassuring."

"I'm saying there's more to them. Dad cares, but neither he nor his brother, it seems, were cut out to be family men."

Several locals came up to talk to Harlan and Angus. Hayes told his father he would catch him later and went to find McKenzie.

Hayes had always wondered about his father. What man let his wife raise five boys alone? Not that their mother wasn't one strong woman who'd done a great job.

"That's your father?" McKenzie asked, studying the elderly cowboy.

"That's him." Hayes had only recently learned that his father and uncle had spent most of their lives working for various government agencies. Both were reportedly retired.

He didn't want to talk about his father. "About earlier when I suggested you come to Texas…"

"I might come down just to see what all the fuss is about sometime," she said and quickly added, "Just to visit."

Fortunately, the band broke into a song. McKenzie put down her beer and, taking her hand, he led her back out on the dance floor.

As he pulled her into his arms, though, he couldn't bear to think about the day he would have to go back to Texas without her.

"ARE YOU ALL RIGHT?" Hayes asked as they walked toward their cabins after they'd closed down the Corral. Tag had stayed behind to talk to Hud on the porch, while Dana had gone into the house to see how the kids were. Her sister Stacy had come up from Bozeman to watch all the kids for them.

The night was cool and dark in the pines. Only the starlight and a sliver of white moon overhead lit their way through the dense trees. In the distance, McKenzie thought she could hear the river as it wound through the canyon. It reminded her of the music back at the bar and being in Hayes's arms.

"I'm fine," she said and breathed in the sweet summer night's scents, wishing this night would never have to end.

He took her hand, his fingers closing around hers, and instinctively she moved closer, their shoulders brushing.

"I enjoyed visiting with your father tonight. He seems sweet." She glanced over at Hayes. "He said he wants to get to know his sons. I can tell he's sorry he missed so many years with the five of you." She saw that it was a subject he didn't want to talk about. There was hurt there. She wondered what it would take to heal it. With Hayes in Houston and his father here, well, that was too many miles, too much distance between them in more ways than one.

"I had a great time tonight," she said, changing the subject. She didn't want anything to ruin this night. She felt still caught up in the summer night's festivities. If anything, she had fallen even harder for the Cardwell family tonight.

"Me, too. So you aren't sorry I brought you here?"

She laughed as she looked at him. He wore his gray Stetson, his face in shadow, but she knew that face so well now that she knew he was pleased she'd had fun.

"I'd rather be here with you than anywhere else in the world tonight."

He squeezed her hand then drew her to a stop in the pines just yards from her cabin. A breeze swayed the boughs around them, whispering softly, as he pulled her to him. The kiss was warm and soft and sweeter than even the night.

"McKenzie, that isn't just the beer talking, is it?" he joked.

She cupped his face in her hands, drawing him down to her lips. All night she'd wanted his arms around her. All night she'd wanted him. As she put into the kiss the longing she had for him, he dragged her against him with a groan. Desire shot through her blood, hot and demanding.

When she finally drew back, she whispered on a ragged breath, "I want you, too, Hayes Cardwell, and that isn't the beer talking."

They were so close she could see the shine of his dark eyes in the starlight. Without another word, he swept her up in his arms and carried her into the cabin.

As THE CABIN door closed behind them, Hayes lowered McKenzie slowly to her feet. His need for her was so strong that he would have taken her right there on the floor. But not their first time, he told himself as he looked into her eyes, losing himself in the clear blue sea.

"Last chance," he said quietly.

"Not a chance."

She started to unbutton her blouse, but he stopped her, moving her hands away to do it himself. He was determined to take it slow. As he slipped one button free, then another, he held her gaze. Her blouse fell open. He slowly lowered his eyes to her white-laced bra against the olive of her skin.

He brushed his fingertips over the rise of her breasts. She moaned softly as he dipped into the bra. Her nipple hardened under his thumb, making her arch against his hand. Her skin felt as hot as his desire for her. He released the front snap of her bra, exposing both breasts. Need burned through him, making him ache.

He'd wanted her for so long. When his gaze returned to her face, he saw her own need in her eyes. In one swift movement, she unsnapped his shirt, making the snaps sing. She pressed her palms to his chest.

He felt heat race along his nerve endings. He bent to kiss her then drew her against him, feeling her full breasts and hard nipples warm his skin and send his growing desire for her rocketing.

His mouth dropped to her breast, his tongue working the nipple. His hand slipped up under her skirt and her panties. She arched against him, rocking against his hand until she cried out and sagged against him.

He unhooked her skirt. It dropped to the floor. Her white lace panties followed it. Naked, she was more beautiful than he could have imagined. He swung her up in his arms again and carried her into the bedroom. As he started to lower her on the bed, she pulled him down into a hot, deep kiss and then her hand was on the buttons of his fly.

Lost in the feel of her, he made love to her slow and sweet, but it took all of his effort to hold back. The second time, he didn't hold back. They rolled around on the bed, caught up in a passion that left them both spent.

Later, as they lay on the bed staring up at the skylight overhead and trying to catch their breath, he looked over at McKenzie. She was smiling.

PATIENCE. HE KNEW things would be hot for a while with the cops, which meant there was no going near McKenzie's condo or office. Killing Gus came at a cost. Now he had to live with the consequences.

Tonight he sat on his porch considering his options. One would be to go back to work. It would look better should he find himself on the suspect list. Anyone who'd been to the open houses would be scrutinized. He wasn't worried. He looked great on paper.

Gus hadn't told the police anything—just as he'd sworn before he died. He'd had to make sure the police didn't have the license plate number of the van he'd been driving that night outside McKenzie's condo. Gus hadn't given the police even the make of the vehicle he'd been driving. He couldn't believe his luck—or Gus Thompson's stupidity. Gus was the only one who could have identified him and now he was dead.

Luck was with him. It buoyed him in this difficult time. He could last a couple of days without seeing McKenzie, without going near her. Unless there was another way.

The idea came to him slowly, teasing him in its simplicity. The only way he could get to McKenzie Sheldon sooner would be if her attacker were caught. He thought of the men he'd seen at the open house. A couple of them had looked familiar. In fact, there was one he knew. He was the right size. All it would take was a couple of pieces of incriminating evidence to be found at the man's house. The police would think they had their man.

So would McKenzie Sheldon.

There would be no reason for her not to go back to work as usual.

He felt good as he got up and went to bed. When he closed his eyes, he relived every moment from the time he hit Gus Thompson and knocked him to his knees until he saw the life drain out of the man. It had been a good day.

But he couldn't stop himself from dreaming about the day he would take McKenzie Sheldon for his own. Normally, he only spent a few hours with each one. Too much time increased the chance of being caught.

With McKenzie, though, he wanted to take his time. He would have to find some place where they could be alone for more than a few hours.

McKENZIE LAY IN the bed, the stars glittering like tiny white lights through the skylight overhead, Hayes Cardwell lying next to her.

"So I have to know," McKenzie said, rolling up on one elbow to look at him. "What makes good Texas barbecue?"

Hayes smiled over at her. "Are you serious?"

"Come on. You can tell me your secret. Isn't that how you and your brothers got your start? It has to be some kind of special barbecue."

He nodded as he rolled up on his side to face her.

"You have to understand. We were raised on barbecue." He closed his eyes for a moment and sniffed as if he could smell it. "You've got to have the smoke," he said as he opened his eyes and grinned at her. "And that takes a pit and a lot of patience. Most people don't know this, but cooking whole animals over smoldering coals is thought to have originated in the Caribbean. The Spanish saw how it was done and called it barbacoa. It's been refined since then, of course, and every region does it differently. Texas is known for its brisket, cooked charred black and bursting with flavor."

She laughed. "What makes your brisket so special?"

"We cover them with special seasonings and then smoke them for twelve to eighteen hours in wood-burning pits."

"Secret seasonings, right?"

"You better believe it. But wait until you taste our barbecue sauce."

"I can't wait. Am I going to get a chance to taste it?"

"Count on it," Hayes said and kissed her. It was a slow, sexy kiss that sent a throbbing ache of desire through her. She knew it wouldn't take much to find herself making love with him again. He'd been so tender the first time. The second time he'd taken her in a way that still had her heart pounding.

Just the thought brought with it the remembered pleasure. But as intimate as their lovemaking had been, she needed to know more about this man. She'd put her life into his hands. She felt as if he had done the same.

"I heard you started with just one small restaurant," she said.

He nodded. "We opened the first place in an old house with the pit out back. It was just good ol' traditional barbecue like we grew up on. You can take a cheap piece of meat and, if you cook it properly and with the right wood, it becomes a delicacy. One whiff and I can tell whether hickory, post oak or mesquite was used. But in the end, give me a piece of marbled pork shoulder and I will make you a tender, succulent pulled pork sandwich like none you've ever had before. The secret is that you've got to have smoky pork fat."

She smiled at him, hearing the pride in his voice. "Coleslaw?"

"Of course. You have to slather some sweet slaw on the pulled pork along with our spicy barbecue sauce to cut the richness of the pork. We also do a mean Southern potato salad and you are not going to believe our beans."

She had to laugh. "You're making me hungry."

"Me, too." His gaze locked with hers, making it clear it wasn't just barbecue he was hungry for.

"So the business just took off."

He nodded, almost sheepishly, as if embarrassed by their success. "None of us saw that coming."

Just like they hadn't seen this coming, she thought as Hayes kissed her. This time she let nature take its course. She couldn't bear the thought, though, that with a killer after her, this could be the last time they made love.

"WHAT'S GOING ON, HAYES?" Tag demanded.

Hayes started as his brother stepped out of the trees

next to his cabin a few hours before daylight. He was surprised and more than a little irritated. "Have you been waiting for me this whole time?"

"Don't try to avoid the question. What's the deal with you and McKenzie Sheldon?"

Hayes thought about telling him it was none of his business. But since the five brothers had been little, they'd taken care of each other. He knew his brother was asking out of concern, not idle curiosity.

"I don't know."

"This is moving a little fast, don't you think?" his brother asked.

"Oh, you're a good one to talk, Tag. You come up here for Christmas and the next thing we know, you're engaged to be married and want us to open a barbecue joint up here."

"I fell in *love*. It happens and sometimes, it happens fast." Tag studied him for a moment. "Are you telling me that's what's happening to you?"

Hayes looked out at the mountains, now dark as the pines that covered them, then up at the amazing big sky twinkling with stars. Had he ever seen a clearer sky—even in Texas?

"What if I am falling in love with her?" he demanded.

Tag laughed and shook his head. "The Cardwells just can't do anything the easy way, can they? Bro, there is a killer after her and probably after you, as well, now."

"Don't you think I know that? I have to find him before..." He pulled off his hat and raked his fingers through his hair. "I have to find him."

"Okay, and then what?"

Hayes met his brother's gaze. "I don't know. I think about Jackson and his marriage—"

"It doesn't have to end up that way," Tag said as he followed him into the cabin. "Jackson was blinded by first love. He didn't see that all she really wanted was his money. Does McKenzie Sheldon want your money?"

"No." He let out a chuckle. "I'm not even sure she wants me for the long haul."

It was Tag's turn to laugh. "I've seen the way she looks at you. You're her hero."

"Yeah. That's what bothers me. I'm no hero. What happens when she realizes that? Worse, what if I get her killed?"

Chapter Thirteen

Hayes looked toward the house where McKenzie and Dana had just disappeared inside.

"Sorry I came down on you like I did last night," Tag said. "It's none of my business."

In the clear light of day, Hayes now understood why his brother had been so upset with him the night before. "Last night shouldn't have happened. It's all my fault. I should never have let it go as far as it did. My life is in Texas."

"Shouldn't you be telling her this instead of me?" his brother asked.

Hayes barely heard him. "Her life is here. She's spent these years building up a business she is proud of. I couldn't ask her to give that up. Not that I would. Not that things have gone that far."

"Take it easy, bro. You made love to her. You didn't sign away your life in blood."

"I take making love seriously."

Tag laughed. "We all do."

"You know what I mean."

"Did you tell her you loved her?"

"Of course not."

"Because you don't?"

"No, because we barely know each other. I don't even know how she feels or how I do, for that matter."

Tag shook his head. "You're falling for this woman."

He could see Dana and McKenzie inside the house. They seemed to be having a heart-to-heart. He could almost feel his ears burn just thinking what McKenzie might be telling his cousin about last night.

"If you care about her, you should tell her," Tag said. "It sounds to me like you need to figure out how you feel about her."

"It's complicated."

"It always is," Tag said. "But God forbid if anything happens to her, you'll never forgive yourself if you don't tell her."

DANA HAD PACKED them a picnic lunch and offered to help saddle horses for the ride up the mountain to the lake. "It's beautiful up there. Crystal clear and surrounded by large boulders. There is one wonderful rock that is huge and flat on top. Have your picnic up there. Or there is a lovely spot in the pines at the edge of the water. I think that is my favorite."

McKenzie gave Dana a hug. "Thank you."

"My pleasure." She smiled as she looked out the window to where her two Cardwell cousins were standing by the corral after a huge Montana breakfast of chicken-fried venison steaks, hash browns, biscuits with milk gravy and eggs peppered with fresh jalapeños from Dana's garden.

Tag was handsome as sin, but nothing like Hayes, McKenzie was thinking.

"He's special, isn't he?"

She gave a start, but didn't have to ask who she was referring to.

"Hayes reminds me of Hud." Dana met her gaze. "He's a keeper."

"His life is in Houston."

"So was Tag's," she pointed out with a grin. "It wouldn't hurt to have two Cardwell cousins up here, making sure this barbecue restaurant is a success. Wouldn't hurt to have a private-investigative business here, either."

"You're a shameless matchmaker," McKenzie joked.

"Just like my mother. Did I tell you that she made a new will before she died, leaving me the ranch? Unfortunately, she was killed in a horseback-riding accident and no one could find the will. I almost lost the ranch. If Hud and I hadn't gotten together again I would have never found the will and been able to keep this place."

"Where was the will?"

"In my mother's old recipe book marking the page with Hud's favorite cookie recipe," Dana said and laughed. "Love saved this ranch."

McKenzie had to laugh, as well. The more she was around Dana Cardwell Savage, the more she found herself wanting to be a part of this amazing family. For a few moments, she could even forget that there was a killer after her.

THE HIGH MOUNTAIN lake was just as beautiful as Dana had said it would be, Hayes thought as he swung down off his horse.

"It's breathtaking," McKenzie said as she dismounted and walked to the edge of the deep green pool.

"*You're* breathtaking," Hayes said behind her.

She smiled at him over her shoulder, then bent down and scooped up the icy water to toss back at him. He'd told himself that last night had been a mistake, that he wouldn't let it happen again. But right now all he could think about was McKenzie being in his arms again.

The droplets felt good, even though he jumped back, laughing. He loved seeing her like this, relaxed and carefree as if she didn't have a care in the world. He doubted she'd ever been like this—even before the attack. The woman had been driven in a single-minded determination to succeed. He couldn't help but wonder if any of that mattered now. Was it the attack that had changed her? Or could it possibly be that she had feelings for him? Long-lasting feelings?

He'd spent the morning on the phone with the police and doing some investigating online. The police had run the license plates of those who had attended, but with Gus Thompson's murder, they weren't giving out any information. All they'd told him was that they were checking into everyone who'd been there both for the attack on McKenzie *and* Gus Thompson's murder.

Hayes had run checks on the two men who had provided McKenzie with their names.

Would her attacker be so brazen as to give her his real name, though?

The first name he ran was Bob Garwood. The man had a military background, special ops, and had received a variety of medals before being honorably discharged.

If anything, it showed that he had special training, something that could be an advantage for a man who abducted women and killed them.

Bob Garwood had no record, not even a speeding ticket. He looked clean. Maybe McKenzie was right and he *had* been merely looking for a date the two times he'd come to her open houses.

Or maybe not, Hayes thought, as he saw that Bob Garwood owned a gym-equipment business. Did that mean he traveled? Hayes bet it did. The company he owned was called Futuristic Fitness, promising to sell the most up-to-the-moment, technologically advanced equipment on the market. That could explain why the man was in such good shape.

The next name he ran was Jason Mathews. He was an antiquities appraiser, another job where he no doubt traveled. Like Bob Garwood, Jason Mathews looked clean. He was married, owned his house and volunteered for several charitable organizations—not that any of that cleared him, Hayes thought, reminded of Gacy who dressed as a clown at charitable functions.

The police hadn't found anything suspicious about

any of the other viewers who'd attended the open house from what he'd been told. They were still investigating.

Hayes had finally given up in frustration. He couldn't even be sure that McKenzie's attacker had driven to the open house. He could have come by foot; in fact, that seemed more likely since when he stumbled upon Gus Thompson, he hadn't hesitated to kill him, even though it was a dangerous thing to do.

"I guess swimming is out," McKenzie said wistfully.

"Not necessarily," Hayes answered as he began to pull off his boots. He could use a cold dip in the lake. Not that he thought it would help. "Dana packed towels as well as a blanket." He raised a brow and McKenzie laughed as she hurriedly began to undress.

"Last one in has to unpack the lunch."

THE CALL CAME forty-eight hours later. The police had received an anonymous tip from a neighbor. When they'd gone to a man by the name of Eric Winters's house to talk to him, they'd spotted incriminating evidence in his car and gotten a search warrant. Inside the house, they'd found the knife believed used to kill Gus Thompson along with items believed to have belonged to female victims that he'd kept as souvenirs—including McKenzie's red, high-heeled shoe.

McKenzie began to cry when she got the news as she thought of his other victims. The name Eric Winters meant nothing to her. Even when the police described the man to her, she couldn't place him, but apparently he'd come through the open house for the ranchette.

He'd just been one of a dozen men who could have been her attacker.

"So it's definitely him?" she asked, weak with relief.

"Given the evidence we found at his house, we have the man who attacked you. Your shoe will have to be kept as evidence."

"It's all right. I won't be wearing those heels again, anyway. Thank you so much for letting me know." For so long she'd thought they would never find him, that she would always be looking over her shoulder. She hung up and turned to look at Hayes. Her eyes welled again with tears as she said, "They got him," and stepped into Hayes's arms.

Dana threw a celebratory dinner complete with champagne that night. "Stay," she pleaded when McKenzie thanked her for everything and told her she would be moving out of the cabin in the morning.

"I wish I could stay. I love it up here, but I have a business to run. I've been away from it for too long as it is." The business had been her world just a week ago. It had taken all of her time and energy as well as her every waking thought. Until Hayes, she hadn't realized what she was missing.

But now he had no reason to stay and she had no reason not to return to her life, even if it did suddenly feel empty.

"And Hayes?" Dana asked, as if sensing her mood.

McKenzie looked across the room where the men were gathered. "I guess there is nothing keeping him in Montana now," she said.

Dana lifted an eyebrow in response. "You could ask

him to stay... Otherwise, he'll be back next month for Tag's wedding...."

McKenzie smiled at her new friend. "He *has* asked me to be his date."

Dana grinned knowingly. "That's if he can stay away from you until the wedding. I guess we'll see."

"I guess we will," she agreed. The thought of the wedding buoyed her spirits a little, but there was no denying it. Things had changed. *She* had changed. While she had to get back to work, it wasn't with the same excited expectation that she usually felt at the prospect. True, she would never feel as safe as she had, not in Bozeman, not in her condo. But it was more than that.

She'd fallen for the man, for his family, for even this ranch lifestyle. Not that she was about to admit that to him or his cousin, for that matter. As she'd told Dana, Hayes had a life in Houston. She had a life here. He hadn't asked to get involved. He hadn't even wanted her to know he was the one who'd saved her that night, she reminded herself.

As Hayes turned to look at her, he smiled and she felt her heart rise up like a bubble. She smiled back, fighting tears.

WHERE WAS SHE?

The words had been rattling around in his brain for four days now. It had taken the police several days to arrest Eric Winters. But now two more days had passed. Hadn't the police told her that her attacker had been caught? What was she waiting for? She should be back at work—and so should he. He couldn't afford to take much more time off. As it was, people were starting to notice. He couldn't keep saying he was taking off time to look for another house.

Unfortunately, his Realtor had disappeared. He'd expected her to hide out for a while after poor Gus Thompson's death. But that was almost a week ago. She hadn't been staying at her condo. Nor had she been going to her office. When he'd called the office, he'd been told that she couldn't be reached. He'd declined another real-estate agent, saying he had talked to Ms. Sheldon and only she could answer his questions.

From the exasperated tone of the receptionist's voice, he gathered that he wasn't the only one trying to reach her. Like him, surely she couldn't be away from work too long. Not a woman like her. She must be champing at the bit to return. These days away must be driving her insane.

Her absence was certainly pushing him over the edge. He didn't know how much longer he could stand it. He had to find her and finish this.

His instincts told him that she was with the cowboy. Before he'd killed Gus Thompson, he'd found out that the cowboy's name was Hayes Cardwell and that he was from Houston, Texas. He was considering opening a restaurant at Big Sky.

Cardwell. Wasn't there a ranch up there by that name? That had to be where McKenzie Sheldon was hiding. It would be too dangerous to go to the ranch. No, he had to find another way to flush her out.

He picked up the phone and called her office. He'd been careful not to come on too strong with the receptionist. He hadn't wanted to call too much attention to himself. But this time— "M.K. Realty, may I help you?"

"I sure hope so. I've been hoping to reach Ms. Sheldon, but now another house with another Realtor has come up—"

"I would be happy to put you through to her—"

"I've already left messages for her."

"Ms. Sheldon is at her desk this morning. I'll put you right through. May I say who's calling?"

HAYES LOOKED OUT the office window at the Houston skyscape. Just hours ago he'd been in the Gallatin Valley looking out at the mountains as his plane banked and headed south. Now here, he couldn't believe there had ever been a time that this had felt like home.

"What's bothering you?" Laramie demanded behind him from his desk. "If you still have doubts about opening a restaurant in Montana—"

"It's not that," he said, turning away from the view. The offices for Texas Boys Barbecue had started out in a corner of an old house not all that long ago. Now, though, it resided in a high-rise downtown with other corporations that pulled in millions of dollars a year.

"What is it, then?" Laramie demanded. "You've been acting oddly since you walked into my office."

"It's nothing." He didn't want to talk about McKenzie. It only made it harder. Better to put her and Montana behind him. "Have you talked to Austin?"

"You really want to talk about Austin?" his brother asked as Hayes took a seat across from him. "I've never seen you mope around over a woman before."

"I'm not—"

"Have you talked to her?"

Hayes gave up denying his mood had nothing to do with McKenzie. "She sounds like she is back at work and doing fine."

"And you probably told her you are back at work, too, and doing fine, right?"

He made a face at his brother. "She's happy with her life."

"Is that what she told you? Hayes, do you know anything about women?"

He had to laugh. "Not really. But I'm not sure you're the man to give me advice. Have you dated a woman more than once?"

"Very funny. One of you has to say it."

"Say what?"

Laramie groaned. "That you're in love. That is the problem, you know. You've fallen for the woman." He raised a hand. "Don't even bother to deny it. The question now is what are you going to do about it? Mope around and feel sorry for yourself or go get your woman?"

Hayes started to tell him how off base he was, but he saved his breath. "Just fly up there and go riding in on my white horse? Then what? I have a house, an office and a job here in Houston."

"Are you serious? You would let a simple stumbling block like those things keep you from what you really want? What did you do with my brother Hayes who has always gone after what he wants?"

"I've just never wanted anything this badly and I

don't even know if I can have her," he admitted and not easily.

"Only one way to find out. Better saddle up and get yourself back to Montana." Laramie picked up the phone. "Take the corporate jet. I'll have the pilot standing by."

"Ms. SHELDON?" He couldn't believe she was actually in her office, actually on the other end of the line. "I'm so glad to catch you in your office."

He'd been following the story about Eric Winters in the newspaper and on the evening television news. The man hadn't even been able to get out on bail. And now they were saying he could be a serial killer, having abducted and killed women all across the West. McKenzie must feel so safe, believing her attacker was finally behind bars.

"My wife and I are interested in seeing one of your houses. I was hoping you would be able to show us the residence as soon as possible. My wife was very impressed by you when we met you a while back. I told her I would see if you were free to show the house yourself. I know you own M.K. Realty." He'd learned that acknowledging that he knew who he was dealing with often worked.

"When were you thinking of seeing the house?" she asked, even though he could tell she had been ready to give him to someone else at the agency.

"My wife is very anxious. She doesn't want this house to get snatched up by someone else. I would imagine that now is too soon?" He heard her surprise.

Before she could draw a breath, he said, "It's the one you have listed as executive, high-end home with a million-dollar view."

"I'm familiar with the house."

"I believe it also has a several-million-dollar price tag. I can't tell you what I would have to contend with if we lost it before my wife even got a chance to see it."

"We can't have that," she said and he knew he had her. "I suppose I could show the house in, say, an hour?"

"I really appreciate this. My wife and I will meet you out there, if that is all right." This was working out even better than he'd hoped.

"I look forward to it. I'm sorry. I didn't catch your name."

"It's Jason. Jason and Emily Mathews."

"Yes, I remember we met at several of my showings." She sounded uneasy and he knew he had to mention the murder.

"I was so sorry to hear about your colleague being killed. That was such a shock. I'm glad the murderer has been caught. You just don't expect that kind of thing in Montana."

"It's rare, fortunately," she said and quickly changed the subject. "I'll see you soon, then, Mr. Mathews."

"Please call me Jason."

Chapter Fourteen

The moment McKenzie got off the phone she walked over to one of the cubicles.

"Jennifer, would you be able to take one of my showings this afternoon?"

The real-estate agent looked up in surprise. McKenzie had never asked any of them to take her showings until this moment.

The woman blinked then said, "I'd be happy to. Are you not feeling well?"

McKenzie almost laughed. "It's just that I have one before it that could take a while. Also I don't want you going alone. See if Rafe can go with you. I've decided from now on, we won't be showing houses alone if at all possible, but definitely any that could run over after dark."

"But aren't you showing one now alone?" Jennifer asked tentatively.

"It will be all right this one time. I'm meeting a man and his wife at the Warner place."

"I'm sure Rafe can go with me."

"Great. Thanks for doing this." As she walked back

to her office, McKenzie felt relieved. She had the other showing covered and after today, she would start relying more on her staff. If being gone had taught her anything, it was that she was not indispensible. For so long, she'd thought she had to do everything herself and yet when she'd returned after being gone for a week, she found that the agency was doing just fine.

There'd been numerous calls for follow-ups on houses she'd shown, but her staff had taken care of all but a couple of them. One of those was probably Mr. and Mrs. Mathews. Jason Mathews came across as the kind of man who only dealt with the boss or owner. Well, she was taking care of that one now.

McKenzie felt as if a weight had been lifted off her shoulders and at the same time, she couldn't help feeling a little sad. She hadn't heard from Hayes other than a quick phone call from the airport after he'd landed in Houston.

She'd gotten an agency call she'd had to take so she'd been forced to cut the call with Hayes short. When she'd tried to call him back, she'd gotten his voice mail. She hadn't left a message. What was there to say?

He'd asked how it felt to be back at work. She'd lied and said, "Great."

She'd asked him if he was glad to be home. He'd said he was.

That pretty much covered anything they had to say to each other, didn't it?

Outside her office, dark clouds had moved in. Thunder rumbled in the distance. The weatherman had warned that they might get some summer storms over the next few days.

Packing up her things, she headed for the door, also surprising her staff. She was always the first one in the office and the last to leave. As she walked out to her car in daylight, she couldn't help thinking of Hayes and Cardwell Ranch.

Was Hayes missing it and her as much as she was him? She pushed the thought away. She'd see him next month for Tag's wedding. The thought lightened her step even when it began to rain.

HE WAS WAITING for her. Anticipation had his heart racing. He'd failed once. He couldn't let that happen again.

Arriving early, he'd waited and gone over all the things that could go wrong. She might see that he hadn't brought his wife and panic, taking off before he could stop her. Or she might send someone else. Maybe even more possible, she might bring an associate.

He just couldn't let anything happen that would allow her to get away. Again.

He'd taken even more precautions since his failure with her the first time. He'd secured a place for them nearby. He couldn't chance transporting her any distance. Knowing Ms. Sheldon the way he did, she would be one of those women who got loose in the trunk, broke out a taillight and signaled for help.

Another precaution he was taking was knocking her out quickly. He'd opted to use a drug. He couldn't take the chance he might hit her too hard and kill her before all the fun began. It felt like cheating, drugging her, but he'd lost her once. That wasn't going to happen again. That's why he'd carefully chosen this huge monster of a house in the middle of the valley—and the abandoned house through the trees, only a short walk away.

Normally, he just dragged them out into the woods. But McKenzie Sheldon wasn't getting his quick and dirty usual fare. No, she was going to get the full treatment and that meant he would need a room inside a house.

He'd found one near the house he'd told her he wanted to view. He was counting on her not telling anyone where she was going. He was counting on it, based on the fact that she was the boss and that she would no longer be afraid since as far as she knew, her attacker was still behind bars.

The hard part would be getting her away from this house quickly and to their private spot. He would have to act fast, taking her in her car then coming back for his own car.

At the sound of a vehicle approaching, he tensed. McKenzie Sheldon was right on time. He checked the syringe in his pocket. Now, if she was alone, then nothing could stop him. He carefully adjusted the large straw hat balanced on the back of the passenger seat. From a distance it would appear his wife was sitting in the car waiting.

He glanced in his rearview mirror. It was McKenzie and she was alone. He smiled excitedly as he opened his car door and stepped out. All he needed was a few precious seconds and she'd be his.

HAYES THOUGHT ABOUT what his brother had said on the flight to Montana in the corporate jet. He also thought about McKenzie Sheldon's well-ordered life.

Like him, his career had taken up the greater part of his life. But that, he realized now, was because there hadn't been anything else that had interested him.

Now, his career, as important as it was, wasn't the first thing he thought of when he awakened in the morning. But was that true of McKenzie?

He'd seen her checking the messages on her phone, especially after a few days at the ranch. She'd been worried about her business. Not that he could blame her. She'd been such a major part of the agency he doubted she thought it could survive without her.

Hayes called McKenzie's office the moment the jet touched down outside of Bozeman, but was told she'd left work early.

"Have you tried her home?" the receptionist asked when he gave her his name. Word must have gone around the office that she'd spent almost a week with him up the canyon at Cardwell Ranch.

"She's already gone home?"

The receptionist laughed at his surprise. "I know it isn't like her. She even asked one of the associates to show a house for her this afternoon. We all thought she might have a date or something."

A date? He heard the woman try to swallow back her words.

"I mean we thought she was going out with you." Another gulp. "Is there a message I can give her if I hear from her?"

"No." He'd disconnected, wondering what he was doing flying to Montana. A *date?*

Well, what do you expect? he asked himself. *It wasn't as if you asked her to wait for you or even told her how you felt.*

Still, he hadn't been gone *that* long.

He tried her cell but it went to voice mail. On impulse, he called the office back and asked to speak to the sales associate who McKenzie had gotten to cover for her.

"This is Jennifer Robinson."

Hayes introduced himself and asked if she knew whether or not McKenzie was showing a house.

"She is, the Warner place."

That was the McKenzie Sheldon he knew, he thought with a sigh of relief. "Can you tell me how to find the Warner place? If she just left, I might be able to catch her."

McKenzie saw the large, newer-model expensive car parked by the house as she came up the drive.

Jason Mathews got out as she approached. She remembered him from the open house where Gus was killed. For a moment, she almost drove on through the circular drive and left.

You have nothing to fear. Your attacker was caught. Not only that, he brought his wife, right? As she glanced to the passenger seat, she saw a large summer straw hat and remembered that Emily Mathews was a tiny woman. Relief washed over her.

For a moment, though, she was sorry she hadn't

brought another agent with her. Her heart just wasn't in this, even though the sale would mean a very large commission. This was one of a number of houses in this area that the bank was anxious to get sold after a rash of foreclosures.

Having two agents go on every showing wasn't the best use of manpower. Also, she knew the nonlist agent would complain about losing money. Still, she wanted her agents to be safe and she would have gladly shared the commission.

Shutting off the car, she turned toward the passenger seat to dig the house keys out of her purse. To her surprise, her car door opened. She turned, startled to find Jason Mathews standing next to her car.

"I appreciate you taking the time to do this today," he said.

She tried to find her voice as she told herself he was just being polite, opening her door like that. "Just let me get the keys."

As she picked them up, she gripped them like a knife. Hayes's words came back to her that keys weren't much of a weapon because by then the attacker would be too close. Women lost their advantage up close because they were often the weaker sex.

At that moment, she was sorry she'd given Hayes back the pistol she used to have in her purse. She still had the can of pepper spray, but it would be in the bottom of her purse, not easily accessible.

All these thoughts hit her in a matter of seconds before Jason Mathews said, "I'll get Emily. She is anxious to see this house. Great location since she likes the idea of no neighbors within view."

He stepped away from the car and McKenzie felt herself breathe again. She chastised herself as she climbed out, dragging her purse out after her.

As she headed toward the house, she saw that Mr. Mathews was leaning into the car talking to his wife. For a woman who was anxious to see the house, she certainly was taking her time getting out of the car.

McKenzie headed for the front door of the house, just assuming the two would follow. Whatever discussion was going on between them, she didn't want to eavesdrop.

When her cell phone rang, she stopped partway up the wide front steps to dig the phone out of her purse. Busy thinking about Mrs. Mathews and hoping this hadn't been a wild goose chase, she didn't bother to check to see who was calling. "Hello?"

"McKenzie Sheldon? This is Officer Pamela Donovan with the Bozeman Police Department. I don't want to alarm you."

Alarm her? Surprised, she didn't hear Jason Mathews come up behind her until she felt the needle he plunged into her neck.

HAYES'S RENTAL CAR was waiting for him with the map inside just as he had requested. The Warner place, as Jennifer had called it, was about five miles outside of town to the south.

That meant it was at least fifteen miles from the airport. The worst part was the traffic. While nothing like Houston's, he'd managed to hit the valley during the afternoon rush hour. Just his luck.

He'd left a message with both Jennifer and the receptionist to have McKenzie call him if they heard from her. That's why when his phone rang he thought it would be her.

He was thrown for a moment when he realized the female voice on the other end of the line was the policewoman who'd worked with McKenzie after her attack.

"Yes, I remember you, Ms. Donovan."

"I just tried to reach Ms. Sheldon."

It was the worry he heard in her voice. "Is there a problem?"

"I didn't want to alarm her, but there is some news about the man we arrested in her attack. It might not mean anything—"

"What is it?" he asked as he drove toward the Gallatin Range of mountains to the south.

"McKenzie Sheldon isn't with you, by any chance, is she?" the policewoman asked.

"No. I was just on my way to the house she's showing. Why?"

He heard her hesitate before she said, "I just tried to reach her. We were cut off."

Unconsciously, he found himself driving a little faster. "Why were you trying to reach her?" Again the pause. "Officer—"

"There is some question whether or not the man we have in jail for her attack is guilty," the deputy finally said. "I can't get into it, but the dates of the other abductions aren't adding up for him and there is some question about the evidence we found in his house."

His heart pounded. "The dates. They don't add up for him, but they do for someone else, someone who was at the open house where Gus Thompson was killed, right?"

"When we went to bring Jason Mathews in for questioning, his wife told us that he'd had to leave town for a few days."

Hayes swore under his breath. "I was told at McKenzie's office that she was showing a house to a husband and wife." He prayed that was true and that the man sans the wife wasn't Jason Mathews. "I'm on my way there now." He gave her the directions he'd been given.

"We'll have a patrol car there as soon as possible."

Disconnecting, he drove as if his life depended on it, all the time mentally kicking himself for ever leaving. Worse, for never telling McKenzie how he felt about her.

McKENZIE WOKE TO darkness. She tried to open her eyes but her lids felt too heavy. For a moment she couldn't remember anything. She cracked an eyelid open as she attempted to move. Her hands were bound with duct tape at the wrists in front of her, her feet were bound at the ankles and she was strapped to a wheelchair.

A shot of adrenaline rocketed through her as memory came back in a wave of nausea. The prick of the needle, the horror of what was happening as she slumped against Jason Mathews, the fleeting glimpse of the empty car except for the carefully positioned summer straw hat on the back of the passenger seat.

She looked around, terrified to see where he'd brought her.

"Well, hello," Jason Mathews said from where he stood nearby. "Nice to have you back."

With relief she saw that she was still dressed, but that several of the buttons on her blouse were open. She shuddered at the thought of this man's hands on her as she lifted her gaze. The room was small. A walk-in closet or maybe a pantry. Were they still at the Warner house? She didn't think so, but all of these high-end houses had similar features.

Drugged, it took her a moment to realize he hadn't gagged her. She opened her mouth and tried to scream. The sound that came out was weak. She tried again, stopping only when he erupted into a fit of laughing.

"No one can hear you. There's no one around for miles. Not that I mind hearing you scream. I plan to make you scream a whole lot more before this day is over."

His smile curdled her stomach. She tried to fight down the terror that weakened her as much as the drug he'd given her. Her mind raced. Had she told anyone at the office where she'd gone? Yes, Jennifer. She'd told her she was meeting a husband and wife at the Warner place. Not that there would be reason for anyone to start looking for her for hours. More like days.

Her heart dropped at the thought as the man stepped in front of her, forcing her to raise her gaze to his.

"Finally, we are alone," he said, smiling. "I was worried it wasn't ever going to happen. We are going to have so much fun. Well, I am," he added with a laugh. "First

I want to show you the house. It is only polite, since you showed me several houses." He stepped behind her and, kicking off the wheelchair brake, propelled her out of the small room into a larger one.

She saw that she'd been right about the space he'd had her in being a walk-in closet, even though there were no shelves or rods on the walls yet.

"The master bedroom!" he announced with a flourish. "I haven't had time to decorate, or even get a bed, so we'll have to make due."

Dust coated the floor. She frowned, trying to make sense of where they were. Not in the Warner place. She'd shown it before and it had been clean, although empty for some time like a lot of other houses in the neighborhood this far out of town. Were they in one of those houses? Some had been abandoned by the contractors when they'd gone broke and the banks had been slow to move on selling them.

Her gaze stopped on a pile of items in the corner of the room. Terror turned her bones to mush at the sight of the duct tape, handcuffs, gag ball and an array of sex toys, including a whip.

She closed her eyes, dropping her head, unable to look. She couldn't let herself give in to this. She had to find a way to escape. This wasn't the way she was going to die, not in this dirty, abandoned house with this madman.

"You need to wake up," he said next to her ear.

She didn't open her eyes. She needed to get away from him. She needed a weapon. She needed even half a chance. She could still feel the drug in her bloodstream. It made her limbs feel lifeless, her reflexes slow.

While driven, she'd still always been a realist. No one was going to save her and she didn't see any way to save herself, bound the way she was. He'd done this before. He knew what he was doing. And since she'd gotten away from him once, he had made sure she wouldn't this time, she thought as she tested the tape on her wrists and ankles.

He was going to kill her.

But not until he hurt her. She had seen the cruel glimmer in his eyes as soon as she'd looked at him moments before. For whatever reason, he liked hurting women. It must make him feel superior, not that his reasons mattered.

"I must have given you too much of the drug," he said, sounding disappointed, even angry. "I don't want you to miss a minute of the fun so you are going to have to wake up."

She kept her eyes closed. Let him think it was the drug.

The slap made her eyes fly open and slammed her head back against the webbing on the wheelchair seat. His face was inches from her own now, his breath rank as he laughed.

"I thought that might bring you out of it," he said with another laugh, and stepped behind the chair again. "Pay attention or the next time, I'll have to do something much more painful to get your attention."

He wheeled her through a door and into the large master bath. Her heart stopped at the sight of a roll of plastic in the bathtub and several new blue tarps spread over the floor. "That's for later. I want to put that part off as long as possible this time. You deserve my best after what you've put me through."

She heard the underlying anger in his voice. It made her blood run cold. He planned to hurt her for as long as he could keep her alive. A sob caught in her chest. "Why?" she cried, hating to let him see how terrified she was.

He laughed as he shoved her into the bedroom again then whirled the wheelchair around to face him. The blade of a pair of scissors caught the light, shimmering in his hand. She gasped and tried to draw back as he moved in closer.

"Why?" he asked mockingly. "Because I can."

The knife blade cut through the tape holding her to the chair an instant before he stepped behind the wheelchair and unceremoniously dumped her into the middle of the master bedroom floor. The sound of the blade cutting through the tape reminded her of it cutting through her hair.

"Tour over," he said. "It's time for the fun to begin."

She looked up at him from the floor where she lay on her side, bound and helpless. If she couldn't get away, then there was only one thing to do. She had to make him so furious that he killed her quickly.

Chapter Fifteen

Hayes hit a rain shower near the mountains. It was still spitting rain as the Warner place came into view. The massive house sat on a small rise with a stand of aspens and pines behind it. From the third floor, he would guess there was a three-hundred-and-sixty-degree view of the valley. The house was just as Jennifer at the agency had described it. Massive, tan with matching stone and a circular driveway. The driveway was empty.

"No!" he yelled and slammed his fist against the steering wheel as he slowed. She couldn't have already come here, shown the house and left, unless… Once off the narrow paved road, the circular drive was an intricate pattern of cobblestones. Unfortunately, Montana winters had done their worst, breaking some and dislodging others. His tires rumbled over them as he neared the elaborate front door.

Unless the couple she was supposed to show the house to had called and canceled. He tried her number again. Again, it went straight to voice mail. Still, he was about to grasp onto that theory like a life raft when he saw the muddy footprints.

Hayes threw on the brakes. The rain had stopped. His windshield wipers scraped loudly across the dry glass. He shut them off, then leaving the rental running, got out.

The prints appeared to be muddy boot tracks. What had caught his eye was how they had trailed onto the cobblestones from the side of the house.

So she had shown the house to someone? He started to follow the tracks along the side of the house. The landscaping had never been finished except for a little out front. Peering in a window, he found the house was empty. It had that never-lived-in look and he was reminded of something McKenzie had told him about overbuilding back in the early two thousands. Building contractors had gone broke, leaving grandiose spec houses for the banks to deal with. This appeared to be one of them.

As he neared the back of the house, he expected the tracks to head for the rear entrance, assuming they must be from whomever McKenzie had shown the house to.

But the tracks veered off into the trees. Strange. The hair rose on the back of his neck as he realized the tracks had been heading out of the woods behind the house—and ended on the cobblestones out front.

What the hell? He'd put on his gun and shoulder holster after the call from the policewoman. He checked his gun now as he realized what he was seeing. Whoever had recently come to the Warner place from the trees hadn't walked back. They'd driven.

"Does your wife know?"

He'd never let the others talk. He'd kept their mouths duct taped. He hadn't needed to hear their screams. The eyes were more than windows into the soul. He had been able to see their terror as their eyes widened in disbelief. None of them had been able to believe it was happening to them. When the realization that they were about to die finally hit them, it, too, was in their eyes. He hadn't needed to even hear more than their muffled screams.

"If Emily really is your wife, then she *must* know," McKenzie said. "No woman could be that stupid."

"Don't talk about my wife. She doesn't know anything," he snapped.

"She probably turns a blind eye, just thankful it isn't her."

"Emily isn't like that. She's sweet and kind and… If she knew…" His voice trailed off, the thought too horrifying. Emily loved him. She trusted him. She looked up to him. She wasn't like these successful bitches who looked down their noses at him. If only she had come along years ago before…the others.

"I bet she can smell it on you when you come home. Does she make you shower? Or does she like it, the smell of another woman's pain on you?"

"Enough!" he bellowed, his voice echoing in the cavernous empty room. "You don't know anything about it."

"Don't I? You know she can see it building up inside you, then you leave and when you come back…"

She met his gaze, hers hard as stone. "Believe me, she knows."

He kicked her, catching her in the stomach and flipping her over. A painful cry came out of her so he kicked her again, shutting her up except for the second groan of pain. He flipped her back over to face him as he dropped down beside her and cupped her face in his hands, pulling her a breath's distance from his own face.

"You want to know why I do this? Because of women like you. You think you're so smart. Bitches, all of you. But once you realize that you're mine to do with whatever I want, then you change your tune. Like the others, you will cry and whine and plead with me."

She spit in his face.

He screamed in fury, releasing her to slap her as hard as he could. Her head snapped back, smacking the floor. He hurriedly wiped her saliva from his face with his sleeve, cringing at the horrible feel of it on his skin. "I am going to kill you!" he yelled. "I'm going to—"

"Big man, killing a woman who is bound and helpless. This is what makes you feel better? If you were a real man—"

He snatched up the whip from the corner of the room and swung it at her. She tried to roll away from him, only managing to flip over once before the cattails sliced the back of her blouse open along with her skin. She screamed.

As HAYES ENTERED the dark stand of trees, he pulled his weapon. Droplets from the rain still shone in the bright green leaves of the aspens and dripped down occasionally as he followed the tracks.

He hadn't gone far when the trees opened a little. He glimpsed the backyard of another house. Around him, everything was deathly quiet. He didn't even hear a birdsong, just the drip of the trees.

Hayes moved along the edge of the trees until he could see the front of the house. No vehicles and yet the tracks were fresh. Two sets. Both disappearing into the garage. His heart began to pound faster as he worked his way toward the back of the house, keeping out of sight of the rear windows.

He passed an old greenhouse, the door dangling open. Inside he would see where the vegetation had taken over, but rather than being green, everything appeared crusted with a thick layer of dust. It was the kind of thing that had creeped him out when he was a kid exploring old houses with his brothers.

He moved past the greenhouse and through an old garden spot, the dried cornstalks giving him cover until he was within a dozen yards of the back entrance to the house.

The muddy tracks ended on the back step. He drew out his phone and called 911. He was headed for the door when a scream pierced the silence.

The back door wasn't locked. That was because the man inside hadn't been expecting company? Or had set a trap for him? Hayes took a chance, slipping through and moving fast through the big, empty house.

He couldn't tell where the scream had come from, but there were tracks in the dust on the floor.

One set of man-sized footprints and two narrow wheel tracks. What the hell?

"NOT SO MOUTHY NOW, are you?" Jason said as he crouched down next to her.

The initial pain had been incredible. She'd never felt anything like it and could no more have held back the scream as she could have quit breathing.

Worse, she knew this was just the beginning. She could feel blood soaking into her blouse, running down her back.

He was kneeling next to her, his face close, so close she could feel his breath on her again. It took all her courage to look up into his face, knowing what she would find there. Satisfaction. He knew now that he could break her. There had probably never been a doubt in his mind. She was the fool for thinking she could trick this man into killing her.

He smiled. "I'm sorry. Did you have something else you wanted to say?"

As he started to move back from her, she swung her arms up, looping her bound wrists around his neck. She brought him down hard, pulling him off-balance and slamming his face into the floor next to her.

McKenzie knew it had been a stupid thing to do. She knew it wouldn't knock him out. If anything, it would only make him more furious and more determined to make her pay. She'd acted out of pain and fear and desperation.

He let out a bellow of pain and fury. She tried to slam his face down again, but he broke free of her hold, swinging wildly at her. She managed to roll away after only one blow, quickly rolling a second time so her back wasn't turned to him when he stumbled to his feet.

Dazed, his nose appearing broken and bleeding, he stared at her for a moment. He was breathing hard and looked unsteady on his feet. As he started toward her, she swung around on her butt and kicked him, knocking his feet out from under him.

He went down hard, hitting the wood floor with an *uhftt*. This time, he got up much faster and even as she tried to push herself back into the wall, he was on her, grabbing a handful of her short hair to drag her out into the center of the floor again.

"You have no idea what you've done!" he screeched at her as he held one hand to his bleeding nose and groped in his pocket with the other hand. Something silver flashed in his free hand an instant later.

McKenzie saw the scissors blade gleam in the late-afternoon light an instant before he lunged at her.

HAYES HADN'T GONE far into the house when he heard what sounded like a battle going on overhead. Of course, McKenzie would put up a fight just as she had the night she was attacked in the grocery-store parking lot, fighting for her life.

Rushing through the massive house, he finally found the stairs. What he saw brought him up short. There were no footprints in the dust on the steps and for an instant he stood confused, fighting to make sense of what he was seeing. He could hear sounds of a fight going on upstairs and yet—

That's when he spotted the elevator and the tracks leading into it—the same ones he'd found just inside the back door—a man's muddy boot prints and the two narrow wheel tracks.

He took off up the stairs at a dead run, weapon drawn. McKenzie's scream filled the air as he topped the stairs. He followed the sound, still running, breathing hard, knowing he would kill the man. Blinded with rage, he wanted to tear the man limb from limb. Hayes had never felt that kind of anger. It scared him and yet it also fueled him as he ran toward the heartbreaking sounds. He just prayed he would reach McKenzie before the madman killed *her*.

As JASON MATHEWS lunged at her with scissors, he let out a roar. She caught a glimpse of the insanity burning in his eyes. He came at her like a wounded animal, only this animal didn't just want to fight back. This animal yearned for retribution as only a human animal can.

He came at her so fast, she didn't get a chance to swing around with her feet. He came at her face, slashing the blades wildly. Had he simply tried to stab her, she might not have raised her hands to protect herself. But then again, she might have instinctively. She would never know.

She felt the blades slash across the backside of one wrist where she was bound by the thick tape. Because of that, she didn't feel the pain at first. She'd drawn her feet up as he'd struck her and managed to kick out at him, catching him in one knee. She heard screaming and thought at first it was her.

His leg buckled and he came down on top of her. She tried to roll out from under him, but he was too heavy. He had her pinned to the floor as he tried to struggle to his feet.

He rose just enough that he could get the scissors between them. He was going to kill her. Not the way he had wanted. But he could no longer hold back. She saw it in his expression as he struggled to rise.

Defeat, it was in his eyes, as well as disgust and pain. His nose was still bleeding and there was a bruised spot on his forehead from where it must have connected to the floor. The bright red blood had run down onto his white shirt.

How would he explain that to his wife?

That crazed, terrified thought came out of nowhere. The random thought of a woman about to die.

Hayes. The thought of him came with such regret she felt tears well in her eyes. She didn't want to die without at least telling him that she'd fallen in love with him.

Jason steadied himself as he timed his next thrust, this one aimed at her heart. They were both breathing hard, his breath making a loud almost snoring sound because of his broken nose. Neither of them heard the pounding of footfalls in the hallway.

Jason raised the scissors, meeting her gaze with one of rage and pain. He looked as if he was about to cry. McKenzie wanted to look away, but she couldn't. Her eyes locked with his. He almost looked afraid of her. He just wanted it to be over, she thought and realized that killing her this way wouldn't give him what he needed so there would be other women—and soon. That thought filled her with more sorrow than the thought of her own imminent death.

With the look of a man about to drive a stake into a vampire's heart, he grabbed the scissors in both hands and brought the blades down.

The sound of the gunshot was like an explosion, even in the large master suite. Another shot filled the air. Then another and another.

McKenzie had accepted that she would die. She'd told herself not to fight it as Jason drove the scissor blades down at her heart. But the gunshots into his back threw off his aim and gave her a few seconds to shift her body to the side. The blades came down into her side in a searing pain. Her cry was lost in the echo of the gunshots.

HAYES THOUGHT OF the first time he'd laid eyes on McKenzie Sheldon. She'd been lying on the ground bleeding and then her eyes had opened....

He shoved the madman's body off her and dropped to his knees next to her.

"McKenzie!" There was blood everywhere. He couldn't tell how much of it was hers as he felt for a pulse, praying with every second that he would feel one. "McKenzie?"

He found a pulse and tried to breathe a little easier as McKenzie's eyes blinked open. What was it about those eyes? "McKenzie. Sweetheart. How badly are you hurt?"

She shook her head and tried to smile through

the pain. "The bastard cut me. His name is Jason Mathews. He—"

"Don't try to talk," he told her. He could hear sirens in the distance. "You're going to be all right. You're safe now."

She closed her eyes as he took her hand. He thought about the first time he'd told her that. It had been a lie. She hadn't been safe. But she would be now, he thought as he looked over at the dead man.

Outside police cars and an ambulance had pulled up. He didn't want to let go of her hand, but he did only long enough to go to the window and direct the EMTs up on the elevator.

As he dropped down onto the bloody floor next to McKenzie again, he realized he was shaking. He thought about what he'd seen the moment he'd cleared the bedroom doorway. McKenzie bound up like that on the floor and that man standing over her, a pair of long-bladed scissors clamped in his hands, the man's beaten face twisted in a grimace—

That was all he remembered until he was on his knees next to McKenzie. He didn't remember pulling the trigger, couldn't even say how many times he'd shot the man.

That thought scared him. He'd been in the P.I. business for ten years. He considered himself a professional. He'd never lost control before.

Suddenly the room was filled with cops and EMTs and a stretcher. He let go of McKenzie's hand and moved back out of the way.

"Is she going to be okay?" he asked as two EMTs went to work on her.

"She's stable. We'll know more once we get her to the hospital."

Hayes wanted desperately to ride in the ambulance with her but one look at the cops and he knew he wasn't going anywhere. "Mind if I call my brother so he can go to the hospital to be with McKenzie until I can get there?"

Chapter Sixteen

McKenzie woke with a start. As her eyes flew open, she saw the woman standing next to her hospital bed. Had she been able to forget yesterday's horror, she might not have recognized the woman at first.

But she hadn't been able to escape Jason Mathews, even filled with anesthesia in the operating room or later in a sedated sleep. He'd followed her into her nightmares.

"Emily Mathews?" She tried to sit up but the woman placed a hand on her shoulder, holding her down on the bed. McKenzie looked up into Jason's wife's face. A pair of dark brown eyes stared back at her.

"I had to see you," the woman said in that small, timid voice McKenzie remembered from the day at the ranchette showing. "Jason's dead, you know."

Dead, but far from forgotten. She tried to sit up again, but she was weak from whatever she'd been given after the surgery. Her side hurt like the devil from where she'd been stabbed. She saw that one of her wrists was bandaged and there was something plastered to her back under her nightgown that burned.

She felt foggy, as if caught between a nightmare and reality. Was this woman even really in her room or was this yet another nightmare?

As she felt the pain and recalled what the madman had done to her, she knew she wasn't dreaming.

"Here, let me do that," Emily said as McKenzie reached for the nurse call button. The woman didn't press it to call a nurse. Instead, she moved it out of her reach.

Fear spiraled through her, making her feel as if she might throw up. Jason was dead but this woman… She tried to sit up again. "What are you—"

The door burst open. McKenzie fell back with such relief that she could no longer hold back the tears. "Hayes." There'd been only one other time she'd been so happy to see him and that had been yesterday. She reminded herself that he'd also saved her the first time they'd met, as he rushed to her bed and took her hand.

"Are you all right?" he asked.

She couldn't speak. Tears rolled down her cheeks as she tried to swallow down the fear that had settled like a dull ache in her chest.

Behind him was a male police officer. "Mrs. Mathews, you shouldn't be in here."

"I had to come," Emily said in her tiniest voice.

"Well, you need to leave now. You're upsetting Ms. Sheldon," the cop said.

"Of course," the woman said, and turned to look at McKenzie. "I'm sorry."

McKenzie thought for a moment that she had mis-understood the woman's intentions. Maybe Emily had only come here to tell her how sorry she was for what her husband had done. But then she looked again in the woman's eyes. There was no compassion. The only emotion burning there was fury.

The woman was sorry, but not for the reasons anyone else in the room thought.

As the policeman led Emily out of the room, she turned to Hayes. "She *knew.* She knew the whole time. Her only regret was that I lived and he died."

Epilogue

"You're going to get sunburned."

McKenzie opened her eyes to look over at Hayes and smiled. "The sun feels so good."

Hayes sat up and reached for the suntan lotion. Since they'd been in Texas, the color had come back into McKenzie's cheeks and she'd gotten a nice tan. She looked healthy, even happy. But he knew she hadn't forgotten her ordeal. Never would. Neither would he.

The scars weren't just on her body, he thought as he rubbed the cool lotion on her back. He'd been surprised when she hadn't wanted to see a plastic surgeon about having the scar on her back removed or the others.

"What would be the point?" she'd said. "For me, it will always be there. Anyway," she'd said, tracing one along his shoulder, "we all have scars."

He remembered each of his scars that he'd gotten growing up with four brothers as well as the ones he'd gotten working as a P.I. Life was dangerous. Sometimes you got lucky and survived it.

"I'm going to be all right, you know," she said when he'd finished applying the lotion.

"I never doubted it."

She sat up to look out at the Gulf of Mexico, her back to him.

"You are the strongest, most determined woman I know."

She smiled at him over her shoulder. She had the most amazing smile. Her hair was even shorter than it had been in Montana. He liked it, but wondered if she missed her long hair. She hadn't known that men like Jason Mathews targeted women with long hair. Women exactly like her. She hadn't known a lot about killers, but she did now.

"I like Texas," she said as she took a deep breath of the gulf air.

He waited, anticipating a "but" before he said, "That's good. You haven't seen much of it yet. It's a big state."

She was watching the waves as she had other days, lying in the sun, wading in the water, seemingly content to spend her days on the beach. The hot sun beat down on the white sand while the surf rolled up only yards from their feet, just as it had all the other days.

Only today, Hayes felt the change in her.

"I've had an offer on the agency," she said after a long moment.

He held his breath, not sure what he wanted her to say. He'd known she couldn't be content spending the rest of her life as a beach bum. That wasn't her. It wasn't him, either. Their lives had been in limbo for weeks now. He'd known she needed time and had been determined to give it to her.

She turned around to face him, sitting cross-legged

on the towel. Her skin was tanned, her high cheekbones pink from the sun, her amazing eyes bright. She looked beautiful. She also looked more confident than he'd seen her in a long time.

"I spoke with your cousin Dana. She wanted to know what our plans are for the wedding."

The sudden shift in subjects threw him off for a moment. "You still want to go to Tag and Lily's wedding?"

"Of course. He's your brother and I adore Lily." She frowned. "You do realize this—" she waved an arm, a motion that encompassed the Galveston beach "—this has been wonderful but only temporary, don't you?"

He nodded. "I've just been waiting for you to get your strength back."

She smiled and placed a cool palm on his bare leg. "What about you?"

"What about me?"

"I know you can afford to spend the rest of your life on this beach if you wanted to, but I don't think that is what you want to do, is it?"

"No, I need to work. Not for the money so much as for the work itself."

She licked her lips, catching her lower lip between her teeth for a moment. He felt a stirring in him, his desire for this woman a constant reminder of how much he loved her and that he hadn't yet told her.

The timing had felt all wrong. He wanted her strong. He wanted that unsinkable McKenzie Sheldon back before he laid that on her.

Now as he looked into her eyes, he saw that she was back.

"There is something I have to tell you," he said as he took both of her hands in his and got his courage up. His parents' marriage had failed. His brother Jackson's, as well. He wasn't sure he ever believed in love ever after, but he damned sure wanted to now.

McKenzie smiled, amusement in her eyes. "Is it that hard to admit?"

He chuckled. "I've been wanting to say it for weeks. I just had to wait until I was sure you were going to be all right."

"I'm all right, Hayes."

"I can see that." He gripped her hands, his gaze locking with hers.

McKenzie looked into his dark eyes, afraid of what he was going to say. They hadn't talked about the future. She knew he'd made a point of not pushing her. He'd given her time to heal and she loved him for it.

"I love you."

She laughed. "And I love you. I have for a long time."

He let out a relieved breath and pulled her into his arms for a moment. "I want to spend the rest of my life with you. I don't care where it is as long as we're together."

"Are you saying you would go back to Montana with me?"

"If that is what you want. I could open a private-investigation business in Bozeman or even in the canyon. Dana was telling me about a ranch near hers that was going on the market. I would need a good real-estate agent to handle things."

She couldn't believe what he was saying. "After staying at the Cardwell Ranch, I'm spoiled to live anywhere but the canyon. Could we really do this?"

"Only if you agree to marry me." He looked into her eyes again. "But be sure. This is a no-holds-barred offer till death do us part with kids and dogs and horses and barbecues behind the house."

She laughed as she threw herself back into his arms, knocking them to the sand. "Yes," she said as she looked down into his handsome face. "Yes to all of it."

"And I haven't even made you any Texas Boys Barbecue yet." He flipped her over so he was on top. "Woman, you are in for a treat."

She sobered as she looked up at him. "You've saved my life in so many ways," she said as she touched his cheek. "Do you think it was fate that night that we met?"

"I don't know. But I think I knew the moment I first looked into your eyes that you were the only woman who could get this Texas boy out of Texas."

He kissed her with a promise of good things to come as the surf rolled up to their feet and Montana called.

* * * * *

"Do they teach you to kiss like that in police school?" she whispered, running her fingers lightly across his lips.

"Basic Interrogation 101," he said.

"I bet you aced the class."

He smiled to himself, and not just because the conversation was silly, but because the sound of her voice did that to him.

"I'm sorry I pointed a gun at you," she said with a quick upsweep of her lashes. "Is it really empty?"

"Yep. That's why I didn't take it with me when I went outside to scout."

"I thought you'd forgotten it."

"Cops don't forget their weapons," he said. But being around her was causing him to forget so many other things, including all the reasons he should stay away from her.

SHATTERED

BY
ALICE SHARPE

MILLS & BOON

Published in Great Britain 2014
by Mills & Boon, an imprint of Harlequin (UK) Limited,
Eton House, 18-24 Paradise Road, Richmond, Surrey, TW9 1SR

© 2014 Alice Sharpe

ISBN: 978-0-263-91360-6

46-0614

Harlequin (UK) Limited's policy is to use papers that are natural, renewable and recyclable products and made from wood grown in sustainable forests. The logging and manufacturing processes conform to the legal environmental regulations of the country of origin.

Printed and bound in Spain
by Blackprint CPI, Barcelona

Alice Sharpe met her husband-to-be on a cold, foggy beach in Northern California. One year later they were married. Their union has survived the rearing of two children, a handful of earthquakes registering over 6.5, numerous cats and a few special dogs, the latest of which is a yellow Lab named Annie Rose. Alice and her husband now live in a small rural town in Oregon, where she devotes the majority of her time to pursuing her second love, writing.

This book is dedicated to my delightful friend
and other daughter, Charmian Lodjic,
who loves herself a good cowboy.
Happy reading, honey.

Chapter One

After giving the congested waiting area a once-over, Nate Matthews approached the flight center of the tiny Shatterhorn, Nevada, airport with his customary long stride. After hours behind the wheel, it felt good to finally move around. A woman standing behind the counter cast him an anxious smile as she looked up from her computer. He guessed the lousy February weather was playing havoc with things like schedules.

"I'm running a little late," he explained, "and I'm supposed to meet some friends here but I don't see them. Can you tell me if they've arrived?"

"In this weather? I doubt it," she said. "No private planes have landed for at least an hour. Let's take a look. What's their name?"

"Jessica and Alex Foster from Blunt Falls, Montana. He's flying his own single-engine Cessna."

She checked the computer screen, then thumbed through a sheaf of papers, leaving for a moment to talk to a man sitting at a desk behind a glass partition. When she returned, she was shaking her head. "There's a record of Mr. Foster filing his flight plan, but none of him landing here. Looks like you arrived first. Really, though, I'm not sure I'd expect him tonight. The weather is deteriorating quickly, especially at higher elevations."

Nate leaned against the counter for a second. The drive had not been without mishap; in fact, he'd barely survived a blown-out tire and the near collision that followed it. And then he'd found the spare was flat, too. Arranging a tow truck to haul him back to Vegas to get the tire fixed had eaten up time. Alex and Jessica should have landed way ahead of the storm.

The man behind him cleared his throat impatiently and Nate moved away from the counter. Finding a quiet corner, he called Alex's house just in case something had come up at the last moment. Jessica answered the phone.

"Hey," he said after identifying himself. "Is everything there okay?"

"Sure," she said, but her voice sounded stressed. "Is Alex with you?"

"No, that's why I'm calling. Did he leave on time?"

"Yes. He should have been there by now."

"I thought you were coming, too."

"I didn't feel well," she said after a brief hesitation.

He took a deep breath. "I don't mean to alarm you, but I hear there's a storm in the mountains."

"Maybe he had to land somewhere else," she said.

"Maybe. Wouldn't he call you?"

"Not necessarily." There was the edge again. "Anyway, if anything can go wrong with phone service or the radio, you can bet it will. All his equipment is ancient."

Nate stared at the snow falling outside the window. "I'll alert them here. I think you should do the same on your end, just to be safe."

"I will," she said. "But he'll show up. He always does. What would the Blunt Falls police department do without him?"

"Yeah," Nate said, certain now that something was going on with Jessica. His immediate concern, however, was Alex, though he didn't have the slightest idea what he could do about it.

He and Alex had made plans to meet at the airport and then hook up with a third man, a guy by the name of Mike Donovan. They'd only met Mike once, but it had been on a Labor Day afternoon none of the men would ever forget. Alex had told him that this time Jessica was coming along for the ride and maybe a side trip down to Reno.

Nate asked the airport to notify the right people about Alex's flight, tried Mike's cell phone and walked back to his truck through growing snow flurries. Chances were good Mike was sitting at the mall, too distracted to even hear his phone.

He'd been that way lately, posting long emails full of conspiracy theories. Being a deputy in a small town in Arizona, Nate was no stranger to people losing their grip on reality. He just hoped Mike wasn't suffering some sort of post-traumatic stress disorder. Nate himself had struggled coming to grips with what he'd experienced that late summer day, and he'd been in law enforcement his entire adult life. Mike had spent his career either working on the family horse ranch or selling appliances in town.

Even driving up to the cluster of pale stone buildings that constituted the Shatterhorn Mall brought back a hundred unbearable memories for Nate. Last time he'd been here, he and Alex had been returning from an Alaskan fishing trip. When Nate's flight was delayed, the two men had hiked down the road a bit, winding up at this mall, where they found dinner in the food court.

Just an idle diversion to eat up some time on a Labor Day weekend when the place was crammed with kids buying back-to-school clothes. Nate's plan had been to return to the airport in a couple of hours and continue on to Reno and, from there, home. Meanwhile, Alex would fly the Cessna, which he'd left at the airfield ten days before, back to Montana.

Things hadn't exactly turned out as planned.

Today, entering the mall through the doors closest to the food court put a knot in Nate's stomach that twisted tighter with each footstep. It wasn't a big mall by urban standards, but for a small town, it was busy. That was probably why the carnage that had occurred here had upset the nation; this wasn't the kind of town that was supposed to suffer random shootings and mangled teenagers.

Then again, what town was?

The food court was a grand name for ten or eleven fast-food outlets grouped around a few dozen tables. The clientele seemed oblivious to the devastation that had once littered the space. The shattered windows had all been replaced, the bullet holes mended, torn flesh healed or buried… Life went on.

For a moment, Nate stood there, buffeted by the acoustics created by the dome overhead, scanning faces for Mike's, then he turned to leave. As he did so, he caught a glimpse of a familiar face, but it wasn't Mike's.

Jason Netters stood fifteen feet away, very close to the cookie kiosk that came complete with a boatload of tortured memories. Nate had herded a group of kids to the shelter of that kiosk and told them to stay put while he went to help another child. The kids had panicked and left the shelter. The two girls hadn't made it far before being shot and killed, just like two other kids a short distance away.

Jason had survived.

The boy was compact in size but muscular like a wrestler. He had straw-colored hair and green eyes. He must have felt Nate looking at him. Their gazes met and it was as if the past five and a half months had never happened.

The knot grew so tight it was hard to breathe, but Nate took a step forward, unexpectedly moved to see the boy again.

Jason looked away almost at once. Within seconds, he'd disappeared, swallowed up by the crowd, and gone in less time than it took to say it. But the look on his face before he turned unsettled Nate in a way nothing else had.

The boy didn't want to see him. No way. Not one bit.

Nate understood in a moment of clarity that this was the real reason he'd come back here. Not because he believed Mike had earth-shattering news but because this place had cost him a whole lot that September day. He'd walked in one man and left as another, something his fiancée had been quick to point out right before she left for good.

It was come here and face his demons or change careers, because you couldn't be a decent officer when you woke up in a dead sweat every night. His boss was pressing him to run for sheriff in the coming election, said he'd win in a landslide because of the positive light the mall shooting had focused on him. Confused, disgruntled and undecided, he'd taken a leave, parked his career at the door, so to say, while he figured out what the rest of his life looked like. Right now, it was just a blur.

As just about anything was better than spending another minute in this mall, he decided to go find Mike. At least it would put a little distance between himself and the past…for a while, anyway.

HIS ACTUAL DESTINATION, programmed into the truck's on-board GPS, was thirty miles west of Reno. He knew Mike lived on a horse ranch he'd inherited from his father and that he was divorced, with one daughter from whom it seemed he was estranged. Nate wasn't sure where the daughter was now. Boston or New York or maybe Washington, D.C., somewhere on the East Coast. He'd read a brief account of Mike's family in the newspaper after the shooting.

Thanks to a cold, brisk wind, the driving was tricky, but the roads were mercifully clear of snow and ice, at least at first. Too preoccupied to take note of the scenery, even if he'd been able to see it through the weather and darkness, he traveled in a cocoon of steel, falling into an odd trancelike state where he could have been anyone going anywhere. He kind of wanted to keep driving forever.

After thirty minutes, the directions had him turn off the highway and drive uphill over another ten miles of increasingly untended roads. Maybe the reason Mike hadn't shown was as simple as Alex's—the storm and the inclement weather had prohibited travel. Nate had snow tires on his vehicle, chains in the back and nowhere else to go, nothing else to do, so he kept driving.

He finally came across a sign hanging from a frame by one rusted chain. He emerged from the truck to find the snow deeper here. He'd get stuck if he wasn't careful. Picking his way forward, he tilted the dangling sign toward his headlights and read, "Donovan's Fine Quarter Horses Since 1936."

The place had obviously seen better days, as was increasingly evident as he drove the remaining distance up the overgrown road. He broke out into a clearing upon which sat numerous outbuildings and what appeared to be empty pastures, though he could hear the noise of a horse somewhere nearby. The house itself was dark and looked abandoned. Nate pulled his vehicle to a stop beside an older truck that could have been sitting there an hour or five years. It was quickly being buried in the snow, which was falling fast now. He had no idea what Mike drove. He gritted his teeth as he dug a flashlight out of his glove box.

Had Mike succumbed to the weather or was it more

serious, something like a heart attack or a stroke? Was he inside that house, dead or dying? That would explain why he hadn't answered any of Nate's calls.

Nate flashed his light over the broken pavers that jutted out of the snow. He stumbled over a planter that had frozen and shattered, spilling its contents sometime in the past. He recovered without falling, catching himself by grabbing a porch rail that wobbled when he grasped it. As he flicked the light over the door, shivers that had nothing to do with the temperature raced down his spine and across his back. The door was ajar but he could see no glint of light through the opening.

Since Sept. 11, police officers were allowed to carry weapons across state lines, but Nate had left his behind with his badge. In his head, the two went together. But now, unarmed, he felt naked, a sensation that echoed the way he'd felt months before when hell broke loose in the mall. Now, he swore to himself, come hell or high water, he would never step foot in Nevada again without a gun.

With the flashlight, he nudged the door open quietly, relieved when it didn't creak or groan. He flashed the light around and took in a large entry with three connecting doorways that seemed to lead to a dining area, living room and hallway.

He tried a light switch and was surprised when it worked. He thought he heard a sound from somewhere deep in the house, but at that second, in the improved light, he caught a glimpse of something that focused all his attention ahead.

A body lay sprawled facedown on the floor right inside the living room. Nate gasped a shallow breath. This sure explained why Mike was late.

Chapter Two

Nate knelt beside the body and rolled it over, knowing who and what he would find when he did so. Or at least he'd thought he knew. The who was easy. Mike was dead. The what was a shock.

Not a heart attack, not a stroke, but a massive gunshot wound to the chest had ended Mike's life. His clothes were soaked in blood, his pale eyes half-open, his lidded gaze fixed and empty. Nate had run across more than his share of shooting victims, and now he scanned the area for some sign of the weapon that had caused this catastrophic damage. He felt for a pulse, knowing he wouldn't find one, and did his best to block out the smell of blood. He quickly searched Mike's pockets for a phone or anything else that might help explain what had happened before he died. He found nothing.

He sat back on his heels. Poor Mike, poor guy. To survive the mall, to actually be the one to wrestle the wounded killer to the ground and hear his dying words, only to end up like this five and a half months later in his own home…

There was that noise again. Was the killer still in the house? From the look of things, an intruder had walked right in and caught Mike coming from the living room. He wore an unzipped jacket, as though he'd been in the process of leaving the house. The room had the appearance of having been searched, and none too carefully, either.

The house was cold, no lights, no fire in the grate, impossible to tell how long ago this had happened. There was no smell of gunpowder in the room, but with an open door that didn't really mean much.

He listened carefully as he stood up, once again scanning for something with which to arm himself. All he could see was a fireplace poker, and that struck him as pretty low-tech when it came to confronting whatever had taken down Mike. On the other hand, it was better than nothing. He crossed the room silently, snatched the poker from atop the hearth and stood stock-still, listening.

Another noise, like a door closing. He followed it across the living room and into the entry. He was certain it came from down the hall. He had a quick look at the kitchen and the laundry room, noting the disarray of cupboards and drawers. What in the heck had someone looked for—and had they found it?

The outside door was locked. He turned around and retraced his steps, switching on lights as he moved. Whoever was here must have heard him rustling around, probably seen the lights come on. There was no possibility to surprise them.

A more prudent plan of action would be to head for the relative safety of his truck and call the police, but then the intruder might escape through a back window or destroy evidence. All but holding his breath, Nate nudged open the first door on his left.

From the threshold, he could see the room held a lone twin bed and nightstand, a small chest of drawers and a few boxes stacked in the corner. The closet doors were folded open and the overhead lamp revealed three hangers. There were a couple of empty cardboard boxes inside the closet, their contents heaped beside them. Ditto the boxes in the corner. The drawers were all open.

The door across the hall led to another small room furnished with a futon, a small television and a desk piled high with papers and books. The drawers in this room were open as well, the items they'd apparently once held now scattered across the floor. It looked as though a computer used to occupy the desktop, but all that was left now was a mouse and a few cords. He checked the closet, but it was empty. He found the main bathroom in a similar state of disrepair and pulled the shower curtain back to make sure no one was hiding there.

The last door opened onto what was obviously Mike's bedroom. It held an unmade queen-size bed, a dresser and a couple of chairs. Piles of clothing littered every horizontal surface and the air smelled stale and unused, but it didn't appear to have been ransacked like the rest of the house. The bathroom off of this room was empty. That left the closet.

Wait just a second. Surely the person who had gunned down Mike in cold blood wasn't now cowering in a closet? Well, it was either that or they'd found a way around to the front of the house or out a window.

Holding the poker high, Nate planted his feet firmly, stood off to one side and yanked open the door. At first he saw nothing but the usual array of hanging clothes and a locked gun cabinet. Then he saw the clothes rustle. Peering into a gloomy jumble of boots on the floor, he glimpsed two smaller shoes. One moved slightly. Someone was hiding in here.

"Come on out," he demanded, his grip tightening on the poker.

"Don't shoot," a shaky voice responded.

Using his free hand, Nate pushed back the clothes and

found a woman scrunched as far back into the closet as was humanly possible. It was so dark back there that she was little more than glistening eyes and a pale oval for a face.

"I'm not going to shoot," he said, resisting the urge to shine the flashlight on her.

"Why did you kill my dad?" she asked, and he could hear the effort it took for her to spit out these words. "What good is that going to do?"

"You're Mike's daughter?"

She caught a new sob in her throat and wiped at her eyes. Even in the dim light, he could see her fingers shake as they grazed her cheek. "I…I was," she said.

He offered her a hand because she appeared ready to keel over. "I didn't kill Mike, but it sounds like you know who did. Please, come out of there. Did you see or hear anyone?"

"No," she said. "Nothing."

"Come on," he coaxed, touching her shoulder. "I'm not going to hurt you. My name is Nate Matthews. I was a friend of your dad's."

"From the store? He quit, you know. He couldn't concentrate on selling things anymore. He said… Well, never mind."

"No, I didn't know he quit his job. I didn't work with him. I'm from down in Arizona."

"Oh, my God," she said, her hands flying to her mouth. "You're one of the men who was at the mall last summer with Dad. You're the deputy sheriff."

"Yeah," he said without correcting her.

She seemed to relax a tiny bit and allowed him to help her from the shadows of the closet.

Seen in brighter light, she turned out to be a little older than his first estimate of late teens, and he adjusted her age to mid-twenties, a decade or so younger than him. She had a very pale complexion, her flawless cheeks moist from tears. A sheath of black hair caught the light and reflected it, setting off the bluest eyes Nate had ever seen. She was tall, probably five-seven or so, with full breasts and a small waist, attributes her black turtleneck sweater clearly revealed. Tight jeans announced the other half of her was just as fit. A pair of worn equestrian boots hugged her calves.

Her eyes grew huge as he pulled his phone from a pocket. "What are you doing?" she demanded, catching his hand.

"Calling the police."

"No! You mustn't. Please."

"Listen…" He paused, not knowing her name.

"Sarah. Sarah Donovan."

"Sarah, if there is one thing I'm absolutely positive I must do, it's call the police. This is not open for debate." But why wouldn't she want him to call for help? For that matter, why hadn't she? "When did this happen?" he added when he found he had no signal.

She was studying her watch, and whatever she found there seemed to alarm her. She looked up as though she'd only half heard him. "What? The shooting? I'm not sure when it happened. I just got here a little while ago."

"From where?"

She hesitated a moment before saying, "What's it to you?"

"How did you get here?"

"I flew."

His brow furrowed.

"I landed in Reno and rented a car. It's out in the barn. Why are you looking at me like that?"

He ignored her question. "Does your dad have a phone?"

"He got rid of the landline, but he has a cell."

"I checked his body. He's not carrying it."

"He always carries it," she insisted.

He frowned at her again. "Do you have any ID?"

"What!"

"Look at it from my point of view. You're the only person in the house with a dead man and I'm supposed to take it at face value that you are who you say you are? For that matter, put up your hands. I'm going to frisk you."

"Why?"

"Because Mike was shot in the chest and I don't want the same thing to happen to me. Put up your hands."

"Or you'll what? Hit me with a fire poker? Really?"

"Really," he said, his tone serious.

She glowered at him as she raised her hands. He patted her down with one hand while still clutching the poker with the other.

"Satisfied?" she said when he was finished.

"You could have hidden a weapon somewhere in the house. What about some ID?"

"I left it in the car."

"Why would you do that?"

"I wasn't planning on being here very long."

"So, you flew here all the way from who knows where, parked in an old barn, came into a dark house—"

"It wasn't dark when I got here," she interrupted. "After I saw my dad lying on the floor, I heard an engine and thought his killer had come back, so I turned off the lights and hid. It must have been you."

"Do you have any idea why the house was searched?"

Her gaze flicked to the floor and back. "No."

He stared at her a moment. "Let's go get your ID."

"I have a better idea. Why don't you drive back into

town where your phone gets reception and summon the cops? I'll stay here. With Dad."

"You'll stay here," he said, his voice very dry.

"Yes. Now what's wrong?"

"I still don't know who you are. I'm not leaving you alone in this house."

She rubbed her forehead as though she was so frustrated with him she had to fight to maintain control.

"Let's go get your ID," he repeated.

She didn't look happy about the prospect, but when he started to touch her arm, she drew away and took off down the hall. He stayed close behind her, telling himself not to get distracted by the way her hips moved inside the black denim.

"I need my coat," she said, gesturing at the chair behind Mike's body. As she spoke, her gaze traveled down to her father's still form and she caught a sob in her throat. She flicked away new tears as Nate handed her the coat. He did his best to look away for a moment.

When she finally spoke again, her voice was a little shaky. She'd zipped a dark blue down parka up to her chin. The color emphasized the sapphire hue of her eyes. "I just wish I'd known him better," she whispered.

Nate felt the same way, but wasn't it odd that Mike's daughter did, as well? Maybe Mike wasn't the easiest guy to get to know.

Sarah turned suddenly and met his gaze. "I'll go get my purse," she said. "No reason for us both to freeze to death."

"I don't mind," he said.

"Which really means you don't trust me."

He shrugged one shoulder. "Shall we?"

"Like I have a choice." Once again she glanced at her watch, this time emitting a small gasp. It gave him the willies. Why was she worried about time? Was she waiting for an accomplice to show up?

He followed her out the front door, amazed how much more snow had accumulated in the few minutes he'd been inside. His own white truck was covered with the stuff, as was the other. The wind had also picked up, blowing icy crystals at their faces as they started across the yard. He held the Stetson on his head and was glad he'd worn his trusty cowboy boots.

"I left the car in that barn over there," she said. She opened the sliding door a couple of feet and they walked inside. Nate flicked on his flashlight as he heard a horse whinny nearby.

"That's Skipjack," she said. "He's the last horse Dad has. Had."

Nate nodded, but his concentration was really on the old green sedan sitting ten feet in front of them. "You rented *that* at an airport?" he asked.

"Sort of," she said.

"What's that mean?"

"It means I rented it from a place that specializes in wrecks. It wasn't exactly at the airport."

"Good grief," he said.

"My purse is in the backseat on the left by my suitcase. It's unlocked."

He moved around the car to the far side. Opening the back door, he shined the light into the interior. "I don't see anything—" he began, glancing up, and for a second, he wasn't sure what had happened. The woman was gone as if she'd never existed. Then reason took hold— she must have run out the door while he was distracted. Swearing, he raced around the car and shined his light across the yard in time to see the driver's door of his truck slam closed.

As he followed the path she'd plowed through the snow, he heard the automatic click of his door lock. He shined the light at the driver's window and saw her searching everywhere for something. She finally turned on the cab light and lowered the visor, patting it as though she thought a key might be lurking up there. He saw her cup her forehead with one hand, wincing in defeat. Her lips moved as if she swore. Then she looked at him through the foggy glass.

Taking the ring of keys out of his pocket, he dangled them in front of his side of the tinted window. Her eyes narrowed and her lips moved again. This time he was sure she swore. He pressed the automatic lock button and opened the door.

"Who in the hell are you?" he asked her.

"Just who I said I was. Sarah Donovan."

"Why are you acting so peculiar?"

"I have to get out of here. Now."

"Why?"

"It's none of your business," she said with a pleading note in her voice.

"Well, actually, grand theft auto is my business when it's my damn truck. Did you kill Mike?"

"No, of course not. Everything happened just the way I said."

"Why can't I quite believe that?" he mused aloud, offering her a hand down.

She ignored his help and jumped to the ground, where she slipped on the compacted snow and started to fall. He caught her shoulders and she looked up at him. "You can't believe me because you're cynical," she said. "Every cop I've ever known gets to be like that."

"And have you known a lot of cops?"

"My share," she said. "I even married one a long time ago. Listen, please, just let me leave."

"The police will want to talk to you," he said, letting her go.

"So, I'll come back."

Sure she would. He shook his head. "Sorry."

"Is your phone working? Could I at least make a call?"

He dug his phone out of his jacket pocket. Maybe he could get a signal outside. The screen lit up with a swipe of his finger, and in that instant, a loud pop cracked the frigid air. His phone blew out of his hand and disintegrated into nothing. He grabbed his throbbing fingers with his free hand, dropping the flashlight in the process. Another shot came next and he actually felt the bullet whiz past his left ear. Without thinking, he grabbed Sarah and pulled her to the ground. The flashlight had landed a couple of feet away and sank into the fresh snow, where it now illuminated a small crater and pinpointed their location as clear as day.

"Are you hurt?" he whispered to Sarah.

"No," she murmured. "Are you?"

His hand throbbed. "I'll live. We have to move."

"Your truck…"

"We'd be sitting ducks. The snow's too deep and we can't dig it out with a gunman taking shots at us."

"Then my car."

Another bullet came dangerously close. "Do you want to race across the yard in this snow with someone shooting at you? Besides, your rent-a-wreck is so low to the ground you couldn't drive through the snow even if we did manage to get it out of the barn."

As though privy to their conversation, a couple more shots and a nearby popping sound announced at least one of the truck tires had just bitten the dust.

"Then where?" she said.

"Back to the house. Stay in the shadows and stick close. Ready?"

He wasn't positive, but he thought he detected a slight nod.

Chapter Three

Sarah's head was filled with so many images and worries that for an instant, she almost couldn't bring herself to move. What in the world was she going to do? A bullet hit the snow a couple of feet from her hand and that cleared her mind, at least for the moment. First things first.

She scrambled to follow in Nate's wake, doing her best to keep her head and butt down. If this gunman was who she thought he was, he wouldn't be firing to kill them but to capture them and force information. There would be no quick, clean death, not for her, anyway. The thought of torture created a layer of sweat on top of her icy skin.

She hadn't known who or what to expect when the closet door opened, but it sure as heck hadn't been a tall glowering cowboy, although now that she stopped to think, she should have realized he'd come. How would she get rid of him?

She'd read about Nate Matthews after the Labor Day shooting. She knew he was engaged, that he was respected down in Arizona and that he didn't tolerate any nonsense. She knew his service record and the fact his parents had been photographed looking as proud as peacocks about their upstanding son. And she knew her father had trusted him and his friend Alex. Maybe they'd been the only people her father had trusted toward the end. She sure didn't have a place on that short list.

Hopefully, Nate Matthews would figure out how to get out of this situation and go for help. That would give her the opportunity to finish what she'd started and try to escape.

There was a sincerity in his eyes that made her uneasy about this possibility, but it was clear he didn't believe much of what she said, and that was good. Sooner or later, if they weren't shot first, he'd grow weary of her behavior and cut his losses. All she had to do was wait him out.

Except that took time and time was something she had precious little of. And face it, she was whisper close to being his adversary, or at least he would see it that way, and he didn't appear to be the kind of man you wanted to be on the bad side of. If he'd just let her leave when she'd tried to, then she'd be on her way back to Reno and none of this would have happened.

You'd be on your way empty-handed, her racing mind reminded her, *driving a stolen truck with this killer on your heels. And don't forget, empty-handed means by this time tomorrow, you'll be an orphan.*

"You still with me?" Nate hissed when he paused behind a row of arborvitae. A shot went off, but it hit several feet to their left, over by a planter that would be filled with wildflowers in three months if it survived the night.

"I'm here," she whispered, bumping into him as she scooted to pull her foot into the shadow.

"Listen," he said, his voice very soft, his lips right next to her ear. He'd grabbed her shoulder with one hand when she'd tumbled against him and he didn't release it now. His strong grip was oddly reassuring and his warm breath against her frozen ear distracted her for a second. "I'm concerned this could be a trap."

"What do you mean?"

"There could be another gunman waiting inside the house."

A serious shiver ran up both her arms, made a U-turn and raced right back down to her fingertips. That was exactly what Bellows would plan—a trap where she'd be forced to spill her guts. But how did you spill your guts about something you didn't know anything about?

"The back door is locked," he added, as if to himself.

"Not if you know where the key is."

"And you do?"

"I think so," she said, hoping it was still where her father used to keep it. She hadn't lived in this house for eleven years. By now the key could be lost, the lock might have been changed... Who knew? "There's a fake brick next to the steps."

"Let's go," he said as he tossed a rock several feet across to the other side of the porch. It hit a drainpipe or something else metallic. A round of deafening shots galvanized her as Nate grabbed her hand and tugged her in the other direction, around the corner of the house. From the sound of things, Nate's truck had just lost a window and a couple more tires, or maybe the shots had hit her father's old beater.

They crawled behind the row of camellias her mother had planted in the far past. The snow was deep, but not as deep as in the yard itself, thanks to the bushes and the overhanging eaves. As a child, she'd had to be bribed to come back here to turn on the water or hook up a hose because of the spiders that lurked in the leafy darkness. Tonight, spiders seemed like a distant threat from more innocent days.

"It should be right around here," she said as they scooted into a small clearing by the back porch. The snow covered

almost everything and they both dug like harried rabbits. "I got it," she said, her voice raw from the cold. She
picked up a brick that appeared slightly smaller than the
others. Her fingers were so numb she couldn't discern the
texture of the stone, but it felt blessedly light, as though
it wasn't really made out of clay. She wiggled the bottom
and a panel slid open to reveal something that twinkled
in the indirect light seeping through the window above.

"Eureka," Nate whispered as she shook the key out into
his hand. She remained crouched while he slowly got to
his feet. A second later, she heard the sound of the key in
the lock. "You stay here. I'll go check," he said, his face
surrounded by a veil of condensed breath.

She didn't respond, just followed behind him through
the back door, closing it quietly behind her, ignoring his
disgruntled expression when he turned around and found
her standing there. No way was she staying outside alone.
Besides, it was at least a little warmer in here and she was
frozen to the bone.

"Did your father own a gun?" he whispered.

"He used to. If he still has it, it would be in that locked
cabinet in the back of his closet."

"And the key?"

"I didn't have time to look for it." Truth was, she'd been
searching for that key when she'd heard Nate arrive.

"I'll find it," Nate said. He stared down at her, his features visible for the first time in what seemed a long time.
His skin was slightly tanned, as though he spent a fair
amount of time outdoors. His hair was long for a lawman,
thick and dark, his lashes luxuriant, his gray eyes wary.
She hadn't noticed his dark eyebrows before, how straight
they were and how they framed his eyes. They currently
furled inward as he studied her. "Can I trust you to stay by
this door and yell like a banshee if anyone approaches it?"

"You mean as opposed to running outside and taking my chances with a gun?" His eyes narrowed now and she could sense the lingering distrust. "Sorry," she said, relenting. "Okay, I'll act as lookout. Just hurry."

He nodded once, quick and decisive. Arming himself with a knife from the metallic strip mounted above the cooktop, he left the kitchen and headed toward the entry hall without making a sound, although he did leave a trail of dirty melting snow behind him.

The knife struck her as an excellent idea, so she grabbed one for herself and slid the deadbolt closed. This time when she glanced at her watch, her heart all but stopped beating. The night was being gobbled up like Christmas dinner and she felt like the main course. For a second she considered dimming the lights, but thought better of it. She could still hear the occasional shot coming from the yard and figured the gunman must be shooting at shadows. No need to alert him the game had moved indoors.

How could she even joke about this being a game? Her dad was dead and it might very well be her fault, no matter how unreasonable he'd been. If she didn't get real clever or real lucky very soon, then her mother would pay the price as well. Nope, this wasn't a game.

A flash of light out in the yard, barely visible now because of the falling snow, caught her attention and she involuntarily jerked. The window in the door exploded and she hit the floor along with a shower of safety glass. Yelling like crazy, she scrambled to her feet and dashed toward the front hall, sure the gunman was seconds away from crashing through the door.

She ran right into Nate, who had managed to find a rifle. He immediately caught her around the waist and swung her behind him, then continued on into the kitchen while she clung to the faux paneling, the knife gripped in her white-knuckled hand. Her gaze followed him as he ran to the door and started firing shots through the broken window.

He knelt to reload, his concentration so intent on the gun and the ammunition that he might have been in a different world. He stood again and aimed, letting off a few rounds, then waited. It had grown ominously quiet outside.

Up until that point, Sarah had thought of Nate as part obstacle and part protector, a leader, but standing there, his jeans wet from melting snow, his taut body ready for action, he came into sharper focus as a fellow human being who had walked into a mess not of his own making and was now stuck.

She lowered her gaze. She knew he would do everything in his power to safeguard her, whether he trusted her or not. That should have reassured her. Instead, along with everything else, it made her stomach roll.

After several very long moments, he turned to look at her and their gazes connected like two hot wires with a spark in the middle. She drew a small, quick breath, surprised by the tension between them that suddenly leaped with awareness. It was almost as if he could read her mind and knew darn well that she was determined to leave this ranch as soon as she could.

"You look scared," he whispered.

"And you're not?"

"Nerves of steel," he said, but he said it with a self-deprecating smile and a soft shake of his head.

"There's nobody else in the house?" she asked.

"Nope, we're alone."

She gestured with her head toward the broken window and the seeming emptiness of the backyard. "Do you think you hit him?"

"Either that or he's circling around to the front."

Sarah turned her head suddenly. "What's that sound?"

He cocked his head and listened for a second, then strode toward her. "That's a two-stroke engine," he said. They both raced into the entry, where it was obvious the noise came from outside the house. They flanked the door and peered through the small inset piece of glass. At first there was nothing to see, then a light blazed on, wavering through the snow. "Headlight," Nate said under his breath.

Sarah looked up at him. "Just one?"

"A damn snowmobile," he said, lifting the rifle. "I should have guessed. How else would anyone get up here and away again? Okay, stay put, and this time I mean it!" He was out the front door and headed into the storm before Sarah could even react to his madness. Wrapping her arms around herself, she turned into the room and recoiled as her father's bloody body met her gaze.

There was nothing she could do to help him—or Nate, either, for that matter. What she did have was an unforeseen few moments alone to try to finish what she'd come for. Otherwise, in less than twenty-four hours, her mother would be dead. Sarah desperately needed to pull a rabbit out of a hat.

No, that wasn't true. She needed two rabbits.

All she had to do was find two hats. And the only place she could think to look that she hadn't already was the safe.

KEEPING TO THE SHADOWS and wishing like crazy he had a flashlight, Nate skirted the yard. The snow was falling so fast and furious it was hard to get his bearings. He could no longer see the dim house lights or a vehicle headlight, either, but he could hear the engine and so far it didn't appear to be moving away. He just tried to follow the sound, but the wind roaring through the overhead branches made even that chore tricky.

Armed only with Mike's six-shot Winchester saddle
gun that was undoubtedly older than he was, Nate's impromptu plan included tackling the gunman and subduing
him. The bonus would be gaining control of the snowmobile, which could then be used to get to a place where they
could summon help. Because it was obvious there was no
way the truck could be fixed and driven in this weather.
And that car of Sarah's was a joke.

He wasn't going to allow himself to think about Sarah
and all the ways she confused him, at least not right now.
There was something strange about her, but he needed to
focus his attention on the matter at hand.

The engine pitch changed, and he knew his quarry was
about to leave. The snow was too deep for him to run, but
he slogged through as fast as he could, his plan seeming
more naive by the moment. By luck, he bumped into what
felt like a pile of rocks, and that at last gave him some
semifirm footing. Using his numb hands and clutching the
rifle with a death grip, he scrambled up on top in time to
see the vehicle's headlight passing to his left. He fired off
a few shots, knowing this was a last hurrah, then threw
caution to the wind and leaped toward the lights, reaching
out to grab where he assumed the driver would be seated.

A sudden burning sensation flared in his left arm. His
fingers brushed hot metal for a microsecond before he
found himself facedown in the snow with a mouth full of
exhaust. He still grasped the rifle and was kind of amazed
he hadn't shot himself, though his arm throbbed. As he sat
up, the roar of the snowmobile sounded like evil laugh-
ter. The taillights had already disappeared. By the time
he got to his feet, even the motor sound had been swallowed up by the night.

The gunman was gone.

He clutched his left biceps and wasn't surprised when

his hand came away bloody. He hadn't wounded himself with his own rifle, but the gunman must have gotten off a parting shot.

So much for leaving the gun and badge back in Arizona. If he'd come armed with a decent weapon, this could all be over now, and once again, the inadequate feelings from being helpless during the mall shooting all but choked him. Why had he thought he could run away from being who he was?

He had to get back to the house, and that meant figuring out which way it lay, then getting there before hypothermia set in. This time when he questioned Sarah, she'd better say something worth listening to.

Chapter Four

By the time Nate finally bumped into his truck and stumbled the rest of the way to the house, he was experiencing an eerie sensation of being frozen and light-headed at the same time. His trusty jacket was more or less toast, but it had probably saved his life by maintaining his core temperature. Good thing he'd never had the opportunity to take it off.

He had no idea where or when he'd lost his hat, and his head was freezing. He loved the old Stetson, but hats came and went just like women.

All this was flittering through his mind while his light flashed over his truck, and he swore. He'd just finished paying the blasted thing off and he was no longer on the receiving end of a monthly paycheck. Look at the poor thing. The windshield had somehow survived, but the passenger window was gone, half the tires blown out, bullet holes down one side, and that was just what he could see in a glance. He swore again and felt like kicking something.

By the time he got inside the house, he was cold from temperature and anger. First thing to take care of was his arm. Hopefully he wouldn't need to depend on Sarah to help him—so far she hadn't struck him as the helpful type.

Where was she, anyway? Why hadn't she been waiting at the door, anxious to hear the outcome of his mission? What was more important to her than staying alive?

Bypassing Mike's body, he grabbed a bright throw from the back of a chair and started to drape it across the dead man, then stopped. The least he could do was preserve the crime scene until the experts got here. The camera on his phone had exploded with everything else, but maybe he'd find another one somewhere in with Mike's possessions.

Which reminded him that Mike's keys, wallet and cell appeared to be missing, along with his computer and who knew what else. Was this a robbery gone wrong or was it something more complicated?

He dropped the throw back on the chair and went looking for Sarah. He found her in her father's room, poking into the now unlocked gun cabinet that Nate had opened by finding the key tucked away in the pocket of the hunting vest hanging beside it.

"What are you doing?" he said.

She turned suddenly, a bulging manila envelope in her hands. There were additional boxes and envelopes piled on the bed as well. Her eyes widened as though she'd forgotten he was there. Or maybe she was just startled he'd made it back alive. "Did you get him?" she asked. "Did you see who it was?"

"No to both," he said.

She swallowed as she pushed her left hand down into her pocket. Was she holding something? The past hour or so had somehow honed her beauty into a grittier, darker form, enhanced by the dirt smudged on her jeans and across her cheek. In all honesty, it made her twice as sexy as she'd been, and that was saying something.

His head swam in the sudden heat of the room and he swayed a little. "What's in the envelope?"

"Dad's retirement stuff. I was looking for some old papers of mine."

"Old papers," he responded, his voice dry.

"Yeah. School papers, my diploma... Listen, it doesn't matter. They're not here."

"Anything else interesting in there?" he asked, nodding toward the safe.

"No," she said quickly. "Just genealogy stuff. Dad got off on that tangent a few years ago when he and Mom split up." She stared harder at him, then gasped. "You're bleeding!"

He followed the direction of her gaze to the torn, blood-soaked sleeve of his jacket and the red smears on his hand. "Yeah," he said and sat down abruptly on the side of the bed.

She was there in front of him almost at once. "What happened?"

"Score one for the bad guy."

"Oh, man, this is my fault," she said, running to the adjoining bathroom and returning with a stack of clean towels. "Take off your jacket. Here, I'll help you."

She very carefully unzipped the front of his jacket, which put her head next to his, and he breathed in the scents of hay and snow, an odd combination and bracingly refreshing. Her hair brushed his forehead and he closed his eyes, not trusting himself to look at her. He'd always been a sucker for blue eyes and this wasn't the time or place for that kind of thing.

"Easy now," she coaxed and gingerly helped him get his good arm out of the sleeve. Then she began peeling away the other sleeve, which hurt like blazes, and he winced.

"Sorry," she said. "Almost done." She dropped the jacket to the floor. "We'd better get your shirt off, too." That took longer and was agonizing for Nate as she freed his good arm from the heather-gray Henley and began the painstaking process of loosening the other sleeve from his injured arm.

"It's stuck to the blood," she explained.

He swallowed and nodded.

"Just a minute, okay?" She went back to the bathroom and returned a moment later with a brown bottle of hydrogen peroxide and bandages. "Maybe this will help," she said and, using the towel beneath his arm to absorb the overflow, drenched the site with the peroxide, loosening the knitted material from the wound. A moment later she managed to slip the shirt over his head and he sighed deeply with profound relief.

She looked a little pale as she considered his arm but, to her credit, didn't shy away. Instead she used more of the peroxide to bathe the site and peered intently at it.

Nate turned his head to try to get a good look. He was way too aware of her hand resting atop his bare shoulder, her fingers trembling as though her external coolness masked an inner repulsion at the sight of bloody flesh. The tip of her tongue flicked across her lips and he took a deep breath. He wasn't sure if his reactions to her proximity were an attempt to distance himself from his injury or because he'd have to be in far worse shape than he was *not* to notice her.

"I think the bullet entered and exited the fleshy part of your arm," she said.

He flexed his hand and tried out a smile. "It must not have hit anything too important on its way. It looks more like a graze to me. More of a nuisance than a danger."

"Spoken like a true he-man."

"Spoken like a guy stuck in the middle of a shoot-out."

"I'll wrap it with gauze."

A few intense minutes later, his biceps was bandaged

and she'd found a wool shirt of her dad's with the tags still attached. "I sent him this for Christmas," she said. "I guess he didn't like the color."

The color looked fine to Nate, kind of a deep blue. She guided it gently over his bandaged arm, then insisted on buttoning it for him. Once again, her face was close to his as she performed this chore, and once again, every one of his senses jumped into hyperdrive.

He caught her hand as she straightened up. "I could tell it was an…unpleasant…task for you," he said, running his thumb over the tops of her fingers. "Thanks."

"No big deal," she said. "I've always tended animals, you know. In fact, I wanted to be a veterinarian."

"What happened?"

"Life," she said. "Now I work at animal clinics. Anyway, I've seen my share of bloody messes."

"Still, your hand shook," he said. "Maybe human gore is worse than animal."

She shrugged and looked away. It was obvious to him that she wanted to let matters drop, but he couldn't quite dismiss the feel of her fingers against his skin. Nevertheless, there were more urgent matters at hand. "I assume that old truck parked out front was your father's only vehicle?"

"Yes. Why?"

"Because someone took his keys and wallet."

"His keys." If possible, she went whiter still. "Oh, my gosh. His garage."

"What garage?"

"One of those storage units over in Shatterhorn. Maybe someone wanted access to it. I didn't even think of that."

"What did he keep in it?"

"Who knows? When I was a kid he kept business-related items there. I'm not even sure he still has it."

"Okay, well, try this. Did he ever say anything to you about someone threatening him?"

"Not directly, but I know he's felt restless and out of sorts since Labor Day and the mall shooting. Being the closest in proximity when the shooter killed himself really affected him, especially after the carnage the guy had created. And there was that last word the man spoke, too. It worried Dad."

"You mean *pearl*," Nate said.

"Yeah."

One of the mall jewelry stores had contracted to keep a pricey shipment of Tahitian black pearls that were in transit to a big casino down in Vegas. The police had voiced the theory that the kid planned to steal them, but it seemed unlikely to Nate. Since when did a nineteen-year-old bring two loaded weapons to a shopping mall on the busiest afternoon of the summer to steal pearls? And if that had been his plan, why kill four people before taking his own life?

"I don't know," Sarah said. "Since the shooter never got around to actually stealing the pearls, Dad worried someone else would step in and try to do it. For a while he drove into town almost every day, watching and waiting. I tried to tell him the pearl shipment had been sent away the very next day, but he didn't believe me, even when I sent him the newspaper article."

"I didn't know he was that troubled," Nate said quietly, but it didn't surprise him. When something horrific happened to a person, they were often driven to try to make sense of it. And sometimes, there just wasn't a way to do that.

"Anyway," she continued, "he'd been questioning everyone, making a nuisance of himself—at least that's what I heard."

"From who?"

"Someone told me."

"Someone reliable?"

"More or less. My, er, source said Dad nagged the newspaper, the mayor, the police—anyone he could get to sit still while he expounded on his theories. I don't think he made a lot of friends lately. And, of course, he knew Thomas Jacks. Everyone knew him."

Thomas Jacks was the name of the gunman. Nate should have realized that in a town the size of Shatterhorn, people were likely to know one another.

"He just couldn't get over the fact that boy caused all that heartache," Sarah continued, "and not to just himself, but to his family. Even his past schoolmates, like Jason Netters. People kept asking themselves if they should have seen this coming, but by all accounts, Thomas was a good kid who loved his family and his country—it just didn't make any sense."

Was that why Jason had survived the barrage of bullets that had killed the two girls who had fled the protection of the cookie kiosk with him? Had Thomas spared his friend, or was it even possible Jason had been part of the crime?

"Did your father know Jason?"

"I don't know. He knew Thomas because I babysat for him and his brother a few times. But Jason's dad, Stewart Netters, is the newspaper editor, so I'm sure he got to know him recently."

"I remember Netters," Nate said. "He interviewed me and your dad and Alex after the shooting."

"I read the article. Mayor Bliss hailed you guys as heroes. He said the whole thing would have been worse if the three of you hadn't kept everyone calm. Dad said he didn't deserve any accolades, that it was you and Mr. Foster who had police experience."

"Your dad underestimated his role," Nate said. The intended compliments she'd passed on about Nate made him cringe inside. He'd lost the lives of the two kids he felt responsible for—he was no hero. Desperate now to get the topic off of that day, he abruptly changed the subject. "Did you happen to find a camera anywhere?"

"It's in the bottom drawer of his dresser," she said. "Why?"

"Precaution," he said, recovering the camera and checking to see if it contained film, which it did. From the corner of his eye he could see Sarah dividing her attention between him and her watch. What had she stuck in her pocket? Would she tell him if he asked? He doubted it, so he didn't ask.

For a few minutes when she'd been helping him, he'd glimpsed a calmer, gentler side of her, but the nervous one was emerging again, complete with quick glances and fidgety hands.

"I need to get out of here," she said under her breath.

"We need to talk," he said.

"I don't have time to talk. I have to get back to Reno."

"Listen, if you won't tell me what's making you so damn anxious to leave in the middle of this storm, will you at least explain why you tried to ditch me and who the heck our visitor was?"

"I don't know who it was," she said with a subtle shift of her gaze that told him she was hedging at best, probably lying.

"Then why did you say my getting shot was your fault?"

"I said that? I don't know."

"You have an idea who this assailant is, don't you?"

"No, none. How could I? Like I said, I hadn't seen Dad in a while."

"Then why did you come here?"

"I just wanted to talk to him."

"About what?"

"How is that any of your business?"

They were back to square one, her defiantly standing her ground, him floundering around in the dark. He shook his head and headed toward the door. "You know, you're a beautiful woman, Sarah Donovan," he said, pausing by her side to look down at her. Big mistake—those eyes looked so innocent and guileless. "Under other circumstances I bet you're fascinating company," he added, "but right now, I'd settle for some straight answers."

"Unfortunately, I have nothing to offer."

"How about ID? Where is your purse or wallet or whatever?"

"It was taken from me. I have no identification with me."

"And yet you managed to rent that bucket of bolts in the barn?"

"My stuff was taken after I rented the car."

"So the rental agreement is in the car?"

"No, it was in my purse."

He took a deep breath.

"Will you try to stop me if I leave?" she asked.

"Unless you can fly, I don't see how you're going to get out of here. But, yes, I *will* stop you." He continued on his way.

For the next few minutes, he busied himself taking pictures of Mike's still form and the surrounding area, covering his friend's hands with plastic bags from the kitchen. He committed to memory any detail that might someday be relevant. While he did all this, he kept an ear out for Sarah, but things had grown very quiet. He was angling a shot from near the fireplace when a photograph propped up on the mantelpiece caught his attention, and he paused to study it.

There was Mike, not too long ago from the looks of

things, and standing with him, Sarah. They stood side by side but not touching or looking at each other, and Nate could practically feel the tension between them. The photo looked as though it had been taken out in the yard. A black horse with a white blaze stood near Sarah. Fall colors in the deciduous trees indicated it was October or November— after the Labor Day shooting, after Mike got caught up in the life-and-death drama. After things changed. There was nothing written on the back of the picture, but at least it proved Mike had known Sarah and that she was probably exactly who she said she was.

He put the photo down, grabbed the throw from the chair and floated it gently atop Mike. Was Mike dead because he'd been poking around, because he'd been asking questions? How unlikely was that? The kid behind the shooting was dead, so who would care that Mike asked questions?

Jason Netters?

Or was Mike dead because of Sarah? Wasn't it pretty coincidental he should wind up murdered on the very night she came for a visit?

He took the film out of the camera and pocketed it. In the hall closet he found several old jackets, hats and wool scarves, even a fur-lined pair of gloves. He borrowed a little of everything and somehow managed to bend his arm to get it into the jacket. He also found a small flashlight with a good beam.

Behind him, he heard a sharp intake of breath and turned. Sarah stood with her mouth open. "You're wearing his work clothes," she said after a moment. "For a second I thought…" Her voice trailed off as she glanced down at her father's covered form. It crossed Nate's mind to ask her about the photo, but really, what was the point? So far she'd told him very little and the truth of what she had said was open to question. "Where are you going?" she added.

"Outside," he said, moving toward the kitchen. This room was a great deal colder due to the blown-out window.

"Are you sure you're up to that?"

"Yes."

"Well, thank you for covering Dad's body," she added, pausing a few feet away from him.

He turned around and looked at her. "You're welcome. Did your father keep some kind of tool chest in the house?"

"In the laundry room. There's not much in it—or at least there never was."

"Would you get it for me?"

She scooted into the laundry room and returned a second later with a rusty-looking metal box. Opening it revealed a few old nails, a measuring tape, chisel, screwdriver and a hammer. That would have to do.

"What are you up to?" Sarah asked as he chose the tools.

"I'm turning myself into a foreman. Unscrew the biggest cabinet door you can find. That one down there looks about right."

When the board was free, he told her to hold it over the yawning hole where the door windowpane had once been. She hefted it into place and he held it there with one hand while she hammered in every nail they could find. The end result wouldn't win any decorating awards, but at least it gave a sense of security and blocked the cold wind.

"Lock the doors behind me," he cautioned, setting the tools aside.

Her brows furled as she quickly turned, straining to see through the window over the sink, which was acting more like a mirror than a portal. "Why are you going out there? Is the gunman back? Did you hear something?"

"I'm just going to look around. Maybe I'll find something that will tell us who it was and why he left so suddenly. You could save me the effort if you would supply a name and a motive."

She bit her lip as her shoulders rose fractionally. "Sorry."

"I'd dim the lights a little if I were you and stay away from the windows." Without another word, he opened the door, straining against the pile of broken glass that caught under the panel. He switched on the pocket flashlight and shone it into falling snow. Visibility sucked, but recalling where he'd seen the flash of their assailant's shots, he made his way down the cement steps and trudged out into the weather, looking for who knew what.

SARAH STARED AT Nate's retreating figure, then took the small paper-wrapped bundle from where she'd quickly stuffed it out of sight. Unfolding it, she found a silver key. Scribbled on the attached tag was the number 118. Maybe everything she was looking for was in the garage her father rented in Shatterhorn, but she doubted it. He'd sat on his treasure for years—it was extremely unlikely he'd have moved it into a rental unit, of all places.

She rewrapped the key and pushed it back into her pocket, then hurried down the hallway. A few minutes ago, she'd remembered a crawl space above her old closet.

She moved the boxes she'd already emptied out into the room, then shoved the nightstand into the closet to create a makeshift ladder. Climbing up on that, she slid open the panel on the top and then had to take time to track down a flashlight in the kitchen.

The flashlight lit up the crawl space above her room. Not tall enough to be called an attic, just two feet or so into which she'd crammed any number of things when she

was growing up. It was empty now, dusty and dirty, cob-
webs shimmering in the light.

She wasn't sure how long Nate had been gone, just that
time was slipping away at an alarming rate. Once he got
back inside this house, she'd have a horrible time exiting,
and even if she did, what would keep him from tracking
her down?

She climbed off the nightstand and kicked aside the
boxes she'd searched hours before, sick at heart, scared out
of her skull. Then she walked back down the hall.

If the people she feared were behind the shooting, they
would return. She had to leave, storm or no storm, Nate
or no Nate. She took a steadying breath, her mind racing through nonexistent options, searching for a means to
leave and, even as important, a way to salvage her mother's
precarious situation, since Sarah was going to be leaving
without finding what she'd come for.

Unless the key held the answer, but in her gut, she knew
it didn't hold all the answers. It couldn't.

Confide in Nate Matthews.

The thought ran through her mind and it was the only
option that seemed to have even a remote chance of making a difference. He seemed to know how to do everything—no, that was just an illusion created by this insane
situation. He wasn't a superhero; he was just a man—albeit
a very well put-together one with muscles in all the right
places and skin that felt warm even though he had to be as
cold as she was.

That was why she'd trembled. Touching him had been
like opening a window of some kind, like stumbling across
the threshold of an unexpected journey.

All an illusion. Anyway, what could Nate do? What
could anyone do? All he'd want was to detain her because
the bottom line was he was a cop and he thought like one.

On top of that, he was injured. She was first on the scene of a murder. She was obviously evading questions. Why should he trust her? She didn't even trust herself at this point. And hadn't her original plan been to drive him into leaving first?

She had no right to be in her father's house, and yet every right. No right to take what wasn't hers, and yet again, every right. Besides, at this point, what was the difference between right and wrong? What did it matter?

If Nate wasn't here, she could start tearing up the floors and walls. At this point, that was about the only place she hadn't looked except for the acres of land around the house, where anything could be buried. And the ground itself had currently disappeared under the snow.

At the back of her mind, an ugly little question bit at her sanity. Why would someone who wanted the very same thing she was looking for try to shoot her before she found it? The only way that made sense was if he'd already killed her mother and he was cleaning up loose ends. And now she was supposed to try to reason with him? That stood about a zero chance of working, but if not that, what?

All she could do was get out of here and try.

There was one last thing she had to do before she left. Well, two more things. The first one was undoubtedly the most difficult task she'd ever done in her life, but she could not leave her father in the middle of the living room for a whole lot of reasons. The most important one being it was wrong. She'd witnessed Nate taking pictures and studying the scene—that would have to be enough for the police. Lifting his hands, she dragged her father down the hall and into the spare room he used as an office, then got a good-sized blanket from the closet and covered him properly.

For a second, she knelt next to his body. "'Bye, Dad," she whispered. "Maybe this wouldn't have happened if you hadn't double-crossed Mom. Maybe it would have. I don't know. But I'm sorry I wasn't here to save you." She added a silent apology to Nate, too, for what she was about to do to him, then squared her shoulders and did what needed to be done.

Chapter Five

Why had the gunman left?

Nate pondered this question as he tramped through the snow, shining his light every which way, looking for blood or some sign the assailant had been injured and that was why he'd left.

But there was another half inch of accumulated snowfall, and if there had been blood at some point, it was covered now. He found a gaggle of frosty trees, saplings, really, and by the look of them—bent, twisted, broken—he figured this must be where the gunman had turned when he ran away. A few depressions hinted at footsteps and there was a convenient outcropping of boulders nearby for cover.

Nate fell to his knees near the boulder that afforded him the best view of the back of the house. Using his good hand and holding the flashlight between shoulder and chin, he cleared off the new snow. Just when the task was beginning to seem fruitless, his gloved hand passed over something dark that smeared on contact. Blood.

Against all odds, Nate deduced he'd hit the gunman, and despite everything, he sat back on his heels and grinned. About time the good guys scored a point.

Next he followed the trail through the saplings and around some larger trees to a spot with lingering parallel tracks. He recognized the silhouette of the rocks from

which he'd leaped and there was a larger depression where
he'd fallen. He shone the light over every square inch and
caught glimmers of blood. The gunman appeared to have
taken a bullet and retreated—at least for the time being.
That probably meant he was hurt seriously enough to com-
promise his ability to fight but not so seriously he couldn't
handle a snowmobile.

There was nothing to gain by following the faint tracks,
so once again, Nate trudged through the snow, this time
shadowing the leftovers of his own earlier trek. He veered
off when he made out the looming shape of the barn. It
was a relief to get inside out of the weather.

Sarah's rental was the obvious sore thumb in the open
area of the structure. He flashed the light around the enclosure until the beam illuminated a switch and he hit it. The
lights flickered on, but they were nothing to write home
about. Better than burning up batteries, though.

The old green vehicle squatted in front of the closed
rolling barn doors. Had Sarah known there was a storm
coming? Was that why she'd parked inside the barn? But
if she'd only arrived just before he did, then why hadn't
he seen tracks on the road when he drove up hours ago?
Hers should have still been there, and Mike's murderer's,
too, unless he had come the way he'd apparently left, on
the snowmobile.

Nate carefully slid into the front seat and looked around.
A small suitcase sat on the backseat, while oversize fuzzy
pink dice hung from the rearview mirror. A bobblehead
blackjack dealer figurine with a green visor leered from
the dashboard. Both items seemed incongruous with the
personality of the woman he knew as Sarah. They also
looked entirely too personal to inhabit a rental car. The
keys were lying in a tray between the seats and he took

them to keep Sarah from doing something stupid—like trying to drive out of here.

He checked the glove box next, propping his arm on the divider between the seats to take the pressure off his wound. It took him a few minutes to wade through cast-off makeup, brochures, maps, show ticket stubs and casino chips, but he hit pay dirt at the bottom when he came across the car's registration.

"Diana Sarah Donovan," he read aloud, complete with a Reno address. He also found a five-year-old receipt for new tires for this car along with an oil-change schedule that had stopped over two years before, all with Diana Donovan's name somewhere on the forms.

So Sarah went by her middle name. Any way you looked at it, she'd lied about renting the car just like she'd lied about almost everything else.

Nate crammed all the stuff back in the glove box before walking around to the trunk, where he inserted the key. Inside, he found work gloves, rubber boots and a shovel along with an empty cardboard box. Fresh dirt and what appeared to be bits of straw were stuck to the blade of the shovel.

He slammed the lid and rested his right hand on his waist, head tilted, thinking. And as he thought, he began to notice details about the barn he'd missed before. Drawers had been pulled open on the workbench, for instance. Cabinet doors stood ajar. Tool racks had been emptied. Things had been moved away from the walls. He walked down a row of stalls, all empty except the first one, which housed a black horse with a white blaze who looked happy to see him. Skipjack, he presumed.

Nate liked horses. He had four of his own that he rode on the national land that abutted his ranch north of Flagstaff. In fact, there just wasn't anything better than saddling up before dawn and riding out to the river, casting a line and riding home a few hours later with fresh fish for dinner. He'd often wished he'd been a lawman back in the early 1800s, before cars, before automated weapons and incidents like the slaughter of kids at a mall or the most recent tragedy to hit the news, the killing of two sailors on a family beach in Hawaii.

The horse made a friendly grumbling noise in his throat and Nate handed him an apple out of the small barrel outside the stall. He continued on, flashing his light into each successive cubicle. They'd been filled during the years of disuse by an amazing array of broken tools and outdated equipment, but here, too, there were signs an attempt had been made to search each one, at least in a haphazard manner. A shallow hole in one corner explained the shovel, though its purpose was as confusing as everything else.

The horse whinnied, rousing Nate from increasingly troubled thoughts. He left the barn with a sour taste in his mouth, his eyes narrowed, surprised the snow didn't melt in his wake.

A minute later he opened the front door, which he noted Sarah had neglected to lock. It was almost as though she wasn't really afraid, and yet she sure acted nervous. Was it an act or was she just careless?

A third option presented itself when he found her right inside the door, back in her coat, waiting to greet him, the saddle rifle jammed against her right shoulder, the barrel pointed straight at him.

"CLOSE THE DOOR behind you," she said, hating the quiver she detected in her voice.

He did as she'd asked, then looked straight into her eyes. "Do you know how to use that weapon?" he demanded.

"I'll figure it out," she said. "Stop right there."

To her astonishment, he stopped.

"I have to leave," she added for what seemed the twentieth time, glancing at her watch as she spoke, unable to stop herself from obsessing about the minutes ticking away. Behind Nate, she could see the snow still fell, but there was something about it that seemed less intense than it had an hour before. "Close the door and go into the living room," she said.

"Or you'll shoot me?" he asked.

"I'll aim for your foot, but I'm not a marksman, so no promises."

"Not in the chest like your father?"

"I didn't shoot my father."

He looked straight into her eyes. "I know you didn't, Sarah."

"How do you know that?"

He shrugged. "I'm not sure. I guess there's a little corner of my heart that isn't as cynical as you thought. I guess you found your way into it."

She stared into his eyes while tears threatened her own. His comment constituted the one warm moment in this frozen hellhole.

"Or should I call you Diana?" he added.

She blinked. "How—"

"I found the registration in your car."

"It's not mine," she said.

Nate sighed deeply. "You have the upper hand now," he said, closing the door and preceding her into the living room. "Where's your dad's body?" he said, stopping abruptly.

"In the spare room."

"You moved him? Why?"

"Because he deserved something better than getting

stepped around. Because I didn't want to leave you tied
up here with Dad lying dead at your feet."

He shook his head, but continued on when she motioned
with the gun. "Sit down on that chair," she said, gesturing with the rifle.

He sat down on the straight-backed chair she'd set up
by the fireplace and looked up at her. "Like I said, you've
got the gun. You're the boss. But why not spend five minutes clearing up a few things before you bolt?" Cradling
his injured arm, he nodded at the roll of duct tape she'd
found in the laundry room and added, "Then you can tape
me to the chair and do whatever you have to do."

Could she really tape this poor guy to a chair, what
with his wounded arm and everything else? Hell yes. If
that was what she had to do, that was what she had to do.
She heard herself say, "Five minutes?"

"That's not too much to ask for a guy who could have
gotten himself killed trying to protect you, is it? Besides,
what do you have waiting for you? A walk in a snowstorm?"

"That's better than sitting here and wondering what's
going on. I hate waiting. I'd rather die trying."

"Well, you may get your chance," he said, imploring
her with those sexy eyes. "Five minutes."

As she took a seat opposite him, she noticed the way
his broad shoulders drooped, the dark shadows around
his eyes. He looked tired, all right, but he didn't look as
scared as she figured a man facing a gun should look. She
sat down, the rifle at the ready.

"Suppose you could help me take off these gloves?"
he asked.

"Sure." She kept the rifle close as she peeled the leather
glove from his right hand.

"I can get the other one," he said and pulled gingerly

on the fingers, obviously in pain when the motion jarred his injured arm. She couldn't imagine how he was carrying on as though nothing had happened when it must hurt like hell.

"Okay, now what?" she prompted.

"Let me tell you what I know, and if you want to further enlighten me, that would be great."

"Okay," she said hesitantly.

"I know I wounded our gunman and he left on his snowmobile. I don't know how badly he's hurt, if he went to fix himself up or get reinforcements and is on his way back. I don't know who it is, if the same person killed Mike, or why anyone would want to do any of this."

She nodded.

"I also know you were here last fall. Don't look so startled. There's a relatively recent picture of you and Mike and Skipjack standing out in the yard. It's on top of the mantel."

She glanced over, saw the photo and swore under her breath. How had she managed to overlook that? And yet, how touching that her father had cared enough to stick it up where he could see it once in a while.

"I know you drove here earlier today and parked in the barn, out of sight," Nate continued. "I also know it's your car, that you were looking for something and that from the way you're acting, you haven't found it. How am I doing?"

"Not perfect," she said, but there was a flower of calm beginning to bud in her chest and that in itself should have been setting off alarms. Since getting to Reno two days ago, she'd been moving like a hamster on a wheel and making just about as much progress. Now Nate was close to figuring her out and she almost wanted to help him go the last distance. That was a horrible sign of weakness her mom couldn't afford. Nate's life was law enforcement; he was a man who liked order, who valued the truth. Sarah swallowed hard as her fingers twitched on the gun. "How did you know I got here earlier?"

"There were no tracks on the road when I arrived. The weather must have gone downhill after you pulled into the barn."

She looked away from his intense gaze.

"Your dad didn't even know you were here while you searched the barn, did he?" he added.

She thought before she spoke, weighing the wisdom of engaging in this conversation, deciding at last a little truth couldn't hurt. He'd kind of gotten to her when he'd expressed that unwarranted—from his point of view—faith in her. She'd remain wary and on the defensive, but a little chat couldn't hurt, could it? "He wasn't home when I got here."

"Obviously, he returned."

"Obviously. I heard his truck. I knew he was planning on driving into Shatterhorn this afternoon, so I was surprised he'd come back to the ranch."

"You knew his plans?"

"Yeah. I talked to him a couple of days ago."

"So you chose a time to visit when he'd be gone."

One of her shoulders lifted a little. Man, she sounded like a coldhearted bitch, even to her own ears. Of course, her dad hadn't helped any.

"Because you needed to find something that you didn't want him to know you were looking for," Nate added.

"More or less. My plan was to search the house first, but he came home almost at once, so I started with the barn. After a while, I heard another car and looked outside again. A silver sedan had parked next to Dad's old truck. A man was just going into the house."

Nate suddenly straightened in the chair, his gaze sharpening. "Who was it?" he asked.

"I don't know."

"But it might have been his killer."

"I know that now. If I'd run outside maybe I could have stopped Dad's murder, but at the time, I just thought it was a friend or something."

"What kind of car was it?"

She shrugged. "A newish one. I don't know what model or make. I only saw it from the side, so I'm not sure if it had a Nevada plate. And before you ask, I never saw the man's face. I didn't really see anything except his legs disappearing into the house."

"What was he wearing?"

"I don't know. Wait. Black boots. A long coat."

"What did you do then?"

"Put my stuff back in the trunk in case Dad came out here and found me and then just hung out with Skipjack, waiting for the other guy to leave. I wasn't really anxious to see Dad, so I kind of hoped he'd just go away with the guy if I gave him time. For all I knew, his plans had changed and Dad had invited the man to the ranch."

"And then?"

She started to speak, then paused, her eyes moist again. It was hard to get the words out.

"Take your time," Nate said softly, his voice tender in a way that further undid her. Tears threatened to roll down her cheeks and she sucked them back.

"I fell asleep," she said.

"What?"

She took a deep breath. "I just fell asleep. It had been a horrible forty-eight hours leading up to that point. I'd closed the door to the stall and it was relatively warm and there was fresh straw…. Dad must have done that earlier. The horse kind of snuffled around and I closed my eyes. The next thing I knew, Skipjack was blowing hot air on my face and it was darker inside the barn. I got up and peeked outside. The weather had really deteriorated since I'd last looked. A couple of hours or more must have passed.... The silver car was gone and Dad's truck was still where he'd parked it. I didn't know if Dad had left with the other guy or not, but I knew I needed to check."

"Why did you need to check all of a sudden?" Nate asked. "You'd been content to stay hidden up to that point."

"I had a dream," she said, amazed with herself for sharing this. "In my dream someone…well, someone I feel responsible for was drowning and I couldn't help. I was frozen in place. Powerless. When I woke up, I admitted to myself that I needed Dad's help, and if he was still here, I had to go ask for it." She didn't tack on the word *again,* but it played in her mind.

"Why would he have refused to help you?" Nate asked gently.

She equivocated just a little. "You have to understand that we parted on a really sour note last fall. We both said things— Well, it's too late for regrets, but I still have them. Lately, we'd been talking by phone and he just started to get odder and odder."

"Like how?"

She took a deep breath. "He talked about Pearl Harbor a lot. He was way too young to have ever been in World War II and I know he's never been to Hawaii, so I didn't get what he was going on about. Maybe he wanted to move. I don't know. Then he started going on about Washington. I explained I had moved from there to Virginia, but he passed that off as though I hadn't even spoken. He was impatient and scattered—I mean, he was all over the map. Talking about the newspaper articles written after the shooting and the mayor of Shatterhorn and how you and he and that other guy had been called patriots for what you did. I really began to think the shootings had unhinged him."

"I know what you mean," Nate said softly. "His emails were getting bizarre."

"Exactly. He was obsessed with reading about terrorist groups and civilian militia movements and a whole bunch of other stuff. Like I said, I know he'd been hounding everybody. Then he went off on a group called People's Liberation. He was sure they were behind some incident—"

"The shooting in Hawaii last December," Nate interjected. "Maybe that's why he was talking about Pearl Harbor. The victims were off-duty sailors."

"Then you know about this group's involvement?"

"I've read things. Some believe their claims, some don't. The Hawaiian shooter was an out-of-work malcontent who had been rejected by the navy. No one ever heard about any motive he might have had. But what did Mike think the newspaper editor of a small Nevada town could do about any of this?"

"I don't know, Nate. I have to admit I tuned him out after a while."

Nate nodded. The look in his eyes made her think that he, too, had occasionally tuned out her father's ranting.

"Okay, so you were going to go talk to him. Then what?"

"I walked across the yard and found Dad's front door open. That seemed really ominous because it was cold and snowing." She paused again, catching her breath. "Dad was right where you found him. I'd never seen any dead person before, let alone someone I...I was close to, so I felt for a pulse, but I think I knew he was already gone. I also knew there was nothing I could do for him and that time was running out for me to save my— So, I...I started searching the house, you know, to see if he'd been robbed."

Nate cocked an eyebrow. "That's why you searched the house?"

She looked away and didn't respond directly. "I found his computer was gone along with a notebook he used to jot things down. I looked to see if there was anything else missing, thought of the safe, and that's where I was when I heard you arrive. You know the rest."

Nate shook his head. "No, as a matter of fact, I don't know the rest. What are you looking for and why? Who are you trying to protect? Why are you lying about owning the car? What difference does it make?"

Sarah leaned toward him, fighting the desire to lay her troubles before this near stranger.

"You have to know how this is going to look to the cops when they're finally notified," he continued. "Your unwillingness to be up front concerning your father's murder makes it look like you were in cahoots with someone and that someone killed your father and now you're protecting him or her. Can't you see that?"

She stood up, the gun at the ready. The back of her nose ached with building pressure; her hands trembled. Of course she knew all this, and when he said how it would look to the cops, he meant how it looked to him because he was a cop. He didn't believe her at all; he was just trying to get her to talk.

"I can't tell you anything else," she said. "It's not my information to share. I'm leaving now. Don't try to stop me. I don't want to hurt you."

Like a striking rattlesnake, he reached up and shoved the barrel of the gun downward with his right hand before twisting it out of her grip.

He was suddenly standing in front of her, his face strained and shadowed. He set the rifle aside and clutched her upper arm with his good hand. "There's a greater enemy than me running around, but you know that, don't you?"

"I could have killed you!" she cried, her whole body shaking now. "What kind of madman grabs a rifle that way?"

"The kind who knows there's no round in the chamber and bets there's no more ammunition in the house," he said. "The kind who is tired of whatever game you're playing."

"It's not a game," she said.

"Don't tell me. Tell your dead father," Nate responded.

She raised her hand to slap him and he caught it. Before she could protest, he'd taken care of quieting her by pulling her closer and covering her lips with his. She attempted to wrench free, but his grip tightened, and then it relaxed and she knew she could tear herself away now, that he'd had a chance to think about his actions and probably regret them.

But she didn't budge.

Chapter Six

For a moment, Nate lost track of time and place. Sarah had fought to get away for about two seconds, and then she'd melted against him. By the time they'd moved into a second kiss, he was as good as lost in a blizzard. There was nothing but the silky moistness of Sarah's mouth, the feel of her breasts pressed against his chest. Gradually, her arm encircled his neck and her fingers grazed his cheek. A dizzying flood of sensations bombarded his nervous system. He forgot about Mike's murder, about gunmen and craziness and crashes in the night and being shot and bloodied. He even forgot about evasions and secrets and lies and uncertainty, all for one glorious minute.

The next time she pulled away, he let her. She didn't go far, and when he looked down at her, there was a speculative gleam in her eyes that wrapped itself around his heart. He'd been fighting awareness of her since the moment he'd met her and she'd made it easier by being so blasted contrary, but here it was, rushing through his blood, pounding in his veins. He kissed her again, softly, the need for her surging through his body.

Nate wasn't sure if Sarah allowed him this intimacy because she figured that was the best way to control him or if she'd been as jolted as he by the events of the past few hours. All he was sure of was that he'd kissed his fair share of women in his life, been married to one and engaged to another, and it had never, ever happened like this.

"Do they teach you to kiss like that in police school?" she whispered, running her fingers lightly across his lips.

"Basic interrogation 101," he said.

"I bet you aced the class."

He smiled to himself, and not just because the conversation was silly and he knew he was acting like a moron, but because the sound of her voice did that to him. He didn't know a whole lot about her but he did know that on some level, he *knew* her.

"I'm sorry I pointed a gun at you," she said with a quick upsweep of her lashes. "Is it really empty?"

"Yep. That's why I didn't take it with me when I went outside to scout."

"I thought you'd forgotten it."

"Cops don't forget their weapons," he said, ignoring the irony of the comment. He hadn't forgotten his gun; he'd chosen to leave it behind in some crazy mind game he was playing with himself. He let that thought go when he sensed her leaning in toward him again. He lowered his head a little and she raised hers. Electricity arced between them as his lips throbbed with anticipation.

They both heard the noise at the same time, a loud crashing and a crack coming from outside as the lights blinked out and the house plunged into silent darkness. Sarah's gasp sent shivers down Nate's spine. A second later, her footsteps pounded across the wood floor, away from him.

He groped his way toward her, at a loss to remember exactly where the furniture was. He sped up when he heard the door open and a shade of lighter gray appeared. Was she choosing this moment to try to run away again? If she was, he was about ready to let her go.

"Show yourself!" he heard her shout.

He switched on the flashlight he'd pocketed when coming inside and found Sarah standing out in the middle of the yard, yelling into the night. If someone was out here, she made a perfect target, as a subtle break in the weather allowed weak gray moonlight to filter down through the trees.

"Do you hear me!" she screamed again. "Are you out here? Answer me!"

Something overhead made a creaking, groaning noise that captured Nate's attention. He shone the light overhead, where he caught a glimpse of a sagging power line. He followed it along until the raw wood of a fresh break high in an evergreen laden with fresh snow stood out like a sore thumb. The break had sent a limb the size of a shopping-mall Christmas tree crashing down on the lines below, yanking on a utility pole, which now leaned at a crazy angle.

Beside him, Sarah yelled again, all but shaking her fist, twirling around every which way. He caught her shoulder and turned her to face him. Tears sparkled on her cheeks. Her eyes looked huge and manic.

"I can't take it anymore," she said, flicking the tears away, looking over his shoulder as though the marauders were close at hand. "Whoever he is, let him come out in the open and announce what he wants!"

"Who?" Nate asked. "Give me a name."

"I can't give you a name. I don't know it. But he's out here. I can feel it in my bones."

"I don't think so," Nate said. "Look." He shone the light and she followed its beam up to the treetops. "It's the power line," he added. "The sound we heard was the wood breaking. The branch got too heavy, but this may be good news. The utility company may send out a crew to fix it."

"How can they help us?" she asked, her voice full of despair.

"I'm not sure," he told her. "On the other hand, anyone not shooting us is better than no one. Come on, let's go back inside. We need to find a better light source than flashlights."

"There are lanterns in the barn," she said.

"Great."

The barn was darker than the outside. The horse must have been spooked by the crashing noise not far from his stall or the sound of Sarah shouting or both, because they could hear him snorting and kicking his stall walls.

"The lanterns are in that cabinet over there," Sarah said. "I'm going to go check on Skipjack."

Nate assumed she either knew where the lanterns were because they'd been there during her childhood or because she'd run across them when she'd searched the place hours before. He found two that seemed to have all their parts and fuel, as well. He lit one of them and it emitted a warm, yellow glow.

"I opened the door to the outside pasture," Sarah said when she finally returned.

She looked hauntingly beautiful in the light from the lantern and it was all he could do not to pull her into his arms. What in the world was happening to him and why did it have to happen now and with this woman?

"Why did you do that?" He handed her a lantern.

"Just in case. I don't want him stuck in here if, well…"

"I'd like to reassure you that we're going to be fine, but without knowing what's really going on, that seems like a naive statement. And you don't strike me as a naive woman, Sarah Donovan."

"No, I'm not," she said, her gaze flitting away under his scrutiny.

"How are you connected to the people you think are behind this?" When she didn't respond, he added, "You know, maybe you could try accepting a little help."

"The price is too high," she said.

"There is no price."

"There's always a price. Besides, you're a lawman."

He bit back a disclaimer. "I'm also a man stuck inside an incredibly volatile situation," he reminded her. "And believe it or not, I do know how to think outside the box." He lit the other lantern and lifted it with his good arm. The jarring motion of stripping the gun away from her followed by everything else had set his shoulder aching anew.

"Let me think," she said softly, turning away from him.

"Just think fast," he warned her. "Sooner or later, someone will return to finish what he started."

"I know."

As they made their way toward the barn door, the light illuminated the green sedan. This time, Nate noticed the faded sticker on the rear bumper: Life Is a Casino, it said. He shook his head. "It's kind of hard to associate what I know of you with fuzzy pink dice and gambling slogans."

He was aware of the deep breath she drew. "It's not my car."

"Right. I keep forgetting that," he said, increasingly frustrated with her.

"It belongs to my mother," she added. "Her first name is Diana. Sarah was her mother's name. It's who I'm named after."

"Why couldn't you just tell me you had your mother's car?" Nate asked. "What's the big secret about that, or did you take it without asking?"

"Trust me, she knows I have it. I lied about it because you're a cop and Mom is mixed up in some pretty dicey stuff."

"And you're trying to help her?"

Sarah nodded.

"That's why you came here. To look for something for her?"

"Yes," she said and, quickening her pace, preceded him out of the barn.

"Were you followed?" he called, but she didn't respond.

He caught up with her halfway across the yard, though she was moving fast.

"Were you followed?" he asked again.

"I don't think so," she said. "I was really careful."

"Then how could whoever this is wind up here, of all places?"

The answer was slow in coming, as though she had to reach deep inside to drag it up her throat and push it out of her mouth. "Maybe Mom told him this is where I was headed."

Nate took her arm and propelled her into the house. There was no better target on a dark night than someone standing still while holding a light. Two such someones just upped the odds.

He closed and locked the door. "Sarah, you need help," he said as he set his lantern down on top of the counter-high divider between entry and living room. "You know that, right? You were willing to risk asking your father. Can't you extend that trust? Let me help you."

"You promise you won't arrest me?"

"I can't arrest anyone in Nevada," he said. *Or anywhere else.*

"You can make trouble for me and I can't afford the luxury of time to straighten things out. I have to find what I came for and return it to Reno or get back there and try to reason with someone who strikes me as really unreasonable."

"Reason with the person who's been taking potshots at us? Do you really think you can?"

"I don't have any other choice. I can't find the coins."

There it was—the object of her search was coins. "Valuable coins?"

She turned her head, her jaw set in a stubborn line.

"For heaven's sake, Sarah, just spit it out."

Her next look was defiant. "Okay. Yes, coins."

"Old coins? Doubloons? Come on, give me a break," he pleaded.

"Silver coins my great-grandfather collected."

"A lot of them?"

"Scads."

He stared at her and finally took a deep breath. "I'm waiting. Define *scads*."

"Rolls of them," she said. "All stacked into three-gallon coffee cans. Dad told me stories about how Grandpa stood in line to buy them when they were first minted. My grandfather passed them along to my father, who refused to put them in a bank because he wanted to keep them close by. He wouldn't even spend them, just liked knowing he had them. 'Rainy-day coins,' he called them, even after the ranch started going downhill and he had to sell the horses. His truck is broken-down, the house is falling apart... Exactly what kind of rainy day was he waiting for?"

"I don't know," Nate said uselessly.

"At any rate, each silver dollar is worth at least two or three hundred dollars. I've looked everywhere, but I can't find them."

"And you need this silver to do what?"

She set her lantern on the fireplace hearth, then plopped down on an ottoman, landing in a heap. She raised both hands in a hopeless gesture and mumbled, "Save my mother. She's in big trouble with some very bad people."

"What kind of trouble?"

"She's addicted to gambling, Nate," Sarah said with a darted look to his face as if admitting a flaw in her own personality. "This time she got into a real mess when she burned up her credit lines with even the semireputable lenders. She had to go to this loan-shark guy."

"I take it that's the guy you think is shooting at us?"

"No, the loan shark is a man named Jack Poulter. He would never dirty his own hands."

"Now I'm confused," Nate said.

"Poulter demanded payment. When Mom admitted she didn't have enough to repay him, he warned her that no one walked away from debts owed him. She said something like, 'You can't get blood out of a turnip.' I gather he disagreed with her. Still, she thought she'd charm her way out of it."

"Really? Loan sharks aren't exactly famous for allowing someone to screw around with them."

"You don't know my mother. I think she just thought he'd view the whole thing as a big mistake and let it go."

"But he didn't."

"Of course not. He disappeared from the front line, so to say, but within a day or so, a stranger showed up at my mom's house. He said he was there to enforce Poulter's claim for a percentage and he had no intention of walking away empty-handed."

"Who was it?"

"He gave the name Bellows. That's all. He's a scary-looking guy with a couple of silver teeth. He had another guy with him."

"I don't understand. Why would Poulter loan your mother that much money in the first place? Did she have collateral?"

"Dad gave her one of the coffee cans when they split, on the condition she would completely relinquish any interest in this ranch. She burned up most of that money, but some was tied up in a CD. As I understand it, this time she took a loan on what she optimistically considered a 'sure thing' using the CD money as collateral, telling Poulter she had a whole lot more than she really did. When the money was gone and the sure thing fizzled out, she was left holding the bag. After Bellows showed up, Mom got creative and asked Dad to bail her out. I guess he agreed and then changed his mind. He told her this time she'd have to face the consequences of her actions."

"'This time'?"

"This has been an ongoing pattern for her as long as I can remember. She's spent her life moving between self-made disasters. I tried to distance myself from her by moving east, but she always seems to find a way to reel me back in. I haven't actually seen her in months."

Nate considered his next question carefully. "You're sure your dad still has these coins?"

"Pretty sure. He agreed to give Mom the money when she asked him, and he knew it was up to almost a quarter of a million dollars, so he must have had it."

Nate whistled. "That's a lot of money."

"Tell me about it."

"Your mother couldn't mortgage her house or—"

Sarah interrupted him with a laugh devoid of mirth. "What house? She lost that years ago. Her net worth is less than zero, way less, and she tapped me dry the last time she got in bad trouble. It wasn't a lot, but it was all I had. I'd been working for years, saving money to go back to college. It took every penny to get her solvent."

Did Sarah understand how she was enabling her mother? "That many coins are going to be very heavy," he said. "You won't be able to walk them out of here."

"I know."

"What really happened to your ID?"

Sarah rubbed her eyes. "Bellows snatched my purse. He didn't want me going too far. That's why I couldn't rent a car and had to take Mom's."

"How long before this guy acts on his threats?"

"Tomorrow at three o'clock. Then he says he'll cut his losses."

"And you believe that means he'll harm her?"

"He broke two of her fingers to convince her to call me for help. I don't know if he'll kill her outright, but I'd bet the ranch he'll take out his frustration in a brutal way, and I don't know how much more she can stand."

"But why call you? They didn't think you had that kind of money, did they?"

"Mom must have told him she had to travel to get the money and he didn't trust her. So he roughed her up until she agreed to ask someone else to go on her behalf. That turned out to be me. This dude met me at the airport, showed me a picture of my mother all beaten and bloody, demanded my purse and gave me the keys to her car along with directions to be back tomorrow by three o'clock. For all intents and purposes, I'm now her hostage. If she bolts and goes to the cops, they come after me."

Nate shook his head. As devious as Sarah had proved herself to be, he believed her. The past few hours had taken a lot out of both of them and he doubted she was up to inventing all of this. "If these people are expecting you to produce that much money, why would they try to kill you? Why not just wait until you brought it back?"

"I don't know. The only thing I can figure is that he made

Mom tell him where I was going to get the money. She must have said I was going to get it from her ex-husband. If he got wind that there was a lot more here than what Mom technically owes, he'll want every penny of it." She sat forward and added, "I have to either find the silver or figure out a way to extend the deadline. Otherwise, my mother is dead, I'm dead and now it looks like you're dead, too. It's as simple as that."

Chapter Seven

Nate's brow furrowed as he looked into Sarah's eyes.

It didn't make sense to him that men as ruthless as these guys had orchestrated the present situation. There was the fact that someone had come into Mike's house and killed him in cold blood but never even looked in the barn to see if anyone else was here. Then, after killing Mike, why did he drive away and come back on a snowmobile? He would probably have had to rent it and that would be traceable when all was said and done. It just seemed sloppy.

But thugs weren't always the most organized of people, and if the gunman was Bellows's lackey, he might be making this up as he went along.

Sarah rubbed her eyes, suppressing a yawn in the process. Running a hand through her hair, she stood and took off her jacket, then offered to help him with his. Although he dreaded moving the arm again, he agreed. The coat came off with a few internalized gasps on Nate's part and a glistening layer of sweat on his brow. Sarah studied his sleeve for a moment in the flickering lantern light and then met his gaze. "Your arm is bleeding again."

"I figured."

"Come on, I'll fix you up."

She grabbed one of the lanterns and he followed her down the dimly lit hall back to the bedroom. He sat down on the bed and began fumbling with his shirt buttons while she went into the bathroom to wash her hands. "Let me help you do that," she said, deftly interceding once she returned. The process was much as before, except that this time they'd recently shared a few kisses and everything seemed charged with awareness. When she peeled the shirt away from his arm, she frowned. He glanced down and saw the bandage had turned red.

"You need to go to bed for a few days," she said.

"That's not going to happen," he said as she unwound the bandage and dropped it in the trash can. She smeared antibiotic cream on a pad, which she placed directly over the wound, then she rebandaged his arm. A couple of seconds later, she'd produced another clean shirt from her father's drawers and helped Nate slide his arm into the sleeve. Mike had been shorter and heavier than Nate, so the sleeves ended above his wrist bones.

"I'll make you a sling out of a bedsheet," she said as she buttoned his shirt. Technically, he could have done two-thirds of these things himself, but the truth was he enjoyed her fussing over him. She disappeared into the hall and re-entered carrying a white sheet, which she tore into pieces to fashion a sling. When she tied it around his neck, he reached up to touch her face and she glanced down at him.

"Thanks," he said.

Her smile was warm and quick. She sat down beside him and put her head against his good shoulder. "I'm the one who should be thanking you," she murmured. She looked up into his eyes and added, "Don't you wish we could just lie down on this bed and go to sleep for a few hours?"

"Yes to the lying down," he said, kissing her softly on the lips. "No to the sleeping."

"And with that arm, how would you go about making love to me? That is what you're talking about, isn't it?"

"Yes it is," he said. "And the answer is I would go about it very carefully but with abandon."

"I thought you were engaged to be married."

"I was. Now I'm not."

"What happened?"

"A few weeks ago I told her I was coming up here to see my friends and she just fell apart. She said I wasn't the same as I'd been, that I was living in the past, that I'd come home from Shatterhorn a different man."

"You, too? Like Dad?"

"Not exactly, but changed. I lost a little of my swagger, wasn't so sure I was leading the life I wanted or that I had all the answers. I failed to save two kids, Sarah. I was there after a vacation, unarmed and vulnerable, and I let two kids die. If I'd been carrying, the whole thing would have ended a lot differently."

"But that wasn't your fault...."

"Maybe not technically, but saving innocent people is what I'm supposed to be able to do, and I failed. I guess I was so disappointed in myself that it affected other parts of my life and I kind of closed down."

"But it's only been a few months, Nate. You have to give yourself a chance. Anyone who goes through a mess like that is going to suffer some changes, don't you think? Your girl should have stood by you and helped you."

He shrugged. "She's a little on the impatient side. She wanted me to be who I was before, and I couldn't do it. Enough about me. What happened to the cop you married?"

"We got hitched when I was seventeen. That's right after Mom's gambling worsened. Dad told her to leave. I had just graduated from high school and I didn't know what to do."

"So you got married?"

"It was more complicated than that," she said softly.

"In what way?"

"We saw each other through some hard times," she said.

"You didn't take his name?"

"No. I had all these dreams of being a veterinarian and I wanted my own name—at least that's what I told myself—but I think I really kept it in an attempt to make my dad proud of me. I always disappointed him."

"That seems so unlikely," Nate said.

She smiled. "Well, that's how it seemed to me at the ripe old age of seventeen. You didn't really know Dad well, did you?"

"No, not at all."

"He could be hard. I mean, as strange as he got, the truth is he was always a little on the odd side and his temper— Well, he had a temper."

"Was your husband like your dad?"

"No, no way. Johnny was kind. He had a good heart."

"What happened between you guys?"

"He left me," Sarah said. "Not by choice, though. He was shot in the line of duty and died before I could get to him."

"I'm so sorry," Nate said softly. He stared at her for several seconds. The light bathed her face with a glow that made her seem otherworldly, too beautiful to be human, too human to be anything else. There was sadness in her tilted blue eyes that he yearned to kiss away. She was so alive her body seemed to hum.

And she was in deep trouble....

"Where did your father used to keep the coins?" he asked.

"The only time I ever saw them, they were in a secret cabinet built into the wall beside the fireplace."

"I assume that's the first place you looked?"

"Absolutely. There's nothing in there now but a photo of Skipjack."

"From the looks of things, you've searched just about everywhere else."

"I tried, but you arrived before I could tackle the floors and walls."

"That's why you were looking in the safe?"

She paused a second.

"I know you took something out of the safe," he told her. "I saw you put it in your pocket."

"Oh, that," she said. "It's nothing. Nothing to do with the coins or my mother, anyway. It's just a key and it's personal."

He nodded. "Okay. Nothing else in the safe, though, right?"

"No. I was hoping the coins themselves would be in there or maybe a clue as to where he might have moved them. Even proof he sold them would be better than nothing. And I wanted to find his will, too, but it wasn't in there, either."

"I guess we better continue the search, then."

"We?" she asked.

"I'm not going anywhere," he said. "In fact, if you want to lie down and close your eyes for a few minutes, I'll take all the pictures off the walls and look for any sign things were disturbed, like new plaster or patches. It'll be daylight in a few hours, and one way or another, we have to get out of here or reinforce our position, so we need to work fast."

"Then I'll help," she said and got to her feet. She offered him a hand and pulled him up beside her. They stared at each other a moment, Nate a little dizzy. She caught his good shoulder with her hand. "You okay?"

"Dandy," he said and, leaning forward, gently kissed her forehead.

For the next thirty minutes, they stripped everything off the walls. Studying every surface with flashlights, they found absolutely nothing alarming or suggestive except faded spots on the paint, which clearly indicated each wall hanging had been in place for umpteen years.

"Any of the rugs new?" Nate asked as he sank down on the edge of the sofa. Sarah had done all the heavy work, but he was still hurting.

"You mean since I was a kid? A few. The area rug in the living room, the one in my old bedroom and the wall to wall in the master bedroom."

"Let's get to it," Nate said. "We're going to need a crowbar."

"There's one in the barn."

"I saw it on the workbench. I'll go get it."

She shook her head as she looked at him. "Not this time. You rest arm. I'll go get it."

"And will you come back?" he asked, challenging her gaze.

She smiled. "Maybe, maybe not." A second later, she was gone.

SARAH, HURRYING AS FAST as the weather and growing fatigue allowed, paused as she entered the barn.

Her mother's old green sedan squatted there like a bloated toad. A couple of hours before, she would have tried to drive it out of here and probably gotten stuck in the snow. It wasn't that she was an idiot; it was inaction that was slowly killing her. That and wondering what was happening back in Reno. And truth be known, even now she was tempted to hop in the car and give it a try.

But she couldn't leave Nate here. Her gut told her this

wasn't over. They had to find the coins and get them out of here before someone returned.

She found the crowbar and hurried back across the yard. The snow was coming in flurries now, cold but dry. In the pasture to her left, she heard Skipjack's heavy breathing as he galloped across the pasture toward her, probably hoping for a handout.

She reentered the house, locking the door behind her. Nate looked up from where he knelt beside the fireplace cabinet.

"You came back," he said, and it was impossible not to note the pleasure in his voice.

"Yeah, well, it amazes me, too." She crossed the room and squatted beside him. "What are you doing?"

"I was just looking at this cabinet. It all but disappears when it's closed. I didn't know Mike was such a craftsman."

"He wasn't. My grandfather built this house."

Nate got to his feet and offered Sarah a hand. "Let's start pushing aside rugs and pulling up floors."

Because of his injury, Sarah did most of the physical labor. It actually felt good to put energy into something besides worrying, and she tackled the wood floor in the living room with abandon. They were old tongue-and-groove fir boards, soft but thick, and pretty soon it became very clear it would take days to tear up all the floor.

Eventually, they changed their tactics and began moving aside rugs and looking for any changes in the flooring, like a patch or different wood. They ended up back in the living room where they'd started.

"I wish he'd left those cans in that cabinet," Sarah said bitterly.

"I wonder why he moved them."

"Probably because Mom knew where they were and he

didn't trust her not to rob him. Isn't that a laugh? Here I am, robbing him on her behalf."

"Unless there's someone I don't know about, I would assume they'd be yours now anyway."

"Maybe. Or maybe he intended to give them to a good cause or his friends. Who knows?"

"When your mother took your college money, why didn't Mike help you? I mean, if he had all this money, I'd think he'd want to support your dreams."

"I couldn't tell him what Mom did."

"Why?"

"Because I had to protect her."

He stared down at her. "Isn't that supposed to work both ways? Isn't she supposed to look out for you, too?"

Sarah shrugged and looked away. "It doesn't exactly work that way in my family."

Nate let it drop as he knelt again, and this time when he stood, he held the snapshot of Skipjack in his hand. "Why was this one lone photograph in that cabinet?" he asked.

"I don't know."

"Is it an important picture?"

Sarah took the photograph and studied it. "Well, as you can see, it's Skipjack. See that upside-down horse-shoe above his stall door? Dad said the string holding it up there rotted away about two years ago and it never got remounted, so the picture is at least that old. So, no, I can't say if there's anything special about the photo."

"Sarah," Nate said, his voice soft and slow. "What if your dad hid the coins in the horse's stall?"

She looked up at him, her grip on the crowbar tight. "That could be it," she said, hope ringing in her head. She lifted one of the lanterns in her free hand. "Come on."

Once again, they put their coats on and trudged across the yard and into the barn, hurrying now, Sarah afraid to think it through because she couldn't bear to face potential holes in this last-ditch theory. She closed the bottom half of the outside door to the horse's stall to keep him from coming back inside and getting in their way. Nate found a pitchfork.

"Let me do that," she said, taking the tool from him. "This is two-handed work."

"Okay, you clear the floor, and I'll check the walls. Okay if I take down that hay rack?"

"Sure."

They each set to work as the black-and-white horse hung his head over the open panel and watched. Within a few minutes Nate had used the crowbar one-handed to take the hay rack off the wall and Sarah had shifted all the straw out of the stall.

"Nothing," Nate said, his voice weary.

Sarah didn't trust herself to speak. The dirt floor looked the same as in the rest of the barn. Nate shined his flashlight along the walls, and it glittered on something metallic, which caught their attention. Moving closer, Sarah identified the old horseshoe. It was hanging on the wall above where the hay rack had once been and the ground beneath it looked freshly disturbed.

"I'm getting the shovel out of my trunk," she said.

"Wait a second," Nate said, digging in his pocket. "You'll need your keys."

She shook her head as she took them from him. He'd known she wasn't leaving or even going to try to when she looked for the crowbar, because he'd had the keys all along.

She returned with work gloves and tools. "I have a feeling about the floor right here," Sarah said, and hefting the shovel, she slammed it down into the dirt. It penetrated the earth. She immediately put some muscle behind the spade and began digging.

She was about ready to admit defeat when the blade hit something that made a thumping, hollow sound. Working faster now, she quickly shoveled the dirt away to reveal a painted wooden trapdoor, which she hastily cleared of dirt before falling to her knees. Nate brought the lantern closer.

There was a handle set into the wood with a small chain attached to it. Nate leaned down and grabbed the chain, raising the lid. The link on the end of the chain was just long enough to slip over one end of the horseshoe to keep it open.

Sarah peered into a hole that appeared to be about two feet deep and three feet across, hollowed out of the earth and reinforced with bricks. Best of all, the shine of metal cans dazzled in her eyes.

"There have to be ten or eleven of them down here," she said, her voice hushed, her heart racing. She swallowed a sob of relief.

"Do you need help lifting them out?" Nate asked, peering over her shoulder.

"No, I can do it."

Years before, her father had poked opposing holes near the tops of the cans through which he'd threaded nylon rope, thus creating handles so they could be easily lifted. Sarah stretched out on her stomach and hooked one with her hand. Her heart sank as she realized it wasn't nearly heavy enough to hold coins.

Nate sat down on the stall floor beside her.

"Is that one of them?"

"No, it's too light. But it's the same kind of can I remember." She sat up, took off the leather gloves and opened the plastic lid. Nate shined a flashlight into the can and Sarah withdrew a few folded sheets of paper stapled together in one corner. Next came a small brown notebook wrapped in purple rubber bands. She handed Nate the notebook and unfolded the papers.

"This is his will," she said as she held the sheets toward the light to read. After a few moments of silence, she added, "He left me everything."

"Then even if the coins are gone, you'll have the ranch and the land," Nate said.

"Yeah. Maybe I can bargain for Mom's life with it. This could help me buy her a little more time." She refolded the papers and slipped them into her jacket pocket, then nodded at the book in Nate's hands. "That's his notebook, isn't it?"

He tried to hand it to her but she stopped him. "That's okay. You look at it. You were with him at the mall shooting. Maybe his ramblings will mean something to you."

"I'll study it later," he said, shining the light at the rest of the cans. "Well, let's get it over with," he added as he lowered his good arm into the hole and hooked another rope. He glanced back over his shoulder at Sarah. "This one is really heavy. I bet it weighs forty pounds."

"I hope it's not full of rocks," Sarah said, holding her breath again as he yarded an old red coffee can from the hole.

Sarah's mouth was dry as Nate pried open the lid. And there they were, roll upon roll of coins that looked as though they'd never even been unwrapped.

"Wow," Nate said on an expelled breath. "There have to be thirty rolls in here." He pulled one out carefully and handed it to Sarah.

The coins were wrapped in heavy brown paper, the ends partially open to reveal the brilliant gleam of silver. The paper was stamped *Carson City Mint*.

"Twenty coins a roll," Nate said. "Uncirculated, to boot. That means each can is worth at least one hundred and fifty thousand dollars and there are—" he paused to count "—ten more of them. If they all hold the same amount, you're talking over one and a half million dollars."

Sarah felt a giggle tickle her throat as despair turned into hope. "Now all we have to do is figure out how to get them away from here."

"That's all," Nate said.

They were silent for a moment, and in that moment, Skipjack whinnied and trotted away from the barn, the sound of his hooves moving fast and sure and toward the part of the pasture that fronted the house. They were both still sitting on the floor, the lantern on the ground with them and the top panel of Skipjack's stall opened to the wooded area behind the barn. There was an ominous quiet as they both got to their feet and looked outside the stall door, but the house wasn't visible from this angle and everything looked peaceful enough.

"I hear something," Sarah said.

"Shh," Nate warned her, dousing the lantern light. He left the stall in a hurry, moving toward the front of the barn. Sarah knew he was trying to get a better view. Sheltering the beam of her flashlight with her hand, she quickly picked up her father's notebook and stuffed it inside her jacket, tucked the roll of coins she still held back in the can and deposited both cans in the hole. Working as quietly as she could, she closed the trapdoor and quickly covered it with dirt, then, using the pitchfork, put down a heavy layer of straw. She couldn't risk the noise of reattaching the hay rack, so she propped it up instead and stuck hay in it. Then she opened the bottom half of the outside stall door before turning and running to the front of the barn, where she found Nate's dark form peering through the slats in the door.

"What is it?" she whispered, coming up to stand beside him.

"I think someone is behind the house. I saw lights and heard an engine. I'm going to go investigate."

"Nate, no, please don't. You're unarmed and you're hurt. Let's just wait here. We can defend the barn if we have to—"

She got no further, because in that instant, they both saw flames licking the side of the house.

Chapter Eight

Sarah cried out. "Dad!"

Nate slid a hand over her mouth and drew her against him, talking softly and close to her ear. "The fire can't hurt him, Sarah. We have to get out of here."

"The snow is still too deep for the car."

"We'll take the horse. Can you saddle him?"

"Yes." She tore herself from his grasp and ran into the dark. Nate took one last look at the burning house. Through the now lightly falling snow, he caught the shape of a man standing off to the side, visible because of the light created from the fire. He stood at a point where it was likely he could see both the front and the back doors, and he had what appeared to be a rifle clutched in his hands. Nate could make out the front half of a snowmobile parked behind him.

It was obvious to Nate that the guy was waiting to pick off whoever ran from the house when they realized it was on fire. When no one showed up, would it finally dawn on him to check the barn?

Turning, Nate moved as fast as he dared. He didn't know his way around the barn as well as Sarah did and there was no way he would risk a light until he was buried in the depths of the stall. By the time he got there, Sarah had managed to get the horse inside and closed the doors.

He saw that she'd replaced the floor so it looked much as they'd found it. He could only imagine how it gutted her to ride away from the coins after just uncovering them.

There was too much white showing in the horse's eyes and his movements were skittish and excited, but Sarah had a magical way with the animal and he calmed under the influence of her soothing voice. "Find anything warm that you can. Saddle blankets, whatever," she said.

He took out his flashlight but searched in near darkness, coming across a couple of mildew-smelling wool blankets stacked in another stall and a length of rope, which he took along for good measure. As Sarah finished tightening the saddle cinch and slipping on the bridle, he stuffed what he could in the saddlebags. He'd carry the rest.

"Okay, let's go," she whispered, switching off her light.

Nate opened both halves of the door and Sarah led the horse out of the stall. He closed the door behind them. Soft flakes fell on his face as he looked up at Sarah, who had mounted Skipjack. "He'll have to carry us both," he said.

"He can do it."

Nate settled himself behind Sarah, one of the blankets rolled and stuffed between them. This was her horse, her stomping ground. He just hoped there was a way out of the pasture that didn't go past the front of the house or they'd be dead meat.

Sarah headed across the back of the pasture toward the darker shapes of the trees, the only noises the creaking of the saddle, the crunch of the horse's hooves in the snow and the wind still blowing through the branches. Sarah seemed to be giving Skipjack his head as he picked his way through the foliage. The snow wasn't as deep under the cover of the trees, and the horse sped up under Sarah's quiet urging.

"Is there a gate back here?" Nate asked, leaning close

to speak softly. Her hair, smelling like cold, fresh hay, brushed his face. He had one hand around her waist, the other still supported by the sling, and her firm body rolled with the gait of the horse. For the first time in a while, he allowed himself a moment to think they might make it out of this mess, after all.

And then he remembered the man standing outside the house, pointing a gun, waiting. Would that man figure out no one had been in the house? Would he notice all the tracks between the house and the barn and would he then find the stall and the tracks leading away from it and toward the trees?

"Yes, there's a gate," she said. "And then there's a couple of miles of downhill terrain to a piece of land Dad bought years ago. There's a river and a fishing cabin on it…. It's abandoned, but it'll give us a place to wait out the rest of the night."

He didn't want to scare her any more than he had to, but stopping seemed a poor idea. "There was a man with a gun at the house," he said.

"What!" She turned her head briefly to look at him. "You're just now telling me?"

"This is the first opportunity I've had. He was waiting for one or both of us to run out the door. I can't believe he won't figure out where we've gone and how we left. Let's just keep riding until we find a phone or an occupied house or something."

"I can't," she said.

"What do you mean?"

Her voice tightened as she dashed words over her shoulder toward him. "Are you forgetting my mother?"

"No, but—"

"But nothing. You want to call the cops. If I get involved

with them, I'll never get the coins if they're still there to get, and I'll never save my mother in time."

"Even if the coins remain undiscovered, the house is on fire. Someone will call the fire department. By tomorrow, the place will be crawling with investigators."

"Maybe not. The place is pretty remote, no near neighbors, and in this weather, well, I have to try, don't you see? This isn't open to debate, Nate."

"Listen to me. If the coins are gone, it means Bellows or his buddies took them. Your mother will be okay."

"Maybe. But I can't bank on them finding the coins. I have to get my hands on some kind of vehicle that can handle cross-country and go back as soon as I can. Nothing has changed."

"That means a snowmobile."

"Yeah, it does, and I can't do that until daylight. I have to stay away from any involvement with the police until I have the luxury of time to explain all of this. You know that."

He swallowed any further comment. It went against his nature to avoid the law, but he could see her point.

"If you want me to let you off somewhere near other houses, just say so and I will. But don't go to the police, please—not until you hear from me that Mom is safe."

"I'll stay with you," he said. "I told you I would help and I will."

She nodded briskly.

They fell silent as the trees began to thin out and a sliver of moon actually showed now and then through the clouds. "The fence is up ahead," Sarah said, "and then the easiest way to travel the next half mile or so is to stick close to the highway. I don't know if we should do that."

"The arsonist had a snowmobile," Nate said. "He probably isn't using roads."

A few minutes later, Nate caught sight of the fence. When Skipjack got close enough to the gate, they both dismounted to open it. This was no easy task, thanks to the drifts of deeper snow pinning it closed. It took both of them digging with their hands to get enough clearance for the horse to pass. No way could they close it again, and so they left it open.

Beneath Nate's grip, Sarah's slim body shivered as they moved forward. Nate carefully unfurled a little of the wool blanket and draped it around her shoulders, making something of an impromptu hood to protect her head, as well. His own was still bare, and he missed his old Stetson with a passion.

"Thanks," she said, her voice a little muffled now by the blanket. He laid his cheek against the back of her head and murmured acknowledgment he doubted she heard.

A few minutes later, they came across the road Sarah had mentioned, a winding stretch of white the width of two lanes, closely banked on either side by dense forest, all leading downhill. For a while, they rode alongside it, but then they saw approaching headlights and Sarah guided Skipjack toward the trees again, where they would hopefully blend into the deep shadows.

"I felt like a sitting duck out there," Sarah said as an older truck slowly passed them by, the clinking noise of the chains on its tires diminishing as its taillights disappeared around a bend. "It'll take a little longer, but we're going to stay off the road."

Nate gripped her around the waist a little tighter. "You're behind the wheel."

An hour later, when Nate judged it to be near two o'clock in the morning, Sarah stopped the horse. The moon had broken through even more, and it reflected off the small river that glimmered through the trees at the bottom of the

shallow glen before them. She urged Skipjack forward and
the horse found footing on the snowy path leading down
toward the water.

"There's the fishing cabin," Sarah said at last, once
more pulling the horse to a stop. It was impossible to make
out the details of the tiny structure through the snow and
in the poor light, but what he did see wasn't particularly
encouraging. On the other hand, it had a roof and seemed
to have only one door, so as a place to guard, it had the
house and barn beat to hell.

He slid off Skipjack's back first, then reached up to
help Sarah dismount. Still half shrouded in the blanket,
she landed right in front of him, and for a second, she
seemed to sag. He leaned down and kissed her forehead a
few times, holding her against his chest, the blanket slipping from her head, her hair a soft cloud against his cheek.

"You can do better than that," she said softly, turning
her face up to his.

It was surreal to kiss her right then as the wind teased
snow to fall from the overhead branches and the horse
breathed warm air down their necks. He closed his eyes as
their lips met, and the kiss he'd planned, a short one they
could improve upon when they weren't cold and bleeding
and wet, escalated in the first second until he'd parted her
lips with his tongue and explored every inch of her tan-
talizing mouth. She responded with equal gusto until the
horse tossed his head, rattling his bridle, snorting into the
cold air and reminding them where they were and what
still had to be accomplished.

"He's worse than an overbearing parent," Sarah whispered as they smiled at each other. She turned to face the
horse. "Okay, big fella, let's get your saddle off." Nate
reluctantly released his grip on her and came away with
the blanket.

"There's a lean-to and a small fenced corral over by the trees. We'll have to trust the fence is in good repair." She led Skipjack into the enclosure and relieved him of his saddle and bridle while Nate used the flashlight to examine the lean-to. He found an old stump under the cover, and embedded in the stump was a thing of beauty, a double-bitted hand ax, the kind used to chop kindling for a fire. He yanked it from the stump and shone the light on it.

"What did you find?" Sarah asked.

"An ax," he told her. "It's a little rusty, but it's sharp enough."

"Sharp enough for what?" she said.

"To use as a weapon if need be. Let's get in out of this cold."

The cabin's tiny porch was more of a covered step than anything else and the unlocked door opened inward to a small square room. As they shined the flashlights around the space, Nate saw a counter of sorts running along one wall complete with a sink and a small hand pump for water. A few shelves above the counter held scattered plates, cups and cooking utensils. There didn't seem to be any food and the nearby stove was the kind campers the world over used.

Two chairs flanked a small table situated beneath the rear window while a small wood-burning stove promised heat. A mattress on the floor of the farthest wall served as a bed. Nate tossed the blankets onto the mattress. As rustic as it all was, that bed looked like heaven to Nate, and he imagined Sarah had the same bone-weary response as he.

"Do you want me to build a fire?" he asked her.

"No. It's too late for that. I just want to sleep. There's a lantern under the sink with all the fishing gear," Sarah said, the beam of her flashlight considerably dimmer than it had been a couple of hours earlier. She found the lantern and they lit it with difficulty with matches from a box someone had left on the table.

"Keep the light turned low and on the floor," Nate cautioned as he hooked one of the chairs and propped it under the doorknob to block access. "No need to advertise we're here." He was glad she'd refused a fire, as the smoke from the chimney would be as telling as a light.

"I agree," she said, unzipping her jacket. She produced Mike's notebook and handed it to him. "Maybe that will do for a little light reading."

They stared at each other for a few moments, then, in unspoken agreement, sank down on the mattress and pulled off their boots. Sarah had to help Nate accomplish this and he smiled as he watched her.

"I could get used to being babied this way," he said as he raised his good arm. She settled in against him, both with their backs against the wall. He'd set the ax on the floor beside the mattress, where he could reach it if need be.

"So, this is your dad's fishing cabin. It must be hard coming here tonight after all that happened today."

She nodded, her eyes growing soft. "His death has kind of been pushed to a back burner because of everything else that's happened. In some ways it's hard to believe he's gone, that he won't come bursting in here with a string of fish."

"I wish he could," Nate said. "I'm starving."

"I know. Me, too."

"Wait a second," he said, shaking his head as he reached into the big coat's pockets and withdrew two small apples. He handed one to Sarah.

"Where did you get these?" she asked and took a bite.

"From the barrel outside of Skipjack's stall. I don't know if they're any good—I grabbed a couple when I was looking for blankets."

"It's delicious," Sarah said, happily munching away.

Nate took a bite of his own. The apple wasn't great, but nothing had ever tasted better, and he wished he'd taken time to gather a few more. They ate in silence for a while, savoring the juicy fruit. "Did you come here often when you were a kid?" he asked.

She swallowed and wiped her chin with her fingers. "Off and on. I wasn't much for fishing, but I loved exploring the riverbank. We had a cocker spaniel named Rosie. She was a swimming fool."

"I like dogs," Nate said.

"Do you have one now?"

"Two. A black Lab and a little scruffy white thing that showed up one day. The Lab likes to go horseback riding with me, but he's a terror in the river, so I can't take him when I go fishing. He scares all the fish away."

"You live somewhere you can have horses?"

He smiled at the enthusiasm he could hear in her voice. "Sure. I have a few acres that border a national preserve. I've got horses, some cattle, a pregnant goat and a handful of chickens. I've also got coyotes and rattlesnakes."

"Sounds like heaven, except for the snakes."

"It is. I take it you've been living in a city."

She polished off her apple. "Yes, but my heart is in the country. It tore me apart to leave the ranch, but at least I had plans to work with animals. Those dreams got me through the marriage and Johnny's death, the meaningless jobs, everything. And then Mom needed the money, and, well…what else could I do but help her?"

"You have money now," Nate said gently. "Thanks to your father, you can go to the best college in the country and become a world-class veterinarian."

She nodded as she took his apple core and laid it on the floor beside her own. He produced a red bandanna from his pocket and they both wiped their hands dry. "Yeah, thanks to Dad."

They were quiet for a minute, then Nate asked a question. "Do you know where you can get a snowmobile in the morning?"

"I think so. Fred and Emma Crawley live a mile or so from here. They used to let me use theirs. If they remember me, I'm sure I can borrow it."

He leaned his head against hers. "They'll remember you."

She pulled away a little and stared up at him. "You sound so sure of it."

"Well, who could forget you?"

She was quiet for a second and he wondered what was going on inside her head, then she murmured, "They haven't actually seen me since I was seventeen."

"When you ran off with an older guy—a cop, to boot. Probably makes you infamous in a small place like this."

"Probably," she whispered, settling against him again. "As long as my mother makes it out of this alive—"

"I'm hoping you and I make it out alive," Nate interrupted.

Again she pulled away to look at him. "That goes without saying. But Mom—"

"—got you into this mess," Nate said. "I hope she's worth what you're risking."

"She's my mother," Sarah said with a note of finality in her voice.

"I understand that," Nate said.

She looked down at her lap. "Do you?" she murmured.

Nate didn't respond. He was glad when she leaned against him again, but it was obvious it was more for comfort and warmth than closeness, and he guessed he'd earned that from her. He closed his own eyes but his mind raced with the images and impressions of the past few hours. Now, in the relative safety and quiet of this remote cabin, every thought revolved around the woman next to him.

She was such an enigma to him. There were parts of her so competent and brazen that she made him shudder in despair that she would do something incredibly dangerous—like try to negotiate with the thug she'd described, Bellows. But there was also something about her that suggested she was no fool when it came to self-preservation. And what about that loyal streak of hers, and for a mother who seemed to have done little to earn it? Nate's own parents were good, upstanding people who had never told a single lie that he knew of. That was the way he'd been raised, too.

How could he take credit for that? His folks had made choices that spared him having to choose between lying to a stranger and forsaking one of them. They had never asked for help in a life-and-death situation, and if they had, what would he have done to ensure their safety?

Anything. He would have done whatever it took. In Sarah's shoes, he would do the same.

He opened his eyes, intent on telling her this, but she'd grown heavier against him, her breathing softer and more steady. He twisted his head and looked down at her, admiring the sweep of dark lashes against her cheeks and the supple peachy glow of her lips. While part of him ached to wake her with a juicy kiss, another part was content to watch her. Had he ever felt this way before?

And what would Mike have made of this instant attraction between his daughter and Nate? Mike…almost forgotten in the rush to save his daughter and his ex-wife.

With thoughts of Mike came equally disquieting ones of Alex. Why hadn't he shown up in Shatterhorn? Had he had to make an emergency landing somewhere else?

If he had, Nate was sure one of the first things he would do was find a phone and try to make contact. However, Nate's phone was history, so any calls would appear to go unanswered and that would concern Alex. Hopefully his friend would call home and Jessica could explain that they'd spoken.

With any luck, he and Alex would soon be downing a beer together and recounting their individual adventures. While Nate looked forward to that, he dreaded the thought of trying to explain Mike's murder.

Which reminded Nate of Mike's notebook that he'd tucked beside his leg. He picked it up now, working it free from the rubber bands, holding it turned to the lantern light. At first he wasn't sure if it was fatigue or poor lighting, but nothing made a lot of sense. Gradually, though, he was able to see that it was part personal diary, part schedules and impressions of interviews and stakeouts, part musings that seemed to be his way of assimilating information. Sometimes Mike had folded a cut-out newspaper article within the pages, or quoted from an article or perhaps something he heard on the radio. It appeared one page had been torn out, as the jagged edge sticking out of the binding attested. And he'd made a list. For an appliance salesman, Mike showed signs of latent detective skills.

The first word on the list was *Fireworks.* The second was *Pearl.* Nate knew that had been the mall shooter's last word. But seeing it here and followed by the date December 7, with the notation of Pearl Harbor Day right after it, startled Nate.

The mall shooting had happened on Labor Day. Mike also mentioned a Veterans Day incident at a library in Arlington, Virginia, five dead. The Hawaii shooting had happened on Pearl Harbor Day. Was it possible the dying man's last word had not referred to a gem taken from a mollusk but the holiday commemorating the attack on Pearl Harbor?

But how could that sorry excuse for the kid at the mall have known anything about shootings that would take place several months down the road?

Nate flipped back a page and found an article about a July Fourth incident. Two months before the mall shooting, a gunman had slain two victims during a fireworks display in the middle of Iowa. The gunman had been killed when the crowd finally figured out that not all the explosions and shouting were coming from enthralled onlookers and gone after him. Nate vaguely remembered reading about it. He couldn't remember if any foreign group had taken credit for it.

The second-to-last word on the list was *Washington*. *Washington*. Sarah had said her father went on and on about it, growing frustrated with her when she kept assuming he was talking about where she used to live. What if he was talking about the city in a different context?

Memorial was the last word. Did that mean the Washington Memorial? Had he meant the *Washington Monument?* Was it possible terrorists were targeting American national holidays? Was that what Mike had thought? Was that why he'd been hounding the editor of the paper and the only politician he knew, the mayor of a small town who had smothered them in accolades after the mall shooting? Had Mike been trying to enlist their aid in reaching a broader audience?

The last few pages held notes on People's Liberation, all written in tiny script and all crossed out with a scribbled *NO!* across the top. And on the very last page that had been used was the number twenty-eight, circled in red ink.

The words began to swim before Nate's eyes and he closed the book. Maybe if he slept for a few minutes, his head would clear enough that he could figure out exactly what Mike had been trying to say. He turned off the lantern and adjusted the blankets to cover Sarah's feet and his own shoulders, then, leaning his head against her, closed his eyes.

He awoke standing beside Sarah. She was dressed in a blue skirt, her hair curled and bouncy. Her white blouse was covered with little red and black flowers that gradually morphed into the suits of a deck of cards—diamonds, hearts, spades and clubs. She pulled on his hand, yanking him to a booth of sorts. She pointed at a pearl necklace.

They were suddenly inside a mall and the place was crowded with tiny children, preschoolers, really, running everywhere, laughing, but Nate felt an all-pervading weight of anxiety. He had to get Sarah away from that booth, which was suddenly crawling with babies who were falling to the floor. He and Sarah each started grabbing the infants, but there were too many to save them all.

Booming gunfire stopped everything and Nate's arm exploded. He was alone except for Sarah lying at his feet, her blouse red now. He knelt beside her and she opened her eyes. "Save my mother, Nate," she whispered. "Nate, Nate…"

He sobbed as she disappeared into smoke. His shoulder ached. He groaned and Sarah said, "Nate? Are you okay? Wake up."

His eyes flew open to face the dark room. "I'm awake," he said at last.

She gently rolled him over. All he could see of her was the slightly lighter shade of her face and the glistening of the whites of her eyes.

"You were having a nightmare," she said, smoothing his hair away from his brow.

He had nightmares almost every night. The only difference with this one was the fact Sarah had been part of it. If he was honest with himself, she'd been the center of it, a focus for his fears, eclipsing even the children.

"Are you okay now?" she added.

He took a couple of shallow breaths, then caught her hand and brought her fingers to his lips. She drew her hand away and he winced inside, but the interruption in physical contact was brief. She lay down beside him and put her arms around him as though he was a scared little kid. No one had done that since he was ten years old; he was used to being the strong one who protected, not the other way around.

The feel of her body pressed against his began to get through the nightmare hangover and arouse him in all the predictable ways. When she tenderly kissed his lips, he closed his eyes and hoped she'd never stop.

She kissed him a dozen times, all over the face, his eyelids, his cheeks, his nose and ears, all sweet, comforting kisses that he found anything but comforting. The next time her lips landed on his, he opened his mouth and that was like throwing gasoline on a fire. He longed to make love to her.

As though she'd read his mind, she unzipped his jacket and unbuttoned his shirt, doing both slowly, driving him mad as her fingertips grazed his skin. Although she was incredibly careful not to touch his left arm, she touched almost every other place she could reach, her strokes light and sexy and urgent, her kisses on his neck and chest sensuous, and as they traveled down his stomach toward his waist, he almost lost it.

He pulled her back up so he could claim her lips once again, knowing if she even fiddled with the buttons of his fly he'd stand no chance of making this last. Limited by the fact he could use only one hand, he made up for it with his mouth, sucking on her earlobe, licking her throat. Her coat and sweater were obstacles and he tugged on them, the need to feel her bare skin invading every organ in his body.

"Take them off," he whispered and she sat up. When she lay back down, she was naked from the waist up, her breasts soft alluring orbs, the nipples hard beneath his touch. She moaned deep in her throat when he put his mouth to one and fondled the other. He would have given anything for light enough to see her as well as feel her.

"Do you have something?" she asked, her voice breathless.

His hand traveled under her low-cut jeans, her heat and warmth and suppleness affecting him like a drug. "Have what?" he managed to say.

"Protection. A condom?"

"No," he said, burying his face in her hair. "Do you?"

"No," she whispered.

He couldn't get enough of her. He would have sucked her into his lungs if it was possible, tasted every little bit of her.

But something had changed, and it finally got through to him. His poor brain was so addled by her that it took a second to connect her request with her withdrawal.

He held her head under his chin and kissed her hair.

"I have to have protection," she whispered. "I can't have sex without it. I mean, I want to have children someday, but not like this. I just can't risk pregnancy."

"It's okay," he assured her. "You're right."

"And you were so recently engaged to someone else."

"And you were going to shoot me just a few short hours ago. Don't forget that." Her soft chuckle made him smile in the dark. "All of this is true, but it doesn't change the fact that I want you so much it hurts," he murmured.

She raised his hand to her mouth and kissed his fingers.

"It's going to be light soon. I'm going to try to get a little more sleep."

Holding her was exquisite torture, but that was okay. Her soft, fragrant body pressed up against him would keep him wide-awake all night. He should never have allowed himself to go to sleep in the first place—it wouldn't pay to forget the image of their adversary poised outside the house ready to pick them off when they tried to escape a fire.

And there was another image he hadn't told Sarah about, because there wasn't much they could do about it. Often, on the ride across the pasture, he'd glanced behind them, afraid they were being followed. He'd never seen anyone, but once the sky lightened, it would reveal the path the horse had left in the snow. For all intents and purposes, they might as well have sprinkled fluorescent bread crumbs in their wake. And down here with the river on one side and a hill on the other, they were as good as trapped.

Chapter Nine

Sarah woke up with a start. Morning had come, and soft light filtered through the dirty, cracked windows of the cabin. She twisted her arm up to look at her watch and saw it was almost 8:00 a.m. She'd overslept.

"Wake up," she told Nate as she extricated herself from beneath his arm. She grabbed her sweater and jacket from where she'd discarded them the night before, aware of Nate's gray gaze watching her dress. She grabbed her boots and pulled them on, then got to her feet.

"Hurry up," she said, moving to the sink, where she pumped ice-cold water into her hands and splashed it on her face. She rinsed out her mouth with more of the same, glanced at Nate and found him slowly buttoning his shirt. She knew it would be hard for him to tug on his boots with the injured arm, but he'd make it.

"I'll go saddle Skipjack," she said and moved the chair to let herself outside the cabin, where she paused for a second as she closed the door. It was a relief to get away from Nate. She hadn't even been able to meet his gaze. She'd been embarrassed by recalling overwhelming intimacy after such a short time knowing one another and clearly remembered rattling on about a baby—something she hadn't thought about in years and something a woman shouldn't start talking about with a man she barely knew.

It was all like a bad dream. Well, maybe not all of it. There was no denying the passion, no denying the desire…and no denying her empathy for his pain.

She just really didn't want to know what he thought about her this morning.

But more important, why had she let down her guard last night and told him so much about her mother's predicament? Who was to say he wouldn't start arguing with her again about going to the police? There wasn't time for a bunch of maneuvering. She had to get back to the house, get the silver and drive to Reno.

Maybe she should leave him here and go by herself. Why had she even woken him up?

Skipjack came to her call as she let herself into the corral. She picked up his bridle from where she'd stowed it the night before and slipped it over his head, then lifted the saddle and settled it atop the saddle blanket. As she flipped the stirrup up to fasten the cinch, something glinted in the rocks downstream. She quickly looked away.

"Let's see that foot, sweetie," she crooned to the horse. She bent down to pick up his foreleg and pretended to study his shoe while she peered downstream. Then she put Skipjack's leg down and wound his reins around the fence. "I'll be right back," she said with a pat to his flank. She let herself out the gate and casually walked to the cabin.

Nate was standing with his back to her at the sink. At the sound of the door, he turned, water glistening on his stubbled jaw, looking twice as worn-out and three times as sexy as he had the day before. "What's wrong?" he snapped after a searching look at her face.

"Someone is out there," she said.

Drying his face with a towel, he started to look out the window, but she stopped him. "Don't—he'll see you. He's downstream, hiding among some rocks. I saw the flash of something like binoculars."

"Could it be a neighbor or someone coming to use the cabin?"

"No. The land is posted, but beyond that factor, the Crawleys are the nearest neighbors and they're eighty years old. I don't think they're running around spying on people the morning after a snowstorm."

"Do you think whoever it is knows you're onto him?"

"I don't think so. I tried to act like nothing was wrong. Nate, I have a plan."

He looked at her and she could tell that he wasn't expecting much. "I don't have time for an argument, so just hear me out," she said. "We need to get this guy off our back once and for all. So, here's what we're going to do. I'm going to go out there again and piddle around while you sneak out the window. If you use the trees for cover, you should be able to circle around and come at him from the other direction. Then you hit him or something, we tie him up, take his snowmobile and go get the coins to save my mother."

Nate's eyebrows shot up his forehead. "Honestly, Sarah, are you forgetting that this person is probably the same one who spent most of yesterday afternoon and evening trying to kill you?"

"He could have shot me while I was saddling the horse," she said as she gripped the doorknob. "Maybe all along he was just trying to get our attention so he could steal the coins."

"Talk about being a sitting duck. I am not going to let you use yourself as bait—"

"I'm depending on you," she interrupted and, without waiting for him to disagree more adamantly, let herself back outside. She heard him swear as she moved off the porch.

It was amazingly difficult to act natural knowing someone was watching. She did her best to look busy as she once again entered the corral and sat on her heels, running her hands up and down Skipjack's front leg as a diversion. This time when she dared a glance, she didn't see any reflection near the rocks and her heart skipped up her throat. Had he moved? Or had she been mistaken? She'd been so sure, but now she didn't know.

She left the corral again and walked toward the river as though admiring the view, glancing at her watch now and again. If she had been mistaken about someone being out here, she and Nate were now wasting time better spent getting to the Crawley place and borrowing a snowmobile.

She wanted to look around for Nate but kept her back to the rocks and the trees. She heard footsteps crunching the snow and realized Nate had reached the same conclusion. She turned to talk to him.

But it wasn't Nate. Instead she found herself looking at a man dressed in gray-and-white camouflage gear with a black ski mask covering most of his face. A pair of green binoculars dangled around his neck and he carried a revolver. That gun was currently aimed at her heart.

"Are you Bellows or one of his henchmen?" she asked, resisting the urge to scan behind him for some sign of Nate.

"Where is he?" the man asked. His voice sounded young and wired.

"Who? Bellows?"

"No, the guy you were with. Matthews."

"He left," she said. "He's off calling the cops."

"I don't think so," the man said. "There are tracks into this place but none out." He cocked the gun, advanced a few steps and repeated, "Where is he?" The tip of the gun inched up to Sarah's forehead.

"Hey," she said. "If you hurt me or him, you'll never find the money."

"What money?"

He didn't know about the coins? "Who sent you?" she asked. "Who are you?"

"Listen, lady, you're going to end up floating facedown in the river in about two seconds if you don't tell me where Matthews is."

"What do you want with him? I'm the one who can help you."

He finished closing the distance between them, grabbed her arm with a viselike grip and propelled her toward the cabin. "Call for him," he said.

"No."

The tip of the barrel pressed against her throat. She could feel her pulse beating against the metal. "Call for him."

Where is Nate?

The gun pressed harder.

She was shaking so hard it was difficult to stand. Surely Nate had left the cabin. Surely he knew what was going on. But where was he?

"One last time," the man hissed in her ear. "Call for Matthews to come out of the cabin. Tell him you need help."

"He'll see you through the window," she said. "He won't come out here."

"Then we'll make him." The man's iron grip slid up to her neck, but before he could tighten his grasp, Sarah stomped on his foot and took off. She knew she'd pay for this action with a bullet in the back, but she had to try. She got an arm's length away before he grabbed her by the hair and yanked her back, shoving her to the ground in the process. He pointed the gun at her. She saw his mouth open through the gap in his ski mask and her heart stopped beating.

No words left his lips. Instead he made a sound as if all the air had been pushed from his lungs. He fell forward onto Sarah, pinning her legs beneath his torso. Sarah found herself staring at a hatchet buried in the brute's back.

She began screaming and couldn't stop. Nate was suddenly there and he pulled her out from under the man. She shielded her eyes by burying her face in his jacket and he led her to the corral, where he gently pushed her onto the stump once used to chop kindling.

"I'll be right back," he said and returned to the man on the ground. She watched as he sat on his haunches and felt for a pulse, then closed her eyes as a wave of nausea rose up her throat. She got to her feet, wondering what they would do if the man was still alive. Common decency said they would have to go for help. But that meant Sarah's mother would perish.

"Is he dead?" she asked Nate as he returned to her.

"Yes. Are you all right?"

"I'll be fine. Did you find his snowmobile?"

"Yeah, it's back in the trees. Is that Bellows?"

"I didn't see his face. He sounded too young, though. And he wanted you, not me."

Nate's brow furrowed. "Me? Why would he want me?"

"I have no idea. He didn't seem to know anything about any money, either."

Nate shook his head. "This doesn't make sense. Are you up to looking at his face?"

"If I have to," she said and followed Nate back to the slain man. His head lay to one side, and Nate pulled up the ski mask. She saw a young guy in his early twenties, maybe late teens. She looked past the bloody bubbles around his lips and studied his features. "I kind of recognize him. Do you?"

Nate ran a hand through his dark hair. "He does look familiar but I don't know why. Damn it, I didn't want to kill him, but it was the only way to stop him before he shot you."

"You don't hear me complaining," Sarah said, turning away from the dead man. "Nate, we need to take the snowmobile and go get the coins."

"It's a one-seater. There are saddlebags, but two people won't fit."

"Then I have to go alone," Sarah said. A little while ago, that had seemed like a great idea, but now Sarah hated the thought of riding out of here without Nate.

"I could go instead of you," he said.

She averted her gaze from the dead man on the ground. "I'm the one who has to drive to Reno, and time is ticking away." She paused before adding, "This is my responsibility, Nate."

A tilt of his head said clearly that he understood what she meant. "And mine is to contact the law. I've just killed a man and then there's your father's murder to try to explain."

"I know you have to do what you feel is right and what's important to you. Tell the sheriff's department whatever you have to—just give me an hour or so to get the coins and get out of here."

"How are you going to do that?" he asked. "Your car may have been confiscated, but even if it hasn't, the snow is still too deep. The fire department could still be there, too. If a spark got to my truck, it might have blown up. The ranch could be a real disaster."

"I know. I don't know how I'm going to get to Reno, but somehow, I will."

"Sarah, there's something else. We have no way of knowing if this man is the one from last night."

She thought for a few seconds before speaking. "You wounded the one last night. Does this guy have any bullet holes?"

"I'll look."

"I have to go," she said.

"I know you do."

"And, Nate, when you talk to the cops, could you just not mention the coins, you know, for now?"

He stared down into her eyes. "I won't mention them, but when this is all over—"

"I'll sing like a canary," she promised. She gazed up into his eyes and gripped his uninjured arm. "Nate, I'm scared. This guy didn't know about the coins or give a hoot about me. He wanted you."

Nate nodded. "It takes a little getting used to, doesn't it? But if it is the same guy from yesterday then Bellows had nothing to do with any of this. That's good news for you and your mother. Pay off the debt and walk away."

"It's not me I'm thinking of," Sarah said. "It's you. He was ready to kill me to get to you. He may not be alone. Be careful."

"I will. But you be careful, too. Just because this guy today was after me doesn't mean last night wasn't all about you."

She nodded and glanced at her watch. "Take Skipjack," she said. "There's a large-animal veterinarian on the east edge of town that Dad has used for years. I'm pretty sure they'll keep him for you."

He raised his right hand and cupped her chin. "I hate

letting you go off on your own. There's so much we have
to finish."

"I know. The police and—"

"That's not what I meant," he said.

She swallowed a lump and blinked rapidly. "Just be
careful," she repeated.

He leaned over and claimed her lips, and Sarah was
shocked to discover in that instant leaving him was the
hardest thing she'd done yet. There had been so much fear
lately, so much loss, and this felt like another. Would she
ever see him again? He kissed her one more time, lightly,
then whispered against her lips, "Go now."

Sarah sucked back tears as she turned away and ran
off into the trees.

As DISTASTEFUL AS it was, Nate pulled off the dead man's
ski mask and gloves and searched for a sign of a gunshot
wound inflicted a mere twelve hours earlier. Then he unzipped his jacket and patted him down. He found no identification, no bloody bandages or injuries, although if he'd
been shot in the back the night before, it sure wouldn't
show now. The ax had made a real mess of things, and for
a moment Nate thought about that split-second decision
to launch the ax rather than take the time to try to run up
to him unheard and hit him over the head.

It hadn't really been a hard decision to make. It was this
guy or Sarah, and she'd won. He suspected she would win
every contest in his head. He heard the snowmobile and
looked up the slope in time to see her erupt from the trees
and disappear over the lip of the cliff.

He collected a dozen rocks from the riverbed, carrying
them back up to the body, then retrieved a blanket from
the mattress inside the cabin. His plan was to cover the
body with the blanket and secure it with rocks. Lying on

the snow as it was, the body should be pretty well pre-
served until the police arrived.

Before he did this, he studied the guy's profile one more
time, and again, there was something about him that looked
a little familiar. Something about the cheekbones and the
jaw. Something—but nothing definite.

Once he climbed on Skipjack's back, he realized he
wasn't sure the quickest way to anywhere—he was totally
turned around—but there was a road up there somewhere.
If he could find that, he could find people, help, a phone.

And then he could face the music for killing a man
and try to explain what had happened at Mike's house
yesterday.

Would he ever see Sarah again? Nate had a gut feeling
that the guy he'd just killed had not been the same one
he'd shot the day before. Like he'd told Sarah, it was possible there were two agendas at work, possible that Sarah
was walking into a death trap and there wasn't a thing he
could do about it.

Or could he?

SARAH HADN'T KNOWN exactly what to expect at the ranch.
Firemen, probably, maybe the police. It was a long shot
that she could sneak in there and steal her own coins out
from under them, so she approached warily, parking the
snowmobile by Skipjack's stall and entering the barn as
quietly as she could.

To her great relief, the stall looked just as she'd left it.
She took a detour to the front of the barn, where she found
the door wide open and the cold, thin wind tunneling inside. Moving in the shadows to avoid being seen from outside, she made her way to a vantage point from which she
could see the house. It took her a second to believe her eyes.
There wasn't a soul around or any sign that anyone had

been. With the exception of partially burned wood siding, nothing looked any different than it had hours before. Had the gunman extinguished it himself or had the house refused to burn? She blinked a couple of times but in the end decided to accept it as a stroke of luck and hurried back to the stall.

She quickly moved the straw bedding and then shoveled up the dirt in the corner. The cans were right where they were supposed to be, and as she hooked the first one with her fingers, she glanced at her watch. She had four hours to get the coins and herself to Reno. She couldn't drive her car, she couldn't take the snowmobile all that way and she couldn't rent a car. As she moved the coins from the cans into the saddlebags, she found herself close to giggling. *Heck, I could buy a car.* She could buy a fleet of cars as long as no one needed to see a license or any identification.

She did the math in her head to come up with what her mother needed. The value of the coins far exceeded their actual weight because of their mint condition—she wasn't sure how to figure it all out, but at this point, she would be happy to fork over too much if it meant ending this nightmare.

Which begged the question, how did she assure her mother didn't get herself back into the same old mess a week or a month or a year from now? She would find out that Sarah had inherited everything from Mike, and as soon as she did, little by little she would eat it all up in her wild gambling sprees. Sooner or later, the money would end up in the pockets of Poulter or Bellows or others of their ilk, and it galled Sarah to death. Her father had sat on most of the coins his entire adult life; he hadn't kept up the ranch or bought himself new cars, nothing, just let the coins sit in their cans and then left them to Sarah, who would now need to figure out a way to assure they did some actual good in the world.

Talk about problems for another day. Right now she had to get into Shatterhorn and beg, steal or borrow a car. Three and a half hours...

Because there were still several cans of coins in the underground vault, she had to take the time to put the stall back together again, working up a sweat despite the cold temperature. A weak sun came out as she rode off, and she squinted at the brilliance as the light reflected off the snow. A pair of goggles hung from the handlebars, but they had to have belonged to the man Nate killed and Sarah didn't want them touching her face. As it was, her face was soon so cold she couldn't feel her lips or her nose.

She looked back once as she crossed the pasture, then concentrated on driving, trying in the back of her mind to figure out how she should go about the next step, her hands half-frozen, her hair whipping about her shoulders.

She still had friends from high school living in Shatterhorn; maybe one of them could loan her a car. But how did she show up on their doorstep after eleven years' absence and ask without delivering a long explanation she didn't have the time for? For that matter, where did they currently live and how did she get to their houses while lugging around almost a hundred pounds of silver coins?

Nor, Sarah admitted, did she want any of them knowing her mother still gambled. Diana Donovan's antics had been the talk of the town once, and once was enough.

Sarah had been driving beside the highway for the past mile or so. The road itself had been plowed and traffic was light. A short time later, the snowmobile belched its first sputter. She was still a half a mile from Shatterhorn. A couple of hundred feet more and it became clear the machine was about out of gas. She managed to guide it behind a spur of old fence before its last gasping moment, hoping to hide it from sight, but what did she do now?

Caught in a web of indecision and rising panic, she started stuffing the rolled coins into her pockets, knowing it was hopeless, not knowing what else she could do. Her watch kept catching the reflection of the sun, twinkling at her, taunting her.

She heard the sound of a car approaching and ducked her head, unsure if Nate had had time to coax the police into starting their investigation, only knowing she didn't want to get involved in any part of that until there was no other choice. She caught the blurred shape of a dark blue truck passing her by, then looked over her shoulder to witness it make a screeching U-turn before stopping several feet away. Nate leaned across the front seat and opened the passenger door. "Need a ride?"

She scrambled to climb inside. "What are you doing here?"

"I'm driving you to Reno if you managed to get the coins. Did you?"

"Yes. Whoever started the fire must have put it out. The house shows where it burned and the barn door was open as though someone looked around in there, too, but that's it. Maybe they didn't want authorities snooping around prematurely. Now that you've gone to the police—"

"I haven't talked to them yet," he said. "I was on my way out to the ranch when I caught a glimpse of you behind that fence."

"That's where the snowmobile is. I ran out of gas. Where's my horse?"

"At the vet. They said they'll board him until you come for him." As he told her this, he positioned the truck as close to the side of the road as he could, and together, they transferred the coins from the attached saddlebags and

Sarah's pockets, piling the rolls in a cardboard box in the backseat. Sarah could see Nate was favoring his arm and wondered how much it still hurt.

At last he made another U-turn and they took off.

She stared at him for several seconds before finally speaking. "Why aren't you spilling your guts to the cops?"

He spared her a quick glance as he merged onto a major highway leading west toward Reno. "What's the rush?" he asked.

She studied his strong profile for a moment before shaking her head. "Well, let's see. A, there are two dead men, and B, you're a deputy sheriff who has, until this minute, seemed hell-bent on following the rules."

"I believe I told you I knew how to think outside the box," he said, but there was something else in his voice that caught her attention. Exactly what it was, she wasn't sure.

"Yeah, but, Nate, think about it. This could get you in a heap of trouble," she added.

"You, too," he said.

"I'm used to trouble. I get the feeling you're not."

The look he flashed her this time was more intense. "Mike is dead and can't be brought back to life no matter when law enforcement gets into the act. The same goes for our visitor this morning. But your situation is immediate and dangerous and I don't want you doing it alone."

"You keep forgetting someone showed up this morning intent on killing you. Not me—you," she said.

"I haven't forgotten. In fact, I finally figured out who it was."

"Are you going to tell me?"

He flashed her a grim smile. "I thought you'd never ask."

Chapter Ten

"It's Peter Jacks," Nate said.

Sarah felt like slapping her forehead. "I didn't really recognize him. I should have, but I didn't."

"People look different when they're dead. Besides, it's been several years since you saw him, right?"

"Over ten. He was just a kid I babysat occasionally. He gave no indication he recognized me, either. How did you figure out who he was?"

"He looked familiar to me. I talked myself into a few minutes of internet use while I was renting the truck. I found a photograph taken of Thomas's family leaving his funeral, and there, front and center, was his older brother, Peter."

"So he wanted to kill you for, what, revenge? Because you were at the mall when his brother went berserk? But you didn't kill Thomas. He killed himself. Why go after you?"

"I'm not sure," Nate admitted. He hadn't thought it all the way through yet.

"Does this mean he killed my father, too?"

"I don't know."

"How would Peter Jacks know you were in Nevada unless my father told him?"

"He wouldn't."

"No, and my father looked as though he was caught coming home or leaving his house, not like he'd been in the middle of a heart-to-heart chat with Peter." She gestured at the road ahead and added, "Can't you go any faster?"

"Sure I can," he said and sped up. The nervous energy emanating from Sarah permeated the cab.

"Did you find a gunshot wound on Peter's body?" she asked.

"No," Nate said. "But that doesn't mean there wasn't one. I could hardly strip him." The truth was, Nate had been happy to have an explanation for the morning's disaster, but now he saw that Sarah made some valid points. "After we talk to the Shatterhorn police, I want to arrange to see a couple of other people. Your dad's notebook mentioned conversations but didn't really specify content. Maybe the people he spoke with will remember what it was about. And maybe one of them will know if there was contact between your dad and the Jacks family."

"You may not be able to arrest anyone in Nevada, but you still approach things as the cop you are," she said. "Do you think they're involved with Dad's murder?"

Nate kept his eyes on the road ahead. "Impossible to say. Until we know for sure, we have to assume the people who have your mother were at your father's house yesterday, busily trying to kill us. We'd better concentrate on keeping a few steps ahead of this guy when we get to Reno. How are you supposed to deliver the money?"

"He gave me a phone number to call before three o'clock. He said he'll tell me where he stashed my mother and we'll make an exchange."

Nate glanced at the dashboard clock. They were about twenty miles from Reno and it was after one. "We have to make time to hit a coin dealer first. You can't just shovel out silver coins in front of Bellows."

"I'll have to call him first and make sure I know exactly how much Mom owes him. Then I'll sell enough coins to meet that debt. I wonder if one dealer will have enough cash?"

"I guess we'll find out. I sure hate the idea of these thugs getting away with it."

"I know you do," she said with a swift glance Nate caught out of the corner of his eye. "But that's exactly what's going to happen. I thought you were okay with this."

"I can agree with you but still not like it," he said.

She laughed softly. "Yeah, that's true."

A half hour later, they pulled into the almost empty parking lot of the first coin dealer they found. Nate was delighted, when they entered, to see the place was also a vendor for other merchandise, including prepaid cell phones. While Sarah talked with the dealer, he bought and activated a new phone, which would serve him fine until he could go back to his original carrier and replace the unit that had been shot out of his hand.

When he joined Sarah, he found her deep in negotiations with a balding Asian man who wore a jeweler's loupe and emitted a fierce aura of concentration. As the dealer carefully unpeeled the wrapper of a roll of silver dollars, Sarah looked up at Nate. "Where have you been?"

"I bought a phone. Why don't you go call Bellows and I'll stay here and watch over things."

Sarah took the phone, and as she walked away, Nate watched her dig in her hip pocket and withdraw a slip of paper that he assumed held the number she had to call. He had to force his gaze from her lithe figure, and when he did, he found the dealer looking at him with a speculative expression.

"She won't tell me where she got these coins," he said, nodding at the stack of rolls they'd deposited atop the cabinet.

"They're hers," Nate responded.

"You expect me to take your word for it?"

Nate wished he could open his wallet and show the guy his badge. "Have a little faith," he said instead.

"The deal is, there are a lot of coins here, and if they're all of this quality, we're talking a small fortune. You know I can't buy them without filing a CTR, right?"

"What's a CTR?"

"A currency transfer report. You know, the government's attempt to try to control money laundering." He rubbed his bald head. "I hope I have enough cash in the safe to purchase the whole lot. If not, I'll have to call my banker and arrange a transfer."

Nate propped his hands atop the cabinet and leaned forward. "We're in a bit of a hurry. How about you purchase all that you can and help us figure out how many more it'll take to come to a certain figure?"

"What figure?"

"We'll know when the lady returns. Just keep examining the ones you can afford to buy outright. We need to be out of here in fifteen minutes."

The man rubbed his head again. "Let me see what I can do."

As the dealer took out a pocket calculator, Nate went in search of Sarah. He found her standing outside with her back against the brick building, and as he approached, she clicked off the phone and looked up at him. There were tears in her eyes and Nate closed the distance between them as fast as possible.

"What's wrong?"

"Bellows put my mother on the phone. She was crying

so hard I couldn't understand much of what she said. I guess this maniac has been passing the time by detailing the ways he's going to torture her to teach us both a lesson if I don't show up."

"Were you able to ask her if she told them you were going up to see your father to ask for the money?"

"She was in no shape to think clearly. I didn't ask her much of anything." She hastily wiped a teardrop from her cheek and added, "We have an hour to get to the Silver Dollar Motel right outside of Carson City. We have to hurry."

"Are you kidding me? The Silver Dollar?"

"I know. Appropriate, isn't it?"

"Damn right poetic," he said. "How much money do we need?"

"Two hundred and twenty-eight thousand dollars."

"Let's go make this happen," Nate said and took her hand.

The dealer came up with all the money they needed to ransom Sarah's mother and asked that they sell him the rest of the coins, though he wouldn't be able to cash them out right that second. As Sarah had no desire to tote a bunch of silver coins around, she agreed to his deal. The dealer supplied a canvas tote for the money and even threw in a black Stetson that Nate had been eyeing. As Nate was mostly dressed in Sarah's father's clothes from the waist up, the hat went a long way toward making him feel a little more like the man he usually was.

"Did this guy say how you're supposed to go about the exchange?" Nate asked as they drove away.

"Yeah. I'm to go to room eight and knock three times."

"He's going to be there?"

"I guess so. He isn't exactly forthcoming."

"She's just quietly sitting in a motel room? That doesn't sound very plausible."

"You have to remember that they're threatening her with my safety. She acts up, they take it out on me."

Nate narrowed his eyes but kept his gaze straight ahead. He didn't know Sarah's mother, but from what Sarah had said about her, he had doubts she was able to think much further ahead than her own welfare. He'd have to trust Sarah's faith in the woman, but it went against all common sense to meet someone like this on their terms.

Options? He couldn't think of any. Not only was he currently not in law enforcement, but even if he was, he would be powerless to act in a different state. Putting aside the ethics of paying off a goon, you had to remember it was only money—and Sarah's money, at that—and perhaps down the line, justice would be served.

He would play his part just as he'd promised. What else could he do?

SARAH STRAINED AGAINST her shoulder seat belt as though willing the truck to move faster. Reno traffic was unexpectedly heavy, but it petered out as they headed south. It took half an hour to get to Carson City and then they had to stop at a service station to ask directions to the Silver Dollar Motel.

The motel itself turned out to be in an almost deserted industrial area of town, bracketed by an old warehouse with its windows shot out and a fenced yard full of old vehicles.

The motel itself might have been cute at one time in its dim past. Now it was surrounded by weeds and didn't even appear to be in business. The sign out front included a huge neon figure of a cowboy lounging with his back against the marquee, his arms folded across his chest, his face set in a permanent smirk. Most of the bulbs surrounding his figure were broken. A smaller sign announced there were no vacancies. The parking lot was covered with dust and the chill February wind blew a few tumbleweeds along the snow-dusted pavement. The one visible car was pulled up in front of unit eight.

"Except for that car, this place looks like a ghost town," Nate said.

Sarah nodded, her mouth too dry to actually make words. How was this all going to go down? As they rolled across the parking lot, she saw Nate reach under his seat. When he caught her watching him, he admitted he didn't want to take his wallet into this situation and she was glad he'd thought to leave it behind.

As Nate locked the rental truck, Sarah slowly approached the door of room number eight, her skin prickling with the sensation of being watched, the duffel bag heavy in her hand. She knocked the prescribed three times as Nate joined her on the step.

A big brute of a man with two silver eyeteeth opened the door. Bellows looked much the same as he had at the airport the only other time she'd seen him. A smaller man with thick curly gray hair and dressed in a golf shirt stood to the side. With a grunt from Bellows, the smaller guy patted Sarah and Nate down. All they found were Nate's truck keys, which he snapped back.

"Where's my mother?" Sarah said after a quick glance around the room, which seemed predominantly green from the carpet to the bedspread to the wall paint and was achingly absent of another person.

"Where's my money?" Bellows said, then, staring Nate in the eye, added, "And who the hell are you?"

Nate crossed his arms, and for a second, he looked like the human version of the cowboy out front. "My name is

Nate," he said in a Western accent new to Sarah. "I'm a friend of the family. Can't expect her to run around on her own, now can you?"

Bellows grunted and turned his back on Nate to address Sarah. "Your mom is close by. We got tired of her caterwauling. This place is empty, so she can yell all she wants as long as we don't have to listen to it. Two days was enough. Woman's got quite a mouth on her. Now, hand over the money."

"I want to see her first," Sarah said.

"You'll see her when I say you see her."

"No dice," Sarah said. "How do I know you'll keep your part of the deal?"

"Here's a—what do you call it?—a gesture of good-will," the big man said and handed Sarah her handbag. She opened it to see her belongings as she'd left them: the phone in a side pocket, her house keys and hairbrush, her wallet with a few green bills showing. Was she supposed to be impressed by his honesty?

She shouldered her bag. "Let me see my mother, then you can see the cash."

The big guy looked at Nate. "Are you as stupid as she is? Has it completely slipped your mind who has a gun and who doesn't? Show them your gun, Benny, and don't be shy about using it if either one of them forgets the facts of life again."

Benny pulled out a lethal-looking gun and then tucked it back in his waistband.

"Just tell me where she is," Sarah pleaded.

"She's here in the motel. Now open that bag."

Sarah zipped open the bag and the two thugs fell on it like pirates on a keg of rum.

"Where is Diana Donovan?" Nate asked.

"Room twelve," Benny said. He was stacking up hundred-dollar bills like an accountant.

Nate reached for the door, but Bellows threw out an arm to stop him. "Not so fast, slick. The girl can go get her mother. You're staying where I can keep my eye on you."

"Is the door of her room locked?" Sarah asked.

"No."

Sarah left the room after exchanging meaningful glances with Nate. She hurried along the cold sidewalk to unit twelve and threw open the door.

Her mother lay straddled on the bed with hands and feet each tied to a bedpost. The gag in her mouth looked torturous, and her eyes, as they landed on Sarah, went from terrified to relieved in a blink. She pulled against the knots to the point that Sarah's fingers hurt trying to untie them.

"Calm down," Sarah kept saying. "You're safe now. Just relax so we can get you out of here." As she struggled with the knots on her mom's right hand, she saw the busted, bruised and swollen fingers and couldn't imagine how much they hurt, though her mother seemed oblivious to the pain.

Eventually Sarah managed to free all the knots and helped her mother sit on the side of the bed. Her jeans and pink T-shirt were studded with rhinestones that looked glaringly out of place in the shabbiness of the room.

For some reason, Sarah had left removing the gag for last, and as that came off, Diana Donovan licked her lips and rubbed her face with a jittery hand.

"Are you all right?" Sarah asked.

"I could have died!" Rivers of mascara had run down her face until her eyes looked like dark smudges. This impression was enhanced by the shiner, which Bellows had probably given her and which was now turning her left cheekbone shades of blue and purple.

Sarah tried to hug her, but her mother stood abruptly. "Did he give it to you?" she hissed.

"Sort of," Sarah said, knowing the *he* her mother referred to was her father.

"What do you mean, 'sort of'? Where is it?"

"I handed it over to the men in room eight," Sarah said, furrowing her brow. What else would she have done?

"All of it?"

"Of course."

"We could have bargained them down," her mother said.

Sarah felt sure her jaw dropped open. "Bargained with them? Look at you. They've…they've beaten you up and your fingers are broken and untreated."

"Right. And how will I afford to fix them now when you gave away all my money? What will I use to get back on my feet?"

"It's Dad's money," Sarah said softly, glancing away from her mother's swollen face. "And if you're talking start-up money for more gambling—"

"Of course I'm talking seed money, but it all belongs to snaggletooth now!" Her mother turned abruptly, staggered as though weak or dizzy, but she caught herself and left the room. By the time Sarah gathered her wits and followed, her mother was opening the door to room eight and disappearing inside.

Startled, Nate watched Diana Donovan storm into room number eight, take a good look around and march on over to Bellows and Benny, who were still counting out their money around a tiny, scarred table. She stood over them and started poking and grabbing, swearing like a sailor and acting about as scared as a bulldog confronting a mouse.

This was Sarah's mother? She was a good six inches shorter, rounder, softer-looking with very pink skin stretched tight over her cheekbones, as though she was no stranger to plastic surgery. Even taking into consideration the woman's running makeup, bleached hair and the black eye, the differences were so striking they seemed impossible to reconcile.

A second later, Sarah erupted through the door, as beautiful as ever, but somehow changed. She lunged for her mother, who shook her off as she grabbed a fistful of dollars. The bigger of the two thugs grabbed Diana's right hand to make her release the dough, and that must have compressed her horribly mangled fingers. The scream that leaped from her throat could curdle milk. The big man slugged her, but it was like fuel to the older woman's rage. She yelled louder.

Nate couldn't just stand there. Using reflexes honed by years of hands-on experience at keeping the peace, he jumped into the fray and wrangled both men to the ground, delivering and receiving a fair number of punches in the process. Fists flew; screams flew; cash flew. He subdued the smaller of the men and was in the process of getting to his feet when the larger man grabbed him from behind with a stranglehold around his throat. He heard a deep thud, and the pressure lessened as the man's hands slid away. With a thump, the guy ended up facedown on the floor.

Nate looked up to find Sarah standing there with a metal waste can in her hands.

"Did you—"

"—whack him over the head?" she said. "I sure did."

Nate brushed his hair from his face and scooped his hat off the floor where it had fallen. His shoulder throbbed again, but that discomfort was mitigated by the sight of Sarah's smile as she surveyed the results of her handiwork. "Thanks," he said.

"Anytime."

Benny's eyes seemed to spin in opposite directions as he came around, while Bellows held his head and groaned. Nate relieved Benny of his gun and patted down the other one for a weapon. "He's clean," he said.

Diana started to scoop up more of the money, but Nate caught her hand. "What the hell do you think you're doing?"

"Taking what should be mine," she said. "There's enough here for a fresh start."

"They'll come after you," Sarah said as she set aside the trash can.

Diana kept cramming money in her pockets. "I'll go far away."

Nate shook his head. "You do that and they'll go after your daughter. Sarah will continue to be in danger."

"No, they won't. She'll be fine."

Nate pointed Benny's gun at her. "Put every penny back on that table."

She looked at him as though he was nuts. "Who the hell died and made you boss?" she demanded.

"Do it," Sarah said. She glanced up at Nate and added, "He's already killed one person today. I wouldn't push your luck."

Diana looked from one of them to the other, shoved her tangled, bleached hair away from her round face and sighed. She dug the money out of her pocket and threw it at the two men on the floor.

"Ladies? Time to go," Nate said, still holding the gun. Benny and Bellows were beginning to sit up and take notice of their surroundings.

He hurried both women to his truck, which had a double cab. He expected Sarah to slide in back with Diana, but instead she got into the front. Nate glanced at her face as he closed her door, taking in her huge blue eyes and mussed hair, her sweet lips and long throat, all absorbed into his brain and recorded for future reference in the time it took to blink. It felt like the end of the road for them—he had things he had to do, and from what he'd seen in that motel room, Sarah's hands were going to be full for a long time.

As he walked around behind the truck, he fought off a wave of melancholy. He wasn't ready to say goodbye to Sarah Donovan but he should have seen it coming.

Shots came out of nowhere, or so it seemed in the instant it took Nate to dive to the pavement. He still carried Benny's gun. Another shot alerted him to the direction from which the gunfire originated and he got off a round of his own before leaping to his feet. Someone was shooting from the abandoned building next door.

Sarah pushed open his door, then hunkered down low as he climbed inside. He jammed the key in the ignition and shifted into Reverse, sitting up fully as he steered away from the building and the shooter. His last sight was of Bellows and Benny standing at the motel door.

They looked as confused as Nate felt and he had the profound feeling they had nothing to do with the ambush. So now who was gunning for him?

Chapter Eleven

"They're still shooting!" Diana Donovan screamed, and sure enough, Nate heard a bullet hit the rear of the truck. He glanced back to see the gunman had come out of hiding and was now standing out in the open wielding what appeared to be a rifle. Nate could make out nothing of the man's features and another bullet hitting the back window took care of him trying to.

"Get your head down," Nate shouted. "You, too, Sarah."

Both women ducked as yet another bullet hit what sounded like the bumper. Undoubtedly, the gunman was aiming for the tires. Another shot was followed by the tinkle of breaking glass and a scream from Diana. A quick glance at the rearview mirror revealed part of the sliding back window was now gone.

If Nate hadn't had passengers, he might have doubled back and headed right for the jerk. Instead he took a hard turn to the right. The small truck skidded a bit but kept to the road, and Nate immediately took a left turn and, at the next corner, another sharp right. There was no sign of pursuit, but he kept up the evasive maneuvers until they cleared Carson City and hit the road back to Reno.

"I think it's safe to sit up," Nate said, glancing at Sarah, whose expression looked terrified, all in all a logical reaction to the past few minutes.

"No, thanks," Diana Donovan called from the backseat. "I'm staying down."

Sarah, however, did sit up and twisted around in her seat. "Are you okay?" she asked her mother.

"No, I'm not okay. I'm covered with glass. What the hell is going on?"

"Good question," Sarah muttered as she turned her attention to Nate. "Did you notice the shots didn't start until you were walking around out there alone?" she asked.

Nate nodded. He'd noticed. It was pretty clear whom the intended target had been.

"Better head to the emergency room," she added with a nod toward the backseat.

"What's the point?" Diana grumbled. "I can't pay for anything."

"I'll cover it," Sarah said.

Diana sat forward, resting her hands on the back of Sarah's seat. "Did your father give you more money?"

"Yes," Sarah said.

"How much more?"

"Everything."

Nate kind of wished she hadn't said anything to her mother about the money, but talk about something not being his business.

"Is there a lot?" Diana asked, her voice anxious.

Sarah turned to face her mother. "Don't you want to know why he gave me everything?"

"Not particularly. Not after he turned his back on me."

"It's because he's dead, Mom. Murdered. I thought maybe you told the killers that I'd gone to Dad's house to get the money to rescue you, but now I'm beginning to think that's not the case."

"Of course I didn't tell anyone where you were going," Diana said. "How did Mike die?"

"He was shot."

"By this man you've taken up with?"

Nate cast his gaze into the rearview mirror, but he couldn't see the older woman.

"No."

"Are you sure?"

"Positive."

"So, how many of the coins do you still have?"

"Enough, but that's not how I'll cover your expenses. I have a little of my own money left after buying the plane ticket to come here. What I have is yours so you can get back on your feet. I'm hoping you'll give that gambling-addiction program another chance to help you."

"I'm not addicted!" Diana insisted. "I just like to have a good time."

"Think about the past few days," Sarah said, her voice soft and in vibrant contrast to her mother's nasal whine. "Do you really think the people who gamble for fun end up dealing with loan sharks and thugs, getting beaten up and held against their will?"

"I'm not other people," Diana said. "Things got a little crazy this time, but with your father's money…"

"No, Mom. You're not going to burn up Dad's money."

"What are you going to do with it?" she demanded.

"I don't know, but I'm not going to hand it over to criminals. You need help. I'm begging you to get it."

"I'll think about it," Diana said, and Nate could tell from her tone of voice that she was placating Sarah. It was probably part of her pattern, a little olive branch of hope extended with no heart behind the words, intended to end an unwinnable conversation without making a commitment.

But Sarah seemed content with the response. "Good. That's a start."

"As soon as I get my hand fixed up properly, I'm going to need my car," Diana added. "Where is it?"

"It's in Dad's barn. You'll have to wait until the police release it."

"Why would the police care about my car?"

"Dad was killed at his house, Mom. There were also other troubles. You don't need to hear about them right now, but I imagine the whole ranch will be a crime scene. Don't worry. I'll help you figure something out."

"I'm sorry I was so short with you earlier," Diana said, her voice suddenly softer. "No matter, we'll have lots of time to talk and get to know each other again. Days and days. Months. Years."

"Well, a little while, anyway. I do have a life I have to return to," Sarah said.

"Where?"

"In Virginia. I work for a great veterinarian there. I told you about it. I love working with the animals."

"Oh. Well, what's more important, people or critters? Besides, thanks to your father, you won't need to work anymore. You can move out here and be closer to me. Won't that be fun? I can show you around. Reno is a great town after dark."

Nate kept his thoughts to himself, but even without looking at Sarah, he could sense the deep sinking of her spirits. Was she wondering if she would ever be free of this woman's emotional grip? There was no way on earth he could help her, and so he concentrated on driving and thought nice thoughts about his own parents, bless their independent souls.

Diana gave him instructions, and within a few minutes, he pulled up next to the emergency-room entrance. Without a word to Nate, the older woman was out of the car in a flash, pausing by Sarah's door. Cubes of safety glass glittered on her shoulders and from her hair.

Sarah glanced at Nate, then opened her door and turned her attention to her mother. "Go get out of the cold, Mom. I'll be with you in a minute."

As Diana walked inside the building, Sarah turned back to face Nate. "Aren't you coming in to have your arm looked at?"

"I'll wait until I get to Shatterhorn," he said. "I don't want to answer questions about a gunshot wound more than once. You should take your father's notebook." He opened the console compartment between them, but she closed it before he could withdraw the battered notebook.

"No, you keep it."

He nodded.

"I'm sorry about my mother," she added.

"You have nothing to be sorry about."

"Yes, I do. She's a little on the self-centered side. She's used to having somebody look after her. After Dad there was a string of guys. She must be between men now. That may have been what triggered the latest gambling episode. I don't know...."

"It's okay," he said. "She's your mother."

Sarah nodded, but still she lingered until at last she reached across the console and touched his arm. He put his hand over hers and leaned toward her. Their kiss was short and circumspect, but as always, there was the pulsating awareness of her that burned beneath Nate's skin.

"I'm scared about you going off alone after what just happened in the parking lot," she said softly, her lips moving against his. "And then there was that guy this morning.... Can you believe that was only a few hours ago?"

"I've known you a little less than twenty-four hours," Nate said, running his fingers along her curved jaw.

"But they've been a very intense twenty-four hours," Sarah said. She closed her eyes and leaned her face against his palm. He could feel a wisp of dampness, as though a stray tear had hidden in her lashes. "I don't want to let you go."

"Come with me," he said, brushing his lips along her temple.

"I can't."

"You're going to have to explain your part in all this sooner or later, you know."

"I know." She pulled away a little and squared her shoulders. "You saw my mother. I have to stay with her at least through tomorrow, help her get settled, then I'll rent a car or something and drive up to Shatterhorn. Will you still be there?"

"That depends," Nate said, not going into detail. It depended on whether he survived the rest of the day, whether he was charged with murder or whether he was free to go back to Arizona, which was the option his gut told him to take if possible. Sarah was buried in issues with her family and he was still half-dead inside and on the heels of a breakup. Twenty-four hours of living on the edge with Sarah had meant a lot to him. She meant a lot to him, but she was unavailable, and perhaps he was, too.

Maybe that was just the story of his life.

"I programmed my cell-phone number into your phone while we drove," she said. "Call me."

"Sure," he said, knowing he wouldn't put himself through any more goodbyes.

"I had such big plans for us, you know, for tonight. I guess I wasn't thinking clearly about reality," she said.

"That happens under duress," he said. "Don't worry about it."

"But—"

He cupped the back of her head and kissed her again, putting an end to words that didn't mean as much as the touch of her lips. This time he didn't care who saw or even if the gunman lurked nearby. Her lips tasted just as good as they had the night before; his longing for her hadn't diminished. She would now join his personal string of opportunities lost and regrets to ponder.

When they came up for air, he released his grip on her. "Your mom is waiting for you," he said. "Take care, Sarah."

"You, too," she whispered as she slipped out of his truck and out of his life.

SHERIFF ALAN GALLANT greeted Nate with a hearty handshake. "It's been a while since we saw you," Gallant said, peering into Nate's eyes. "After what happened the last time you were here, I guess you haven't felt much like visiting us. How's your pal Detective Foster?"

"Alex is fine," Nate said. "He would have been here with me, but he couldn't land because of the weather. I'm not here for a visit, though. I have a story I have to tell you and I'm afraid it includes a couple of dead men."

"Cripes," Gallant said with a grimace as he forced his ample frame into a protesting wooden chair. He looked over his shoulder and said, "Larry, bring coffee. Patty, you better get this on tape." After the coffee was delivered and the equipment switched on, Gallant looked straight into Nate's eyes. "What's going on?"

"I'm not sure," Nate said. "First I should ask you if anyone called in a fire at the Donovan horse ranch or reported a body."

"What? Hell no. You mean Mike Donovan? What did he do now?"

"Nothing that I know of. He's dead, Sheriff."

"He finally pissed someone off bad enough to get himself killed?" Gallant immediately shook his head and looked contrite. "Sorry, I know he was a friend of yours. That wasn't a nice thing for me to say. Tell me what you know."

Nate launched into an account of what turned out to be a multilayered story. It took him an hour to tell it, and by that time, Nate had handed over the film he'd used to record the original condition of Mike's body, crime-scene units had been sent out to both the river cabin and the ranch house and investigations had been launched. Once they were alone, Gallant swiveled to face Nate and lowered his voice. "Tell me again about Peter Jacks."

Nate once again repeated the morning's events. He downplayed Sarah's role, but there was no way to leave her out of everything, as her fingerprints would be all over the cabin and the abandoned snowmobile, so he also explained about her family trouble and how she would be here the day after tomorrow to clear up her part in the proceedings. As promised, he left out any mention of the coins.

And that made explaining the origins of Benny's gun, which he handed over at once, a little tricky. He couldn't keep the weapon nor did he want to—who knew what crimes it had been used to commit—so in the end he gave a good description of Benny and Bellows and told a watered-down version of the situation in Carson City. Finally, he kind of threw up his hands. "Sarah will clear it up when she gets here."

This lame statement caused the sheriff's thick brows to furl, but he bagged the gun and let it go—for now.

Nate also admitted that yet someone else had taken shots at him. He really had no choice in the matter as the rental company was sure to notice all the damage and report it. The sheriff asked if he wanted protection and he waved the offer away. Protection from whom? Unfortunately, he could provide precious few facts and Gallant informed him he would take care of alerting Carson City police. He seemed to be under the impression the shooting was related to the ransom and Nate let that assumption stand.

"Which brings us back to Peter Jacks," the sheriff said with a shake of his big head. "I knew the boy was having trouble. Him and Stew's boy both."

"You mean Stewart Netters, the editor of the paper? So we're talking about Jason?"

"Yeah. The kid hasn't been right since the shooting. Having both those girls gunned down right in front of him, to say nothing of the other two dead kids— I don't know. Maybe it's survivor's guilt."

"Yeah," Nate muttered. He'd thought a lot about survivor's guilt. Unfortunately, he hadn't come up with a way to turn it off.

"Not that people haven't tried to help," Gallant continued. "There's a relatively new organization around, started by a man named Morris Denton. He calls it B-Strong. It concentrates on building character and self-esteem. Some of the local kids have attended summer programs and weekend workshops, things like that. The hope is positive reinforcement will empower them. It certainly seems to have empowered Thomas Jacks."

"Thomas had been part of this camp?"

"Yeah. Of course, after the shooting we interviewed anyone who had ever talked to the kid. No one up there had a thing to offer."

"Did you meet Denton?"

"Briefly. He was out of the country when the shooting occurred and was horrified by Thomas's actions, just like everyone else." He shook his head. "Lots of people rallied round Peter after the shooting, but there were some, too many, who seemed to be waiting around for him to do something terrible like his brother did. I've known the Jacks family for years. Peter and Thomas were on the same soccer teams as my own kids, went on the same campouts, attended the same church. When Thomas went berserk in the mall, the whole town suffered, but no one worse than his folks and his brother. There was no warning, no nothing."

"Is there anyone who thinks a foreign terrorist group might be involved?"

"Well, I think Netters did at first. He ran a couple of articles about something called People's Liberation, right after they took credit for the Hawaii shooting last December, but I think Thomas acted alone."

"Are you sure?"

"The sheriff's department found no link between him and any terrorist group. Neither did the city cops or the feds, at least as far as I know."

"How about the possibility Thomas was in league with another individual, you know, another kid, maybe?" Nate stopped short of naming Jason.

"Nope. It's pretty much like the mayor says. In recent years there has been a rash of domestic acts of violence across the country, where one citizen directs his rage at a random group of others."

"The mayor said that?"

"He's running for office. His bottom line is America for Americans, take care of yourself, do for government, don't wait around for government to do for you. His rhetoric might sit easier if he was a self-made man, but he's riding on family money. Still, what he says makes sense to lots of folks. I wouldn't bet money on the other guy winning."

"Do you think the mayor's sentiments made sense to Mike?" Nate asked.

"Up to a point. Mike took things a step further. He was convinced these random acts were related, that there was someone behind them. In my humble opinion, teenagers aren't generally disciplined enough to organize some clandestine movement."

Gallant paused to scratch his jaw. He wore horn-rimmed glasses, and those came off next for a quick inspection before once again returning to the perch on his nose. "Around here, gun permits doubled after the shooting," he said, his voice softer. "No one felt safe. And now this thing with Peter. It's going to absolutely kill his parents."

Nate's gaze drifted to the view out the window. There was still snow on the ground and the skies were a clear, cold gray. A winter world, to be sure, but was it really such a threatening place that people were afraid to go outside without a weapon in case their neighbor went nuts? Scary thought.

But look at Peter Jacks. What had gone wrong?

Peter, lying by the river with an ax in his back, thanks to Nate. "Did Mike try to help anyone?"

The sheriff sipped at his cold coffee before answering. "Mike was in here all the time, spouting his favorite conspiracy theory about some evil mastermind at work behind the scenes."

"Did he say who he suspected?"

"Not to me."

"Did he ever mention anything about the Washington Memorial or Monument?"

Gallant looked slightly pained. "Yeah. I heard about that."

"Did you tell anyone with the authority to guard, say, the Washington Monument on Presidents' Day?"

"Nate, now listen. The feds are always on the alert during crowd situations and especially on holidays. You think the little old sheriff from Shatterhorn, Nevada, is going to tell them something they don't know? For that matter, do you think they'd actually listen to me?"

Nate took a deep, frustrated breath. "I guess you have a point."

"Well, Mike sure as heck didn't think I had a point. I told him to leave the matter to the government and all those counterterrorist experts. If there was really some kind of conspiracy, domestic or foreign, they'd find it. But he wouldn't listen. If he wasn't lecturing me or the city council or trying to get things published in the paper, he was showing up at meetings where he didn't belong. Made a real nuisance of himself."

"Enough so that someone wanted to kill him?"

Gallant shook his head. "Heck, I don't know. Does his daughter have any idea who wanted her father dead?"

"No," Nate said and, anxious to change the subject away from Sarah, added, "I'd like to get my truck towed into town and repaired."

"You're kind of hard on your vehicles," Gallant said with a chuckle.

"Very funny. I'm not the one who keeps shooting at them."

The sheriff sobered right up. "I'll let you know as soon as you can. I need to go talk with the Jacks family and then drive out to the Donovan farm. You come back in the morning, okay? Don't leave town, by the way."

"Am I being charged with something?"

"Not right now. But you're in the business—you know there will be more questions."

"I've taken a leave of absence for a few months," Nate said.

Gallant looked surprised. "Mind if I ask why?"

"Just trying to get some things straight. I needed a little time."

"I see." He pried himself out of his chair and took his jacket from a hook on the wall. "If Sarah doesn't show up by tomorrow night, I'm going to get a warrant to bring her in for questioning."

"She'll be here," Nate said, not sure if she would or not. "All right if I go now?"

"Sure. Where are you staying?"

"I don't know."

"Try the Motorcoach Inn. It's a little on the old side, but they got cable TV, a free breakfast, and the coffee shop next door isn't bad for dinner."

Nate stood and offered a hand. The resulting shake just about jarred him out of his boots. He put his hat back on his head and buttoned up Mike's old coat, something else he would need to replace.

"How about your arm?" the sheriff asked, apparently noticing the gingerly way Nate pulled on the jacket. Nate had told him about the shot, of course, and the fact that he believed he'd wounded the shooter in return.

"I'll have it looked at tomorrow," Nate said. "All I want now is something to eat, a hot shower and eight uninterrupted hours in the sack."

He figured he'd be lucky to get even one of those.

NATE ASKED FOR a corner table away from any windows at the back of the restaurant and took the chair that faced the door. He'd come across the parking lot to eat as soon as he'd checked in, before taking a shower, even, and imagined he looked like something his dog had pulled from under a rock. He'd had a feeling, however, that once undressed and clean, he'd fall into a coma. It had been a good long time since he'd had anything to eat, and his stomach was grumbling.

Now he watched everyone who entered, looking for anyone who acted uncomfortable or out of place. A man would have to be nuts not to be cautious when two different people on two different occasions tried to kill him on the same day. And maybe yesterday, too… What had he done to deserve all this very unflattering—and deadly—attention? He had absolutely no idea.

Though he detested using a cell phone in a restaurant, there was no one else seated close by, so he employed the time between ordering and eating to make a call to Alex Foster's house. Hopefully he'd be home by now or Jessica would know where he was. But Nate's call went straight to voice mail. The message he left was short and to the point.

Dinner was hot, substantial and filled some of the hollow spots that had been growing inside him for the past couple of days. His waitress resembled Debbie, his ex, right down to her lush curves and black curls. She had the same high-pitched laugh, too, the same way of using a hundred words to say what could be accomplished with ten, and it came as something of a surprise to Nate that he was glad he wasn't going to spend his life dealing with Debbie's nonstop chatter.

Which brought to mind Sarah's way of talking, the words she chose, the sound of her voice, and from there, it didn't take too big a leap to zero in on the shape of her lips as she formed those words, the taste of her mouth and the stirring in his loins that thinking of all this created.

He needed some cold air on his face, and he paid his bill, leaving a big tip for his waitress in a vague, convoluted apology to all the ways he'd failed Debbie. Maybe she'd been right. Maybe she hadn't left him; maybe he'd left her.

Before Nate walked back into the night, he asked to

borrow the restaurant's phone book. He wasn't sure the motel room would have one, and he knew once he was close to a shower and bed, he wouldn't want to leave again. Using his own cell, he first dialed the airport, where he asked if Alex had landed his plane and was assured he hadn't. Then Nate called the mayor's house. A male employee with a crisp, cultivated voice answered and revealed the mayor was out of town until the day after tomorrow. Leaning against the wall, Nate flipped through Mike's notebook and decided to call the editor of the newspaper, Stewart Netters. Though it was late, the man answered the phone himself. He seemed pleased to hear from Nate and agreed to meet him in his office the next afternoon, even though it was a Sunday.

Nate had to find Mike's killer, not only to avenge his friend, but because there was the off chance that the attempts on his own life were somehow connected to Mike's murder. Nate wanted to figure this out, put a stop to it and get back to Arizona and his ranch and his life. He'd hoped to find answers of some sort in Shatterhorn, but what he had gotten were more questions.

It was dark by the time he walked outside, and the melting snow had started to refreeze, making it slippery as all get-out. He kept to the shadows, waiting for something to happen—a gunshot, a racing engine, heck, a bomb landing at his feet. He found himself looking over his shoulder, walking as fast as he dared. He hated feeling vulnerable, and it was a relief when he closed the door and locked it, sliding home the deadbolt, claiming his space.

"His space" was hopelessly old-fashioned, but what it lacked in character, it made up for in cleanliness. The drapes were closed, the bed looked comfortable and he'd hope for the best when it came to the shower behind the closed bathroom door.

He wasted no time easing his arm out of the sleeves of the jacket and shirt, both Mike's. On his way back to Shatterhorn, he'd stopped at a clothing store, where he'd bought himself some essentials. That bag sat on the chair beside the door, promising clean, warm clothes that actually fit for the next morning. He fought off a yawn as he stripped off the rest of his things.

He was putting his watch on the nightstand when he heard a shower go on so close by it had to be right next door. He groaned. If his neighbor was using this exact time to shower, what would that do to his own water pressure in a place this ancient?

Wait a second. Did he really care? No, not really. A hot trickle would do for tonight.

He opened the bathroom door to find that the water sounded as though it was running in his room because it was. Steam billowed out of the corner shower. Did the unit next door share this bathroom or had the motel mistakenly double-booked the room? He stared at the opaque shower door, trying to discern if the trespasser was male or female, but it was useless. He grabbed a towel from the rack and tied it around his waist as he considered the best way to handle the situation.

And that was when the clothes hanging on a hook behind the door caught his attention. He didn't recognize the white dress, but the equestrian boots sitting in a corner— they were a different matter. He blinked a couple of times and really opened his weary eyes. A purse the color of an old saddle perched on the back of the vanity and beside it sat a brand-new box of condoms. A smile spread his lips. He was suddenly wide-awake.

Chapter Twelve

Sarah jumped as the shower door opened. Even though she knew whom to expect, the past couple of days had cautioned her to be prepared for surprises, but this time there was no gunman, no threat, just Nate standing there giving her a lingering once-over, wearing nothing but a white towel.

And from the look in his eyes, to say nothing of the obvious engorgement beneath the terry cloth, he was just as happy to see her as she was to see him. She hadn't been sure he'd feel that way. Every inch of her body burst into excited flames that made the steamy water feel tepid against her heated skin.

"Are you going to stand there all night and ogle me?" she said.

"Not *all* night. Mind if I join you?"

She smiled. "What do you think?"

"I think I've never seen anyone in the world look better wet and naked." He threw aside the towel as he stepped into the small shower and closed the door. He slipped his arms around her waist. "How in the world did you find me?" he asked.

"I looked in every motel parking lot until I found a truck covered with bullet holes with a cardboard insert in the back window. Then I told the guy in the office I was your wife."

"So much for security."

"Has anyone else tried to…well…"

"Kill me? Not since Reno. And now you're here. The sheriff will be beside himself."

"And how about you?" she asked, staring into his eyes. "Are you beside yourself, too?"

"I'm giddy," he said and nuzzled her neck. She knew how he felt about seeing her, at least in a physical way. There was no hiding that.

"I brought you a present," she added.

He opened his hand and she found that he'd opened the box of condoms and brought one with him into the shower. She threw back her head and laughed. He put an end to that by pulling her against his powerful chest and claiming her lips.

The kiss started out hot and quickly boiled over. Sarah had never quite been kissed that way before, even by Johnny. So deep and long, like intercourse with tongues. Maybe it was because she'd brazenly initiated this scenario with Nate or maybe it was because she hadn't been positive he would welcome her, but she felt dizzy with the desire to touch and explore every solid, throbbing inch of him as his fingers set off discovering her.

He backed her against the tile and leaned in to kiss her neck, licking her ear, his hands gently fondling her breasts, his mouth dipping to suck rock-hard nipples, his erection hard against her abdomen. "I want to take it slow," he said, his voice almost a whisper, but that just fanned the fire, and she knew if this wasn't consummated within seconds, she would come completely undone. Kiss led to kiss, water sprayed and dripped. He touched her between her legs, his fingers gentle but insistent, his need echoing her own. She closed her eyes, consumed with passion, desperate to be closer. He lifted her bottom in his hands and she wrapped her legs around him; somehow he'd managed to put on the condom while she'd been soaring who knew where, and then he was inside her.

She gasped with the pure vibrancy and strength of his thrusts, the way he filled every crevice of her body from her brain to her toes, like an invading army with a take-no-prisoners approach. Her eyelashes fluttered against her cheeks and she saw his face through the water, both confident and lost, suffused with ecstasy that drove her over the edge at the same moment he leaned his head against her throat and exploded inside of her.

For several minutes, he kissed her, still holding her against him, then her feet touched the tile and she opened her eyes.

The smile on his face as he looked down at her was one of wonder. He smoothed her hair away from her face. "You're the sexiest, warmest, most slippery lover in the world," he whispered, his eyes devouring her. "So much for making it last," he added.

She touched the skin around the wound on his shoulder, but he didn't flinch. "You can make it last next time," she said. "Let me wash this wound for you."

He leaned against the shower wall as she found the tiny bar of soap and worked it into a lather against the hair on his chest, gently rubbing the resulting suds against his wounded skin. It really did look 100 percent better, and from the way he'd made love to her, she knew it must feel better, as well. From his biceps to his well-defined pectorals, down lower to his washboard abs, she followed the newly cleaned and rinsed skin with small kisses, smiling when he groaned with pleasure.

This time, they ended up in the bed, still damp but obliv-

ious to anyone or anything but each other. And this time
he made it last so long that the sheets all but incinerated.

When at last they were both replete, they lay in the dark,
wrapped in each other's arms, tucked beneath the quilt and
blankets, warm and content. Sarah had been exhausted
when she got off the bus from Reno, but now she felt all
tingly and strangely ravenous.

"I didn't expect you here tonight," he whispered against
her hair.

"I like to be unexpected."

He kissed her forehead. "Come on, Sarah, tell me."

"Tell you what?"

"Where's Diana? The last I heard, you felt you had to
stay in Reno a day or two to help her get settled."

Sarah cuddled deeper in the crook of his arm. "Nate,
come on, I don't want to talk about my mother right now,
okay?"

The bed shifted as he transferred weight to his side to
reach the bedside lamp. Sarah blinked against the light,
and when she looked at him again, she found his gray gaze
focused on her face.

"Oh, all right," she said, partially sitting up but keeping the blankets close for warmth. "She refused to stay at
the hospital and they said it wasn't necessary anyway. She
wanted to go back to her apartment, so I took her there."
Sarah rested her head atop her bent knees. All the peace
she'd discovered in this room with this man seemed to
be fizzing away like fragile bubbles escaping a glass of
champagne.

"What happened?" he asked, sitting beside her now.
He kissed her shoulder, and when she turned her head to
look at him, his lips moved to her mouth.

"I took a shower and borrowed some clothes from her.
She asked me to go down the block to the store to get

something we could fix for dinner, so I did. When I got
to the counter, I found I didn't have any cash."

"Had Bellows robbed you?"

She shook her head. "I know there was money in my
bag when he gave me back my stuff. I saw it. But at the
store, I literally didn't even have a single dollar. I'd paid
for Mom's care at the hospital with a credit card. There
was only one person who had been alone with my wallet
since then, and you can guess who that was."

"How much did she take?"

"A hundred dollars or so. I put the groceries on a debit
card and went back to her place, but I was on foot, so this
all took a while. She was gone when I got there. No note,
no nothing. I wondered if those two men had come after
her again, or maybe Poulter had heard she suddenly had
money.... I don't know. I was just about to call the police."

"Why didn't you?"

"Because one of her neighbors knocked on the door and
asked if she was back yet. He wanted the twenty bucks she
owed him. I assumed he'd been aware she was missing for
a few days and started to explain, but he stopped me. He'd
met up with her while walking down the sidewalk an hour
or so before and had asked her for his money. She'd told
him she was just going to go get it. She'd be back soon."

"Uh-oh."

"Yeah. I obviously went down the same sidewalk. The
first place I came to was a hole-in-the-wall bar, and sure
enough, there she was, black eye, bandages and all, playing the slots, drinking whiskey and flirting with someone I imagine she saw as a good prospect. Don't ask me
what the guy was a good prospect for because I'm not
going to tell you."

"What did she say when you spoke to her?"

"Who says I spoke to her?"

"You didn't?"

"Nope. I walked back to her place and left her a note telling her I was going to Shatterhorn to settle things with the police and would bring her car back in a few days. I'm not even sure why I did that much." She sighed deeply.

"But, Sarah, this is a pattern with her and her addiction, isn't it? Why did you choose this time to walk away?"

She looked straight into his eyes. "Because of you."

"Me?"

"Yeah. I could tell you were disappointed when I didn't agree to come back here with you. I could also tell that you were about to walk away from whatever is happening between us."

He didn't respond, so she continued. "When I saw her sitting in that bar and going at the slot machine, it all just gelled in my head. Someone is trying to kill you, and there I was, wasting my time with someone who didn't need me, not really. You've done nothing but protect me from practically the moment we met. With you, I can make a difference. I can watch your back. My presence will mean something. With her, I'm just an obstacle on the way to getting what she wants, and that's been true my whole life. So I chose to go where I could make a difference. I chose you."

He smiled at her, but was there also a flash of panic in those foggy gray eyes? Maybe she'd said too much. She smiled to lighten the mood. "Honestly, I'm just tired of being angry with her. She sneaks around, she connives and she lies. I'm done." Sarah chanced another glance at Nate. "Does that make me a horrible person?"

"I'm the wrong person to ask," Nate said.

"Why?"

He rested his forehead against her shoulder. "I've lied to you, too, Sarah."

"Oh, God, I don't want to hear this," she said. "Okay, what are you, still engaged? Oh, no, you're not already married, are you?"

"No, nothing like that. It's just that I'm not a cop anymore."

"That's it? Why?"

He swallowed and studied his hands. "Why am I not a cop or why did I keep it from you?"

"Both, I guess."

"I didn't want to say it out loud. I guess that's the answer to why I didn't tell you. As for the other, well, I took a leave to try to figure things out." He cast her a swift look and added, "The sheriff of our county is a real political type with eyes set on becoming governor. He wants hungry go-getters on his team. When I admitted that didn't really define me anymore, he encouraged me to run for sheriff when he left. I don't know if I want that. I don't know who I am anymore."

"I know who you are," she said, looking deep into his eyes as she ran her fingers along his jaw and up into his hair. Her last relationship had ended over a year before, and since then, she'd sworn off men, thinking they were all alike and you couldn't trust a single one of them.

She'd been wrong.

"You're kind and generous and sexy as all get-out. You're strong, Nate."

"Strong men don't run away," he mumbled.

"Do you call what you've been doing the past two days 'running away'? Really? Listen, I read something once that makes sense to me now that I've gotten to know you. It was about a study done with people who survive horrendous accidents or incidents. They found that the more a person was actually responsible for the safety of others or perceived themselves to be, the harder recovery was for them. So a pilot or a stewardess suffered a heck of a lot more than a passenger. That's what you're fighting, the feeling that you should have been able to subdue Thomas Jacks, when the truth is you were as unarmed as everyone else at that mall."

"But—"

"No, Nate. No buts." She kissed his neck. "You know, actions speak louder than words. How about you come closer and I'll demonstrate what kind of man you are?"

She didn't have to ask twice.

THEY AWOKE EARLY the next morning, still tangled in each other's arms. Nate had wondered if Sarah would feel shy or awkward with him after the night they'd spent, but her eyes and lips were as warm as ever, and a dangerous warmth glowed in his heart.

"You didn't have a nightmare last night," she whispered against his neck. "Or did you?"

"No," he said. "I'm not sure if it's because I barely got any sleep or because you're here. Either way, you get the credit."

She kissed his nose. "I'll put it on your therapy bill."

He dressed in his new clothes while Sarah put on the white dress that must belong to her mother. It was a little short and loose, but she cinched it in at the waist with her own leather belt. Dressed in the white wool sheath with the boots covering her legs, she looked incredibly put together. Nate fought down the desire to strip her out of her clothes.

They were too hungry to settle for the frozen waffles, tiny boxes of cereal and basket of bananas the motel served as their free breakfast. Instead they walked across the parking lot to the diner where it appeared half the town ate. Nate scanned the parking lot as they crossed, uncertain how best to shield Sarah in such a wide-open spot. In a way he wished she'd stayed in Reno, where she would have been safe.

Oh, hell, who was he kidding?

They ordered pancakes, bacon, coffee and juice and sat side by side at the only two open seats, which happened to be at the counter. It was the first real meal they'd ever eaten together.

Nate had given the place and its patrons a once-over before they sat down. If it had been him looking for an opportunity to pick someone off, he would have staked out this café the night before and would now be sitting behind a newspaper, biding his time, waiting for the opportunity to attack, which would present itself sooner or later.

He could see no one lurking suspiciously behind the morning paper. It might have been a big relief if he had.

Sarah finally had the opportunity to study her father's notebook as they ate, and she finished scanning the pages as they drove to the sheriff's office. "It looks like one's been torn out," she commented.

"I saw that."

"That might be important," she said.

"Or it might be part of his editing process. Maybe he just didn't like what he'd written."

She closed the book and wrapped a rubber band around the pages. "I can't believe the leaps he made. *Pearl* refers to Pearl Harbor? And he connected a Fourth of July shooting with these other situations. But really, they happened all over the country, didn't they?"

"Yeah. What they have in common is young shooters who all either killed themselves or were killed, and holidays like the Fourth of July, Labor Day, Veterans Day, the anniversary of the attack on Pearl Harbor," Nate said.

"And what national holiday is next? Presidents' Day?

That's, like, tomorrow, isn't it? I've sort of lost track of the date."

"Tomorrow," Nate repeated, a little stunned. He'd lost track, too.

"What about the twenty-eight circled in red?"

He shook his head. "Not sure. By the way, have you ever heard of a guy named Morris Denton?"

She seemed to consider his question for a second before responding. "Can't say I have. Should I know who he is?"

"Not necessarily. I've heard his name mentioned in connection with a support organization focused on youth."

"Dad didn't mention him, too?"

"Not in those pages, which seems odd."

"Maybe that's the page he ripped out."

"And maybe he just discounted the guy. Maybe, maybe."

"What about Washington and a memorial?"

Nate cast her a quick glance. "I'm wondering if he meant 'monument,' as in the Washington Monument."

"Oh, no. Nate, who do we warn? Maybe there'll be another shooting tomorrow. We've got to try and stop it."

"This is all suppositions and connecting dots that may or may not go together. Just because there've been several events on weakly linked days doesn't mean the explanation is a huge plot. What would be the point of such a thing? Anyway, your dad was trying to make this point, but no one was listening to him. No one took him seriously."

"Not even his own daughter," Sarah said with a shake of her head.

"If it helps anything, I didn't score high on the list, either."

"At least you came when he called."

"I didn't come for him. I told myself I did, but it's not the truth. Anyway, we have a full day ahead of us. First the sheriff and then the editor of the paper."

"You're going to ask Netters what he and my dad talked about?"

"Yeah."

"I wonder how Jason is doing. I heard he was at the mall that day and that a couple of his friends were shot—" She stopped abruptly.

Nate knew his whole body had tensed as she spoke.

Her hand floated over to touch his thigh. "Me and my big mouth," she whispered. "For a second I forgot you were there with them."

"I wish I could forget," he said, and they finished the drive in silence.

SHERIFF GALLANT GREETED them with the news that he'd released both cars, and as he spoke with Sarah privately, Nate arranged to have the vehicles towed from the ranch while one of his deputies went out to catalog the damage to the rental. He was lucky the garage was willing to tow on a Sunday—a lot of small-town businesses shut down completely on the weekends.

Nate joined Gallant and Sarah after an hour or so. He was relieved to discover Sarah had been totally honest about everything, including the coins. Her father's will lay on Gallant's desk and the sheriff informed them they would all drive out to the ranch to clear up a couple of issues.

"The tech guys were out there all night gathering evidence," he said. "Looks like your attacker was shooting a .22. As for the coins, I don't see that the coins your father left you had much to do with anything. Still, best we recover them and get them someplace safe until this is all figured out."

"How did Peter Jacks's mom and dad take the news?" Nate asked, but if there was a dumber question in the world, he didn't know what it was. How many times had he had to tell someone's parents they'd lost their child, and how did they always take it? The fact Peter had been killed while attacking people only made it harder to hear, let alone understand.

"Pretty bad. I had the doctor come out and give Betty Jacks a tranquilizer. Peter's dad is just sitting there like a zombie."

"I wish I hadn't had to kill him," Nate said.

Sarah touched his arm. "You had no choice unless it was to let me die, and then he would have come after you."

"Sarah's story confirms what you told us, so we're not bringing any charges against you, Nate. The team that went over the cabin crime scene found out where Peter had been waiting over in the rocks, probably a couple of hours or more. There were a half dozen cigarette butts and some binoculars. If he hadn't been downwind from you, you probably would have known he was there because of the smell of the smoke."

"I wonder why he didn't just burst into the cabin while we were sleeping," Sarah said.

"I think he was working up his courage," the sheriff said, "but he might have also worried Nate was armed and wanted you out in the open to use as leverage."

Nate thought about it a moment and realized he'd probably never know the truth. The only man who knew was dead.

Wait—was that so? If it was, who had shot at him a few hours later in Carson City?

"Funny that Peter Jacks wasn't carrying any identification on him," the sheriff added. "Same with his brother, you know."

"Yeah."

"His folks say he's been out of town, just got back the night before he was killed."

"Did the M.E. find any gunshot wounds on Peter's body?"

"No. If you wounded someone out at the ranch, it wasn't him."

"Did his parents say where he'd been?"

"No. They say he's been hanging around with the Netters boy, Jason. I'll talk to him later. Still, I don't get the timing and I don't get the vendetta against you. It doesn't make sense."

"Did you hear back from the cops in Carson City?" Nate asked.

"Yeah, but there wasn't much to tell. By the time they got there, rooms eight and twelve had been wiped clean of prints. It's not even clear who owns the property. The gunman wasn't still hanging around the parking lot next door—no one thought he would be. And there are no neighbors to speak of, so no witnesses." Gallant paused before adding, "The police would like to ask you a few questions. They asked me to tell you to come on back and help them clear this up."

"I'll settle with them later," Nate promised. He had no idea what he could tell them—he simply didn't know much.

Revisiting the ranch was a gloomy, depressing affair. As Sarah had reported, the scorched house still stood. Mike's body had been removed the night before by the sheriff's department, but his ghost hovered just the same, tangled in the crime-scene tape, mingled with ashes, blowing in the breeze. Sarah got more and more withdrawn as they retraced the movements of two days before. The signs of their struggles—the broken glass, discarded saddle rifle, bloody bandages, bare walls and turned-up carpets—all looked garish in the cool light of day.

She'd grown up here, and in the past two days, her dad had been gunned down in cold blood and her mother had imploded. When they entered Skipjack's empty stall, her gaze went to the corner under the feed rack. By the time it was necessary for Nate to leave in order to meet up with Stewart Netters, she'd walked outside and stood staring up at the sky.

"Do you want to come to the newspaper office with me?" he asked her.

"I don't think so," she said. "Sheriff Gallant says he'll help me get the rest of the coins into town. He'll keep them safe in a police vault until the bank opens tomorrow, then I'll transfer them until the will is probated and all this legal stuff is worked out. That means I need a lawyer, too. I wonder if everything will be open on Presidents' Day."

"I don't think the banks are open," Nate said.

"Then I'll wait around until the day after tomorrow."

"Which begs the question of what we're going to do about this perceived threat your dad danced around concerning Washington and Presidents' Day," Nate muttered, as though talking to himself. He came up with an answer. "I'll call Dan Perry. He works with me, well, worked with me when I worked. His brother is an FBI agent. Maybe Dan can get him on board. I don't know."

"It's better than nothing," Sarah said, but her face revealed she thought it had as much chance of making a difference as he did, and that wasn't much.

"I also want to grab my suitcase out of Mom's car and go to the vet to see about boarding Skipjack for a while longer," she added.

"What will you eventually do with him?" Nate asked.

"I guess I'll sell him. Breaks my heart, though."

"Sell him to me."

She finally looked at him. "You?"

"Sure. I've got room for another horse. I can hook up a trailer to the truck and haul him back to Arizona with me. Truth is, I've grown pretty fond of him."

"There's a trailer out behind the barn you can use," she said. "In fact, you can have it."

"Deal. And you can come visit him whenever you're down my way."

Sarah smiled, the first one Nate had seen since she'd stepped foot on the ranch. He cupped her chin with his fingers and kissed her.

"Watch your back," she whispered as his lips left hers. "Don't forget someone wants you dead."

Chapter Thirteen

The newspaper office consisted of a half dozen rooms all accessible through a lobby outfitted with a glass door. It was empty on a Sunday afternoon, but there was a note on the receptionist's desk addressed to Nate, telling him to come back to the editor's office. As Nate had visited the past September, he knew his way around.

He entered a large office with a black desk at one end and a gathering of soft chairs at the other. The walls were covered with plaques and framed photographs surrounding a cabinet that Nate recalled housed marksman trophies that Stew Netters had collected over the years.

Netters, a compact fifty-five-year-old with a prominent Adam's apple, sat behind the desk. He was wearing a gray sweater and jeans. He had hair like his son's, though the blond strands were sprinkled with gray. He was busily taking notes while the mayor, seated in front of the desk, spoke.

Mayor Bliss was older than Netters by a couple of years and appeared extremely fit, sporting an out-of-season tan that showcased the brightness of his teeth when he smiled. He looked prosperous and sure of himself, and Nate had read that he won every election by a landslide. According to Gallant, this November would bring the same results.

A small lapel pin shaped like a waving American flag festooned the lapel of a dark blue suit.

There were hearty handshakes all around before Nate sat in the chair Netters indicated. "I understood you were out of town," Nate said, addressing the mayor.

"Just got home this morning."

"George flies himself all over the state," Netters said. "He's got his fingers in a dozen enterprises."

"Family business," Mayor Bliss explained. "My grandfather started Bliss Chocolate fifty years ago. The old man would turn over in his grave if I let it flounder, and that takes a hands-on approach, despite my elected office."

Netters drummed his fingers on the desktop as though he'd heard this spiel before. "Did you fly up from Arizona?" he asked Nate.

"No, this time I drove. I came to see Mike Donovan."

"I just heard he was killed the day before yesterday," Netters said, sitting forward.

"Yes, I know."

Enlightenment dawned on Netters's smooth face. "Of course. Gallant wouldn't release any names, but the buzz around town is there was a standoff of some kind out there. Did you have anything to do with that?"

Nate shrugged.

"How about giving me the story?"

"When the sheriff says it's okay," Nate said.

The mayor shook his head. His buzz-cut hair and the tan made him look ex-military. His mouth was on the small side and his lips were currently pursed. "It's the people's right to know what mayhem is brewing in their own city," he said. "Especially after last Labor Day. People are nervous, and another killing is just going to make things worse."

"There'll be more gun permits issued, you wait and see," Netters said.

"Speaking of which, didn't you just buy Jason a gun?" Bliss asked.

"I did," the editor said, nodding. "Although I debated the purchase."

"Why?" the mayor asked.

"He's young," the editor said.

"You're never too young to protect yourself and your family in these troubled times," Bliss commented. "People tend to think the government is going to take care of them. How much did that belief help those poor children at the mall last year?"

"Yeah, well, that's what Morris Denton told the boy. Anyway, I'm hoping it will give him a leg up come fall."

Nate thought of that troubled kid with a weapon and inwardly cringed. He also decided to play dumb about Denton. "Morris Denton? Who's he?"

"A philanthropist," Netters said. "He started this whole grassroots camp located on several acres up in the mountains. B-Strong, it's called. He gets kids from all over. Jason went to one of his workshops not long ago. He really seemed to change after that."

"In what way?" Nate asked.

"More sure of himself. Knows what he wants now. He's going to join the military when he turns eighteen in October. Helped him find himself."

"Have you ever met Denton?" Nate asked.

Netters shook his head. "Not yet, but I will. I think it's high time someone interviews Denton and takes a look around B-Strong. Too little is known about it and about Denton himself, especially since Thomas Jacks spent a few weeks late last summer at his camp."

"As a matter of fact, I wanted to ask about Thomas's

brother, Peter," Nate said. "Did he attend the workshop with Jason?"

Netters nodded. "I think he's the reason Jason wanted to go. They've been hanging out together."

"It doesn't sound as though you know Peter Jacks is dead," Nate said, watching both men.

Netters sat forward. "Dead? When? How?"

"Yesterday," Nate said. "He was about to shoot someone else."

Netters looked truly shocked. "My God."

Bliss spoke up. "Who was he going to shoot?"

"Mike's daughter, Sarah Donovan."

"Sarah is back in Shatterhorn?"

"She's the one who found her father's body," Nate said.

Stew Netters ran a hand through his sandy hair as though giving himself a moment for all this to sink in. He stood abruptly and took a few steps toward the door. "That damn Gallant is keeping things from me. I've got to get some reporters in here."

"Did you hurt yourself?" Nate asked, his voice kind of quiet. Netters had a pronounced limp.

"Damn arthritis in my left knee. Doc wants to replace it—I don't know, guess I'm dragging my feet. Where does that secretary keep my phone book?"

Nate studied the man as he searched a nearby shelf, looking for any sign of equivocation. Was arthritis really why he limped or had he been wounded by a bullet from Mike's saddle rifle, a bullet Nate had fired? There was just no way to tell without saying a lot more than he had any intention of saying. Instead, he asked, "Before you get back to work, would you please take a few minutes to tell me what you and Mike talked about the last time you saw him?"

Netters seemed to look longingly at the door, but eventually he limped back behind his desk and sat. His turned-down mouth and wrinkled brow suggested he didn't much like recalling Mike's last visit. Before he could launch into his story, the mayor spoke up.

"Was that the day Mike burst in here?" he asked. "You remember, Stew. You and I were just chewing the fat when Donovan showed up."

"Yeah, I remember," Netters said. "How could I forget? It was last week sometime. He pushed his way past the receptionist and plowed through the door."

"Why was he so angry?" Nate asked.

"Because I wouldn't print his half-baked theories about some countrywide conspiracy."

"He talked to you about those?" Nate asked.

"He talked to everyone. Man couldn't get enough of hearing his own voice," Netters said. "He thought there was one person behind all of the shootings with some crazy agenda, but he had no facts, just a lot of jumping from one big idea to the next. I don't think his feet ever touched down."

"So, he wanted you to interview him and float his theories?"

"That's about it. When I refused, he started insinuating I was part of the conspiracy. He called my newspaper 'biased.' Those are fighting words to a newspaperman like me. He was steaming hot under the collar, calling me names and threatening me."

"Threatening you in what way?" Nate asked.

"I don't remember," the editor said, his gaze shifting to the floor.

The mayor jumped in. "He said if he could prove you were part of this so-called conspiracy, he'd see you hang."

Netters seemed to blanch. "Donovan kept waving an old leather book wrapped up with rubber bands in my face.

He swore he had proof. He was fishing—I don't think he knew a damn thing. I mean, does he think he's the only one who's been working on figuring all this out? I've got my suspicions about what's going on, too, but you don't find me attacking people. Man, the jerk was practically foaming at the mouth."

"He wasn't the only one," Mayor Bliss said softly.

Netters frowned. "Okay, I admit it. I got angry, too. Who did he think he was, coming in here and acting like he had a right to say any damn thing he liked? I punched him, okay, I did, but it was provoked, wasn't it, George?"

The mayor shrugged. "Violence rarely solves anything, Stew—you know that. And Mike Donovan along with Mr. Matthews here and Alex Foster did come to the town's aid last Labor Day and help prevent that tragedy from being any worse. You yourself called them 'heroes.' I hailed them as patriots.

"Mike said he was going to call you and Alex," he added. "He said he wanted to get your feedback. Did he have a chance to talk to you before he died?"

"No," Nate said.

"You shouldn't have come here," the editor mumbled. "It's like you're a catalyst or something."

Nate didn't respond to the comment.

"Anyway," the editor continued, "all our compliments must have gone to Donovan's head." He looked at Nate and added, "After all, you didn't go psycho."

"Everyone copes in their own way," Nate murmured. "By the way, does the number twenty-eight mean anything to either of you?"

The mayor scrunched his brow. "Twenty-eight what?"

"I don't know," Nate admitted.

"Like a date?" Netters asked.

Nate shook his head. "Just wondered," he said.

The editor studied his hands for a moment, then looked defiantly at Nate. "I guess I shouldn't have punched Mike. I didn't like what he was insinuating. Rumors get started, a man's career goes up in smoke. You have to be careful what you say about people. Truth is, he was lucky I wasn't packing a piece or I would have shot him then and there."

His words, spoken softly and in light of what had eventually happened to Mike, fell like an atom bomb. And then someone cleared his throat and all three men turned to find Netters's son, Jason, standing right inside the door.

"Jason?" Netters said. "What are you doing here?"

Jason looked from his father to the mayor to Nate. "Nothing," he mumbled.

At that moment, the desk phone rang. Netters grabbed it, listened without taking his eyes off his son, then glanced at Nate. "It's for you," he said.

AFTER THE COINS had been locked in the evidence room at the sheriff's office, Sarah walked out to the sidewalk and checked her watch. Nate would still be at the editor's office and Sarah wanted no part of that. She'd heard the rumors about her father's behavior and she couldn't stand the thought of facing Stewart Netters.

But since she had some time and the garage was just a couple of blocks over, she might as well go get her mother's car and, more important, retrieve her suitcase from the backseat so she could put on some warmer jeans. As she walked, her brain finally kicked into gear. Now was her chance to drive out to the storage garage and see if her old boxes were in unit 118. She walked faster.

The garage was shorthanded on a slow, cold February afternoon. The green toad looked more dejected than ever as the man on duty, who had just finished replacing Nate's tires, looked up from his work.

"Bud," Sarah said, recognizing an old high school friend. "I didn't know you worked here."

Bud hit the button to lower the truck from the lift. "Hey, Sarah, it's been years," he said, reaching out to shake her hand, seeing the grease smudged on his and smiling instead.

She grabbed his hand and pressed it.

"Hey, your dress," he said.

She laughed. "It's okay. Boy, it's good to see you."

"You, too." He took a surprisingly clean rag out of his pocket and handed it to her. "I've been working with Dad since the economy took a downturn and I lost my job at the market. This pays better anyway, and seeing as I've got three kids to support, every bit comes in handy."

Sarah looked up from wiping away the tiny bit of grease on her fingers. "Three kids? Did you marry Janet Hawser?"

"Right after high school."

"That's great. You guys were a cute couple."

"Thanks. Hey, I heard about Johnny. Sorry. And now your dad. I don't know what this town is coming to. Getting so you're afraid to walk outside."

"Don't talk like that, Bud. You're raising kids. You have to have faith."

He grinned. "And a concealed-weapon permit. Listen, do they know who—"

"No, I'm afraid not. Not yet, anyway." She gestured at the car. "I came by to see if I can take this old wreck off your hands."

"Didn't Gallant tell you?"

"Tell me what?"

"It won't start. That's why we had to tow it in the first place."

Sarah's brows wrinkled. "Why wouldn't it start?"

"Heck if I know. I think the starter is shot, but Dad will have to check to make sure, and he won't be in until day after tomorrow. Then he'll have to order the part, but it won't take long to get here. Less than a day, probably."

Sarah sighed. "Rats."

"You need to get somewhere?"

"Yeah, just a couple of miles from here on the other side of the tunnel.... Wait, is Nate's truck drivable?"

"I guess so. It doesn't have a passenger window, but I got new tires put on and I vacuumed up the glass and stuff. It'll be pretty cold and you won't be able to lock it, is all."

"Then I'll borrow that, okay?"

"Do you have a key?"

She sighed again as the memory of Nate holding his keys in front of the window and repocketing them later surfaced in her mind. "No, he has them."

"I found a spare in a magnetic box in the rear tire well. Here, I'll get it for you and drive the truck out of the garage, okay?"

A few moments later, Bud gave her a hand up into Nate's truck, which he'd left running. She headed down the highway while cold air blew in through the broken window, chilling her to the bone. She zipped her jacket up to her chin with one hand and wished she had gloves and a hat. The road led through a long curvy tunnel at one point and the air in there seemed to have welled up right from the coldest spot in the world.

When she arrived at U-Lock Garages, she thought she'd made the trip for nothing, as the gate was closed. But as she sat there wishing she could figure out what code to input into the security lock, a white van approached. Sarah moved Nate's truck out of the way. The newcomer put in their number and the gate slowly opened, a sign on the inside warning that only one car should enter at a time. She quickly got behind the van and trailed it inside the gate, hoping it didn't take a code to get back out.

The row of tapioca-colored garages with red roofs stretched on for what appeared to be miles, crisscrossed now and again by roads leading to other rows of the same thing. The place had a desolate appearance. The van made the first left. Sarah followed the original row until a sign directed her to turn right. The numbers 114 to 118 were printed on a door that sat in the middle of a block of buildings. She parked the truck and tried the knob, which wasn't locked. A weak light went on, revealing four more metal rolling doors, two on each side of a ten-foot hallway. One-eighteen was the last unit on the right. She propped open the outside door with a wedge of wood that looked as though that was its intended purpose.

She could hear the buzzing of the timer light and hurried down the hall as she felt around for the paper-wrapped key in the depths of her handbag, where she'd deposited it the day before. Emerging with just the key, she closed it in her hand as she spied a piece of pink paper taped to the door. She unfolded that to find an eviction notice dated several weeks before, warning that the lock would be changed and the contents of the unit confiscated if her dad didn't settle his bill by the previous Friday. That was the day he had been killed. She stuffed the paper in her purse.

The padlock opened easily and she rolled up the door to reveal a very cold, very dark space piled high with shadowy boxes and other paraphernalia that looked as though it hadn't been sorted or attended to in years.

An electric lantern hung beside the door, and she flipped the switch, rather surprised when the light flickered on. Illumination did not mitigate the mess, but she did find that the boxes had been labeled with a black marker. Most seemed to hold old tax records and business papers from a decade or more before; some seemed to be her mother's old clothes, left behind in the divorce, but eventually, in the nearest corner, she came across the boxes she remembered packing so long ago. They had her initials printed on them in her dad's writing.

For a second, she stood there and tried to feel his presence in the tiny room, but she couldn't. He had to have been the one to bring everything here. She found a solid box to sit on, knowing the white wool dress would need a trip to the cleaners after this, and opened the first of three boxes.

Stuffed animals, rolled posters, boxes full of cheap jewelry, a collection of old CDs. She moved the box aside and opened the next one.

Under a layer of folded sweaters from a lifetime ago, she found the letters Johnny had written her, all stacked together, tied with a blue ribbon. She knew the exact date of the one she wanted and riffled through them until she found it. She opened the letter and stared at the words, reliving for a second that May day when Johnny had slipped it into her hand.

Baby, it began, *don't cry. I promised you...*

The resounding slam of a closing metal door banged nearby and Sarah almost fell from her perch atop the box. Still holding the stack of letters, she peeked out into the hallway, which was now heavily shadowed as the hall light had gone off and the outside door was no longer open.

Had the wind blown it closed?

Sarah stuffed the dozen or so letters into her purse and walked toward the door. She was afraid to open it because it felt as if someone was out there, waiting for her to emerge. She switched on the overhead light again and went back to relock the garage, then worked up her courage, finally opening the outside door.

The truck sat just as she'd left it, looking more than ever like a casualty of war with its broken window and line of bullet holes running down the side. She couldn't see anyone else, but there was a feeling of being watched that raised goose bumps on her arms. She glanced toward the highway, but it appeared empty, too. The wind had come up and blew down the narrow storage-lot roads like the icy breath of a ghost.

Sarah's heartbeat thumped in her throat as she scurried around to climb inside the truck. She locked the doors despite the missing window. Gunning the engine, she made a quick U-turn and headed toward the gate.

It turned out she did need a code to exit. Opening her window, she tried her father's birth date on the number pad, then the ranch address and a half dozen other numbers until she actually ran up against a memory of coming here with her father when she was a little girl. He'd made a big deal out of revealing the code was Sarah's birthday. She'd assumed he'd changed it. She popped in the numbers and watched as the gate rolled back.

She glanced at her watch as she turned onto the highway and realized this had all taken longer than she'd thought. Nate was probably wondering where she'd taken his truck. She drove faster, switching on her lights when she got to the tunnel.

It was about twenty feet long and made a curve in the middle. Sarah had driven through it a thousand times in her life and she knew you had to slow down to make the turn. The exit was also on a curve and as a kid she'd been terrified the first time she sat behind the wheel, then exhilarated as her expertise increased and it became something of a challenge to accomplish the turns smoothly.

Today she barely thought about it at all until she was aware of lights suddenly popping up in her rearview mirror. They were right behind her as though they'd come out of nowhere, dropped from above or wrenched from the roadbed. Her instinct was to hit the brakes, but that would have created a collision, so she was forced to speed up instead. The lights moved out from behind her as if to pass, and she gripped the wheel tightly because the idiot was going to be in the wrong lane at a critical moment on the curve. If someone was coming the other way, it was going to be nasty....

The larger vehicle suddenly loomed beside her. The next thing she knew, it had rammed in her door, shoving Nate's truck against the rock sides of the tunnel. The sound of screeching metal filled the cab as pieces of the truck flew off and disappeared in a flurry of sparks.

She tried applying the brakes, but the other truck was still pressing her inward. And then with a roar, it took off and sped out of sight around the curve. Meanwhile, Nate's truck was still ground against the wall as though it couldn't break free. She was almost around the bend herself. The truck finally broke away and shot out of the tunnel, Sarah fighting for control as the next curve was immediately upon her. She almost made it, too, but at the last minute, one of Nate's tires climbed a boulder, rearing like a stallion before falling back to earth in a lopsided crash. Sarah took a breath, thinking the worst was over, but it wasn't. The truck found a passage through the boulders and took off down the slope of the ravine, gaining speed.

Her foot still on the brake, Sarah rode the truck through bushes, headed for trees, snow flying in the wake until it came to an abrupt halt. The deployed air bag pinned her back against the seat.

By then she couldn't feel a thing.

Chapter Fourteen

By the time Nate left the editor's office, the skies above were dark and foreboding. While inside the windowless room, he'd overheard rumors that another storm was in the offing. Now, walking into the cold wind, it wasn't hard to believe.

He'd been called in by Gallant because Morris Denton had made an appointment to talk to the sheriff's department and Gallant thought Nate might want to sit in on the interview. While it had been hard to leave the editor's office at that exact moment, Nate had come, curiosity about Denton overcoming curiosity about how Stew Netters would get his giant foot out of his mouth and save face with his son.

"Now, what can we do for you, Mr. Denton?" the sheriff asked.

Denton was thin to the point of bony, with hands that seemed too large for the rest of his body. Dressed in jeans and a black sweater, he looked to be about forty, give or take a few years. Most disconcerting to Nate was the vague look in the man's eyes. Hardly the dynamo Nate had expected. He smoothed his longish brown hair away from his brow, rubbed his bearded cheek, then folded his hands in his lap. "I heard about Peter Jacks," he said, his gaze shifting between Nate and Gallant. His voice was soft, his speech hesitant.

"Did you know Jacks?"

"I never met him. But a couple of the counselors expressed concern about him. I guess he's been hanging around the facility with Jason Netters. What happened to Peter?"

"I'm afraid it's an ongoing investigation," Gallant said. "I can't really discuss it with you."

Denton shifted in his chair. "Sure, I can see that. Okay."

"Is there anything else?" Gallant asked.

Denton shrugged. "No, I don't think so. I...I just wanted to tell you you're welcome to come out and ask questions or take a look around—whatever. I mean, the fact he's been hanging out up there with us and then committed a crime, well, that could look bad, and you know, we depend on the community for support."

"I thought you were independently financed," Nate said.

"Sure. Yeah, we are. I mean, I am. I don't mean financial support. I mean as in goodwill."

"Oh, I see."

He wobbled a little as he stood. Gallant heaved himself upward in response. "Are you okay?"

Denton nodded. "I've had the flu," he said.

"Are you driving back up to the mountains tonight?" Gallant asked.

"No, I'm staying in town. I'll go back tomorrow. Don't worry about me. Good luck on your investigation."

The sheriff thanked Denton for coming in, then saw him out of the office. When he returned, he looked Nate straight in the eye. "What do you think of that?" he asked.

"Drugs?" Nate mused.

"I'm going to make sure the lab does a full toxicology on the Jacks boy. I've met Denton before, but the past five months haven't been kind to him. Sounds to me like an official visit is overdue up at that camp."

"That's just what Stew Netters said," Nate commented. As he left the office, he thought again about Jason Netters. Before he'd left the editor's office, Nate had made a point of greeting the boy. Jason had shaken his hand but hadn't made eye contact. But more than that, the kid had given the impression it was taking every ounce of his willpower to stay in that room and not spin away. He'd brought an undercurrent with him, or maybe his father had introduced it with that ill-advised comment about shooting Mike Donovan. All very odd, and Nate found himself wondering if the editor had any idea how troubled his boy seemed to be.

Nate tried Sarah's phone as he parked the rental in front of his motel room, but she didn't answer. To be on the safe side, he went inside the room to make sure she wasn't waiting for him, but the place smelled and looked as though it had recently been cleaned, and there was no sign that Sarah had been back there since before breakfast.

He knew she wasn't at the sheriff's office, so he veered toward the garage, thinking maybe she'd gone to get her stuff out of her mother's car, though why she wouldn't answer the phone if that was the case he didn't know.

The guy at the garage turned as Nate approached him. He was in the act of locking the front door and he winced when he saw Nate. "Oh, man, I was afraid you'd get back before she did," he said, pocketing his keys. "I gotta get home. I don't know what's taking her so long."

"Are we talking about Sarah Donovan?"

"Yeah. She wanted to run some errand or other, and since her car won't start, she asked to borrow your truck. She said she wouldn't be long, but it's been, like, three hours."

"Do you know where she went?" Nate asked.

"Out past the tunnel. Just two or three miles, she said."

"What's out that way?"

"Not much. A truck yard and an old mining operation.

Oh, and one of those storage places." He pulled his coat tighter around his thin frame and added, "My dad is going to kill me when he finds out I let her take your truck. I guess I shouldn't have, but I used to go to school with Sarah." He flashed a shy smile and added, "I had a thing for her, but she only had eyes for Johnny Pierce. Still, she's got a way about her."

"I know exactly what you mean," Nate said. "Don't worry about it. Did she take her suitcase out of her mother's car?"

"No. Did she want it?"

"Yeah. Mind getting it for me?"

"Not at all. Wait here. I'll go in through the garage door."

He trotted off, opened a small door behind the office and disappeared. He was back a few minutes later with Sarah's suitcase, which he handed to Nate.

NATE KEPT THINKING about that key Sarah had taken from her dad's safe. She'd explained it away by saying it concerned a personal matter. She'd also talked about a locker or garage her father rented in town. He had the gut feeling this personal matter concerned that storage locker and that she'd gone there to take care of something important to her. Reason said he should give her space to deal with whatever this was. He shouldn't intrude.

But on the other hand, she'd been gone far longer than she'd told the guy at the garage she would be, she was driving a truck with no window and it was getting dark. Plus, there was a storm coming. What if the truck had given her trouble?

Or what if another kind of trouble had come her way? There'd been so much violence in the past few days he couldn't rule anything out. In the end, he took off down the road.

U-Lock Garages was located 2.3 miles from town and was set down a slope from the highway. It was well lit with high overhead stanchions, and as the road passed it by, the whole thing could be seen from above. There wasn't a single vehicle visible on any of the honeycombed lanes, or a human, either, for that matter. Nate drove down to the gate, but it was locked and the office inside the gate looked empty and dark.

Sarah wasn't here.

He drove back toward town with his high beams on. About halfway through the tunnel, the lights revealed debris on the pavement and he slowed down. As the road was part of a blind curve at this point, he couldn't stop the truck on the off chance someone would come up behind him, despite the fact he hadn't met a single other car for at least a half mile. He drove out the tunnel and parked on the shoulder, grabbed a flashlight out of the center console and walked back into the tunnel.

The debris turned out to be broken red plastic from what looked like a taillight housing. He also saw the sparkle of glass. He swung the light in a circle and picked up what appeared to be a side mirror with a small convex mirror lens stuck to the only unbroken piece, just like the one he had mounted on his own vehicle to increase rear-view visibility. Most of the mirror was shattered, which explained the glass.

He picked up the mirror and shined the light around again, and this time he saw white paint on the tunnel wall. That made his heart skip a beat. Running now, he headed for the opening, suddenly aware a vehicle was coming, its engine noise filling the tunnel. A second later, blinding lights came up behind him and passed with a blare of the horn that about shattered Nate's eardrums. He kept running, following the red taillights until they broke into the night and disappeared around another turn.

Using a flashlight to investigate the side of the road, he found tire tracks in the snow that careened down the slope. His hands and face were freezing by this time, and his lungs stung from taking deep breaths, but all that disappeared as he started down the slope, shining the light at his feet so he wouldn't trip and fall, noting the deep gouges and steamrolled bushes, until the light finally glinted off a silver bumper up ahead.

His white truck, all but invisible in the snow, appeared to have hit an old stump headfirst, popping the hood and stopping forward progress. Moving as fast as he could, Nate hurried to the driver's door and shined his light at the window, but not only was it tinted glass, it was also covered with condensation on the inside. He could tell someone was in there. He just couldn't see in what condition that someone might be. But it didn't take a rocket scientist to figure out who was behind the wheel.

He yanked on the handle. It was locked. He suddenly remembered he carried his keys in his pocket and swore at himself as he fumbled with numb fingers to find them and hit the auto lock button. The truck beeped and the door finally opened, triggering the cab light.

Sarah sat behind the wheel, staring at him as though she'd been asleep and had just woken. She still wore her seat belt. The deflated air bag extruding from the steering wheel covered most of her lap.

"Sarah," he said, touching her face, her shoulders, her arms, moving aside the air bag, looking for blood or jutting broken bones. She watched him in a distracted way until finally she whispered something.

He leaned closer. "What did you say, sweetheart?"

She licked her lips. "Sorry."

"Sorry about what?"

"Your truck."

"Don't worry about that," he said softly. "All that matters is you're okay. I'm calling the police and an ambulance."

She closed her eyes, but she'd slipped her hand into his and held on to him tightly. While they waited, Nate asked her if she hurt anywhere and she admitted her right leg ached. The crash had pushed the front end of the truck inward, pinning her inside, so there was no way he could check things out for her. He draped his coat across her body to ward off chattering teeth, held her hand and waited.

It seemed to take forever until he heard an approaching siren, but it was probably less than ten minutes. Searchlights appeared as another siren sounded off down the road. Pretty soon medics had pushed Nate aside and started attending to Sarah. When they were satisfied with her stability, the cops went to work freeing her from the mass of metal. Eventually she was transferred to a stretcher. Nate held her hand as they struggled up the hill until they reached the road and the welcome sight of the waiting ambulance.

Sheriff Gallant got out of his squad SUV. "That your truck down there?" he called to Nate.

"Yeah. Sarah was driving. She must have had an accident coming out of the tunnel."

Gallant looked down at Sarah, whose face was as white as the blanket tucked around her body. "Is she going to be okay?"

"Of course she is," Nate said, unable to entertain any other possibility.

But Sarah tugged on his hand. "Not an accident," she said.

Gallant heard her and both men leaned closer. "Then what?"

"Another truck. I went off the road."

"When did all this happen?" Nate asked.

"I looked at my watch a little while before. Around four o'clock."

The medics lifted the stretcher and Sarah disappeared into the back of the ambulance. Nate knew there wasn't room back there for unnecessary personnel, and he told Sarah he'd meet her at the hospital.

"You okay to drive?" Gallant asked.

Nate hurried to his rental. "Fine."

"I'll be by later to talk to her about this other vehicle," Gallant said.

"Fine," Nate repeated.

Gallant caught his arm. "Keep in mind it was *your* rental truck, and in the dark and from behind, no one could tell who was driving," he said.

Nate nodded. The number one important thing was Sarah's safety. Nate swore to himself. He wouldn't rest until he found out who had done this to her.

SARAH WAS EXTREMELY relieved when, after umpteen tests and X-rays, she was released from the hospital with little more than a mild concussion, a very sore neck and shoulders, and a sprained leg acquired when the truck floor pushed upward. She knew she was lucky to walk—well, limp—away from the crash and tried, as Nate drove toward the Motorcoach, to remember what had happened after the truck came to an abrupt standstill.

It was all blurry in her head, though. It had to have been a couple of hours that passed with her falling in and out of a strange slumber, growing colder and colder, unable to move herself out of the truck, always knowing in the back of her mind that Nate would look for her, Nate would find her, all she had to do was survive until he got there.

She hadn't been able to tell the sheriff much about the other vehicle except it was a truck slightly bigger than Nate's and dark in color. Judging from his deep sigh, she assumed that description fit a whole lot of Shatterhorn's vehicles. She did point out that it was likely to have suffered damage on the right side when it had slammed against Nate's truck. She hadn't seen the driver, hadn't even tried to as she'd been struggling with the steering wheel in an attempt to avoid what eventually happened.

"How are you doing over there?" Nate asked, his hand coming to rest atop hers.

"Worried about tomorrow," she said. "Worried that we're going to hear there's been a senseless shooting at the Washington Monument and that more innocent people are going to die and we don't know how to stop it. Did you call your department in Arizona?"

"Yeah, while you were in X-ray. I talked to Dan. He promised to pass on the word to his brother. He tried to assure me that the FBI would be on top of any conspiracy, domestic or foreign."

"That's what everyone says," Sarah remarked as they pulled into the motel parking lot.

As Nate unlocked the door, his cell phone rang. In a way, he hated to answer it. It was late, both he and Sarah were exhausted, and there just wasn't anyone he wanted to talk to except the person or persons behind what was going on, and he doubted they would phone to explain themselves.

"Go ahead and take that call," Sarah said, dropping her handbag on the bedside table and heading to the bathroom.

He dropped into the chair by the small desk and saw on

the screen that it was Gallant. "What are you doing still up?" he asked in lieu of a greeting.

"Acting like your darn answering machine. First Diana Donovan called, supposedly to hear what we'd found out about her ex-husband's murder, but I got the feeling she really wanted to find out where Sarah was."

"Okay," Nate said. "And speaking of Sarah, what kind of vehicle does Netters drive? And how about his son? And the mayor, too. And Morris Denton."

"Let's see. Netters drives a dark green four-door truck. George Bliss has a white car and a dark truck. Jason drives his dad's old—wait for it—truck. I don't know about Denton, but he was in my office with you when Sarah was run off the road." He paused a second. "Besides, why would any of them run your truck off the road?"

"I don't know," Nate admitted.

"There's something else," the sheriff continued. "Jessica Foster has been trying to get ahold of you. She finally called my office, and they called me, and I called her and promised I'd pass along a message. She wants to talk to you right away, no matter what time it is."

"Do you know what this is about?" Nate asked.

"I'll let her explain," Gallant said and smothered a yawn. Nate thanked him and clicked off his phone, then clicked it back on and called the Foster house.

Jessica picked it up before the ringtone finished. "Nate? Is that you?"

"Yeah," he said. "I tried calling last night and left a message—"

"You did? I must have erased it or something. Oh, Nate, Alex is missing!"

"Missing?"

"No one has seen or heard from him since the day he flew out of here. The last communication put him over the mountains during that storm. As soon as the weather cleared, they started a search, but there's nothing. Nothing!"

"Wait a second," Nate said. "What about the aircraft's emergency beacon?"

"Nothing," she insisted. "Absolutely no trace. You know how he likes his old equipment and refuses to update. And now another storm is brewing, so they have to call off tomorrow's search, and he's out there in the cold—" Her voice broke off while she excused herself and blew her nose, then she was back, a little calmer but not much. "We had a big argument before he left, Nate. I told him not to bother coming home. What if those are the last words I ever say to him?"

Nate took a deep breath. Alex was his best friend, so Nate knew about the occasional arguments. Money was tight at times; in-laws were an issue; his work was demanding. Hers was, too. They both wanted children and yet had struggled conceiving.... Things almost everyone had trouble with at times. But Nate hadn't known things had gotten this bad between Alex and his wife.

After a long hesitation, she spoke again. "I'm just going to blurt this out, Nate. Maybe Alex disarmed his own beacon. Maybe he decided to cut his losses with me and start fresh."

"No," Nate said. "He wouldn't do it this way."

"How do you know? He's a detective in the Blunt Falls police department—if anyone could figure out how to disappear, it would be Alex."

"He wouldn't bail on you or his career or his family," Nate insisted, hoping with all his heart he was right.

"You never know what really goes on with people," she said, her voice ragged, tired. "You can know them so well and yet not know them at all. Anyway, I didn't want you to find out he was missing on the news or read it in a paper."

"I appreciate that," Nate said.

"Sheriff Gallant told me that Mike Donovan is dead. 'Murdered,' he said. Nate, what's the world coming to?"

Nate had no pithy reassurance to offer. His head was reeling with the images of Alex crashed, injured, helpless in the bitterly cold mountains. "Are you alone?" he asked Jessica just as Sarah emerged from the bathroom wrapped in a towel, damp hair clinging to her beautiful face. She limped over to the bed and perched on the edge, staring at him. Apparently the tone of his voice and the urgency of the conversation had alerted her to his distress.

"My sister is here. I'm okay. How about you, Nate?"

"I'll come as soon as I can," he said. "We'll find him."

"I hope so," Jessica responded, and she just seemed to fade away.

Nate quickly filled Sarah in on the details, explaining he would leave for Montana the day after tomorrow. She nodded thoughtfully, then winced as the movement apparently hurt her strained muscles. "What a horrible coincidence," she said, rubbing her neck with one hand.

He got up and approached her. "Let me do that," he said. "Come sit in the chair."

She sat down in his vacated chair and he gently began massaging her neck and shoulders, delighting in the petal softness of her skin and the pure beauty of her back. But even while he enjoyed the scenery, he found himself thinking, at first to himself and then aloud.

"Is it a coincidence?" he said, trying out the words.

"It has to be," she responded. "How could it be anything else? I mean, one man is shot and another's plane disappears. The only thing they had in common—"

"—was a shooting they were part of in Shatterhorn, Nevada, months before. And me."

She grabbed his hand and pulled him around to face her. He sat on the bed so she wouldn't have to strain herself to look up at him. "And someone's been trying to kill you since that same day," she said.

"I've been thinking about something that happened outside of Vegas when I was on my way up here. One of my tires blew on a nasty piece of highway. At the time, there was a lot of dust blowing across the road, so I'd slowed way down, and traffic was relatively light. I remember thinking had I been going the speed limit or if traffic had been heavier, the resulting crash and repairs might have been a whole lot worse. As it was, it delayed me by two or three hours."

"So now you're thinking it wasn't an accident?"

"In light of everything else, yes. I'd stopped for a late breakfast at a real busy truck stop because I'd left home at the crack of dawn. I was there about twenty-five minutes. The tire blew five miles down the road."

"I'm getting chills," Sarah said, hugging herself.

"If I'm right, that means Mike, Alex and I were all targeted on the same day, which just happens to be right after Mike asked us to meet him here. Both the editor and the mayor heard Mike say he was asking us to come and who knows how many people they told. I think from what I've heard since then that your father was shut down by so many people he was getting desperate to be heard. He thought he saw a pattern, but he was too mixed-up in his thinking. He thought something horrible was coming tomorrow."

She nodded and winced again.

He looked at her closely. She was shivering and pale, and he was suddenly ashamed he hadn't insisted she spend the night in the hospital. But how could he protect her there? Time was running out and their enemy was faceless. The attack on Sarah had changed the stakes. "I retrieved your suitcase from the garage before I found you," he said. "I'll go get it out of the truck. You need something warmer than that towel."

"Don't go," she said.

He took her hands and pulled her to her feet. The action jarred loose the towel and his breath caught as it slipped to the floor. "And your mother tried calling you today," he added around the sudden lump in his throat.

"My phone is dead and the charger unit is in my suitcase."

"I'll go get it."

"Not now," she said. "It's a car charger. Anyway, I'm very tired." She rested her head against his shoulder. "I don't need to talk to my mother right now, and I certainly don't need clothes to stay warm—not when I have you."

He picked her up in his arms and held her, kissing her soft lips as he gently laid her down on the bed. A few minutes later, they were under the sheets, making heat of their own. When they finally parted, Sarah fell asleep almost at once, but Nate lay awake, staring into the dark, thinking....

He kept picturing the last page in Mike's notebook. A big number twenty-eight circled in red ink.

A cold fist seemed to punch him in the gut as his brain ran through dates and months until he reached May. What day was Memorial Day on this year?

He'd bet it was the twenty-eighth.

Had Mike suspected another shooting would occur in late May?

Chapter Fifteen

Sarah woke up first. She must have groaned when she rolled on her side, because Nate's arms suddenly surrounded her. She could tell he'd fallen back to sleep when his breathing once again turned slow and steady.

Her handbag lay on the bedside table, and carefully, so as not to awaken Nate, she reached inside for Johnny's letters.

Nate's embrace tightened. She left the letters where they were and turned in the circle of his arms to kiss him awake.

"Morning breath," he warned her without opening his eyes.

"I'll take my chances," she said, giving him a chaste kiss.

"How are you? How do you feel?"

"Fine," she said. "Antsy."

"Me, too," he said as though coming fully awake, and she could sense him thinking: this was *the day*. What exactly that meant might still elude both of them, but there was no denying the relentless feeling something was going to happen soon. This was the day the country celebrated its presidents both past and present. Sarah hoped Nate's buddy Dan had made more headway figuring this out than her father had.

Nate disengaged himself and got out of bed, walking to the bathroom in that sure-footed way of his, totally at ease with his body. There was no reason why he shouldn't be. The man was built perfectly, muscles defined without bulging, good health exuding through his pores. She was still staring at him as he looked back from the bathroom door and winked at her.

Eventually, Nate retrieved her suitcase from the truck cab and they made it into their clothes. Then Nate called his friend Alex's wife for an update, and from the stoic look on his face and the paucity of conversation, Sarah could tell nothing had changed. She was unsure why he asked the woman to consult a calendar, or why he nodded as she spoke.

"Alex is still missing," he said. "And according to Jessica, Memorial Day falls on the twenty-eighth of May this year, as in the number twenty-eight circled in red ink. It makes sense something would happen on that date, as it ties in with all the other shootings on similar holidays."

"Of course," Sarah said.

He handed her the phone. "Your turn."

It was obvious Sarah's early-morning call had awakened her night-owl mother from a sound sleep. She hung up after five minutes of hedging to find Nate staring at her.

"What's up?" he asked.

"She apologized for going to the bar. She wants me to come back to Reno. She wants to talk to me."

"And?" he said.

"And I've heard it all before." She cupped her forehead and closed her eyes for a minute. "I told her I'd come when I could. Let's get some breakfast."

"How about I bring something back from the motel office and we eat it here?"

"That sounds good," she said and laid her head back

against the chair. A second later she heard the door close and lock behind him. "Come on, painkiller," she whispered.

It felt good to be back in jeans and a sweater, although she'd had to trash her boots after the medics cut apart the right one to remove it from her injured leg. She'd brought along running shoes and laced the right one gingerly. As she waited for Nate to return, she thought about going to the nightstand and getting Johnny's letter, but her leg hurt and she just wanted to sit still. Five minutes later, she heard a noise at the door as though Nate was having trouble opening it, maybe because his hands were full. It wasn't until she swung it open that the thought crossed her mind—what if it wasn't Nate?

But it was, and he entered the room in a rush. It was obvious by his expression something was wrong. He closed the door and slid the deadbolt, turning to look at her.

"Now what?" she asked, her heart suddenly racing.

"Stewart Netters is dead."

Sarah stared at him a second. "Jason's father? The editor of the *Shatterhorn Gazette?*"

"The motel management had the television on. He was shot sometime early this morning."

"Poor Jason."

"They're looking for Jason in connection with his father's death," Nate interrupted. "Someone saw him leaving the newspaper office in a dead run. They interviewed the sheriff's department."

By this time, Sarah had turned on the set in their room and found the Reno news station covering the story. A woman's anguished face filled the screen. Sarah looked up at Nate. "That's Giselle Netters, Jason's mother."

"Turn it up," Nate urged.

"I don't believe it, not for a minute, not any of it," Giselle was saying. "Jason would never, ever do something like this.

He loves his father. He would never hurt him. Stew couldn't sleep last night—he was troubled about something—so he went in early to the office. The sheriff's department has this all wrong, I swear. They should be looking for the person who murdered my husband, not wasting time trying to make a case against our son. Jason, please, if you can hear me, come home...."

Her tear-streaked face was replaced by that of an anchorwoman sporting rigidly coiffed red hair. "You've been listening to the alleged attacker's mother, Giselle Netters, wife of shooting victim Stewart Netters. Mr. Netters's body was discovered early this morning by an employee. He'd been shot once in the chest with what sources claim is a .380. Shatterhorn mayor George Bliss was unavailable for comment."

The newswoman paused before adding in a more modulated voice, "Viewers will remember the small community of Shatterhorn faced another disaster just last Labor Day, when a nineteen-year-old gunman by the name of Thomas Jacks injured five and killed four in a crowded mall before turning his weapon on himself. And in a strange twist of fate, the man who was with Jacks as he took his dying breath was shot and killed three days ago by an unknown assailant. Speculation is growing that perhaps Jason Netters was involved with that shooting, as well. In other news..."

"Turn it off, please," Nate said.

Sarah was happy to do as he'd requested. For a moment they both sat there staring at each other, and then Sarah took a steadying breath. "Maybe this is it," she said. "Maybe it's over."

"What do you mean?" Nate asked her.

"Dad speculated something would happen on Presidents' Day, and it has."

"I don't think so," Nate said.

"There are similarities," she insisted. "A shooting committed by a young man—"

"But not random," Nate interrupted. "A son killing his father is never random. And Jason didn't then kill himself—he apparently fled. If he's guilty. If he did this."

Sarah, feeling deflated, nodded. As horrible as this recent event was, she'd experienced a few moments of pure relief—the worst was over at last. But now she could see there was no way to know that, not until they found Jason.

"Are you hungry?" he asked her.

"Not anymore."

"Me, neither. Let's drive over to the mayor's house and ask him what happened in Netters's office yesterday after I left. Maybe he's not making a public comment because he has information the sheriff doesn't want him to reveal."

"Would he tell us?"

"Probably not, but even knowing he has something might help and maybe Gallant would share. It's someplace to start."

They left the room soon after that, pleased to see the weather system that had appeared so threatening the night before had barely dusted the streets with snow. Both of them were on the quiet side. In an abstract way, Sarah recognized the care with which Nate checked the cars behind them, the pedestrians on the street, his eyes constantly scanning everyone and everything as though he was looking for a killer.

Perhaps that was because he was.

IT WAS OBVIOUS to Nate that Mayor George Bliss lived in a style befitting his family's wealth, from the locked rod-iron gates at the head of the curving driveway to the white mansion visible inside the fenced grounds. An American flag, beautiful against the grayish sky, waved above the roof. A call box sat next to the gate complete with a video monitor, which Nate got out of the truck and activated.

A decisive voice he recognized from a phone call made a couple of days before responded. The image showed a balding man with a prominent, thin nose. "Yes?"

"I'm here to see Mayor Bliss," Nate said.

The man looked annoyed as he said, "You media people have been told over and over again that the mayor isn't giving statements right now."

"I'm not with the media," Nate said, giving his name. "And you are?"

"The mayor's secretary, William Tucker. I'm sorry, sir, but I was just leaving. If you'll try again tomorrow—"

Nate tried out a smile. "Mr. Tucker, I need to ask Mayor Bliss a couple of quick questions."

The man's irritated frown curved a little. "Are you the Nate Matthews who was at the mall last Labor Day?"

"That's me."

"I see. Nevertheless, the message is the same. The mayor is indisposed."

"In what way?"

"Sir, in deference to the high regard in which the mayor holds you and your friends, I will tell you what I haven't divulged to the media. Mayor Bliss is not presently in Shatterhorn."

"Can you tell me where he is?"

For a moment, it appeared a challenging glint flared in the man's eyes. "He flew out this morning for Helena. I'm not supposed to advertise that information, so please don't share it. The mayor and Mr. Netters were good friends. This horrible…event…has hit him hard."

"May I ask what he's doing in Helena?"

"He's attending a Presidents' Day celebration to show support for the governor. He agreed to go just last night."

Presidents' Day. "Okay. Well, thanks for your time."

"Come back tomorrow morning," the man said curtly. "I'll make sure the mayor is expecting you."

Nate got back in the truck and faced Sarah, who had leaned her head against the window and closed her eyes. She looked delicate and beaten, her face a little black-and-blue, her lips pale. He swallowed a knot as she opened her eyes and met his gaze. "Well?"

"Bliss isn't here," he told her, his voice choked. What was he doing with this woman? She was hurt; she should be home in bed. If he truly cared for her, would he keep dragging her into danger? Wouldn't he insist she go back to Reno or Virginia, where it was safe, instead of subjecting her to this awful series of violent situations that just never seemed to stop?

Because it was suddenly very clear to him that the situation with her mother, while volatile, had never put Sarah's life in imminent danger. He and Mike had brought the violence, and it was still following Nate around like a very cruel shadow. Sarah was a victim every bit as much as her father, and all Nate had done was replace her needy mother with his own needs. True to form, Sarah had followed that misguided sense of loyalty that seemed inherent to her soul and almost died because of it. Again.

He cleared his throat. "I'm going to take you back to the motel, where I hope you'll lock yourself in the room and not answer the door unless it's for food you ordered yourself."

Her eyes widened. "Where are you going?"

He told her about Helena as he started the truck. "Do you know where it is?"

"A couple of hours driving, far less by plane," she said.

"What about the roads? If the storm dumped snow, they could be impassable." Unbidden, he pictured Alex lost in those mountains, freezing, hurt.

"No, they should be fine. It's not a bad drive." She narrowed her eyes. "*Why* are you going to Helena?"

"To see the mayor."

"But why? The chances you'll even be able to get close to him seem remote, and you said he'll be back by tonight."

"Tonight I'm going up to that B-Strong camp."

"Why?"

"I want to get a feel for the place, because tomorrow I need to drive to Blunt Falls to see what I can do to help find Alex."

She was quiet for a second. "I can't leave tomorrow. I have to take care of moving the coins and contacting a lawyer."

"I know," he agreed. "And your mother wants you back in Reno."

She looked down at her hands, then at him. "What are you really saying, Nate?"

He paused for a second, measuring his words. "I'm saying maybe it's time we each took care of business. You have your family. I have this."

"Do you?" she asked.

"What do you mean?"

"Why can't you let the police take care of it?"

"That's not the way I work."

"You're beginning to sound like my father."

His mouth opened, but no words came out. He wasn't even sure what they were fighting about, only that her accusation hurt like salt rubbed in an open wound. After several seconds of tense stillness, he muttered, "When you've been in law enforcement as long as I have, you get a sixth sense about things."

"You're talking about a gut feeling," she said. "What is your gut telling you?"

"That the mayor is in danger."

"From Jason?"

"I'm not sure. But he and Stewart were both in Jason's father's office yesterday, and Jason is hiding something. I can guarantee you that. It's worth a drive to Helena and that's why I have to go. But there's no reason for you to tag along."

"No need for me to tag along?" she repeated, obviously annoyed. "Well, it's not that easy. This isn't just about you, Nate."

"I didn't say it was."

"Didn't you? I'm going, too."

"Sarah—"

"Don't you know by now that there is no point arguing with me?"

"That's kind of scary, isn't it?"

"I'm usually pretty reasonable," she objected, her voice dry.

"No, I mean it's kind of scary that I know that about you." He glanced at her as he said this and his expression struck her as uneasy.

"I see your point," she said softly. "But isn't it kind of nice, too?"

"Yeah," he said, but it came with a quick turn of his head and, after that, utter silence.

SARAH CLOSED HER EYES, drifting in and out of restless slumber. Nate had the heat turned up and that felt good, because everything hurt more today than it had the day before.

Why was he acting so odd? How had he gone from the lover of the night before to this hard-to-read, all-too-typical guy? Was it her fault? And why had she insisted on accompanying him when it was clear he'd rather she didn't? In the back of her mind, she asked herself a question: Was it possible she'd made the error of mistaking sex for genuine feeling? Mistaking passion for compassion?

Or was Nate rediscovering his old self, the cop under his skin, and with that, his swagger? And if that were true, perhaps it was also possible he was beginning to reexamine his severed relationship with his fiancée. Perhaps letting her go now seemed a huge mistake he needed to rectify.

She dug in her purse when they stopped for gas and Nate got out to stretch his legs. The whole stack of Johnny's letters came out and with it, a much folded and unfolded piece of paper she recognized as having been wrapped around the storage-garage key. She was about to stuff it back in her handbag when she saw writing on one side.

"What's that?" Nate asked as he climbed back in behind the wheel of the rental.

"A name. Morris Denton, with *Seattle* written under it followed by a question mark. What do you suppose that means?"

"Is that the missing page from the notebook?"

"It looks like it. It was wrapped around the key I found in Dad's safe. I'm so stupid. I should have recognized it, but this is the first time I really looked at it." She handed the paper to Nate.

"I have no idea why he'd include Seattle unless Denton is from there or was going there. We'll get Gallant to check on it tonight." He gestured at the letters still in her lap. "What are those?"

She looked him in the eyes. "Johnny wrote me these before we were married."

"That's what you went to the garage to get," he said.

"Yes. I wanted to read them again."

"You really loved him, didn't you?" he asked her.

She nodded. "I really did. I'm funny that way. When I give my heart, I give my heart."

"I'm sorry I pried," he said, starting the truck, and from the tone of his voice, it was clear the letters held little interest for him. Sarah took a deep breath and thanked her lucky stars. If he'd asked why they were important to her, she would have told him, and now was not the time—not when things had gotten so strange between them. She stuffed the letters back in her purse right as a road sign announced Helena just ahead.

Chapter Sixteen

The town of Helena was home to a small college, which considerably boosted its wintertime population. And on this chilly Monday afternoon, the one-way street leading into town was jammed with traffic. Even the sidewalks were crowded, and everyone moved in the same direction toward the center of town.

"This is Union Street," Sarah announced as they crawled along. "It leads to Memorial Plaza, and if I remember correctly from the one and only time I've ever been here, there's a big old statue of George Washington right smack in the middle. I never put the two together before."

"Washington Memorial," Nate whispered, his gut sending signals again. "This is it. Something is going to happen here." He stopped for a group of people who were crossing the street and added, "Where is everybody going?"

"Judging from the red-white-and-blue banners, I'd say a parade or something. Look, the road is blocked off up ahead."

Nate followed behind a trolley until he saw a sign directing him to a makeshift parking lot and pulled out of the traffic. "We'd better walk from here," he said as he turned off the engine. "Are you up to it? Maybe you should stay in the truck."

"Why do you keep trying to get rid of me?" she snapped. "What's gotten into you?"

"I don't want you to get killed," he grumbled as he slipped Mike's old leather notebook into the breast pocket of his jacket. He wasn't proud of the childish way his emotions were getting the best of him. If something happened to her that he could prevent and he somehow missed the mark, like he had on Labor Day with those kids, he'd never forgive himself. He'd never make it back to anything approaching normal. For both their sakes, he wanted to park her in a steel vault until this was over.

"I'm a big girl, Nate," she said as she took his hand, clenching it in hers and tugging slightly for effect. He stopped to look down at her, but the crowd swept them up and they moved with everyone else toward the town square.

Helena's elevation was lower than Shatterhorn's, hence the pavement was clear of snow and nearly empty. As they staked out a piece of curbside real estate, a chill wind carried the sound of an approaching brass band. Across the road, Nate could see the grassy square and the top of Washington's head. His pulse raced as he looked for anything amiss.

Within minutes, everyone seemed to turn in unison to watch the distant corner with murmurs of expectation. As the music grew louder, two brown quarter horses made the turn, their riders carrying the state and national flags.

The crowd cheered as the horses, followed by the Helena High School Tigers band, pranced by. A float complete with three young women draped in period clothes topped with fur coats, as well as two guys dressed as Abraham Lincoln and George Washington, came after the band. The girls waved like prom queens while the guys looked embarrassed and cold. A dozen or so kids riding decorated bikes and so bundled in parkas their own mothers probably couldn't tell them apart followed the float. A half dozen brave girls in brief uniforms twirling batons preceded the next float, which featured a seated woman hand sewing the Stars and Stripes—à la Betsy Ross—onto a huge flag. Every so often she reached into a sack and threw a handful of candy to the kids.

Nate grew increasingly anxious. This was exactly the kind of venue these "random" shooters had been choosing—crowded, everyday Americana events, complete with families and celebration, as though the whole point was to underscore that no one was safe, not at school or in a library or on a beach. He looked back at the parade as an open car drove by. Two men were seated in the backseat, and by the banners affixed to the door, Nate figured out one was the mayor of Helena and the other was the governor of Nevada. Nate was kind of surprised Bliss wasn't in the car with them.

He tore his gaze away from the men and went back to scanning the crowd. A few minutes later, his heart leaped into his throat as he recognized a face in among the strangers.

He grabbed Sarah's arm, propelling her forward with him lest he lose sight of his target. "Go get the police."

"Why?"

He tore his gaze away from the opposite side of the street. "I just saw Jason Netters. I have to follow him." Nate began walking again, aware Sarah was close behind. He apologized to an older woman as he sidled past her, moving faster than the parade now, out in front of the horses in an effort not to lose sight of Jason.

"I'm coming with you."

He glanced down at her again. "Go find help," he pleaded.

"Tell them anything you can think of to get this crowd dispersed. I have to keep up with Jason."

"Where's he going? Can you tell?"

"It looks like he's headed to the end of the parade route."

He ran off, not pausing to look back. He had to find Jason and stop him before it was too late.

SARAH LOOKED AROUND desperately for someone in a uniform, and when she finally spotted an officer working crowd control, she hurried to speak to him, her leg throbbing in protest.

The man was several inches taller than she was, and the noise of the crowd drowned out her voice. Plus, he was involved in another situation and was only paying her cursory attention. When he turned the opposite direction to control a horde of little kids, she grabbed his arm, and he turned to face her, annoyed now that she'd interfered with him.

"A guy wanted for questioning in the shooting death of a man in Shatterhorn this morning has been sighted on his way to the end of the parade," she explained breathlessly. "Is there a gathering down there?"

"Yeah," he said, shooing the kids back.

"Get on your radio and tell the others to be alert. There's reason to suspect this person is armed and might be getting ready to fire into the crowd."

"Are you serious?" he asked.

"Dead serious."

"What's his name?"

"Jason Netters. About eighteen, blond, medium sized."

"That describes two-thirds of this town," he said, but he was fingering his radio as he spoke. "And who are you?"

"It doesn't matter who I am. Please, do something. I have to go."

A CONGESTED BARRICADE at the end of the sidewalk directing pedestrians to cross the street and continue down toward a park Nate could see through the trees caused him to lose sight of Jason. He crossed with everyone else, keeping his gaze peeled for a glimpse of the boy, but Jason wasn't a big guy and he wasn't particularly distinctive.

Wait—he'd been wearing a green camouflage-type coat. Those were hardly rare in rural Nevada, but at least it gave Nate something to be on the lookout for.

Checking the street, he saw the parade was now making its way to the park, where bleachers were beginning to fill with people. He, along with two dozen others, got stuck behind the last float, and by the time Nate made it to the park, the car with the dignitaries had come to a halt. The governor and Helena's mayor were in the process of climbing up to a platform where a podium had been situated. There was no sign of Mayor Bliss, which seemed odd. The band launched into another march song and people cheered. The noise and confusion made concentrating that much harder. Where was Jason?

He caught a glimpse of the back of a head covered with straw-colored hair and took off after him. Three minutes later, he touched the guy's shoulder. A man spun around and raised his eyebrows. He was ten years too old. "Something wrong, pal?" he asked.

"Sorry," Nate said. He made his way back to the bandstand and climbed up three or four levels. Since the park sat on a slight incline from the town, it gave a panoramic view of things. Nate scanned the almost deserted streets and saw nothing and no one suspicious. Turning his head, he caught traffic and a glimpse of movement headed toward a freeway underpass not too far away. He kept staring until two figures emerged from some deep shadows and came briefly into view before disappearing again.

One guy had buzz-cut silver hair and wore a long coat; the other one wore a camouflage jacket. The mayor and Jason walking together, Jason's hand on the mayor's arm as though forcing him to come along, the mayor's gait stiff and labored.

Nate jumped off the bleachers and started winding his way out of the park in the general direction of the freeway, his eyes peeled for some sign that Sarah had managed to find a cop. No such luck. For a second, he thought about returning to the stands to warn people, but warn them about what? If Jason's goal was to conduct a random shooting into the crowd, he wouldn't be taking the mayor the opposite direction, would he? And panicking a large group of people could lead to a stampede and trampling.

For about the fortieth time since leaving Arizona, Nate wished he'd kept his badge and his gun. Who had he been trying to kid? He was who and what he was—a deputy, plain and simple. He didn't want to sit behind a desk as sheriff. He didn't want to spend his life hiding on his ranch. He just wanted to be a decent lawman again, but this going at it through the back door was crazy. At least Sarah wasn't in the middle of it for a change, and that was something to be thankful for.

The noise of the crowd behind him quickly began to fade, but traffic picked up and cars sped by on the road to his left. Nate stopped running after a few minutes in order to slow down and look around. Where had the two men gone?

The sky had clouded over, the shadows under the overpass ahead deep and dark. Nate stopped altogether and stood with his back against a signpost, listening. A car whizzed by followed by another car, and as the noise of their engines drifted away, Nate heard a voice coming from the dark part of the overpass.

"Come to your senses, son," the mayor said, his tone reasonable and calm. "Shooting me won't bring back your father."

"I'm not your *son*," Jason said. In contrast to the mayor's voice, the boy's reply was raspy and raw with emotion.

Nate peered into the gloom and saw the flash of metal. There were two men in there. How did he approach them? They'd see and hear him the moment he got closer.

Headlights coming from the other direction were mounted high enough to announce they belonged to a large semi-truck. Nate looked off to his right and glimpsed a subtle path etched into the dirt leading up the embankment and under the overpass. He pictured a shelf of sorts where people with nowhere better to be waited out rain and snow. Using the roaring noise of the approaching truck as cover, he scrambled up the dirt trail, and sure enough, erupted onto a narrow ledge littered with cast-off garbage. He hunkered down and considered his options.

He was now directly above the two men, whose voices were still drowned out by the sound of the retreating truck. They were standing on a very wide sidewalk, facing each other. Jason was holding a gun close to his own body, pointed at the mayor's chest.

Nate knew he had one chance to get this right. He had to throw himself down the ten feet of slope, hit Jason dead-on and knock the gun out of his hand. He knew the moment the kid became aware of Nate's presence, instinct would guide his next move. He would turn his weapon and fire without hesitation.

"You don't get it, do you?" the mayor was saying as Nate's muscles bunched in his legs.

"I get it," Jason said. "I just don't want any more. I can't do it." He reached out and shoved the mayor, who stumbled backward.

Another car was coming, and once again, Nate used the distraction to cover himself. He started down the slope. When he saw Jason's head begin to turn, he launched himself into the air. A second later, he collided with the boy, who folded under the impact of Nate's body.

For a second, they struggled, then Nate wrangled away the gun. He stood, keeping the kid under cover, breathing heavy from exertion and adrenaline. His hat had flown off in the attack and lay in the middle of the road. The mayor had stumbled backward after Jason's shove and now stared at the boy, his face red beneath the tan, his eyes all but popping out of his head, the tendons in his neck bulging.

"You okay?" Nate hollered as a car roared by, its tires flattening his hat.

The mayor limped toward him, heavily favoring his right leg. With a start, Nate realized this was the first time he'd seen the man stand since getting to town. "Thanks to you," he said.

"Stop him!" Jason shouted, still on the ground.

Nate's brow furled. "'Stop him'? What are you talking about?"

"He shot my dad," Jason said, sitting up now, holding his head.

"You can't believe that," Bliss said. "The boy is obviously crazy."

"I'm not," Jason said, and for the first time this trip, he met Nate's gaze with his own. He got to his feet, lurching a little, unsteady, rubbing his chin, then he turned his attention to the mayor. "You shot Dad because I told him who you really are. He went to work early. He said he was going to call you and demand you come talk to him. And you shot him, you bastard!"

The mayor looked at Nate's hand. "Give me his gun."

Nate clutched the weapon tighter. "The police will show up here sooner or later. We'll let them figure this out."

"This isn't any of your business," Bliss said.

Nate glanced at Jason again. "What exactly did you tell your father?"

It took Jason a few moments to speak. Tears streamed down his face and his voice trembled. "Dad said he was going up to B-Strong to interview Morris Denton. I told him the truth. Horrible things."

"You're not making sense," the mayor said. He'd moved to within four feet of Nate and Jason.

"Morris is a doper," Jason said.

"Watch what you say about people," Bliss hissed.

"You really run the camp," Jason continued, his voice icy calm. "You choose people to do what you want. You chose me. Today was my turn. I was supposed to shoot into the crowd, keep my bullets low so little kids would get it in the head and adults in the gut. You said—"

The mayor struck fast, hitting Jason in the face with his fist, knocking the boy to the ground. The action jarred Bliss's body and he wheeled away. A truck drove by and Nate caught a momentary glance of startled faces. No doubt they thought there was some sort of drunken brawl going on. Good—maybe they'd call the police.

"What the hell is going on?" Nate demanded of both of them.

"The boy is off his rocker," the mayor said, wiping spit from his chin with his fist. "Give me his gun and I'll take him back into town."

Nate reached down to grab Jason's arm and haul him to his feet. Another car sped by.

"Ask him how he hurt his leg," Jason said.

"You shoved me," Bliss spat.

The image of the two men walking away from the park flashed in Nate's mind. "You were walking funny way before Jason shoved you," he said.

"That's because you shot him," Jason said, looking at Nate. "That's why he sent Peter after you and now Peter is dead just like his brother." Jason once again glared at the mayor as he added, "You called us your foot soldiers, but the truth is we were your puppets."

"What are you talking about?" Nate asked, but he knew. *He knew.*

"It's him, don't you see? He's got this crazy idea that if people are afraid all the time, they'll fight to keep men like him in power. They'll oppose gun laws. He uses their fear. He finds guys who are troubled or weak—"

"I'm not going to stand here while this brat slanders me," Bliss sneered. "Put a bullet in him and save the taxpayers the cost of paying for his trial."

At that moment, someone touched Nate's shoulder and he turned to find Sarah facing him. He'd been so involved in what was going on, he hadn't heard her approach. She looked positively worn-out, pale and breathless.

"Where are the cops?" he asked her, wishing with all his heart she hadn't arrived at that moment.

"They must still be in the park. Someone said they saw a tall man in a hat run off this way, so I followed, and then I heard yelling, so I hurried. Nate, what's going on?"

Nate took a chance he understood everything correctly. "Jason, run back to the park. Get the police to come out here. Don't tell them your name or they'll stop to arrest you and there's no time. Go now and hurry." He wanted to send Sarah with the boy, but he didn't think she had speed in her right that moment.

In a flash, Jason was running back to the park. His exit

created just enough chaos for the mayor to take advantage of the distraction. Once again moving way faster than Nate anticipated, the older man grabbed Sarah and pulled her against his chest, his arm moving up to circle her throat. "Give me that gun," he growled, "or I push her in front of the next car that comes by."

"It's too late. It's over," Nate said, looking for a way to shoot the mayor without hitting Sarah. There just wasn't one. "You killed Mike. You must have taken his computer and phone, and then when I called him, you listened to the message and knew I was in town, that I'd survived that near accident down by Vegas. Did you pay someone to sabotage my car? And why kill Mike? Did he figure out your involvement in the B-Strong camp? What the hell were you doing out there? Recruiting gunmen to sacrifice for your own agenda?"

"You have no idea how many of us there are," Bliss growled. "I'm just one man, but there are others all over the country. The malcontent losers we choose are all on a one-way bus to nowhere. We have to stay vigilant. This is not the time for restraint and caution. This is the time to fight back, to take control. I gave those boys' deaths a meaning."

"And the innocent people they killed?"

"Every single one of them died for their countrymen. What greater honor?"

"You are a warped, twisted man," Nate said, Bliss's claim there were more like him a chilling thought. But how else could they attack Hawaii and Nevada and Iowa and heaven knew where else? "You're hiding behind the flag and corrupting the very ideals you say you stand for. You don't want people to be free to make choices. You want to decide for them. You followed us to Carson City, you ran Sarah off the road, and what the hell did you or someone like you do to Alex's plane?"

"Mike Donovan was a miserable little weasel. He poked around and poked around. I had to stop him. He would have ruined everything. And you and your buddy are no better." He took a deep breath and lowered his voice. "We're not going to talk anymore. One last time, Matthews. The gun for the girl."

"Don't do it," Sarah said as a car raced by. A big truck was right behind the car. Bliss yanked Sarah closer to the street. He smiled at Nate and pushed her with abandon. Sarah stumbled backward toward death. The truck blared a horn, swerved and kept going, but another car was on its heels. Nate grabbed for Sarah with one hand. Her fingers slipped from his and he dropped the gun in his effort to grip both her wrists. He was vaguely aware of the screech of brakes. For one second, Sarah's terrified eyes stared into his, then he pulled with everything he could muster. They both rolled to the pavement as the car continued on its way. Sarah must have hit her head. Her eyes were closed and her body was limp. Nate struggled to his feet and quickly pulled her body to the sidewalk, lifting her to safety just as another car went by.

When he looked up he found exactly what he'd expected to find—the gun was gone and George Bliss was running away from town, practically dragging his injured leg in his rush to escape. Nate took off after him. Bliss turned, took aim and fired.

Nate crumpled to the sidewalk but not before he saw a dark car swerve onto the sidewalk and hit Bliss head-on with such purpose and speed that the mayor's body flew over the hood and landed with a dreadful thump several feet away.

The car's engine roared as it regained the road and

disappeared up the highway, leaving Mayor Bliss's body in its wake.

Nate closed his eyes as the world drifted away.

Epilogue

One Month Later

The sun felt great coming through the windshield, the breeze from the open window warm and welcoming. Sarah checked the rearview mirror as she did every few minutes, just to make sure the horse trailer was where it was supposed to be, fastened to the back of her new truck, Skipjack safe and secure and on his way to his new home in Arizona.

She then glanced over at her passenger and saw he'd woken up from drifting off somewhere in Nevada. The past month in the hospital had robbed his skin of its light tan, but that would come back, as would his strength. She would make sure of that.

"Where are we?" he asked, stretching his long legs, then wincing as the movement hurt his still mending wounds. He'd almost died four weeks ago, and in fact, if it hadn't been for the slight cushioning impact of her father's leather notebook, which Nate had carried in his jacket, he probably wouldn't be sitting here.

"About two hours from your place," she told him.

"What do you think of Arizona?" he asked.

"It's beautiful."

He waited a second before following his question with

another. "Think you could go to school and live here?" he asked, his hand coming to rest on her thigh.

She looked over from the straight road ahead and smiled. "I think it's possible."

"Yeah, me, too," he said softly, gently squeezing her leg.

She glanced at him again. "You haven't heard from Alex's wife lately, have you?"

"Not for a while. From what I gather, there's been no sign of him anywhere. If he's still alive, he must be somewhere no one expected him to be, either injured or snowed in. I can't believe I wasn't able to help look for him."

"I know it's been gut-wrenching," she said.

"Yeah. Well, a lot of things have been gut-wrenching lately, right?"

"Yes. Don't think less of me, Nate, but I have to admit I'm glad someone killed Bliss. I don't know who it was or what the motive was or anything else. I'm just glad Bliss is history."

"You have every right to feel that way," he said, his voice kind, but she knew he worried about the who and why aspects of Bliss's murder. "The man was behind killing at least four kids as well as your father and Stew Netters," he added.

"And Morris Denton."

"Gallant doesn't think so."

"But Denton was found overdosed in his motel room the same day Netters died."

"There's no proof to link Bliss to that motel room. Besides, drugs seem to be kind of outside his operational pattern. He was more of a 'shoot now, ask questions later' kind of guy. And since his secretary disappeared soon after Bliss's death, there's just a paucity of information. Too bad he burned a bunch of papers before he left."

"Maybe Denton accidentally killed himself."

"Maybe," Nate agreed. "The important thing is B-Strong has been seized by federal agents, and law-enforcement agencies are ratcheting up antiterrorist investigations in the hope of ferreting out other militia groups."

"That is important, but equally so, at least to me, is that you and I survived," Sarah said as she cast him a loving look. "I have something to tell you," she added.

Nate looked over at her. "Yeah?"

"Open my purse and take out the paper inside."

He did as she'd asked. "This is one of those letters, isn't it? One that Johnny wrote you before you were married."

"Yes. Read it. Out loud, I mean. Please."

He cleared his throat. "'Baby,'" he began, and in some odd way, he sounded a little like Johnny. "'Baby, don't cry. I promised you that I would marry you and that hasn't changed. I know losing the baby hurts and I know your dad celebrating the miscarriage hurts even more. But you belong with me now, Sarah, and together, we'll have a bunch of kids, as many as you want. So don't cry. Nothing has changed. Love, Johnny.'"

Nate lowered the letter and took a deep breath. "Well, now I see why you loved him so much," he said.

She blinked a couple of times. "Yes. Well, I always fall in love with really good men. Both times now. It's like I've got a gift for it."

"I'm sorry you lost the baby," he added.

"Thank you for saying that. It was really early in the pregnancy, but I guess that doesn't matter sometimes. Dad was overjoyed. He told Johnny to get lost and made plans to send me to live with an aunt in Alaska. My mom had flitted off to who knows where by then. What Dad couldn't wrap his head around was that Johnny and I wanted that baby. It hadn't been planned, but from the moment we knew, everything just changed. It was a tragedy to lose it, not the blessing Dad claimed it was, and it broke my heart."

"Did you try again?" he asked softly.

"No. There was school and work and loans. And I was afraid. You know. And then it was too late. He was dead."

She saw a rest stop ahead and pulled off the road, parking the rig in the shade of a big tree. By unspoken agreement, she and Nate both got out of the truck and met in the front. He took her hand and led her to a picnic table, where they sat side by side on the table itself, their feet on the bench, their shoulders and hips touching. The sun beat down on their heads. To Sarah it felt as though the rays infused themselves right into her bones, spreading light and warmth through her body.

"I love you, Sarah," he said, gripping her hand and looking into her eyes. "I have from the beginning and I don't see it ever changing. But if I learned anything in this last month or so it's this—I'm born to be in law enforcement, on the front lines, taking care of business. As soon as I get home I'll tell my boss I want my badge back. I know it's a lot to ask of you, but do you think you could handle being married to another cop?"

She smiled as she stared at their interlocked fingers. "I know who you are, Nate. I would never want you to be anything or anyone else."

"Ditto," he said. A moment later, he added, "So, you will marry me someday? You'll have our babies?"

She nodded, too emotional to speak.

The smile started in his eyes, then spread to his lips, and the next thing she knew, he'd wrapped her in his arms. Wounded or not wounded, he held her so close she wasn't sure where he stopped and she began. And when he kissed her, the sensation of their bodies and lives merging into one completely overwhelmed her.

Whatever the future held, they would face it together. Always.

* * * * *

Don't miss Alice Sharpe's STRANDED,
the second book in her miniseries
THE RESCUERS, *on sale next month.*

A sneaky peek at next month...

INTRIGUE...

A SEDUCTIVE COMBINATION OF DANGER AND DESIRE

My wish list for next month's titles...

In stores from 20th June 2014:

❑ Wedding at Cardwell Ranch – BJ Daniels

& Stranded – Alice Sharpe

❑ Explosive Engagement – Lisa Childs

& Undercover Warrior – Aimée Thurlo

❑ Hard Ride to Dry Gulch – Joanna Wayne

& Sanctuary in Chef Voleur – Mallory Kane

Romantic Suspense

❑ Lone Wolf Standing – Carla Cassidy

Available at WHSmith, Tesco, Asda, Eason, Amazon and Apple

Just can't wait?

Special Offers

Every month we put together collections and longer reads written by your favourite authors.

Here are some of next month's highlights— and don't miss our fabulous discount online!

On sale 20th June

On sale 4th July

On sale 4th July

Save 20%
on all Special Releases

THE
CHATSFIELD®

Enter the intriguing online world of
The Chatsfield and discover secret
stories behind closed doors...

www.thechatsfield.com

Check in online now for your exclusive
welcome pack!

The World of Mills & Boon

There's a Mills & Boon® series that's perfect for you. There are ten different series to choose from and new titles every month, so whether you're looking for glamorous seduction, Regency rakes, homespun heroes or sizzling erotica, we'll give you plenty of inspiration for your next read.

By Request

Back by popular demand!
12 stories every month

Cherish™

Experience the ultimate rush of falling in love.
12 new stories every month

INTRIGUE...

A seductive combination of danger and desire...
7 new stories every month

Desire™

Passionate and dramatic love stories
6 new stories every month

nocturne™

An exhilarating underworld of dark desires
3 new stories every month

For exclusive member offers go to
millsandboon.co.uk/subscribe

Which series will you try next?

HEARTWARMING

Wholesome, heartfelt relationships
4 new stories every month
Only available online

Awaken the romance of the past...
6 new stories every month

The ultimate in romantic medical drama
6 new stories every month

MODERN™

Power, passion and irresistible temptation
8 new stories every month

True love and temptation!
4 new stories every month

You can also buy Mills & Boon® eBooks at
www.millsandboon.co.uk

WORLD_ M&Bb